Night And
The City

Night And The City

Gerald Kersh

With an introduction by John King

LONDON BOOKS CLASSICS

LONDON BOOKS
PO Box 52849
London SW11 1SE
www.london-books.co.uk

First published 1938 by Michael Joseph Ltd
This edition published by London Books 2007

A catalogue record for this book
is available from the British Library

ISBN 978-0-9551851-3-7

Printed and bound in Great Britain by
William Clowes Ltd, Beccles, Suffolk

Typeset by Octavo Smith Ltd in Plantin 9.75/12.5

CONTENTS

INTRODUCTION

For generations raised in the fading post-First World War suburbs of London, the older circles of red-brick terraces and tenements had – and to an extent still have – a near-mythical status. Greater London is built along futuristic Fritz Lang highways, smooth arterial roads heading out to the satellite towns, straight tarmac cutting through huge estates of semi-detached youth, a brave new world that helped create the mods and skinheads in the Sixties, the boot boys and punks in the Seventies, at the same time preserving the Teds and rockers well past their Fifties heyday. These interzones were where the worker's dream came true, but the glamour remained further back inside London, in the streets our parents and grandparents left behind.

Growing up in the Seventies, it was football and music and sometimes markets that pulled us towards this older London, a chance to mingle with the ghosts of ancestors we hardly knew existed. Cut-glass boozers tugged us inside, into fading gin palaces where men and women drank and enjoyed their music – through the fingers of a piano player hammering out 'Knees Up Mother Brown' or 'Shout For Joy', or the vinyl of a jukebox filled with Eddie Cochran, The Who, Sham 69. It was very different from today's sterile gastro-pubs and characterless theme bars, where a hundred years of tradition can be erased with the swipe of a yuppie's credit card.

England was still littered with bombed-out buildings, doodle-bugs and V2 rockets things we heard about first hand, daily war films and documentaries reinforcing our imagery. The Blitz seemed very real to us, the dirty walls of Old London reflecting the bravery of tougher times, as if the bricks were scorched by terror and relief. Television added a parade of post-war geezers to my impression of London – the Steptoe totters of Shepherd's Bush and the cockney rebel Alf Garnett in the Sixties and Seventies; Jack Regan cleaning up the streets as Harold Steptoe and Alf began to fade; Arthur Daley and Terry McCann dodging their way through Fulham in the Eighties, Del Boy doing it for South London well into the Nineties. These boys were loveable rogues, but they also reflected the pride of a fading London in their humour, slang and outspoken views. They had codes of behaviour, a firm morality limiting their law-breaking.

Experience and storytelling merged, so for me West London was represented by the Uxbridge Road and The Shed at Chelsea, The Clash and The Sex Pistols, the Westway and the Chiswick Flyover, The Ruts and The Lurkers, Southall curries and the pubs of Fulham, Hammersmith and Brentford. North London was Camden Town and The Electric Ballroom, Irish fiddles and the nutty sound of Madness, Finsbury Park muggers and running battles on the Seven Sisters Road. The East End, meanwhile, was the daddy of London legend, the oldest corner of Old London. It was the Blitz Spirit and Jack The Ripper, West Ham dockers meets Fagin's under-fives, cockles and mussels on Petticoat Lane, Jewish tailors and The Last Resort skinhead shop. I didn't know South London at all, vague impressions of Brixton reggae, Millwall aggro and the fumes from Frankie Fraser's car battery drifting across the river.

Then there was Soho, where all these Londons merged.

I first saw Soho in the late Seventies. In my teenage mind it was famous for punk, peepshows and Kray Twins fruit machines, but once there it was obviously worth much more. The buildings were stacked close and shut out the sun, dim alleyways connecting the narrow streets, a Dickensian flavour dominating the bright lights and gangster trim. Time warped, the Artful Dodger mutating into Johnny Rotten in a mash-up of drunk film men and walk-up brothels, the strip clubs fronted by speed-skinny women in PVC mini-skirts, sex shops staffed by scruffy herberts in NHS specs, middle-aged hard men showing off velvet-collared Crombies and some serious mutton chops as they guarded blank doors.

Soho had pubs and eccentrics galore, a sleazy postcard sauce and an air of villainy, and yet it felt safe somehow, with none of the casual violence of the suburbs or inner cities. It was said to be past its best, trading on a reputation that was never made clear, but which seemed to revolve around a cosmopolitan mix of vice and creativity. Journalists and artists had their special hang-outs, presented the bohemian case, but Soho's image had to go back further than the Swinging Sixties. It was a mystery. Twenty years later, in the mid-Nineties, I came across a book that brought this lost world to life.

I was walking down from The Blue Posts on Berwick Street, heading for Chinatown, the fruit-and-veg market dismantled for the night, the record shops shuttered, continued along Strippers Row, coming out the other side and ducking into a discount bookshop, the upstairs dealing in cult fiction and glossy art books, the downstairs peddling porn. Scanning the shelves through an eight-pint haze, a title clicked. Wasn't *Night And The City* the name of that old black-and-white film starring Richard Widmark, the one set in the clubs and wreckage of post-war London, a charged merging of wide boys, crooks and a great old wrestler who wants to keep fighting? But if so, what was Robert De Niro doing on the cover? And who was the author? Gerald Kersh? Never heard of him.

Luckily I dipped into the text. The effect was instant. The writing was strong and stylish, the locations familiar yet exotic, the prose pounding in from the pavements outside, slang easily shifting into sharp observation. I bought the book, enjoyed my chow mein and, within days, was a Kersh fan, his writing showing that maybe there was a world of London fiction I'd missed. Robert De Niro was explained – the book had been turned into a film *twice*.

Night And The City was a revelation. Later I would discover the likes of *Fowlers End*, *The Angel And The Cuckoo* and *Prelude To A Certain Midnight*. And other forgotten London authors. Men such as James Curtis, Alexander Baron, Frank Norman. Cult books by Robert Westerby, Mark Benney, John Sommerfield. Others had been on their trail for years – Nick Robinson, Iain Sinclair, Chris Petit – but I didn't care. Better late than never.

It was clear that *Night And The City* ranked near the fiction of Alan Sillitoe, the only English author I knew who wrote about everyday people in a familiar language. Sillitoe's novels had themselves been a discovery years earlier, and while he came from a different background to my favourite English author George Orwell, the two men obviously shared the same humanity. Sillitoe's novels added a first-hand knowledge of the working world, the fact he often wrote about his native Nottingham unimportant as the language and warmth and defiance connected. From my first brush with Sillitoe I was hooked. The same happened with Gerald Kersh.

Night And The City is set in the Soho of legend, itself a focus for the glitz of the West End. The book recreates a trail of pubs and clubs and Italian-run cafés from back in the days when a bowl of spaghetti was still exotic. Kersh knew this world, and his sentences shine bright, his locations peopled by a nutty bunch of fluorescent characters with nuttier more fluorescent names – Anna Siberia, Figler, Phil Nosseross, the Black Strangler. They drink and plot in Bagrag's Cellar, Saxophone Joe's, The International Political Club.

Kersh's creations are flamboyant and believable, the novel's central character going by the name of Harry Fabian, a cockney wide boy who puts on a fake American accent and talks big, forever trying to impress but too often failing to convince. He is a small-time crook who throws away the money he has, desperate for some sort of recognition. He is also physically frail and from a poor background, the Dodger or Rotten in a flash suit. He is a vulnerable, Dickensian character. He is also a ponce.

The term 'ponce' was taken seriously when the novel was written. It was a term of abuse, even for the likes of Harry. Language changes, but it's interesting reading a book such as *Night And The City* to see how much slang is still in use. Kids learn from their parents and grandparents as much as their peers, maybe more so, though the teenage-rebellion industry would never admit this truth. Slang dips and rises, changes emphasis, wordplay something that Kersh and a small number of his contemporaries relished.

Today, the pimp has replaced the ponce, the term introduced via rappers and their corporate managers. Living off women has been glorified, yet a ponce or pimp remains among the lowest forms of lowlife. This term 'lowlife', meanwhile, is another interesting one, and was applied to a genre of fiction that seems to centre on Soho. The description does the writing itself and the social observations it makes a disservice, while there is probably a hidden edge to the term. Is the Marquis De Sade considered 'lowlife' fiction, or is this a double-edged insult for working-class fiction? Especially when it is written by someone from outside the establishment? And when the style applied breaks their rules?

Applying the first meaning, *Night And The City* and other so-called lowlife novels offer an uncensored glimpse of a vanished London. The descriptions and observations are probably impossible to find elsewhere, the same role covered in later decades by criminal and hooligan memoirs, and, to an extent, by modern films and television series.

For much of the novel there's something likeable about Harry Fabian, his vulnerability possibly the result of his poor upbringing, but his dealings with Mr Clark challenge any sympathy the reader feels, show the depths to which he will sink in his pursuit of a pound note. He crosses a couple of lines, and in the end it's personality not background that make Fabian what he is, the regular appearances of Bert the costermonger emphasising the fact. The final twist in the tale drills the message further home. This is an important element of the book. Bert is a decent, hard-working man with a lot more courage than Harry. He is the book's working-class champion.

Harry Fabian has no morals and no backbone, but Gerald Kersh clearly has both. He doesn't lay down the law like so many authors of the past but coaxes the reader along, plays his cards carefully, ultimately delivering a condemnation of greed and materialism.

Learning about Kersh's life is a bonus and adds to the novel. The researcher and editor Paul Duncan has been piecing together his story over the years, and much of the available information is down to his hard work. Gerald Kersh was one of the chaps, knew the pubs and characters of the West End, the lie of the land further into the suburbs. His movements make me feel closer to his work, as if I was destined to find that copy of *Night And The City*. He drank in The Fitzroy Tavern, a pub used by Fabian Of The Yard and the likes of George Orwell and Julian

Maclaren-Ross, somewhere I've known for a quarter of a century; he has connections with the Uxbridge Road which I know well; his roaming knowledge of Soho and its pubs means he probably used some of my favourites – The Ship, The Blue Posts, The Lamb And Flag. His younger years further out in Metroland offer a tentative link with the mental high roads of JG Ballard, the suburbs and M25 badlands another personal interest.

Kersh led a full life away from London and the West End, of course. He was respected for his short stories and articles as well as his novels, wrote about events during the Second World War, in which he was a soldier, was a survivor of bombing and wasn't scared of a fight, a man who travelled and experienced the world and lived in the United States, home of so many free-thinking writers over the years, men he had something in common with – Jack London, Charles Bukowski, John Fante, Hubert Selby Jr. Kersh was an original talent and seems to have died dodging creditors, largely forgotten, his books drifting out of print. He was never going to fit into the official canon, was too imaginative for the literary élitists.

We all build our own legends and myths, create histories, hear old stories and build new ones, tales that mutate and spiral out of control, real and imagined events stretching and bending and finally merging as they're pulled together in more sober moments. Gerald Kersh and *Night And The City* represent a starting point for my interest in London's forgotten fiction, the vibrancy of his writing and storytelling proving once again that good literature is timeless, even when it is recording the past.

John King

Book One

TWO WAYS OF GETTING
A HUNDRED POUNDS

ONE

The barber squeezed the rubber powder-bottle – *bop, bop, bop* – and a faint white bloom settled upon the chin of Mr Harry Fabian. As the chair clicked back to an upright position, Fabian had the pleasure of seeing himself, massaged pink and shaved like a film-star, twice reflected in a couple of mirrors before and behind him. If there was one spectacle that pleased Harry Fabian better than the reflection of his own face it was that of the back of his head. He uttered a breathy 'Ah!' expressive of complete gratification.

'Nothing like a massage to liven you up, sir,' said the barber.

'You said it,' said Fabian; and then added abruptly, like a man struck by inspiration: 'Say! That's not a bad idea for a song. Listen: "There's nothing like a massage to liven you up"' – he sang this to the tune of the last line of 'Minnie The Moocher' – 'Get it? Did I say not bad? Why, it's swell! It's the sort of thing that gets everybody humming it. They put it over in vaudeville acts; fellers say it to their girls. Massage . . . you know what I mean.' Fabian grinned.

'It's very good, sir.'

'I'll say it is. That's the way you get ideas. You look at a trombone, and you say: "The music goes round and around." Then the whole world sings it. You look round a place like this, and you say . . . well, say: "Hot Towels". "Hot towels, I'm in trouble; Oh, hot towels, I'm in trouble,"' sang Fabian, to the tune of 'Black Coffee', 'and there you are!'

'I wish I was clever enough to do things like that,' said the barber.

'Well, you know how it is: either you've got the talent or you haven't. Trouble is, there's no money about over here. I can always pick up a living, but not real money; nothing like what I got used to in the States. I have to work damn hard to pick up twenty pounds a week over here. But in the States, I used to make . . . ha, four hundred dollars a week, and without over-working at that.'

'What doing?'

Fabian looked up at the barber with indignant suspicion. 'Whadda you think? Writing songs. That's my *job*. But over here, there's no money about.'

'Thinking of going back?'

'Oh, I don't know.'

'There long, sir?'

'Ten years.'

'New York?'

'Yes.'

'I've got a brother in Brooklyn. What part did you live, sir?'

'Listen, are you going to be all night? Snap into it, will you? I've got a date.'

'Brilliantine, sir?'

'No, cream. Take care of that wave . . . That's right: just sort of push it in with the back of the comb . . .'

Harry Fabian stood up, adjusting his tie, and surveyed himself from head to foot. He was a little man, no more than thirty years old, excessively small-boned and narrow between the shoulders. He had a large head, perched on a neck no thicker than a big man's forearm, and a great deal of fine hair dressed in the style affected by Johnny Weissmuller. His face was pale; too wide between the ears and too narrow at the chin – a face like a wedge. He looked like a man with a good capacity for hatred. His eyes did not match. The left was large and watery, and it continually wavered and blinked with a flickering of whitish lashes; but the right was smaller, harder, steadier and of a more concentrated blue. Out of this eye he watched you. When he wanted to look dangerous, he simply closed his left eye, slamming the eyelid down like a shutter with an effort that twisted up the whole left-hand side of his face. He had a nose like the beak of a sparrow: that, together with his upper lip, which was pressed out of sight, and his lower jaw, which protruded like the head of a chopper, gave him an air of insolence, spite and mal-evolent calculation. He dressed far too well. There was a quality of savagery about his clothes – hatred in the relentless grip of his collar, malice in the vicious little knot of his tie, defiant acquisitiveness in the skin-tight fit of his coat – his whole body snarled with vindictive triumph over the memory of many dead years of shabbiness.

'Give me a good brush down,' he said. 'I hate dust. What d'you think of this suit? I will say one thing: clothes are dirt cheap over here. Look at this suit. Hand-made, and only nine pounds. You'd pay a hundred dollars for a suit like that in New York. What do I owe?'

'Vibro, shave, brush-up: four shillings, sir.'

Harry Fabian smacked down two half-crowns: he made them sound like twenty.

When he had gone, one of the assistants said: 'I wonder why Yanks go in for face-massage so much.'

'What Yank?' said the barber. 'Him? He's no American.'

'No? What did he say he was? A song-writer?'

'Yes; he writes songs like my tomcat writes songs.'

'What is he, then?'

Upon the slightly steamy surface of a mirror the barber wrote with a forefinger one letter – 'P'.

'Well, would you believe it!' exclaimed the assistant, taking off his white coat.

Ping! went the clock, on the first stroke of eight. Up and down the streets shops began to close. West Central started to flare and squirm in a blazing veinwork of neon-tubes. Bursting like inexhaustible fireworks, the million coloured bulbs of the electric signs blazed in perpetual recurrence over the face of the West End. Underground trains from the suburbs squirting out of their tunnels like red toothpaste out of tubes disgorged theatre crowds. Loaded buses rumbled towards the dog-tracks. Cinema vestibules became black with people. Vaudeville theatres, like gigantic vacuum-cleaners, suddenly sucked in waiting queues. Behind upper windows lights clicked on and blinds snapped down. Gas, wire, wax, oil – everything burned that would give out light. The darkness of the April night got thicker. It seeped down between the street lamps, poured into basements and lay deep and stagnant under the porches and the arches of the back streets. The last of the shop doors slammed. The places where one could eat, drink and amuse oneself alone remained open, and burned with a lurid and smoky brightness. Night closed down upon the city.

Harry Fabian, who had time to kill, walked where the crowds were thickest. He liked to be seen. He trod the streets with the confident step of the man who has money in his pocket. He stopped to look at a poster with a drawing of a classically nude woman and an inscription, BERNARD'S BRINE BATHS BUILD THE BODY BEAUTIFUL; struck a match against the picture so as to draw a short black line that rendered it legally indecent, and went on his way grinning. '*Say a policeman saw me do that: how could he prove that it wasn't an accident?*' he said to himself. He felt that he had scored a point against the forces of law and order; the cigarette between his lips glowed hot as he drew in defiant draughts of smoke. The next time he passed that poster, he decided, he would remember to bring a pencil. At the corner of Rathbone Place a prostitute nodded to him and said: 'Hallo, Harry.' Fabian replied: 'How's things, Marie?' but did not wait for an answer.

He crossed Oxford Street like a man in a hurry, but paused at the entrance to a pin-table saloon. He spent a dozen pennies at the Electric Crane, won a tooth-brush in a yellow celluloid case, but did not deign even to pick it up; sauntered through an avenue of clicking and clattering Jack Rabbit, Jig Saw and Merry-go-Round machines manned by intense, speechless people who feverishly crammed them with coppers; elbowed his way through the Skee-ball crowd at the back of the saloon, and put a penny into the slot of an automatic peep-show labelled THEIR HONEYMOON NIGHT. 'Rifle Range downstairs! Rifle Range downstairs!' bawled an attendant. Fabian went down.

There, where a sleepy girl brooded over four battered Winchesters, Fabian threw down a shilling.

'Gimme seven shots, beautiful, and keep the change. I just want to see if I can still hit anything. In the States I used to be able to split the card edgeways nine times out of ten at fifty yards with one of these little Twenty-twos, but lately my eyes have been getting bad . . .'

Spang! . . . *Spang!* went the rifle. The card came back jerkily along the wires, perforated with a little cluster of five holes in the centre bull and two in the outer bull.

'Very good,' said the girl.

'Lousy,' said Fabian, 'but I haven't had a gun in my hand for over six years. I'm used to heavier calibres – I can't get out of the habit of sighting low. Hell! *we* could of showed you some shooting back in 1927 in Chicago. Did you ever hear about Bugs Moran? . . . Chicago? Sure I lived there most of my life . . . No I quit the racket while I had my health and strength. It may be yellow, but who cares? Hymie Weiss wasn't yellow; Dion O'Banion wasn't yellow; Louis Alterie wasn't yellow – but where are they? Who laughs last? You know they used to call me Last Laugh . . . No, I left the booze racket for the movie business. Acting? Hell no; producing. I don't take the mug's end of any racket.'

'It must be nice to get on the films,' said the shooting-gallery attendant.

Fabian instantly turned his hard little right eye upon her and looked with thoughtful appraisal from her round young face to her plump precocious breasts. Then he replied: 'It struck me as soon as I saw you that you'd photograph well. You're not beautiful in the same style as Garbo or Dietrich; but you got sex appeal and personality. That's more important. Look at Margaret Sullavan. Just lately, I been concentrating more on the musical side; but I got contacts with some of the biggest men in the industry. Me and Goldwyn,' said Fabian, crossing the first two fingers of his left hand, and holding them up for inspection, 'are like that. I can always put you in touch. Get some photographs done. I'll call in again. You won't forget? Good. I'll be seeing you.'

Fabian went out into the street.

The shooting-gallery attendant remarked to one of the pin-table barkers: 'Says 'e can get me on the films! Takes me for a fool or somefink. Does 'e fink I don't know what 'e *is*?' She put her tongue between her lips and made a rude noise.

* * *

The habitual liar always imagines that his lies ring true. No miracle of belief can equal his childlike faith in the credulity of the people who listen to him; and so it comes to pass that he fools nobody as completely as he fools himself. Fabian walked on slowly, unimpaired in his self-esteem. But when he reached the corner of Charing Cross Road and saw that it was already nine o'clock, he moved faster. He crossed to High Street, Bloomsbury, and entered one of those innumerable back-doubles which spring, like tortuous capillaries, out of the larger, congested arteries of ancient cities. A man came towards him.

'Hallo, Duke,' said Fabian.

'Ah-hah!' said the man called Duke. He was short and heavy, with the ashen complexion of the man who never sees daylight, and a heavy face knocked out of shape in some forgotten back-alley skirmish; thin purplish lips, compressed to a line like a dried-up pin-scratch; quite expressionless. The vague light of the street-lamp filled his eye-sockets with shadows, and he spoke to Fabian without moving his lips, in the hurried undertone of the old convict. Force of habit caused him to hide his cigarette in the palm of his hand as he smoked it. Smoke came out of his nostrils, but the glow of the cigarette was invisible.

'How's life, Duke?'

'On the ribs.'

'You skint?'

'Dead skint.'

'Catch hold of this,' said Fabian, passing two half-crowns.

'Thanks: I won't forget yer, Harry.'

'You been up the club?'

'Just left there. You know what they done? They put the bar on me.'

'Is that a fact?' asked Fabian, with sympathy. 'Well, you should worry. Did you notice Figler up there?'

'No. One o' these days I'm gonna do that gaff; I'll smash the bloody place up.'

'Don't you be such a mug, Duke. You don't want no trouble with that mob. If they bar you, let 'em. Don't you care. Stick around: I may have something in your line in a day or two.'

'Thanks, Harry; I won't forget yer.'

Fabian went to a door under a little electric sign, INTER-NATIONAL POLITICAL CLUB, and entered.

The International Political Club was quiet, even respectable. It had a subdued atmosphere, like a committee-room. Upon an old dumb-waiter near the door stood an old eighteen-pounder shell-case, filled with paper chrysanthemums, and a pile of shabby back numbers of the *Cornhill Magazine*. The walls were decorated with portraits of King Edward VII, Queen Victoria and King George V; an engraving of a prize Hereford bull; a chromo labelled LOVE ME, LOVE MY DOG and a picture of a little girl sitting on the shoulders of her father and saying: 'I'se bigger than 'oo.' The rules of the club occupied a big green frame. Above them hung a notice:

THE WRITING OF BETTING SLIPS IS
STRICTLY FORBIDDEN IN THIS
CLUB!

below them another notice:

MEMBERS ARE STRICTLY FORBIDDEN TO USE
THE TELEPHONE FOR THE PURPOSE OF
BETTING.

At the end of the club-room stood the bar, with a glass case for sandwiches, some shelves full of bottles and a dozen huge Salami sausages hanging on strings; bound round, dried and blackened, marked with pallid patches of exuded grease – the corpses of wicked Salamis, hanged and strung up as a warning to the rest. Just below them hung a third notice:

ANY MEMBER USING BLASPHEMOUS OR
INDECENT LANGUAGE IS LIABLE TO
SUSPENSION, WITHOUT NOTICE,
FROM THE CLUB.

It was a club into which you might, without hesitation, have taken your grandmother.

Its staid atmosphere was spoiled only by the face of the proprietress. This woman had something about her that was indescribably terrifying. Imagine the death-mask of Julius Cæsar, plastered with rouge, and stuck with a pair of eyes as small, as flat and as bright as newly cut cross-sections of .38 calibre bullets; marked with eyebrows that ran together in a straight black bar; and surmounted by a million diabolical black hairs that sprang in a nightmarish cascade up out of her skull, like a dark fountain of accumulated wickedness squeezed out by the pressure of her corsets. She painted her lips bright carmine, but had a habit of pressing them together so firmly that lipstick was smeared over the surrounding skin. This made her look like a newly fed ghoul that has forgotten to wipe its mouth. She never had very much to say. She was supposed to be a Russian. Her name? Scarcely credible: Anna Siberia.

'Gin, Anna?' asked Fabian.

'Thanks.'

'I'll have a Haig. Ah! there's the man I'm looking for. Anna, another Haig for Mr Figler. Hallo, Figler!'

It may be said that the International Political Club was a meeting-place on the shifting frontier between the slough of small business and the quagmire of the underworld. But on which side of the frontier did Figler belong? It was hard to decide. He was a business-man; but that word 'business' is so comprehensive, it is almost meaningless. Many commercial gentlemen are called 'business men' until they are found out; then they are described as 'crooks'. Many commercial gentlemen are called 'crooks' until it is discovered that they are merely sharp business men. Figler belonged to no definite class. It was said that he was an honest man in his dealings. Nevertheless, he had been known to do some curious strokes of business. He was one of those men who have been everywhere, know everybody, pick up a smattering of every trade, learn the exact market value of every conceivable commodity, are incapable of anger or astonishment or disappointment, and are out of place in any society. Such was Figler. His activities were manifold and diverse. He was the perfect type of the agent or go-between. He lived almost entirely on percentages, commissions, corners, rake-offs, fivers from buyers, fivers from sellers – he was the kind of man that goes into the world with nothing but an eye and a tongue, and makes money without laying out a penny. Figler could find a market for whatever anybody had to sell, or a seller for whatever anybody wanted to buy; clean or dirty, fair or foul. He had the self-contained hardihood of the born salesman. Kicked out at the door, he would come through the window. He simply would not take No for an answer. The man never lived who could move him with insults: if you called him a bastard, he shrugged his shoulders and said: 'Perhaps.' He was armour plated against derision. By such qualities he made his living – certainly not by attractive sales talk, personality or prepossessing appearance. Looking at him you had an impression of a large quantity of something soft poured into a smallish black suit with a pin-stripe, and overflowing at the wrists and collar; a long body supported by little crooked legs; a curved spine, round shoulders, a pot-belly and a face of the colour and texture of a Welsh rarebit. In order to reproduce the way Figler spoke, put your tongue between your teeth, stop up your nose, half fill your mouth with saliva and try to say: 'This is the end of the matter.' He suffered with an interminable cold in the head, a bottomless nasal catarrh. He could blow his nose from morning to night without clearing his head. Goldsmith's villagers wondered at the school-master; you would have wondered at Figler – how one small head could carry all he blew. He breathed laboriously. It was necessary for him to exhale with a vehement snort so that he could snatch a quick inward breath before a stoppage occurred; and so he managed to save himself from drowning on dry land.

'Hallo, Harry,' said Figler.

'I been looking all over the place for you.'

'What's on?'

'I want to have a word with you. I got a proposition on hand, and I thought you might be interested.'

'What's your proposition, Harry?'

'What are you drinking? Finish that and have another.'

'No, thanks. No more. What's the idea, Harry?'

'Listen, Figler: I'll put the matter to you in a nutshell. I've been figuring out a scheme for running some all-in wrestling.'

'All-in wrestling? Well, you could do a lot worse. There's money in it, on the promotion side.'

'You bet, on the promotion side! Do you think I'd take the

sucker's end of that racket? I got it all figured out. There's still some dough to be made out of it.'

'Do you *know* the business?'

'I wouldn't be such a mug as to go into any business I didn't know, Figler. I can't see any reason why I shouldn't make up a few programmes. I want you to come in with me.'

'Why me?'

'Simply because in the first place I know I can trust you; in the second place, you've got brains; and, thirdly, you can put up a bit of money.'

'Oh, can I? Uh . . . How much do you think you can do it on?'

'Two hundred pounds.'

'Can't you raise two hundred?'

'Listen, Figler, things are not so good. I've had a bad month. I've had a lot to pay out. I'll be quite frank with you; I've been a bit of a mug. First of all, I thought I could beat the ponies, and I lost a lot. Then I made a book up at the Crystal Stadium, with Yosh the Chopper, and he let me down for over ninety quid. It left me short.'

'So you mean to say you want me to put up the whole two hundred quid? Huh . . .'

'It's a cinch, Figler. It'd pay you back a thousand per cent.'

'Listen, Harry, I don't trust those thousand per cents.'

'Listen, Figler, why be a mug?'

'I may be a mug, Harry –'

'Listen, just for a second. I know the business from A to Z. I could start tomorrow. Look at the money Bielinski's making out of it. And there's room for more. The most important thing is to get a good hall and a popular name to top the bill. The rest is easy. I'm in touch with two good halls. I can get 'em tomorrow. I know all about tickets, and I've got a feller that works for Bielinski to do the publicity for me on the side. Wrestlers I can always get. I know 'em all. All we need is a gym and some mats, and we can build up our own men. Don't you get what I mean? Tie 'em up on long-term contracts, the bastards! There's a hundred big fellers that'd be only too glad to do it –'

'There always is. But will the public be only too glad to pay good money to see them do it?'

'Listen, Figler. I know this game and you don't. It's a racket, from top to bottom. Tell me, what does the English public know about wrestling? They've never seen it and they don't want it. It's too slow for them. They ain't educated up to it. The only real wrestler they ever heard of is Hackenschmidt. They can't *understand* scientific wrestling; it don't mean a thing to 'em. They won't pay to see Græco-Roman, or Judo, or catch-as-catch-can; they want blood, and rough stuff. And I tell you, you can train any bloody lousy coal-heaver to do that. Listen. Over at the Roman Club, the other night, there was a guy called Cropman. I'm giving you this as an example. He was a classy wrestler, Continental style – he must have spent twenty years learning the holds. What happened? All the public started whistling him off. "Give him a coupla cushions and let him go to sleep!" That's what they said. They laughed him out of the ring. But on the same bill there was a guy called the Black Strangler, and they went raving mad about him. Now listen, Figler; I can tell you all about the Black Strangler. Three months ago he was a nigger fireman on a Jamaica banana-boat. Wrestle? Wrestle my foot! He knows exactly two things – a hammerlock and an elbow nudge. The rest of the time, he spits, he shouts, he bites, he kicks, he goes cuckoo – and the public fall for it. They love it. All the women run miles to see him. They get in the ringside seats and they bounce about like they had red-hot bricks under their backsides. And Bielinski picked him up one day in the Black Man's café and slammed him into a bill the same night. He had to borrow a jock-strap and a pair of shorts, and fought barefoot. And now? The Black Strangler. Hell, Figler, you can't tell me a thing about building up wrestlers. Me and –'

'Listen, Harry, and don't get excited. I ain't got no two hundred pounds to throw away. You know very well I'm always game for a go at anything. But I ain't a financier.'

'I know you're not, Figler. I know you're a business-man and I want your help.'

'As a matter of fact *I've* been thinking of going in for a bit of wrestling promotion myself. I ain't putting up money for other people to play with. If you can put up one hundred I might find the other. And *if* I came in, we'd have a joint account. It would be on a straight fifty-fifty basis.'

'Is that a promise?'

'I don't make no definite promises. You see, Harry, I make it a rule never to make any business arrangements with people who have nothing to lose. Find a hundred pounds. Show me that hundred pounds and then I'll come in with you.'

'Will you shake on that?'

'Sure.'

'I think I can get a hundred,' said Fabian.

'Well, you must get it within a week. If you can't raise the money by then, count me out.'

'Ah, Figler, have a heart!'

'A week. I can't be bothered to mess about.'

'Jesus, Figler! A week?'

'Well, I got to be going, Harry. See you tomorrow or the next day. Best of luck. So long, Harry. Don't forget.'

Figler left the club, but Fabian sat still, biting his upper lip.

'A week,' muttered Fabian. 'Oh hell, one week!'

TWO

A man approached Fabian's table and sat down opposite him.

'Well, if it isn't Mr Clark!' said Fabian.

'Good evening, Fabian,' said Mr Clark. 'I believe I have a little debt to settle.'

'No hurry.'

'I may as well settle now and get it clear,' said Mr Clark, taking out a note-case and selecting a five-pound note. 'Five is the amount, I believe. Would you prefer small notes?'

'It's all the same,' said Fabian. 'Money is money. Were those men all right?'

'Quite.'

'Did you have to pay them much?'

'As much as I expected.'

'You could get those guys to do anything in the world for a fiver apiece.'

'Could you? However, I can use some more men like that.'

'Well, Mr Clark, I think I can find you a few more, but they look pretty lousy.'

'I don't care if they haven't a shirt to their backs. Just let them be unmarried. I'll take care of the rest.'

'Who got the Greek? Louise?'

'No. Nobody you would know.'

'Well, she should worry, whoever she is. A husband's a husband. But listen, Mr Clark: that other guy, the Irish one.'

'Well, what about him?'

'You want to keep your eye on him. He might try some funny stuff.'

'For example?'

'Oh . . . I don't know. But he looks the type, and you don't want any funny stuff.'

'I think,' said Mr Clark, and if a refrigerator had a voice it would speak in just such a tone, 'I think I am competent to deal with that. People who deal with me do their part and get their share. No more, no less. I have conveyed to your Irish friend just how silly it would be to attempt any . . . funny stuff. I have no time for it. I'm a business-man.'

Mr Clark had a subdued voice with cultured undertones: a very cool voice. He was freezing point made articulate. He spoke as if he preferred not to be heard. Cold reserve, also, was written in the expression of his face. He had the discreet, tight mouth of a family lawyer – a burglar-proof safe, for the locking up of secrets, double-bolted by the muscles of his long square jaw. His face was remarkably symmetrical. There was a cleft between his eyes and in his chin: these marks looked like the remains of a central line about which his head had been mathematically constructed. Out of unwrinkled olive skin his large black eyes, clear cut, bright, and seemingly lidless, stared steadily into space. You might have said that he was an ex-theological student who had deserted the seminary for one of the learned professions. There was something clerical about his clothes: his straight-cut black coat, his narrow trousers, his two-inch collar, and his thick shoes. But precisely placed in the middle of his sombre tie there was a small, but extremely beautiful diamond. He had an air of detachment. How did he live? His associates, who knew, would not say; and the police, who also knew, had no proof. Reports connected him with the white-slave trade and the traffic in narcotics. Rumours hinted at the organisation of jewel robberies and other things which verged upon the fantastic. He ran an office near Great Marlborough Street. His brass plate said ARTHUR MAYO CLARK, COMMISSION AGENT: his shelves were filled with law books. All sorts of people had been seen in his waiting-room – sometimes hard-bitten, black-browed Parisian prostitutes; sometimes gauche country girls, always good-looking, nursing large cardboard suitcases; sometimes morose Italians, with their hands in their pockets; sometimes international-looking gentlemen in American overcoats, German hats, Belgian gloves, French shoes and Austrian neckties, carrying elegant cowhide bags plastered with patchworks of hotel labels; sometimes middle-aged gentlemen who radiated an aseptic aura of indubitable respectability; sometimes chorus-boys, with more powder on their cheeks than men are accustomed to use; sometimes Cypriots, with half-rations of forehead and double allowances of chin; or sub-human types whose abysmal faces were posters advertising fifty-seven varieties of human wickedness. What they had to say to Mr Clark and what he had to do with them remained a mystery. He left his office by seven every evening. Furtive mice crept out of their holes to sniff suspiciously at the scattered butts of cigarettes and cigars on the floor of the waiting-room – the familiar Player's, the outlandish Gitanes, Toscani, Cigarette Macedonia, Camels and Lucky Strikes. Mr Clark merged with the crowds in the streets and did several little business deals in some unlikely places before he went home to sleep.

'Yes, sure,' said Harry Fabian, who in his presence found it particularly difficult to concentrate his refractory left eye. 'Sure, sure. We don't want any funny business. Only about that Irish feller: I just thought I'd better tell you, that's all.'

'I know,' said Mr Clark, showing one or two excellent teeth in a prim little smile, 'and I'm much obliged to you. What will you drink?'

'A small Scotch.'

'Anna! A large Haig for Mr Fabian and a small beer for me.'

'Listen. Mr Clark,' said Fabian earnestly, 'there's a proposition I'd like to talk to you about. Can you lend me a hundred pounds? I'd give you back a hundred and fifty in eight weeks. I –'

'Simply lend you a hundred pounds, eh?'

'Yes, but I'd pay back a hundred and fif –'

Mr Clark shook his head.

'You can't?' said Fabian.

'Couldn't possibly. Bring me forty unmarried men tomorrow and I'll give you twenty five-pound notes the day after,' said Mr Clark.

'Forty! Hell! What am I? A matrimonial agency or something? Honest to God, Mr Clark, I got a red-hot proposition on hand.'

'Can't Zoë find the money for you?'

Fabian shrugged his shoulders.

'Won't you have another drink, Fabian?'

'No.'

'Not even a small one?'

'No.'

'What is this proposition of yours, anyway?'

'All-in wrestling promotion! It's a cin –'

'Ah, not in my line at all, I'm afraid. But I wish you every success,' said Mr Clark, nodding courteously, taking one tiny sip of beer and pushing the glass away. 'Half-past ten. How time flies in your company! Excuse me. Good-night.'

'Tightwad,' said Fabian, in an audible mutter. An exact transcription of his thoughts at that moment would have read like this: '*A hundred pounds. Oh, hell, hell, hell! A hundred pounds. A hundred pounds. Helllllll! Zoë'll have to find it. If I have to break her neck, Zoë'll have to find it.*'

His lower lip came within less than half an inch of his nose. He stood up with an abrupt gesture that sent his chair tottering backwards and stamped out of the International Political Club.

Harry Fabian walked now in straight lines, like a man with a definite objective. *Tap, tap; tap, tap* went his sharp little heels as he made his way southward through the humid night to his flat in Rupert Street.

* * *

Fabian had a talent for keyhole-espionage, and he was an eaves-dropper by vocation. As he approached his flat he walked quietly. He went up the stairs and down the passage like a prowling cat, and when he reached his own door he stopped and listened, turned the key with indescribable caution, closed the door soundlessly and listened again. As soon as he was sure that he was alone, he went into the little living-room next to the bed-room and put on his overcoat, which was hanging behind the door. But just as he turned to go out again he heard the sound of feet in the passage. Fabian was something of a connoisseur of footsteps: he recognised the sharp click of Zoë's Cuban heels sounding above the slower and heavier tread of unknown masculine feet. He slipped back into the living-room, bolted the door and switched off the light a second before Zoë's key grated in the lock. He waited in the dark. Zoë, as usual, led her visitor straight to the bedroom. Fabian heard her voice say: 'Just a second while I put the light on . . . Come in, dear.'

The walls of the flat were thin, but not quite thin enough for Fabian, who, being of an inquisitive disposition, liked to have a glimpse of all that went on about him. He had privately per-forated the bedroom wall with three or four gimlet-holes, care-fully boring them through the dark parts in the pattern of the wallpaper so that Zoë was unaware of their existence. Through these holes Fabian could see without being seen, and hear things which no third party was meant to hear. He applied his sharp right eye now to a spyhole which gave him a long view right across the bedroom.

It was a small room, lined with paper of a Chinese pattern, illuminated by a cheap standard lamp with a fringed yellow shade, and carpeted with an imitation Chinese rug in blue and yellow. There was a big double divan, with a bedspread of electric blue decorated with pink rosebuds; a wardrobe; a dressing-table, littered with brushes, broken scent-sprays and cheap ornaments such as one wins in the Christmas fun-fairs; a crucifix.

Zoë stood by the lamp, taking off her hat.

She was a handsome girl, built in the almost indecently voluptuous proportions of a woman in an Indian carving – one of those girls whose breasts, mature at fifteen, rapidly swell to a flaccid over-ripeness in a humid atmosphere of eroticism, like tomatoes in a hothouse. Now, at twenty-three, Zoë had almost reached the zenith of her physical development: men who did not know her name referred to her not as 'the girl with black, frizzy hair' or 'the dark girl with the mole on her chin', but as 'the girl with the bust'. Fabian, in his invisibility, looked straight into her eyes: '*What a woman!*' he said to himself. '*What a hell of a long way she could go if only she wasn't so soft!*' In full face, in the light of the lamp, Zoë really was extraordinarily beautiful; but as she turned her head to speak to her visitor she displayed a profile that expressed no will – the loose, rolling physiognomy of a woman in whom ovulation had overbalanced cerebration.

The visitor, on the other hand, was one of those men whom it is impossible to associate with any idea of sex – one of those slight, timid gentlemen who, through congenital respectability, seem never to have had the power of enjoying their virility. He had taken off his hat on entering the bedroom. Fabian could see his face distinctly – very pale, bony and elongated by the baldness of his forehead. Such hair as remained on his head was of an indeterminate colour; so were his scanty eyebrows and his clipped moustache. You see five hundred similar faces in a ten-minute walk through the City – see them and forget them – but there was one thing which would have made you look twice at this little man, and that was his expression of abject unhappiness. He had a dull, grey look of patient misery. The deep dark rings under his eyes might have been cut into his face by the passage of tears. The dripping of water can wear away stone – let alone the face of a poor little man! '*He looks as if he's lost a fiver and picked up a penny*' – that was how Fabian at his spyhole defined this look.

Fabian looked, without much interest, at the visitor's plain grey overcoat, hard felt hat and stiff collar. He had seen the type before, in that bedroom – the type of the man of the suburbs, in the late forties; reserved, cautious, scared out of his life; the bread-winner, earning about four hundred pounds a year, twenty-five years married, and somewhat tired of an indifferent wife; seized by an amorous spasm as drastic as a suicidal impulse, and taking a terrible plunge into a prostitute's bedroom. Fabian twisted his face into a scornful grimace in the dark: he knew exactly what was going to happen. The little man would lie down and enfold Zoë in a shaky embrace, then remember all the gruesome tales he had heard about chancres and general paralysis, become impotent and apologetic, plead tiredness, put down his money and run away . . .

Zoë switched on the radio. The voice of a dance-band vocalist came through: 'Struttin' like a peacock, feelin' like a millionaire' . . . Zoë danced down the room, throwing off her dress, and appeared in black lace cami-knickers. Fabian nodded approvingly. But the visitor sat on the edge of the divan, without removing his overcoat.

'You know,' said Zoë, 'I rather like you. You've got a nice face. Dance?'

'No, thank you,' said the visitor. 'I . . . you know, I didn't really come here for . . . for anything like that. I didn't want to . . . to . . . do anything. I was merely lonely. I hope you're not offended. I . . . I liked the look of you, and I . . . I thought perhaps you wouldn't mind just . . . just keeping me company for half an hour or so – just sitting down quietly with me.'

'*Well, of all the mugs!*' said Fabian.

'Why, you poor man!' said Zoë, with immediate sympathy. 'As if I'd mind. I'm sorry you're lonely, dear. Would you like me just to sit down and talk? Shall I switch the wireless off?'

'You wouldn't mind?'

Dop went the switch, and the singer was silent.

'You look dead beat,' said Zoë. 'What have you been doing to yourself?'

'Nothing; only not sleeping.'

'Why not?'

'I don't know.'

'You'll get all run down if you're not careful. You can't do without sleep. Listen, I'll tell you what – you get into bed and have a rest for half an hour or so and I'll lie down with you and talk to you. Eh?'

'It's very kind of you but I'd rather sit, thanks.'

'How would you like me to make you a cup of tea?'

'No, thank you. But it's kind of you to suggest it. I'm much obliged to you.'

Zoë could think of nothing else to say for a minute or so and there was an awkward silence, until the little man said: 'Have you been here long?'

'Two years.'

'Do you . . . do well?'

'Not bad.'

The visitor pointed to a photograph of Fabian on the mantel-piece and asked: 'Who's that?'

'Oh, that's a friend of mine. He writes music.'

'Really? . . . Er, have you been in this business long?'

'Since I was nineteen: about four years.'

'Do you like it?'

'Oh, I don't know. It's not so bad. You know, I've seen you many times round about here, just lately, and I often wondered who you were,' said Zoë. 'One of my friends thought you was a detective, but I knew you wasn't. But I thought it was funny seeing a man like you hanging around all those low-down places, at all hours of the night. Tell me, what's the matter? Are you unhappy at home, or something?'

'Not exactly. It's just loneliness. It's a funny story.'

'Well, tell me.'

'I should *like* to, but . . .'

'Well, if it's a secret, don't tell me, then. Just lie back and have a rest. My God! you look as if you need it.'

'You know, you're very sweet. I feel I can talk to you in confidence.'

'Of course you can. I wouldn't breathe a word.'

'Well, you see, it's like this. I'm a married man.'

'But your wife doesn't sort of understand you.'

'Nothing like that. I've been married for over twenty years, quite happily. But some time ago my wife was taken ill.'

'What with?'

'Cancer.'

'I wouldn't wish my worst enemy to have cancer,' said Zoë.

'Well, you see, I'm a bacteriologist.'

'Hn?'

31

'I worked for a yeast company, you understand, on night work – seeing about fermentation, and all that kind of thing.'

'That must have been interesting.'

'Yes. But shortly after my wife was taken ill my firm amalgamated with another firm, and I lost my job. And at my age, in my line of business, it's not so easy to find another.'

'*Jesus! is this little rat going to say he's got no money?*' wondered Fabian.

'So what did you do?' asked Zoë.

'Well, my wife's in a nursing-home. She hasn't got much longer to live. She was always of a worrying disposition – the slightest mishap could upset her for weeks. I didn't want to poison the last few months of her life by telling her that I'd lost my job, so I kept up a pretence of going to work every night and coming home every morning. Then her sister came to keep house for me, and I had to go on keeping it up.'

'Couldn't you have told the sister?'

'She wouldn't have kept it to herself. So every night I leave for work; and every morning I come home; and every week I produce a pay-envelope. I draw on my savings.'

'Didn't they pension you off?'

'No, but they gave me a year's salary as compensation. Besides, I've saved a little. We weren't spendthrifts. We lived fairly well, yes; but nothing lavish. Cinema once or twice a week. Perhaps once or twice in a year – on our wedding anniversary, for example – we put on evening-dress and came up to Town to go to a theatre and have supper at some restaurant where we could have a bottle of wine and listen to the band. Nothing luxurious. We got on very well together. You know, when people call your wife your "better half" there's something in it. If two people live quite happily together for a long time they really do grow together. They become one. And if you cut them apart . . .'

'Ah, you poor dear!' said Zoë. Her eyes filled and overflowed. Two large sentimental tears dropped, with two tiny splashes, on to her bare right thigh.

'The trouble is,' said the little man, 'that I have to kill time. I daren't confide in anybody.'

'Haven't you got any friends?'

'None that I could really talk to. I've always kept myself very much to myself. I have to go and sit among strangers – all these people who live at night. I daren't go where any of my neighbours might be. I have to go to the places you've seen me in.'

'Why don't you take another room somewhere?'

'Simply because I can't bear to be alone. This has knocked my life to pieces. I can't sleep, or anything. I have to keep roaming about . . .'

'Couldn't you say you'd been put on to day work?'

'It still wouldn't make any difference. I can't sleep at night. In the daytime I can show myself in my own neighbourhood: that's not so bad. But you have no idea how awful it is for me to be alone now, at night. No, no; let me see her out in peace and then I don't care. Poor woman, cancer is quite enough without anything else.'

'Your wife's sister must be a bitch.'

'She's a very malicious woman. It's very nice of you to listen to all this. I'm very grateful, I am indeed.'

'You know, I think you're awfully nice,' said Zoë. 'Don't you be afraid of me. Get it off your mind. Why don't you lie down and have a little rest? Just for a quarter of an hour. It'll do you good: you look terrible.'

'No, I couldn't rest.'

'Shall I go out and get you a drink?'

'No, thanks; I drink too much, lately.' The little man patted her leg with a grateful gesture; then, becoming suddenly conscious of what he was doing, withdrew his hand abruptly.

On the other side of the wall Fabian grinned from ear to ear.

'It's good to be able to talk to you,' said the little man. 'It's a load off my mind. It's all very innocent – not like confessing a crime or anything like that – but it means a great deal to me. I simply couldn't *dare* tell anybody I know. It may sound ridiculous, but I couldn't. Thank you. I'm extremely grateful. I shan't bother you any longer; I shall be off in a minute . . .'

'*By God! This looks like a real break!*' thought Fabian, as an idea occurred to him. He clenched his fists in the darkness and glared at Zoë through the gimlet-hole. He wanted to cry out: 'Get his address, you nitwit!' He trembled with excitement.

'Where are you going from here?' asked Zoë.

'I don't know. I think I'll go and have a cup of coffee somewhere.' The little man dipped two fingers into his breast pocket and took out three pound notes. 'Thank you. Please take this. I've wasted a lot of your valuable time,' he said.

'No, that's all right,' said Zoë. She pushed the money back and, with a sudden impulse, kissed him on the forehead.

In the darkness Fabian ground his teeth.

'No, I insist,' said the little man. 'A present. Not a fee – a present. Buy a hat or something. You're a sweet girl. I'll come again, just to talk to you, if I may. God bless you. Good-night!'

'*Hellll!*' Fabian actually kicked himself. '*What a mug I was not to have slipped out five minutes ago and waited for him.*'

'Wait a minute,' said Zoë. 'Let me put your tie straight. And you've got a lot of bits of fluff on the back of your coat; just a second, I'll brush it for you –'

Fabian did not wait to hear any more. He slid back the bolt, edged out of the living-room and opened the front door, all without a sound. He had a technique of closing doors silently: he passed out of the flat like a shadow, and darted downstairs.

'Thank God for that!' said Fabian, who was not devoid of religious principles.

It was raining. He stood, as if for shelter, in the entrance to the house.

The yellowish light of the street-lamps vacillated in falling sheets of water. With a savage east wind behind it the heavy rain shot down at an angle, as if it meant once and for all to wash away all the vermin that swam over the feverish face of this dreary and interminable City.

The little man came down and walked away.

Fabian put up his coat collar and followed him.

THREE

At any other hour Fabian could have stuck to the little man's heels as surely and unobtrusively as his shadow, but at this time the theatres were closing, and dense crowds, squeezed out of every vestibule, began to break up and block the pavements. The streets became black with pedestrians, rushing the suburban buses, pouring towards the openings of the subways and tumbling in cataracts down to the outgoing trains. The City was emptying itself. In Regent Street and Shaftesbury Avenue the traffic streams grew thicker and slowed down. Through avenues of trembling radiators, in the red-and-yellow glow of traffic-lights and the roaring of a hundred thousand motors, men and women scampered from beacon to beacon over the safety-crossings. There was an atmosphere of panic: you thought of Sodom under the thunderbolts. In Rupert Street, jammed bonnet to bumper, a line of quivering cars waited for the lights to change. Under the shaky scarlet light of the neon signs, Chrysler nuzzled Austin, and Morris sniffed at the hindquarters of Ford, as if that humid spring night had brought about some nightmarish mating season of machines – some madman's vision of the coupling of panting iron beasts in a burning jungle of stone.

The little man reached Shaftesbury Avenue, with Fabian elbowing after him, and stepped into the road. But just as Fabian approached the curb, the traffic-light flashed green, and with a screaming of klaxons and tortured brakes and gears, a solid bar of traffic slid up to Piccadilly, while Fabian stood, sucking in his upper lip, sticking out his lower jaw, and presenting a profile like the outline of a broken window under the hooded lamps of the beacon. He watched, and saw the little man arrive at the opposite pavement. The sober grey overcoat fluttered for a second on the edge of a crowd, which immediately closed over it.

It was as if the City had swallowed the little man as a hippopotamus might swallow a fly. Indeed, no ordinary person would have attempted to look for him in the tangled passages of the quarter into which he had so suddenly disappeared. But Harry Fabian, born in a slum, bred in the gutters, versed in the tortuous geography of the night-world and familiar with every rat-hole in West One and West Central, had no intention of giving up the chase. He was not quite an ordinary person: he had highly developed intuitions, proceeding from long and cumulative experience of the customs of the City. I have mentioned how he could appraise a footstep. He could, by a similar method of

35

spontaneous reasoning, read a face, interpret an expression, calculate how much money you were in the habit of spending, or even decide by the look of you which restaurant or café you would probably frequent. He saw London as a kind of Inferno – a series of concentric areas with Piccadilly Circus as the ultimate centre. The shape of a human face, like a key, touched a series of springs beneath his consciousness, and set in motion a complicated mechanism of comparative memory which, juggling with permutations and combinations of a thousand observations, could deliver an immediate and reasonably accurate estimate of the qualities behind that face and the circle to which it belonged. The same kind of thing takes place in your own mind when you recognise a wanton look on the face of a woman or a lascivious expression in the eyes of a man. Fabian could say: 'This girl works in a dress-shop' or 'This man is a coward,' though, like an experienced doctor diagnosing some ambiguous pathological condition, he could not have explained how he arrived at his conclusion.

But now, considering the little man, Fabian's mind became blank. A respectable person of the middle class, out to kill time in Piccadilly, will probably go to the Corner House. But if he wishes to avoid such places, where any of his friends may see him, who can say where he will go then?

Fabian's intuition had failed him. He was compelled to fall back on common-sense reasoning. This took place quite unconsciously: he was aware only of a kind of geographical confusion, full of the names of clubs and cafés . . .

'He's gone to have a coffee. He's scared of meeting anybody he knows. He'll keep out of the big places. He'll feel everybody's staring at him in the little places. He won't have the nerve to walk into Peter the Greek's or the Calabria. He'll feel shy mixing with all the girls in the Vesuvio or Primavera's. He'll be afraid to go downstairs into any of the dives. He hasn't been around here long enough to be a member of any of the clubs. He won't go into Volpe's; too many sightseers. He won't go to the first place he comes to; he'll turn down a side-street – not a dark one. He'll look in at Domenico's, but he won't go in – he's the kind of mug that can't make up his mind first time. He won't go to the Continental; the boys'll be in, back from the dogs. The Glorious

Cyprus? No. He'll feel nervous, standing about – he'll cross the road quick, and go to the East and West –'

'I got a hunch! He must have gone to the East and West!' said the conscious mind of Harry Fabian. The idea seemed to come out of nothing – a heaven-sent inspiration. Fabian would have wagered his last penny on it. He stepped forward briskly, with perfect confidence, crossed Shaftesbury Avenue and, humming 'Pal of My Cradle Days', a song of which he was inordinately fond, hurried to the East and West Café.

* * *

When Fabian reached the café, he opened the door five or six inches, inserted his wedge-like face, and looked around. The place was full. After the rain-cooled night air, the atmosphere of the café, heavy with steam and the fumes of Toscani cigars, struck him in the face like a damp blanket. Fabian's chest expanded: he was breathing his native air. He went in and passed from table to table, scrutinising every face with his sharp right eye. The front part of the café was crowded with shrieking Italians, prodding at crumpled newspapers, or smashing match-boxes with their fists, re-enacting the fall of Addis Ababa. At the back, two huge old Greeks, as grey and motionless as Stone-henge, brooded over a game of chess; surrounding them, a dozen spectators clawed at the air in uncontrollable excitement. Standing in a corner by the electric crane a fat little Frenchman, red with triumph, waved a twopenny cigarette-holder which he had just won, and invited all the world to come and have a cup of coffee. Beside him, utterly absorbed, unconscious of every-thing else, a cadaverous old gentleman with an inflamed nose sat removing wax from his left ear with a pipe-cleaner. Nearby, two or three young men, heavy-eyed and putty-faced, carried on an interminable and incomprehensible argument over a handful of champagne corks, while at the same table, a smartly dressed Neapolitan, as dark and as miserable as sin, made rings with an empty coffee-cup upon a crumpled greyhound-racing pro-gramme.

But there was no sign of anybody even resembling the little man. Fabian walked out, biting his lips. He stopped outside the café to exchange conversation with a man who was standing at the kerb with a fruit-barrow.

'Hi, Bert,' said Fabian.

Bert was a short, strongly built man; fair, narrow-chinned and sharp-faced, like Fabian, and having the same imprint of the slum tenements. But he was not at all well-dressed. His head was covered by a cap with a broken peak. Instead of a collar and tie he wore a dirty white muffler. His coat was blackish with ingrained dirt. His trousers, of a different colour, were drenched with rain; from under their frayed and water-logged bottoms there protruded a pair of broken patent-leather shoes. He had an air of absolute poverty, but he carried his disintegrating clothes with a curious impudent jauntiness – the swagger of the Cockney costermonger, the indomitable fruit-vendor, tougher than leather, more indestructible than the stones of the City; wiry; sleepless; sharpened like a needle by perpetual vigilance; devoid of criminal instinct, but accustomed to regarding the police-man as his hereditary enemy; humorous, touchy, uproarious and quick with his hands – the only permanent type of the Londoner, speaking an individual jargon and upholding an old and characteristic tradition. He opened his mouth a sixteenth of an inch, keeping the rest of his face perfectly rigid, and said in a hoarse voice: 'Watcher, 'Arry.'

'Listen, Bert. You seen a little feller in a grey overcoat and a bowler hat around here just now? Miserable-looking old feller; looks like a schoolmaster. Short clipped moustache. Seen him?'

'Gord stone me over the 'urdles, 'Arry, London's full of 'em. If I saw 'im I wouldn't notice. Well, 'ow's fings?'

'So so. How's trade?'

'On the bleedn' Rory O'More, 'Arry, me old cock sparrer. I got bleedn' lumbered up Oxford Street last Fursday night. I got a barrer-load o' bleedn' tomatoes goin' orf, see, an' I got to get meself a few bob for me next bit of fruit; an' Gorblimey, I got a wife an' Gord-forbids at 'ome; so I takes a chance an' stands for a minute by Tottenham Court Road Station. An' up comes a bleedn' rozzer an' lumbers me. Wot a life! Coppers! That's wot we pays 'em for – to take the bleedn' strike-me-dead out of yer children's mouf. Forty bob or a month. It left me 'earts-of-oak.'

38

'If you could do with half a quid –' began Fabian.

'Nah, that's all right. I'll be all right.'

'Don't be a mug.'

'Thanks all the same; I can manage.'

Fabian's left eye closed. 'What's the matter with you?' he asked. 'Isn't my money good enough? You had to borrow a couple of quid off Mrs Lee to pay your fine, didn't you? What's wrong with my money? Catch hold –'

The costermonger pushed his hand away.

'I don't want it, 'Arry, straight I don't.'

'Independent, eh?'

'I ain't independent. 'Ow's Zoë?'

'Never you bloodywell mind about Zoë,' said Fabian through his teeth. 'Are you going to take this, or are you not?'

'No.'

'Why not?'

'All right, 'Arry, if you want to know. I don't take that kind o' money.'

'What kind of money?'

'Wimmen's money.'

'You —, are you asking to get done?'

'You couldn't do me, 'Arry; not single-'anded.'

The two men glared at each other, their faces almost touching: the costermonger sticking out his lips; Fabian thrusting out his jaw. They stood like this for several seconds. Then Fabian, finding it difficult to sustain the other man's steady cool stare, lowered his eyes and muttered: 'I can raise a mob. I can keep you out of the West End.'

'You can't.'

'All right,' said Fabian; 'but you're a mug, all the same. You make me laugh. I offer you half a quid and you won't take it. You're bust and you won't take it. Why? Because you don't like where the money came from. Get out of it, you bloody fool! How many whores' shillings do *you* take round Soho in a night?'

'I gives 'em somefink for it. I don't ponce it orf 'em.'

'One day I'll put you in hospital for that!'

'Go to 'ell! Take a ball-o'-chalk!' said Bert. 'I know you. I've known you ever since you was a baby in arms. All your talk don't frighten me. You couldn't do me single-'anded, and you wouldn't 'ave the bleedn' nerve to do me mob-'anded, 'cos yer know what I'd do to yer when I met yer again. Put me in orspital, an' I'll come aht an' do yer! I'd find yer alone. I –'

'Hah! That's what I get for offering you a few bob when you're on the ribs!'

''Arry, we've all done some funny strokes in our time, but, may I be paralysed, I draws the line at poncing. Goo'-night.' Bert laid his hands to the shafts of his barrow and rolled away down the street, uttering a law-defying yell: 'Lovely! All ripe!' in a voice which penetrated the ears like a bradawl.

* * *

Abruptly, like the turning off of a tap, the rain stopped. Fabian stood still. He was enraged and bewildered. He looked in at the Café Calabria; the little man was not there. He crossed the street, to the Vesuvio; except for a taxi-driver and two or three languid women, the café was empty.

'Then where the bloody hell can he have got to?' Fabian asked himself, walking along.

From above, heavy grey clouds pressed down. The rain, already evaporating, filled the air with a tepid vapour. Fabian had the balked, irascible expression of a man lost in a maze; he became suddenly aware of the frightful complexity of the City. He had followed a possibility to its logical conclusion and found nothing at the end of it; now, he was prepared to take the first line that presented itself to him. In such circumstances, one always tends to the improbable. Fabian retraced the path he had followed earlier that evening, and went back down Charing Cross Road.

As if by magic the crowds had vanished. The street was beginning to assume the sombre and lifeless air of the small hours. Traffic still flowed in the road, but it was thinning out. Even the Italian restaurants were closing. Nothing but a snack-bar and a chemist's shop remained open, and the lights in these places seemed to blink in the first, stages of exhaustion. Fabian crossed to Denmark Street; he had decided, in a vague kind of way, to walk round, in a wide circle, from café to café on the outer edge of Soho. He looked in at the Café Papa-doupoulos. There was nobody but the proprietor, who stood combing a superb head of rich black hair, and two dark Cypriot peanut-vendors playing dominoes. *Click-click* went the shuffled pieces, while from an ancient portable gramophone there proceeded the strains of some immemorial melody of the mountains of Smyrna, an unending tune played on a high-wailing flute in combinations of four notes in a minor key, which seemed to weave in and out with the cigarette smoke in a subtle pattern, cutting that place and those people off from the rest of the City.

'Seen a little guy in a bowler hat?' asked Fabian.

The proprietor shook his head.

Fabian went to the end of the street and turned again to High Street, Bloomsbury. The rain had driven everybody away; it seemed that the City was dying. Struggling through the opacity of the clouds the moon sent down a wan and watery light upon the west railings of St Giles's Church. From a nightclub in a nearby cellar there came the stifled thumping of a snare-drum and the shriek of a trumpet. Fabian stopped at Number 19A.

This had been a shop, but the windows had been painted black from top to bottom, and nothing but a hair's-breadth of light under the door gave indication of life inside. This funereal, sealed place was devoted entirely to negroes: here you could see the flash American smokes, with accents as thick and slow as syrup; hatchet-faced Guianians with yellow eyes; turnip-headed Yorubas; Ashantees of the colour of an old sweat-band, their faces slashed with the tribal markings; jabbering Trinidad half-breeds; chattering chocolate-coloured Cubans; and grinning Jamaica shines: yellowish, shapeless men, whose veins might have been slaughter-house drain-pipes carrying the watery overflow of a dozen different kinds of waste blood.

'Seen a little guy in a bowler hat?' asked Fabian.

Two or three of the negroes shook their heads.

'Hell, I . . .' began Fabian. He stopped, stared through the smoke, and plunged towards a corner table. 'Strangler!' he cried. 'You old son of a bitch!'

The man whom Fabian called Strangler was a colossus. You

must imagine the Farnese Hercules in ebony, dressed in a nigger-brown suit with a yellow chalk-stripe, a sky-blue shirt and a crimson tie with a greenish domino motif. He had an extraordinary head. You could reproduce it by shaving the head of the Neanderthal man, polishing it with stove-polish and then smashing up the features with a hammer. The ears no longer resembled ears – they had been beaten and rubbed into indescribable shapelessness – while the nose, a dozen times broken and never repaired, spread in a two-inch width almost flush with the rest of the face. Beneath it a pair of vast pink lips, remarkably pale and prominent and as thick as beef sausages, sucked at the sodden remains of a dead cigar.

'Well, if it isn't the Black Strangler!' exclaimed Fabian. 'Hell! it's good to see you again. How's life?'

'So.'

'Fight this evening?'

'Yuh.'

'Win.'

'I won.'

'Who d'you fight?'

'Pete the Finn.'

'Hard fight?'

'Yeah. He put a good scissors on me once, but I broke loose. That guy's tough. I puts a wrist lock on him, but he won't quit. I says to him: "Quit, Pete, or I'll break your wrist." He won't quit, so I breaks his wrist. He says: "I'll get you for that." Referee says: "Quit, Pete," but Pete's mad and he won't quit – he hits me with the basin. I says: "Pete, quit." He's fightin' with one hand 'cause he's mad. I puts an elbow-lock on him, same arm as the wrist I bust, and I says: "Quit, Pete, or I break your arm." He says: "I don't quit." I puts another coupla-pound pressure on and I can hear the joint crack. This Pete's tough. It hurts him so much his nose bleeds, though I ain't touched his nose; but he doesn't say a word. I says: "Quit, Pete, for Christ's sake, quit, or I got to bust your arm." He says: "Bust it, you nigger bastard." So I busts it and he passes out. He hated me like poison, that man. He wanted me to take first fall, but I wouldn't . . .'

'Where was you on the bill?'

'Middle.'

'Who was top?'

'Legs Mahogany.'

'You could pin that big palooka in two minutes.'

'Two seconds.'

'Listen, Strangler,' said Fabian. 'Bielinsky's a crook. What d'you want to wrestle for Bielinsky for? You know what I heard him say the other day? I heard him call you a nigger. You're a mug to stick with him.'

'I got a contract.'

'You got a contract. Listen, Strangler: tell me what's going to happen say you break that contract? Is Bielinsky going to waste good money suing you when you got damn all to lose? What does he pay you? Three pounds a fight? Two pounds? Hah! Listen to this, Strangler, and keep it under your hat: I'm start-ing promotion in a week or two. Come to me. I'll pay you more. I'll pay you five pounds a fight, and see you get five fights a week. I'll stick you on top of the bill. I'll make a star out of you. I'll get you publicity. I'm going to see the wrestlers get a square deal. Will you come when I give the word?'

'But I got a contract with Bielin –'

'Listen, Strangler: will you let me do the worrying about that? Bielinsky's making a mug out of you. He gets you to sign a bit of paper, and he scares you. Me, I know the law. The law's on your side. Wrestling for Bielinsky, what have you got to show for it? A tin ear and an empty kick, and not enough money to buy iodine for your cuts. You fought tonight. Tomorrow you'll be bust. You crippled Pete the Finn. All right. Say one of these days you're unlucky and some guy cripples you? Say you come up against Red Hammerfest, and he busts your foot in a toe-hold, the same as he did to Mad Maguire? Will you have any dough saved up for while you get better? No. Now me and Joe Figler are going to put this racket on an American basis. The English boys are going to make as much out of it as guys like Londos, not a lousy two pounds a fight. I'll see you fellers right if it's the last thing I do. Come to me; I'll do all the worrying. I'll work new stunts for you. I'll get you a swell new red satin dressing-gown with your name embroidered in gold letters and a panther in black on

43

the front. Boy, can't you see it? THE BLACK STRANGLER. The women'll go mad. Well? What say?'

'I'll come!' said the Strangler, grinning from ear to ear.

'Shake on it, and don't forget. I'll be seeing you! So long.'

'*Mug!*' thought Fabian, as he reached the street.

An aged woman, dressed in the tattered remains of three over-coats and a fantastic straw hat, crawled past, pushing a broken toy perambulator laden with the pickings of a hundred dustbins, trailing a horrible odour of decay. The sight of her made Fabian want to scratch himself. He unbuttoned his huge overcoat, designed to make him look twice his normal size, spat out his cigarette and went up towards New Compton Street, glancing at every man who passed, and looking into every café on the way.

If you could have seen him you might have been struck by a strange thought: '*If Harry Fabian could have devoted such keen-ness, such perseverance and such energy to something legitimate – say, for example, to selling a pennyworth of bismuth and sodium bicar-bonate for two shillings – he might easily have become a respectable character in modern commerce.*'

But as matters stood he was like a sinister figure in a sombre morality-play: a creature of the gutters, sniffing after a trail along the dank and shadowy roads of the night, hunting somebody down.

FOUR

With all that, how could Fabian find the little man? No calcula-tions could help him, and no intuition could guide him: it only remained for him to trust to pure chance – the kind of chance whereby one happens to pick up a five-pound note in the street. But Fabian, true to the type of the little criminal, walked through life with his eyes in the gutter, in anticipation of exactly such strokes of luck. He went back. Steinke's coffee-shop was closing; the Syrian Café was closed. There was no living thing abroad in New Compton Street – not a policeman, not a cat, nothing. He returned again to Charing Cross Road. There was an unutter-able desolation about this mournful street, with its high, thin lamp-posts and its black pavements which glistened with rain-water; always recurring in Fabian's wanderings like a dreary theme in a sombre and monotonous nocturne. Fabian began to feel the lassitude of the small hours – the dead hours when everything seems impossible.

Perhaps it might be best, he felt, to abandon hope and go to sleep. He quickened his pace, with some such idea in mind; but just as he reached the corner of Manette Street a man came out of the all-night snack-bar and called to him: 'Hi, Harry!'

'Hi, Mack,' said Fabian. 'What's up?'

'Zoë was looking for you.'

'Was she? When?'

'Half an hour ago.'

'She gone home?'

'I suppose so. Come in and have a coffee.'

'I got no time, Mack. How's things?'

'Pretty umpty. You doing all right?'

'So so.'

'Zoë had a good day today . . .'

'Yeh? Whadda you know about it?' asked Fabian, screwing up his left eye.

'All right, all *right*! Young Phoebe saw her get hold of a rich mug outside the Plaza this evening – some Spanish steamer that always gives five quid. And I saw her pick up another one later on. Ain't that –'

'What was *he* like? Little middle-aged mug in a grey over-coat?'

'That's it. Is he –'

'You haven't seen him around just now, have you?'

'Funny you should ask, because I was just going to tell you. I saw him a little while ago up the Honkatonk Bottle-Party, knocking back a beer . . .'

'When was that?'

'Just now.'

'Yeh? Good-night, Mack,' said Fabian, walking away as fast as his feet could carry him. He stopped a passing taxi and snapped: 'Honkatonk, Regent Place! Step on it!'

The Honkatonk Bottle-Party was situated on the topmost

floor of a high office building. As Fabian went up he questioned the liftman: 'Listen. Have you seen a little man in a bowler hat and a grey overcoat in the last half-hour or so?'

'I dunno, sir. I'm relieving the other man for a quarter of an hour: I've only just taken over while he goes and gets something to eat, sir.'

'All you god-damned working-class do is eat, eat, eat,' said Fabian. 'Busy up there?'

'No, sir. Very quiet.'

The lift stopped. Fabian rang at the door of the Honkatonk Bottle-Party. A grille opened, revealing a rectangle of a face – two puffy eyes underhung with pouches like crumpled lead-foil and half of a bridgeless nose. A voice said: 'Okay, Harry.' Then the door opened and Fabian went in.

There, under a sloping ceiling daubed with dark blue and stuck with silver-paper stars, everything reeled in an atmosphere of stale crapulence. A dozen people in evening-dress, attended by a waiter with the face of a diseased welter-weight boxer, lounged at tables, drinking themselves out of the last stages of drunkenness into a nauseated state of sodden half-sobriety. On the little parquet dance-floor a few couples slid round and round in a perfunctory quick-step, while a piano, a saxophone, and a set of drums played – probably for the thousandth time – the 'Tiger Rag'.

'Gord! Ain't I ever going to hear the last of that toon?' muttered the proprietor.

'What's up? Nerves?' asked Fabian.

'Me? I ain't got no nerves. Only it gets you fed up, that's all. "Hold that tiger, hold that tiger, hold that tiger, hold that tiger" – a lotta crap.'

'How's business?'

'Can't grumble.'

'Listen: I'm looking for somebody. I heard he was up here: a little feller, in a grey overcoat and a bowler hat.'

'I don't think he's been up here. Joe Figler looked in this evening.'

'What for?'

'Oh, you know Figler. He wanted to sell me some chairs. "Look at the chairs you got," he says, "all wore out," he says.

46

"Look at them covers, how shabby they look," he says. So I says: "Figler," I says, "them chairs have the finest covering in the world," I says. So Figler says: "What d'you mean? What covering?" So I says: "Back-sides." Ha ha! Good, eh?'

'Dead clever. Well, so Mack told me a lie. You haven't seen the guy I'm looking for?'

'Wait a minute. Did you say a little feller in a grey overcoat – looks, sort of, like a schoolmaster?'

'Yes!'

'Was he wearing a little-tiny ruby-and-diamond tiepin, worth, maybe, fifteen bob or seventeen-and-six?'

'That's right. Hell! Where'd he go?'

'Gord knows.'

'Oh, hell!' exclaimed Fabian, turning to the door.

'Why, what d'you want him for, Harry?'

'Want him for? Say, he owes me a hundred quid! So long.'

Biting his lips with rage, Fabian hurried down into the street. Two or three women still wandered near the Café Royal. Fabian spoke to one of them: 'Hallo, Blanche . . . Listen. Have you seen a little middle-aged steamer in a grey overcoat and a bowler hat passing here just now?'

'Nobody like that. How's things?'

'So so. You?'

'So so.'

'Well, so long, Blanche.' Fabian turned in the direction of Oxford Circus, walking quickly, hardly noticing where his feet were taking him. His brain was numb with anger and disappointment. He sucked savagely at his cigarette; in the still, damp air the smoke hung languidly, gradually disintegrating. One of these wisps of smoke, floating by the side of Fabian's head, attracted his attention, and abruptly penetrating to his consciousness through a fatigue-dulled layer of his mind, caused him to start violently in nameless terror, ducking his head. The shock aroused him. He looked about him and saw that he was in Old Burlington Street. Mayfair after dark has an atmosphere of security and privacy, and a blanket of silence. It was a part of the City which aroused, in Fabian, a peculiar surge of self-justification, a spasm of bitterness. '*All right,*' he would say to himself, '*I'm a ponce; they marry money. Zoë lumbers for a fiver; them women lumber for a million. They ain't no better than me, only they make more at it . . .'*

He walked at top speed now, across Regent Street, through Great Marlborough Street, up Wardour Street, back – inevitably back – towards Charing Cross Road. But as he reached Soho Square tiredness again took hold of him. The bell of a nearby church sent out into the night two extraordinary slow, reverberating strokes. Their echoes beat about Fabian's head. He experienced a sickening spiritual depression, a sense of futility and wasted time, as he stood, damp with sweat in his heavy overcoat, looking down at the reflections of the lamps in the puddles. 'Two o'clock,' said Fabian.

Rain started to fall again.

'I give up,' Fabian said. He shrugged his shoulders. He was defeated. The only thing to do now was to have a drink of beer, eat something, and then sleep. He went through to Charing Cross Road. In the doorway of an empty shop something resembling a man lay in a heap; from beneath a heap of rags and newspapers there protruded one boot, which had burst like a seed-pod, disclosing a row of atrocious red toes.

Life had reached its lowest ebb.

Fabian walked up to New Compton Street, to one of the oldest and darkest of all the houses; passed through a stinking passage lit by one dim night-light bulb, and went downstairs to Bagrag's Cellar. As he went in he gave such a start that his heart nearly stopped beating.

There, at the bar, sipping a glass of lager, sat the little man.

* * *

Fabian would sooner have expected to find a mouse nibbling cheese in a cage of cats.

Bagrag's Cellar is a dragnet through which the undercurrent of night-life continually filters. It is choked with low organisms, pallid and distorted, unknown to the light of day, and not to be tolerated in healthy society. It is on the bottom of life; it is the penultimate resting place of the inevitably damned. Its members comprehend addicts to all known crimes and vices. Mingling with them there circulate indefinable people, belonging to no place or category; creatures begotten of decay and twilight, enslaved by appetites so vile that even text-books never mention them, drifting in silent putrefaction to their unknown ends. In this place a ray of smoky light falls upon the mystery of what happens to the lowest criminals in their extreme old age: the waiter, for instance, is an ancient bandit, seventy years old, attenuated, twisted, with a face such as Gustave Doré might have drawn to symbolise cold and silent wickedness. His hollow grey cheeks are mottled with a scarlet rash. There is not a single hair on his head. His domed skull is covered with curious red lines, as if somebody has been striking matches on it. Between unblinking lids, blood-red with trachoma, his eyes, as bleak as the last circle of ice, stare without seeming to see. He has no lips, only a kind of crack which never opens. His name is Mike. Some say that he is Bagrag's father, others that he has some hold on Bagrag, but nobody knows.

Concerning Bagrag, nobody knows anything at all. Who is he? What is he? He looks not unlike Mike – but crime, with its attendant violence and vice, and its similar passions, leaves the same marks on many faces. Bagrag, above all men, is symbolical of that world of winks and inaudible half-whispers in which he moves. No man in the world is more secretive or ambiguous. He cannot give a direct answer. He cannot look you in the face. His Yes may mean No; his gestures are vague and sinister. He hates talking. His eyes are not mirrors of his soul: they are spyholes, camouflaged by heavy eyebrows, through which he secretly watches you, like a snake in the grass. Is his name really Bagrag? The monogram VCT on his signet-ring contradicts this – but so, also, does the name HUGO, which is written in rubies on a silver ring on the adjacent finger; and the gold medal on his watch-chain, which has the inscription P. WATTS, DEVIZES BOWLING CLUB, 1901. The top of his left ear is missing. Ask him how he lost it and he will say: 'Through listening too much.' From the corner of his right eye to the left-hand corner of his mouth runs a most shocking scar: mouth, scar and eyebrows form a jagged letter Z. Ask him how he got that and he will say: 'Through not minding my own business.' His nose is smashed to the four points of the compass. Ask him how he broke it and he will say:

'Through not keeping it out of things which didn't concern me.'

His club used to be a coal-cellar: there is a coal-hole over the piano. Daylight has never penetrated to this place since it was built, three hundred years ago. Picture it now, at two o'clock in the morning. With its shadows, its windowless walls and its single flyblown electric light which burns with a reddish radiance, it resembles a photographer's dark-room. It is strewn with stamped-out cigarette ends and beer mats sodden to pulp. High up on the keyboard of the battered piano, with its tired strings and its cigarette-burned case, the right hand of the pianist picks out a tremolo, at which the dancers writhe as if his fingers were tickling the soles of their feet. The tinkling music barely finds its way through the rumble of voices, the clink of glasses, the scraping of chairs and the unending shuffle of restless feet. A kind of high fever permeates the crowd. A grotesque fat woman flings herself on to the floor and performs a bizarre tap-dance – her body oscillates like the shuttle of a loom, but her bust, like something separate and more abandoned, whirls, swings, quivers and bounces, while her breath comes in tremendous alcoholic gasps. Half-exhausted people throw lip spasms of febrile energy: they rise in groups without purpose, move round, then sink back again, like stirred-up filth on the bottom of a pond. In an airless atmosphere, heavily impregnated with alcohol, mildew, nicotine, and the ammoniacal smell of unwashed women, Bagrag's customers lay the foundations for tomorrow's hangovers; gulping the wine of madness from questionable glasses, against a damp-raddled background of gangrenous yellow distemper . . .

'I could slap my face for saying the things I said!' sings the pianist; and pauses to refresh himself with a heart-rending yawn while his fingers still rattle on the keys: 'EEEEYAH! . . . Gonna send myself a telegram to tell myself what a fool I am – Oh, I hate myself for being so mean to you . . .'

To take a deep breath in Bagrag's Cellar, now, is like inhaling the combined vapours of a distillery, a dosshouse and a burning tobacco factory. Through a thick blue cloud the electric bulb blinks like a sore eyeball. The tables are swamped with spilled beer. Tired people light cigarettes and then forget them: these abandoned cigarettes burst, shed their tobacco and, in puddles of stale drink, disintegrate to form an unspeakable yellow soup. In a corner a young woman, whose ravaged face shows signs of a recent beating, opens her mouth in a tearful and bloody grimace, and holds up two front teeth, recently knocked out. By her side, a middle-aged man with a face which might be made up of the ruined leavings of half a dozen spoiled physiognomies, wearing somebody else's hat, yells at the top of his voice: 'One more word from you . . . !' At this, the woman, shrieking like a demon, smashes a beer-glass into a kind of jagged trephine, and tries to reach his face with it, making a horrible twisting gesture. One waits, tensely, for a deluge of blood, a cataract of frightful oaths, a bombardment of awful blows and a shower of teeth; but Mike, whose aged body seems to be endowed with a remarkable strength, holds the man and the woman apart, and gives them each a look of such malignity that they sit down quietly.

And in the midst of this – all this – the little man sits like a silent ghost of respectability, sipping straw-coloured beer from a tumbler painted with the words ENGEL'S LAGER. To the right of him sits some razor-slashing ruffian of the racecourse; to the left, a prostitute of sixty, used by fifteen thousand outcasts, slumps on her stool, a painted bag of corruption on the verge of bursting point; while Bagrag, behind the bar, covertly watches everything and says not a word.

* * *

'Mike,' said Fabian, 'who is that little feller?'

'Dunno.'

'Has he been here before?'

'Once.'

'Well, get me a Guinness and a couple of hard-boiled eggs.'

Fabian waited. Three o'clock struck. The little man got up and buttoned his overcoat. Fabian ran upstairs. The rain poured down, now, much heavier than before. Pale, used up, and with the air of a man whose life is ebbing away, the little man dragged himself to Cambridge Circus and called a taxi.

Fabian was scarcely a yard behind him. He heard his weary

voice say: 'Hassan's Turkish Baths.' Then the taxi slid off into the rain.

'Taxi! Taxi!' shouted Fabian. He ran across the Circus to leap into a cab that crawled past the Palace Theatre. 'Hassan's Turkish Baths; and step on it!'

He leaned forward, breathing hard with excitement. He saw his face in the mirror, illuminated by the lights of the City which flashed through the rain-blurred window. The more Fabian saw himself, the more he loved himself. He smiled affectionately at his image, shut up his left eye, and said: 'Fabian the Bloodhound.'

The taxi stopped under a red bulb-sign with a star and a crescent. He got out. The meter pinged as the flag snapped up.

'Thank you, sir,' said the driver: *thud-thud* went the swinging doors as Fabian charged into the Turkish baths. He said to the clerk in his best American accent: 'Pardon me; did a middle-aged gentleman in a grey overcoat just come in here?'

'Yes, sir; he's gone in.'

'Gimme a ticket,' said Fabian. 'I'm going in, too.'

FIVE

In the Turkish bath there was absolute silence, a tropical atmosphere of somnolence and heat. In the low, dim ante-room, an attendant moved noiselessly over the thick carpet. Fabian was embarrassed; this was the first time he had ever been in such a place. The attendant took off his shoes and led him to a curtained cubicle.

'Listen; what do I do?' asked Fabian.

'Just take off your clothes and go right through to the hot rooms, sir.'

'All my clothes?'

'Yes, sir.'

'I just wondered. In New York it's different. Here, catch hold of this,' said Fabian, giving the man a shilling. He took off his clothes and hung them in his locker. He felt uneasy; this place was far too quiet, too clean. From an adjacent cubicle came the sound of a long, deep snore. Fabian was troubled, also, by the fact that his feet were dirty; for in spite of his punctilious shaving, dressing and haircutting, and his almost fanatical aversion to soiled collars, he had not the habit of frequent bathing. As he shed his clothes he felt more and more angry; less and less significant. He pulled the curtains close before taking off his delicate blue silk shorts, and then he felt as feeble and as unprotected as an oyster out of its shell. Adjusting the blue check loincloth about his waist, he stepped out; then, ashamed of his dingy feet and soiled ankles, he darted back, spat on a towel, and scrubbed them tolerably white. Then he went out again, lit a cigarette and paused. At that moment, the light clicked off in another cubicle, and the little man stepped out. Divested of clothes, he was indeed a pitiful figure. Misery must have ground him down, like famine. Fabian noted the bent back, along which the vertebræ stood out like a string of beads; the limbs like sticks; and the insignificant neck precariously supporting the weary head, which trouble seemed to have made too heavy.

He went into the Frigidarium. Fabian followed. Here, cooling off in the lukewarm air, two old men lay asleep in great canvas chairs. One of them had let his loincloth slip to the floor; he lay snoring in an abominable nudity, unsexed by the obesity of indolence, senile decay and gluttony. Between huge legs, stretched out to their full extent, a stupendous white belly sagged down, quivering as he breathed, and exuding streams of sweat. One might have thought that the man was melting in the heat, and that in a little while nothing would be left of him but a pool of warm oil and a set of false teeth. The other old man was drunk, extremely drunk. He was not actually obese, but shapeless; a kind of cylinder of soft flesh with extraordinary long thin limbs. His loincloth hung round his neck. In sleeping he had twisted round until his legs hung over the back of the chair, while his arms, with his head between them partly obscured by the blue check cloth, dangled in front. One had an uneasy feeling that the man really was like that – that in due course he would get up and walk away on his hands, holding a cigarette between his toes and drunkenly singing 'Sweet Adeline' through his anus. The little man went to the drinking fountain and drew a beaker of water. Fabian, feeling that this was something that had to be done, did likewise. Then they both sat down.

'Warm,' said Fabian.

'Oh, quite,' said the little man.

'I've never been here before. Do you come often?'

'Oh, quite frequently.'

'To keep your weight down?'

'No.'

'Well, well, well,' said Fabian: 'So this is a Turkish bath. Well, well, well . . .'

The little man turned, and looked at him.

'Do you know,' he said, 'I seem to have seen your face before.'

'Why not?' asked Fabian, easily. 'Do you read the American papers?'

'No, why?'

'Because that's where you would of seen my picture. I'm Harry Fabian, the song-writer. Heard of me?'

'Oh-er – yes, yes, I think I have . . .'

'I wrote one or two popular numbers. You heard "Hot Towels"? And "In The Dead Of The Night I'll Be Waiting" – it goes like this: "In the dead of the night – I'll be waiting for you . . .' sang Fabian, in a tune suspiciously reminiscent of 'When The Blue Of The Night Meets The Gold Of The Day'.

'Oh, really? I seem to have heard that tune before.'

'Sure you did. Well, I wrote it.'

'Oh. You're American?'

'Uh-uh.'

'New York?'

'And Hollywood.'

'Oh. I suppose you must have met all the film actors?'

'Hell, actors?' cried Fabian, crossing the first and second fingers of his right hand. 'Me and Garbo were like *that*!'

'Interesting, I should think.'

Combining with the heat, the novelty of the situation was going to Fabian's head. Upon the potency of his own lies he became drunk, as with wine. He replied: 'Hell, no. In the end they give you a pain in the neck. They ain't *real*. I like London best. Are you in business in London?'

'Well, no, not exactly.'

'Live out of town?'

'Well . . . yes.'

'Long way out?'

'Not very.'

'I'm going to settle in England. I'm looking for a little house out of town. Whereabouts do you live? Maybe they might have something there?'

'Oh, I doubt whether you would find anything there to suit you.'

'Hell, one never knows –'

'Er – if you'll excuse me, I think I'll go into a warmer room.'

'Me too,' said Fabian. They went into the Tepidarium. Fabian broke out into a sweat. 'Hell, this is hot!'

'Yes, isn't it?'

'They have some swell Turkish baths in the States. You ought to take a trip over there some time. It'd make a change from Hampstead.'

'No? Oh, pardon me. Where did you say you lived? I didn't catch . . .'

Fabian sat down; then jumped up again, with a shriek: 'Jesus these seats are *hot*!'

'Well . . . that's what people come here for.'

'It's dangerous to stay too long, isn't it?'

'Well. I suppose so.'

'Do you stay long?'

'Oh, not very. I usually leave at six.'

The little man rose, restlessly, and went into the next room, the little oblong Calidarium. Fabian was reminded of an occasion when, as a child, he had put a cockroach into a tobacco-tin and put it on a hot stove. The cockroach had writhed, sizzled and burst. Fabian's heart thumped. Sweat streamed over his back and chest, and the check towel clung to his thighs.

'You know, it's not wise to stay long if you're not used to it,' suggested the little man.

'Who, me? Not *used* to it? Say, listen: once I walked through Death Valley at midday. Ha ha! You call this warm? Hah!' exclaimed Fabian, hopping in agony on the burning floor. 'Places I've been to, we'd of put our winter overcoats on if it was only as warm as this!'

The other man's emaciated body seemed to draw in some fresh vitality out of the intense, dry heat. He looked at Fabian with a faintly malicious smile, and said: 'Good; then let's go on into the next one. You'll be able to get a really good sweat out of that.' He led the way into the last of the hot rooms, the Radiatus. This tiny room had an atmosphere of terror. One could hear the perpetual moaning of hidden pipes. The floor was too hot to stand on. Heat, night and unearthly quiet cut the place off from the world and life. Fabian felt that he was buried, miles underground. He was entombed, lost. The mercury in the thermometer hung above boiling-point. The pulse in his solar plexus bounded like a rabbit in a bag.

'Jesus!' was all he could say.

'Warm enough now?'

Vanity breeds heroism. Fabian replied: 'Well, yes; but I've been in warmer places.'

Five minutes passed.

'I like the suburbs,' said Fabian.

'So do I,' said the little man.

'The trouble is, being a stranger here, I don't know who to ask for advice about where to look for a place.'

'I should try a reliable estate-agent.'

'Ah, but you can't rely on 'em. I'm funny that way. I know what these guys are. I rely on personal recommendation. Do you –'

'Excuse me; I think I'll go to the steam-room.'

'Hah? Sure. I was going to say, "Do you think we ought to go to the steam-room?" Let's go.'

They passed through swinging glass doors. Beyond, in a room white with hot steam, two or three men lay stewing on marble shelves. The wet heat hit Fabian's lungs; he sat down, coughing. 'Kheh . . . kheheh! How will you get back home so early in the morning?'

'Oh . . . train, or bus.'

'Edgware, Highgate, and Morden line, I suppose?'

'Not exactly.'

'Take you long?'

'Sometimes twenty minutes; it depends.'

'Now that,' said Fabian, grinding his teeth, 'is what I call darned convenient! It'd be round about Hendon way, eh?'

'No.'

'I got to get out of London. How can I compose music with all the noise?'

'Well . . . I have no idea, I'm sure.'

'Are they putting up any houses your way?'

'Well, they're building everywhere, nowadays.'

An old gentleman, abominably naked, looking like a Surrealist vision of pumpkins, marrows and varicose veins, turned the steam on higher, and began to smack himself in the belly. Another man, young and exceedingly drunk, stood trembling under the cold shower and mumbled something about forgetting his umbrella. The heat became intolerable. Fabian's stoicism broke down.

'Hell, I'm getting out of this!' he exclaimed. He went back to the Frigidarium and sat down, faint and sick. He was disgusted, nauseated: he had had enough of all this. Then a chair creaked next to him, and he saw the little man sitting down. Hope recurred.

'I *say*!' he said, with an air of inspiration, 'you look the image of a man I used to know, years ago, a fellow called Edwards, from Ponders End. Not a relation of yours, I suppose? Hell, that would be funny –'

'No, no relation of mine.'

'Well, you might be his twin brother. Might I ask what your name is?'

'Eh? . . . My name? Oh . . . Smith.'

'Of Ponders End?'

'Er – no.'

'Where, then?' asked Fabian, at the end of his patience.

'Farther west,' said the little man.

'Pardon me,' said Fabian, gnawing his upper lip, and smiling the mirthless grin of a skull.

The little man rang the bell. An attendant came up, yawning.

'You ring, sir?'

'Will you bring me a pot of tea and some buttered toast, please?'

'Sir.'

The attendant went away, then came back with the order on a tray.

'I'll put it on your card, sir. What's the number, please?'

'Eleven.'

'That's the number of your cubicle, sir. I mean the number of your card.'

'Forty-nine.'

'Thank you, sir.'

'*Eleven!*' said Fabian to himself.

The little man finished his tea and toast.

'Well, excuse me,' he said, 'I think I'll go back to the steam-room for a little while.'

'And I,' said Fabian, 'am going to get my cigarettes and sit around a bit.'

He waited. The little man went back to the steam-room. Fabian went out. There was nobody in sight. The cubicles were dark and quiet. He stopped at number eleven, and slipped between the curtains. There hung the dark suit, the plain shirt and the round stiff collar. He felt at the jacket and thrust his hand into the breast pocket, pulled out some loose papers and peered at them in the light that filtered in. He could recognise the shape of a long, official envelope and the letters OHMS – an income-tax demand. He pushed this under his loincloth, and slipped out all in a second; banged noisily into his own cubicle, switched on the light and lit a cigarette.

The envelope was addressed to Arnold Simpson, Esq, 'The Nest', The Crescent, Turners Green.

'Smith, eh?' said Fabian. He put the letter in his coat pocket and took his cigarettes back to the Frigidarium. He was in such a good humour that he actually sang aloud: 'Pal of my cradle days, I needed you always . . .' Whereupon, from the lips of the drunken man with his head on the floor, there proceeded a long-drawn bubbling growl: 'Oh, Daisy, Daisy, Daisy, Daisy, give me your answer, do!'

The little man returned, and rang for a masseur.

'Me, too,' said Fabian.

He lay on a marble slab. A giant in a red shirt whisked off his loincloth.

'For God's sake, don't tickle me,' said Fabian.

From the little man's slab came the sound of slapping, and a wan, polite voice saying: 'The right shoulder, please.'

'Ho-ho-he – !" laughed Fabian, as the masseur kneaded his ribs; then, mentally addressing an image of the little man, he said: '*Okey-doke, Simpson; this Turkish bath costs you fifty nicker extra, after what you made me go through!*'

* * *

The masseur wrapped him in hot towels.

'Better, sir?'

Parboiled, limp, baked, bruised and utterly enervated, Fabian replied with a groan: 'Sure. There's nothing like a massage to liven you up. I once wrote a song about it . . .'

The masseur laid him on his bed and covered him with more towels. Fabian gave him half a crown.

'Tell 'em to send me a big cup of strong black coffee, two hard-boiled eggs and some toast – snap into it!'

'Yes, sir. Thank you, sir.'

'You see, I don't get time to sleep. I've hardly been to sleep in three weeks. And I've got to go and collect fifteen hundred pounds off of a guy this morning.'

Fabian lay still. His ears, sharpened by years of eavesdropping to a high selectivity, picked out the sounds in cubicle number eleven. At half-past five the little man began to dress.

'*Now he's going to let the neighbours see him coming home from night-work, the little rat!*' thought Fabian. He heard the little man go out. Then he went into the ante-room and sat on a settee. He had half an hour to kill. He looked again at the envelope he had taken from the little man's pocket. It contained an income-tax demand letter, and another letter which had slipped inside, a note in pencil on paper headed CAVELL NURSING HOME:

MY DEAR ARNIE,

I cannot sleep on account of the pain, and I do not get my injection for another hour, so I am writing you this because it makes me feel better to say something to you. I do so wish I were with you. I feel so worried about you. I was worrying whether you

59

would take care to keep on your winter woollies now that the weather is warmer, dear Arnie, do keep them on up to the middle of May at least. *You* mustn't be ill too. Darling, Arnie, I love to see you all the time, but don't take any more time off from business to see me or they will be sure to get annoyed, so come in the mornings. Do take care of yourself, and I hope Martha sees you get proper meals. I can't write any more, Arnie, I do feel so ill.

Love,
AGNES

'Hah!' said Fabian. He went out giving sixpences to everybody he passed, and called a taxi. '"The Nest", The Crescent, Turners Green,' he told the driver.

'Sir.'

The rain had stopped, and the sun was rising. Through the open windows of the taxi, the cool wind of the morning blew gently on the heated face of Harry Fabian. At Marble Arch, the taxi stopped in the silent road, in obedience to the traffic-lights. From the throat of a remote bird, pure clear, and of an amazing sweetness, there came the notes of an ecstatic song:

Pheewepp! . . . Pheeweep!
Ptyoo-weep: – Plyooweep!
Papatink! Papatink! Papatink!

The broken outcasts on the Bayswater benches began to pick themselves up and drag their misery away from the pitiless daylight.

SIX

The suburb still slept. In The Crescent the street lamps were still burning. Fabian saw a light in the front room of 'The Nest'. Evidently the little man had just arrived. He knocked at the door. The little man appeared. As he saw Fabian his face became red, then white; and he staggered back, too shocked even to gasp.

'Good morning, Mr Smith,' said Fabian, 'I've come for the eggs.'

'Eggs? Eggs? What do you mean?'

'The nest-eggs,' said Fabian, sucking in his upper lip, and sawing at the other man with his jagged profile. 'Come on, now; lemme in.'

'What do you want?'

'I want to have a word with you, and you better make it snappy before Martha gets down. It's nothing you'd want Martha to hear.'

'You . . . there's some mistake. My name's not Smith. I don't . . .'

'Yeah. I know your name's not Smith. It's Arnold Simpson; and there's no mistake.'

Mr Simpson led him into the drawing-room. Fabian glanced, with a knowing grin, at the furniture – so typical of the average best room of the comfortable men of the middle-class – the brown leather suite, the oak sideboard, Axminster carpet, standard lamp, brass fire-irons, knick-knacks and pictures. The little man sat down, trembling like a man dying of cold.

'What have you come here for?'

Fabian replied in a cold, precise voice: 'This evening you interfered with my wife.'

'Me? When? Where? How? I –'

'About eleven o'clock, in Rupert Street. You were followed. You were watched. You were overheard. You were photographed.'

'I swear I didn't do anything.'

'You tell that to the Marines. You were sitting on her bed, with your mitt on her knee. Just brotherly affection, eh? I suppose you think you'll get away with it, eh? Well, you won't, see?'

'What do you want? What are you going to do?'

'Do? Tell your wife. Tell your neighbours. Tell your sister-in-law. Raise hell. That's what.'

'But I assure you, upon my soul, there was nothing at all in it. Nothing! I was lonely. I wanted somebody to talk to. You –'

'Oh, yes. Sure, sure. Oh, yes. You just wanted somebody to talk to. So you picked out a girl of Zoë's figure, and went back to her flat, and made her undress, just so as to talk to her. Sure you did. We all know all about that!'

'I didn't make her undress –'

'Of course not. Sure you didn't. I know you didn't. Her dress just walked off. Everybody knows that. Girls' dresses just jump off. We all know what men take good-looking girls up to bedrooms for. Just to talk. It's an understood thing. All the same, brother, you know what dirty minds some people have. Will they believe it? And what's your wife going to say?'

'But you can't possibly tell her that! It would kill her!'

'Now you know what?' said Fabian reprovingly. 'I'm ashamed of you. To go and pretend you're going to work like a respectable family man, while all the time you're larking around in night-clubs and dives like Bagrag's, and women's bedrooms –'

'Stop it!' said the little man. 'For God's sake stop it! I can't listen to all this. Can't you see I'm a sick man? Can't you see I'm a sick man? Can't you see I can't stand all this? Can't you say what you want of me and stop –'

'One-fifty smackers.'

'Eh? Eh?'

'What d'you mean, "Eh? Eh?" You ought to say: "I beg your pardon." I'll repeat it: one hundred and fifty pounds.'

'Good God, you must be mad!'

'Oh, I must be mad, must I? Why –' snarled Fabian, with sudden ferocity, 'you bloody louse, you: do you know what's going to happen to you if you're not polite?'

'Do . . . do you mean to say you want me to give you a hundred and fifty pounds?'

'Yes. And quick.'

'I haven't got it.'

'Yes you have. I know you have. What about the money you've got saved up?'

'It's . . . it's invested. I can't touch it. I –'

'And the cheque you got when they sacked you from your job – which your wife doesn't know about?'

'It's nearly all gone. My wife –'

'Now don't you bring your wife into it. Never mind her. Just for the moment, let's talk turkey. It's easy. All you got to do is write out a little cheque for one-fifty pounds, go to the bank as soon as it opens, draw out the jack in one-pound notes, hand it to me, and say "Good-bye". And if you don't, by Christ I'll be up at the Cavell Nursing Home before you can say –'

'How did you know that?'

'Ah!' said Fabian, opening his mouth very wide.

'I shall go to the police!'

'That'll do no good. You've got no proof of anything. You could charge me. But it wouldn't get you anything. It'd only cause a scandal –'

'Blackmail cases can be heard *in camera* . . .'

'You don't seem to understand,' said Fabian patiently. 'This isn't blackmail. It's your word against mine. If you wanted to be unpleasant, I'd be unpleasant, and I'd tell your Agnes a tale that'd make her jump right out of bed and dance a Rumba. And Martha – what wouldn't Martha do; dear old Martha!'

The little man drooped in his chair as if his backbone had turned to water. There was silence for a minute or so. Fabian smoked, and waited. Finally, the little man said: 'And if I gave you this money. What guarantee would I have that you wouldn't keep on and on? Would you sign an undertaking – ?'

'Look at my eye,' said Fabian, pushing forward his grinning face, 'what colour is it?'

'Oh . . .'

'What colour is it?'

'Blue.'

'Ah. I thought perhaps you might of seen some green in it. Listen, my name's Fabian, not Muggins. I want that money now, and in cash. Small notes. Pay, and I keep my lip buttoned. Don't pay, and I'll give you the works. I keep my word either way. Suit yourself. Which is it to be?'

'Listen. I swear to you, I haven't got much. I haven't got a hundred and fifty pounds in cash. I could show you my pass-book. My whole cash balance isn't more than a hundred or so. My expenses are heavy. Can't you realise that?'

'Get it.'

'How *can* I?'

'Borrow it.'

'My God!' cried the little man. 'Aren't you even human? Can't you understand the terrible trouble I'm in? For God's sake, can't you put yourself in my place and have a little . . . a little . . .'

'Well, all right. I'll be soft. You'll laugh at me, but I'll be soft. How much did you say you had in ready cash?'

'At the most, a hundred and nine, or ten.'

'All right. You don't deserve it, but I'll be lenient. I'll take the hundred and ten, provided I get it right on the spot. I don't leave this place until I do. I'll wait with you here until the banks open, and if I don't get it then, in one-pound notes, I'll put the scissors on you. Can I say more?'

'But my sister-in-law –'

'That's all right. For your sake I don't mind stooping to deception. Tell her I'm a chemist from where you work.'

'But you promise – you absolutely promise – never to come here again?'

'Word of honour of a gentleman,' said Fabian.

* * *

At ten o'clock, weary but exultant, Fabian rode back to Rupert Street in a taxi. From time to time, he felt at a stiff wad of new green notes in the inner pocket of his waistcoat. Zoë was asleep. He crept in quietly. As he undressed, she awoke.

'Where the hell have you been?' she asked.

'Turkish bath. Look how nice and clean my legs are.'

'Mm!'

'Listen, honey-baby; I'm on a big thing. You'll be riding in a Rolls-Royce before you know where you are –'

'Ooooaaaaaah!' yawned Zoë.

'Snap out of it!' said Fabian. 'Wake up. Tell me, how d'you do last night?'

'Listen, Harry; I'm sorry, dear,' said Zoë, in a persuasive voice, 'I didn't do any good.'

'No? How much you take?'

'Only two quid.'

'Liar.'

'Don't call me a liar!'

'No. You're telling the truth. Sure you only took two quid. But what about the old steamer who gave you three quid for nothing?'

'What . . . what . . . How did you know? Honestly, I think you must be a devil or something, the way you find things out!'

'Ah-ah!' grunted Fabian, putting on flame-coloured pyjamas. 'Now, how much?'

From under her pillow, Zoë took a purse, and pulled out five pounds.

'Now why hold out on me? Have I ever been mean with you?' asked Fabian.

'I've got to get some shoes.'

'Well, why didn't you say so?' asked Fabian, taking the five pounds, and giving back two. 'Here you are, two quid.'

'You are a pet, Harry!'

'Nobody could ever call me mean,' said Fabian. Before putting on his pyjama-jacket, he turned round and round, with outstretched arms, 'Look. Am I clean! . . . Hell, move over. It ain't worth while going to sleep. I got to phone Figler about one o'clock.' He got into bed; then pushed one foot out from under the cover, and, pointing to it, said: 'Look how white!'

SEVEN

Fabian telephoned Figler at one o'clock.

Figler changed his address several times a year, but was usually to be found somewhere in the residential area between Southampton Row and the Gray's Inn Road – that sombre, comfortless jungle of smoky apartment-houses, inhabited by a shifting population of men without property who arrive in a hurry and frequently leave by night; where tradesmen give no credit, and rent is payable strictly in advance. Figler was a bachelor, and occupied a single room on the ground-floor of a house in Tavistock Place. Why Tavistock Place? It sounded good. Why the ground floor? He found it comforting to be within leaping distance of the street.

When Fabian rang, he was poring over a sixpenny scrapbook bulging with mysterious newspaper-cuttings. He closed it, and put a heavy vase on top of it before going to the phone. When he spoke: 'Hallo?'

'Figler?'

'I don't know if he's in. Who's speaking?'

'Harry Fabian.'

'Oh, hallo Harry. What is it?'

'Listen, Figler; about that hundred quid . . .'

'Yes?'

'I got it.'

'You what?' exclaimed Figler, with something like consternation.

'Sure. Now we're ready to start.'

'Oh sure, sure, Harry. But listen –'

'When can I meet you?'

'Uh . . . Almost any time. But I'm a bit rushed at the moment. Better make it tonight.'

'Tonight? Where, up at Anna's?'

'Yes.'

'Say, listen. Got the money?'

'Who, *me*? I can write out a cheque.'

'No cheques, Figler; cash.'

'What? You don't trust me?'

'Sure, sure I trust you. But anybody could write out a cheque. Would you pool in a hundred pounds cash on *my* cheque?'

Figler could find no reply to this; he simply said: 'What, have you got cash?'

'Listen!' Fabian rustled a newspaper in the mouthpiece of his telephone. 'One hundred in notes. D'you hear 'em? Ain't that music? If you got money in the bank, you can easy draw it out, can't you?'

'Ha-ha-ha-ha-ha! Can I draw it out! . . . But all the same, you ought to trust my cheque.'

'Would you trust mine?'

'Between friends –'

'There ain't no friendship in business. You said so yourself; *I* say so too. I got my half. Now let's see yours, and get going. Let's do real business for a change – we're in on the heavy sugar. No funny stuff –'

'Don't adopt that attitude just because you got a hundred quid in your pocket for the first time in your life, Harry! I'm willing to come in on a straight fifty-fifty basis, but if you think you can order me about –'

'Now don't be silly, Figler.'

'All right. Meet me at half-past ten in Anna's.'

'Half-past ten in Anna's, okey-doke.'

'Good-bye.'

'So long.'

Ping went the receiver as Figler rang off. He went back to his room, seething with anger. '*Damn him!*' he thought. '*How the devil did he manage to get hold of a hundred quid so quick? And how the devil am I supposed to get a hundred by tonight?*' He took out his pass-book, and found that he had exactly thirty-one pounds and ninepence to his credit. '*A hundred pounds he gets! Since when has he been a business-man? The little rat!*'

Figler paced the room. Then he took out a fat, old-fashioned note-book with glossy black covers. This was Figler's Bible: it contained his Gospel, and the rules in accordance with which he ordered his life. It was packed with names and addresses of wholesalers, covering every imaginable line in merchandise. Figler had compiled it gradually, during a lifetime of tortuous research in the snake-haunted hinterland of questionable commerce. It was a kind of Kabbalah of buying and selling. If you approached Figler with a consignment of spoiled bird-seed, perished elastic garters, rusty umbrella-ribs, warped butter-patters, out-of-date calendars, or shaving papers left over from the 'nineties, he would run a finger up and down the pages, smoke a cigarette, look up, choke, recover, and say: 'Uh . . . I can dispose of this stuff on a fifty-fifty basis . . .' Buyers attached to film companies had offered him considerable sums for his note-book; but that was the one thing in the world which Figler would not sell. It was more than his living – it was his life.

He sat down with it, and smoked a cigarette.

Smoke bubbled through his congested bronchial tubes, as through a hookah. '*Uh!*' exclaimed Figler. He threw away his cigarette end, and put on his hat; locked up the book, tapped himself on the bosom with a clothes-brush, and went out.

First of all, Figler went to Mortimer Street to a ground-floor office with a plate which said: RETAILERS' SUPPLIES LTD, P. PINKUS. He walked in. A secretary stopped him.

'Pinkus?' said Figler.

'Aoh, Mr Pinkus is awfully busy; he can't see anybody today.'

'Ah. In that case, I'll go right in,' said Figler. Looking straight in front of him, with a calm, preoccupied expression on his face, he brushed past the secretary and went into an inner office. This was a small, plywood room, not much larger than the average bathroom, and ankle-deep in papers. The waste-paper basket overflowed with catalogues; incalculable accumulations of bills, chits, receipts and pro-forma invoices, impaled on old wire files like skewers of cats' meat, hung in festoons around the walls, and curled up in the warm, damp air. On the desk an electric heater, in the form of a copper bowl, breathed waves of stifling heat into the face of Mr Pinkus. He was a short, heavy, excitable man, with a cigarette in his mouth. The smoke rose in a straight blue bar, until the heat waves caught it and spun it out into nothingness.

He looked up as Figler came in.

'What is it? What is it? What is it, Joe? Busy, busy. What is it?'

'Listen,' said Figler, 'tell me; how are you fixed for bentwood chairs?'

'Bentwood chairs!' shouted Pinkus. 'A fire on bentwood chairs! All I get, all day long, is bentwood chairs and bentwood chairs! I've been sitting here on pins and needles with bentwood chairs – and now *he's* here with bentwood chairs!'

'Ssh! All this excitement. You can't get them, eh?'

'Of course I can't get 'em! If I want to buy off Lipsky, I can get a million of 'em. But who's going to buy bentwood chairs off Lipsky, that twicer!'

'Listen. The sort of bentwood chairs you want is the little round chairs with curly backs, eh?'

'Curly backs! You can't get a bentwood with a curly back –'

'Lipsky bought 'em all up.'

'So he's telling me! I've been spitting blood over it, and he's telling *me*!'

'All right. I can get hold of some.'

'How many?'

'Twenty gross.'

'Twenty gross? How much?'

'Lipsky's charging seventy bob a dozen. I'm cutting his price.'

'How much by?'

'Eleven bob a dozen.'

'Go on! Fifty-nine bob a dozen you're asking?'

'Fifty-nine bob per dozen.'

'I can use twelve gross.'

'Yes, I dare say you can. But you are having no more than three gross.'

'Now why should you *be* like that? I can clear you out the whole stock without nonsense –'

'Listen,' said Figler patiently, 'and don't talk so silly. You know as well as I do that Lipsky's got every small round bent-wood chair on the market. Is that so?'

'Well?'

'Give me a straight answer, yes or no.'

'All right, well?'

'All right. I got a few gross. So if I got 'em to dispose of at a cut price, you got to consider, Pinkus, I also got two-three friends in the business apart from yourself who I want to do a good turn to.'

'Well?'

'So if you want three gross at fifty-nine bob a dozen, say yes or no, and I can deliver this afternoon on receipt of cheque. If not, all right. Well?'

'All right, I'll take the three gross. You said fifty-five bob a dozen?'

'Fifty-*nine!*'

'Ah come on! Don't be silly! You can knock me off fourpence on a chair.'

'Pinkus, don't make a fool of yourself. Here am I, cutting the price down' – Figler clicked the nails of his thumb and fore-finger, as one who kills an invisible louse – 'like *that,* and you argue! Listen; don't let's have no argument, because I got no time. I can't cut another farthing. Ain't I got to live? Now you

69

know me; I'm straight. I got a reputation to lose. The three gross; fifty-nine bob a dozen. If you said "Fifty-eight and elevenpence three-farthings," I'd say "No! Definitely no!" A hundred and six pounds four shillings for three gross. Yes, or no.'

'A hundred and six pounds.'

'A hundred and six pound *four*.'

'Forget the four shillings!'

'A hundred and six-pound four!'

'All right, I'll take 'em.'

'Seven-and-sixpenny chairs I offer him for fifty-nine bob a dozen, so he's doing me a favour by taking 'em! I'll deliver this afternoon to your warehouse. I want your cheque the minute the goods arrive.'

'All right. You'll wait a week.'

'Listen, Pinkus; you know me. I don't give no credit. I can't. Ask yourself. How am I going to give hundred-pounds of credit. Cash are the terms. Otherwise, no deal.'

'Well, I can do with the stuff. As a matter of fact, I got an urgent delivery to make –'

'I know. To Wilson.'

'Who told you about Wilson?'

'Never mind. I know. When have you got to deliver?'

'At once, if not sooner. I should have delivered yesterday.'

'Yes, I heard. All right, I'll let you have the stuff today, as soon as I get your cheque.'

'Figler, we've been doing business for years, and I trust you like my own brother. If you say the stuff's all right, I know it's all right. When can I see it?'

'Four o'clock.'

'I can't get away. Say six.'

'All right, six.'

'I'll make a note of the amount. I'll give you the cheque right away. A hundred pounds . . .'

'A hundred and six pound four.'

'Four! Four! A hundred and six pound!'

'– Four shillings.'

'All right. See you later.'

Figler went out.

Now Fabian, in Figler's place, would certainly have taken a taxi; but Figler, who was a connoisseur of traffic congestion and relative speeds, ambled into the Underground. Twenty minutes later he was sniffing and coughing in the offices of Lipsky and Company, in Bishopsgate. Lipsky junior was a young, sharp man, expert in the ways of buyers, wise to the habits of salesmen; calm; detached; a Darwin of the restaurant-supply business, who might have undertaken a scientific classification of the vague flora and elusive fauna of the catering world.

Figler said to him: 'I would like some of those little round bentwood chairs – number seventy-two X.'

'Seventy-two X? Certainly! As many as you like! Very nice line. Can't get them anywhere else, you know. Seventy shillings a dozen to you.'

'Well, it's like this, Mr Lipsky. I'm getting these chairs for a fellow who's opening a new place up North.'

'Oh, up North, eh? What kind of place?'

'A sort of lecture-hall, or something.'

'Might I ask where?'

Without hesitation, Figler replied: 'A town near Blackburn, some place called Darwen.'

'Darwen . . . Yes?'

'Well, business is business. I want to make a few bob out of it, so you'll drop a few bob on a dozen –'

'Can't be done, I'm afraid.'

'Ah, yes it can! You know me. We've done business together for years. *You* won't be down! I'm buying these chairs on my own responsibility, myself. So be a good fellow and let me have them for sixty-five.'

'Well, I'll tell you what I'll do. You can have three gross at sixty-seven and six.'

'I think you might be a little more generous with me, considering we've been doing business together for so many years –'

'That's just it. Business is business. Apart from business, I'll be as generous as you like. If you're on the floor, come to me and you're always sure of a ten-pound note. But business is business.'

'Come on!' wheezed Figler, in a coaxing voice. 'Sixty-six bob. That's five-and-six a chair.'

'Yes, and you couldn't get that chair anywhere for seven shillings.'

'Well, look here. Give me three months to pay.'

'I can't do it.'

'You trust me?'

'I trust you. I've never heard of you letting anybody down. All the same, you're an individual, not a firm, and I can't do it. But look here. I'll tell you what I'll do. I'll meet you half-way. Pay me half down and I'll take your cheque for the other half, post-dated twenty-eight days.'

'At sixty-six bob?'

'I'll make it sixty-seven shillings a dozen, and not a farthing less. That's rock bottom.'

'Look here: make it a third down –'

'No, I've told you the best I can do, and I wouldn't do that for anybody else.'

'Well . . . could I have the stuff at once?'

'Day after tomorrow?'

'Say I wanted it *now*?'

'Can't be done. All the vans are out.'

'Oh, that's all right. I've got a van.'

'Since when?'

'Oh, I been doing business on a bigger scale just lately. I hired one. Well, all right, get the invoice out, and I'll let you have my cheque.'

'All right, Mr Figler. It'll be sixty pounds six shillings.'

'Call it sixty pounds.'

'And six shillings.'

Figler wrote a cheque for sixty pounds, and pushed it across the desk. Lipsky took it very calmly, thanked Figler, and said: 'In that case make out your second cheque for sixty pounds twelve shillings.'

'Sixty pounds.'

'– Twelve,' said Lipsky.

Figler wrote the second cheque for sixty pounds ten shillings.

Lipsky laughed. 'All right, you old devil. You can give me a cigar for the other two shillings.'

'Pleasure!' said Figler. He took out a large Bolivar which

somebody else had given him a month or two before, and which he had brought out with him in anticipation of some such friendly gesture.

The men shook hands. Figler went out.

As soon as he reached the street, Figler began to hurry. He found himself, now, in one of those fantastically precarious positions in which the fiddler not infrequently finds himself. He had given Lipsky a cheque for £60, when there was no more than £30 to his credit in the bank. He knew that that cheque would be paid in by three o'clock. If it were not met, his credit would be killed: he would be ruined. Curious as it may seem, Figler was able to exist almost entirely on account of his unspoiled reputation as a man whom it was safe to trust; and this reputation now hung in the balance. He changed a shilling into pennies and went into a telephone-box. Then he rang the Magniloquencia Cigar Co.

'Hallo! I want to speak to Mr Cohen . . . Figler . . . Hallo, Cohen? Listen. I shall want a thousand of your Coronas, at once . . . Yes . . . No, I couldn't pay before the middle of next month . . . All right . . . Of course! You know me, don't you? . . . Thanks very much, Cohen . . . Yes, a little better, thank you; only a bit stuffy in the head. You quite well? The family? . . . Good, good! Good-bye!'

As quick as lightning, Figler's fat fingers twirled the dial again.

'Hallo! Figler speaking! Is that Mr Gold? Here, listen, Gold; could you do with a thousand Magniloquencia Coronas? You can have 'em for thirty-two pounds, cash . . . What? . . . *What?* . . . Stocked up with 'em? What d'you mean? Eh? . . . Don't be silly, of course you could sell them! . . . Is that definite? You got ten thousand in stock? *Ten thousand!* Oi! . . . All right. Good-bye.'

Figler broke out into a cold sweat. He rang Havana Cigar Distributors, but the proprietor was not in. Cheapside Tobacco (1937) Ltd had more Magniloquencias than they knew what to do with. At this point, Fabian would have said: 'Bloody hell!' but Figler never swore. He changed his tactics, and rang the Liquid Gold Egg Company.

'Hallo!' said Figler. 'Get me Mr Shiptzel . . . Figler . . . Hallo, Shiptzel, this is Figler . . . Figler, not Tiddler! . . . How are you? . . . I'm lovely . . . A little stuffy in the head. Listen, is my credit good for a few tins of frozen eggs? . . . Oh, not more than forty pounds' worth . . . Sure, middle of next month is all right, isn't it? Well, thanks . . . Yes, I've tried syringing my nose, but it does no good . . . Well good-bye.'

Without hesitation, Figler rang the Appleton Bakeries.

'Appleton? . . . Figler here. Listen: what are you paying for eggs? . . . EGGS! Not legs! . . . You are, eh? Well, I can let you have Liquid Gold three-farthings a pound cheaper . . . It's a fact! I got hold of a few that Bobzer was storing before the price went up . . . Yes, I can deliver now if you like, but I got to have cash . . . Of course they're genuine! You know me, don't you? . . . Yes . . . Yes . . . Yes . . . Cash on delivery, then. Very good. Good-bye.'

Figler breathed again. He dialled the Bullet Transport Company.

'Hallo! Bullet? Figler here . . . Hallo, Isaac! How's Betty? . . . Oh, a little stuffy in the head . . . Listen, I want a van – a one-ton van . . . Twenty hundredweights, one ton; are you deaf, or what? . . . Only for the day . . . Shut up, do you take me for a millionaire? . . . Make it a quid . . . Oh, all right, twenty-five bob. Have it ready at once. I'm coming right over.'

Figler rang off, and then got another number.

'Hallo! Cleartype Signs? Figler speaking . . . Hallo Yossel! How *are* you? . . . Oh, a little stuffy in the head . . . Listen. I want you to put your quickest man on to a streamer, about five feet by eighteen inches . . . Ordinary paper – I just want to stick it on the side of a van . . . Here are the words: FIGLER MERCHANDISE CO. Got it? Plain black letters on yellow. I got to have it within an hour . . . Don't kid me, I don't pay a penny more than three-and-six. Good-bye.'

He came out of the telephone-box, mopping his forehead, and rode on a bus to the Bullet Transport Company. Squeezed beside the driver, he went in a one-ton van to Cleartype Signs, where the conspicuous black-and-yellow streamer – FIGLER MERCHANDISE CO. – was pasted where all the City might read it; sped, with a roaring of exhausts, to Stepney, where he picked up the eggs;

delivered them at the Appleton Bakeries, where he received a cheque for thirty-five pounds two shillings and sixpence.

'Lipsky's, Bishopsgate,' said Figler to the driver.

As the chairs were being loaded, he took a taxi to his bank, and paid in Appleton's cheque. Then he rang Pinkus.

'Listen, Pinkus, I got the chairs in the van. Should I deliver them straight to your warehouse, or where? Say quick; I'm in a hurry . . . All right, meet me at the warehouse with the cheque, in half an hour. Good-bye.'

They met at the warehouse. Pinkus looked at the chairs with approval, which he expressed in the following words: 'Well . . . You haven't altogether swindled me.'

'Swindle you? You ought to go down on your bended knees and thank me!' said Figler.

'Here's the cheque,' said Pinkus, 'a hundred and six quid.'

'A hundred and six pounds *four!*'

'Ah! A business for four lousy shillings! Here, here's a cigar, and shake hands on it!' And putting a hand into his breast pocket Pinkus pulled out a scabrous and battered Romeo y Julieta, which Figler recognised, by the cracks, as one which he had given to Pinkus nearly four months previously.

* * *

Figler dragged himself to a tea-shop, sat down heavily, and made notes in a penny note-book.

He had bought three gross of chairs for £120, and sold them for £106. He had bought a load of liquid eggs for £40, and sold it for £35. This made a dead loss of £19. £19, plus cost of hiring van; streamers, telephone-calls, taxi, etcetera – say £21.

Then what had Figler done that was clever?

He had simply started another little circle of credit. He had a hundred pounds in hand. With this capital, he intended to become a wrestling-promoter. He owed Lipsky £60, and Liquid Gold £40. When these bills had to be met, he would buy, on credit, say half a dozen grand pianos, with the proceeds of which he would punctually settle the two debts. Then, his credit being still more firmly established, and his reputation being further strengthened, he could always rely on a consignment of goods from Lipsky or Liquid Gold, with which he could pay the piano-manufacturer. By this time, Mr Gold would have got rid of his stock of Magniloquencia Cigars, with the manufacturers of which Figler's credit still held good – and so Figler could go on and on, always owing somebody something, always robbing Peter to pay Paul, always digging one pit to fill another, always managing to keep a little bank balance and a good name; all by means of words and paper.

Innumerable tradesmen of good repute contrive to keep their heads above water in much the same way.

'Pot of tea,' said Figler to the waitress, 'two poached eggs on toast, and a bath-bun; and if ever a man worked hard for his bit of grub, my dear, that man is before you!'

* * *

Figler met Fabian at ten-thirty that night, and showed him the cheque.

'You said cash,' said Fabian.

'Look here, young man!' said Figler. 'I'm getting fed up with you. All you know is cash, cash, cash. A business-man doesn't go about with pockets full of *money*! My cheque's good. What do I want cash for? What do you think business is, a racecourse? A business-man works on credit. The whole world is based on trust!'

'Okay, okay, *okay!* . . . Listen, Figler, I been looking over premises, and I've seen a classy place in Regent Street –'

'Regent Street! Fah! You listen to me. There's a basement to let in Bristol Square for thirty bob a week. They'll take twenty-five. Bathroom attached. What more do you want?'

'Shower-bath?'

'I can get a rubber thing to fix on for seven-and-six.'

'Okay. And I went along to Smith's today and got a catalogue. We'll need mats, and apparatus, and stuff . . .'

Figler tore the catalogue in two, without looking at it.

'Smith's! . . . Fah! I can get stuff at half the price. Besides, what's the matter with second-hand mats with new covers? Why new mats?'

'Furniture –'

'Leave it to me. You worry about wrestlers.'

'I can get some good men cheap.'

'Hall?'

'We'll take the Olympia, Marylebone, for a start.'

'Staff?'

'I've been talking to some fellers. We won't have no difficulty. Listen, what'll we call ourselves?'

Figler shrugged; he was not concerned.

'Fabian and Figler.'

'Byeh!'

'Figler and Fabian?'

'Ffeh!'

'Fabian Promotions!'

'Not so bad.'

'Sounds good, eh? Fabian Promotions. By Christ!' cried Fabian, overcome with emotion. 'That don't sound so bad!'

'All right, let it be Fabian Promotions.'

A girl passed their table.

'Hiyuh, Vi!' called Fabian.

'Hallo, Harry,' said the girl called Vi. She was a tall, slender, red-haired girl in a black lace evening gown. Under her rouge, one could distinguish the papery greyish pallor of the night-bird – the dead opacity born of dank dance-halls, where, in thick blue smoke and the exhalations of steamy bodies, the crude, raw rhythms of red-hot gut-bucket jazz seem to shake the blood out of women. 'Listen. I heard a new "knock-knock".' She had a curious, chirping voice, extraordinarily high. 'Knock-knock!'

'Who's there?' said Fabian.

'God.'

'God who?'

'God-night, baby, the milkman's on his way!'

'Ehr!' groaned Fabian. 'Well, where you working these days?'

'Up at the Silver Fox.'

'New show?'

'Lovely place, Harry. Come up and see me sometime. He-he-he-he-he!'

'Who runs it?' asked Fabian.

'Phil Nosseross.'

'Good band?'

'Lovely.'

'What they rush you a bottle?'

'Thirty-five bob a bottle of Scotch.'

'Robbers!' said Fabian. 'Still, I might look in. Gimme a card.'

Vi gave him a card: THE SILVER FOX CLUB, LEICESTER MEWS, LEICESTER SQUARE. 'Just mention my name, Harry.'

'Like to look in there?' asked Fabian, toying with the card.

'No thanks.'

'What d'*you think* of Fabian Promotions, Figler?'

'I told you. All right.'

'But what about your name?'

Figler laughed. 'Me? My name? Never mind about my name.'

'I'll have some cards done. Jesus! "Fabian Promotions"! Hell, have a drink.'

'Grape-fruit,' said Figler.

'You, Vi?'

'Gin and lime.'

Anna Siberia took the orders.

'But are you sure about the name?' asked Fabian.

'You can have all the glory; only let me see the money,' said Figler, drinking his grape-fruit juice with the strangled gurgle of a drowning man. '*Uh . . . gu-gub!* . . . Well, I got to go. I had a busy day. I'm tired. Meet me here tomorrow at twelve, and we'll go and see the place.'

'Half-past eleven!' said Vi, looking at the clock. 'I've got to go to work. Coming along, Harry? It's a lovely place.'

'No, not tonight; I'm going to bed. I'm dead beat, too. Tomorrow night, kid; not tonight.'

Figler went into Leicester Square station.

'Good-bye.'

'So long, Figler.'

Through Cranbourn Street, Leicester Square burned red with neon; a flower of inflammation on a spangled stem.

'Knock-knock,' said Vi.

'Oh, who's there?' asked Fabian, with resignation.

'Agatha.'

'Agatha who?'

'Agatha feelin' you're foolin'! He-he-he!'

'Oh, scram!' grunted Fabian.

They parted.

* * *

One struck. Then two. Fabian slept like a dormouse, curled up in his flame-coloured pyjamas.

Three. 'Pr'motions,' said Fabian, talking in his sleep.

'Ah . . .' murmured Zoë, sighing at some lost sorrow sealed in the cellars of her consciousness.

Four.

There was no moon, and the night was bitterly cold. One tiny blue star twinkled, light-years away.

There is always the icy light of some distant star to guide us, lost and bewildered wayfarers in the wilderness of this world.

Four.

INTERLUDE: MAN AND THE CAT

Then, from the shadowy doorway of a shop, noise burst out; loud, deep, prolonged, quivering with melancholy, dragged by strong passion out of living cat-gut: '*Mwowowowow! Woe, owowowoWAAAAOW ow!*'

'*MiaaaOUW! . . . Ow . . . Owowow!*'

'*Myaaaaaaaaaaaaaaaaaaou, wow, wow!*'

'*Ouw . . .*'

A non-descript grey female cat sat, with an air of disdain, while a heavy tom-cat, as black as midnight, prowled around her. Nearby stood a disconsolate little black cat with white paws.

'*Krr-ouw?*' suggested the big black one.

The female shrugged her shoulders.

The black-and-white cat ventured an insinuation: '*Mmrrouw?*' The grey female washed her armpits.

'*Ngrrr!*' growled the big black tom. The two males paused, watching.

'*Khaaaa!*' spat the black-and-white, feinting with his right. Next moment they were hooked together in a fizzing, howling, spinning ball. Dogs replied furiously to the voices of their ancient enemies. The whole night was sawn open by a snarling

79

chorus of hate. Then dog replied to dog, dog awoke dog for miles around. Barking broke out in ripples which flashed over the city – over the face of the whole land. Sound runs smooth by night, and dogs have good ears. Blindly answering, the dogs of Land's End, Dover, Cardiff, Barrow-in-Furness, Hull, Glasgow and the remote villages of the far north lifted their voices; raw-edged, penetrating sound, flying at a thousand feet a second, disturbed the sleep of the entire land. Ten thousand men sat up and shouted: 'Lie down!' Ten thousand women awoke their husbands, and whispered: 'Burglars!'

The grey cat licked her belly.

The tom-cat with white paws fled, shocked but uninjured. Cats may be terrible to mice, but they have no equipment for heavier game. If they had long claws, cats would be extinct: they dilate with hatred, they shriek with hatred – they want to rend, devour, torture, and obliterate each other; but they can't. So they pour out all their venom in their voices, their howling and malevolent voices; exactly like the gossiping women of the villages.

The big black cat returned to the female.

'*Krrr-mrouw?*'

'*Mmmm-iaouw*' . . . she replied, without enthusiasm. Never the less, she swung her tail from side to side. He sidled over to her and embraced her.

'*Yaaaaaaooooooouuuuuu! . . . Ghrooooooooooooouwowow!*' howled the black cat: his voice slid up and down the scales in sickening glissandos. He was crying out with pain.

Why do tom-cats do this thing? For them, love is by no means all moonlight and roses. The genital organ of a tom-cat bristles with spikes, like a pipe-scraper: it is a severe surgical instrument of reproduction, not pleasure. He loses blood and fur in frenzies of impotent rage, and almost bursts with bitterness, simply to achieve a torture-chamber.

What good does it do? It generates more cats.

Who wants more cats?

'*Owow!*' moaned the black tom-cat. From across the street, the black-and-white cat listened with envy and disgust.

The grey female contemplated a lamp-post. All this meant

nothing to her. What did she not know about sex and mother-hood? She had had fifty kittens and forgotten about them. Tom-cats, yes, tom-cats were all right; but for her part, she found more sensual pleasure in an empty sardine-tin . . .

'*Wow!*' A policeman shone his lamp down upon them, and laughed. 'Shoosh!' The black tom-cat fled: the grey female sat quite still. The policeman walked on. Then the little black-and-white cat stepped daintily across the road.

He said again: '*Mmmrrrouw?*'

She replied, more graciously: '*Krrrrrr.*' . . .

The black-and-white cat vibrated and cried out forlornly, like a tortured violin.

The grey cat was unable to suppress a yawn. How mono-tonous, how miserably familiar, were the oscillations and out-cries of these passion-intoxicated males! They were all alike . . .

An old man with a sack shuffled up to investigate the con-tents of the dustbin in the doorway. The black-and-white cat fled. 'Puss, puss, puss!' cried the old man.

The grey cat cut him dead. She walked. In Old Compton Street she decided to try one of her tricks. She knew that here-about, human beings still prowled; lords of life and death, fifty feet high, masters of fish and fire. She went into a café, hung her head, and uttered a hesitant cry: '*Er . . . eeyow?*'

A friendly hand stroked her . . . She purred. Then, abruptly, the same hand gripped her, with unfriendly violence, by the loose skin at the neck, and a voice said: 'I tella you once! I not tella you no more! 'Oppit!' She was flung out in a wide arc, and landed, unhurt, on her feet. She shook her head, and trotted north-west.

It was impossible to embarrass this cat.

She was shameless and heartless, a cat of the city; elusive as an eel, resilient as rubber, indestructible and persistent as chewing-gum; a tile-begotten hybrid, born among salmon-tins and broken bottles, whose pedigree had slunk in offal from dust-bin to dustbin since Egypt. For a thousand years her ancestors had survived being flung downstairs and pitched out of doors. She, above all creatures, had learned the technique of self-preservation; her life was based on the apothegm: '*Preserve yourself.'* At aggression, she was mediocre, but Yukio Otani himself could not have taught her anything about the art of falling down. Every muscle in her body seemed to have been designed for prowling, sneaking, ducking and running away. She lived for herself, parasitically: the perfect type of the Strange Cat – abhorred in well-ordered households like the Strange Woman of the Jews. In hundreds of homes her presence had been suspected by a smell, proved by the disappearance of food and disposed of by hisses and blows. Ratepayers often took her in and christened her with fancy names; but in the end, they always gave her away, with false and hypocritical eulogies and regrets. She had no idea of the significance of a box of ashes, and regarded the practice of Rubbing Her Nose In It as a charming human eccentricity rather than a lesson, or punishment.

She liked householders as people who considerately placed legs on their chairs for her to rub her spine on; and who built furniture of good hard mahogany to enable her to get her claws clean. She had no great objection to toying with a mouse, if it happened to walk into her mouth, but would see herself damned before she would go out of her way to look for one; did not mind an occasional canary, but found that the feathers gave her heartburn; and enjoyed a few gold-fish, but only as a snack between meals.

Why hunt mice? Only fools work. There is always food. The city is full of people, most of whom are mad. Poor crazed creatures – they give away food! The only proper thing to do with food is eat it all. Give nothing away. Preserve yourself! Preserve your*self*! The world is your cat's-meat. The Great Tom-cat, who plays with the world like a ball of wool, created man to give you warmth, milk and chicken-bones, and put the sun in the sky to make you purr . . . You are the Great Tom-cat's Chosen Pussies.

The grey cat saw, in the distance, a red glow. She could smell fire. She went towards it. At the back of Primrose Hill the road was up; the fire burned in a night-watchman's brazier. The cat sniffed. Then she trotted faster. Simultaneously, her ears and nostrils caught the sudden crackle and pungent odour of frying bloaters.

Two men were sitting by the fire: a big man; and a smaller one, the watchman, who was cooking the bloaters in a pan over the fire. He was saying: ''Ow old are yer?'

'Twenty-seven.'

'And what's yer name?'

'Adam.'

'And what sort o' work are yer looking for?'

'Any sort.'

'But ain't yer got no *trade*? You tells anybody you just wants any sort of job, blimey that means nuffink. See? . . . What sort o' work you done before?'

'All sorts.'

'White-collar jobs?'

'And no-collar jobs.'

'But ain't yer got no *profession*? I mean to say, if they asks me: "What's your profession?" I says: "I'm a skilled night-watchman." Now if –'

'Well, I'm a sculptor.'

'Statues, eh?'

'That's it.'

'Ah.' . . . The watchman turned the bloaters over thoughtfully. 'There's nuffink o' that sort goin' round 'ere. I know a feller, a pastry-cook, an' 'e can make marzipan roses; blimey, you could wear 'em in your button'ole. But . . .' Grease at the edge of the pan caught fire and blazed up. For one second, Adam's face jumped out of the half-light – big-boned, pale with fatigue, calm, expressionless. Then, *phut!* the flame went out, and only his square lower jaw was visible, red in the light of the fire-bucket. 'What you say to a bloa'er?'

'Not for me, I'm not hungry. You carry on.'

'I don't like eatin' alone. Come on.'

'Couldn't eat a thing, thanks.'

'Prahd, eh?'

'Who, me?'

'Well then, 'ave a bloa'er. I got plenty.'

'Couldn't touch one.'

The watchman smacked down a bloater on a large slice of bread, and placed it on Adam's knee.

'You don't 'ave to be prahd. Carm on.'

'Well . . . all right. Thanks.'

'*Mrouw?*' cried the cat, in a piteous voice. '*Mrarouw?*'

'Dumb animals,' said the watchman, throwing down a piece of fish. 'So you're a sculpture, are yer?'

Adam nodded, his mouth full.

'Any money in it?'

'Hardly any.'

'Then what you want to go and take it *up* for?'

'Couldn't help it.'

Ptss-Ptssss! went the pan, as the watchman put in two more bloaters. He brewed tea.

'*A-rouw?*' suggested the cat. Adam gave her the naked backbone of his bloater. He had eaten the rest, even the skin.

'Drop o' tea?'

'Very kind of you.'

'Ass all right . . . You ought to get a bit o' sleep. You looked whacked.'

Adam admitted: 'I haven't had very much sleep.'

'What d'you fink of Mrs Simpson and the Dook o' Windsor?'

Adam yawned. 'Who cares about Mrs Simpson and the Duke of Windsor?'

'My old woman cried all night long, the night 'e abdicated. She 'eard 'im over the wireless. 'Is voice was 'usky wiv grief.'

'Was it?'

''Usky wiv grief . . . They didn't 'arf make up some jokes.'

'I heard them.'

'Where d'you kip?'

'Nowhere.'

'Tried the Salvation Army?'

'To hell with the Salvation Army!' The warmth of the fire was making Adam sleepy.

'Can you roll yourself a fag?' The watchman passed him a tobacco-box. 'Papers inside.'

'You're a good fellow,' said Adam, 'and I shan't forget this.'

'Ah,' said the watchman, 'one o' these days, I'll be able to say: "Adams? Wot, the sculpture? I knew 'im. We once dined together."'

Adam laughed.

'You'll ride by in your bloody great Rolls-Royce, and you won't notice me, fryin' me bloaters over me fire.'

Adam smiled and shook his head modestly. A sure way of

cheering a man up is to tell him that when he is rich he will for-get you, his old friend.

'Do you always do this sort of thing?' Adam asked.

'What sort o' thing?'

'Give your food away, and –'

'I ain't a 'eavy eater. Anybody's welcome to a bit o' *my* bloater. Some o' the night-club gels what live rahnd the square, they often stop on their way 'ome, for a warm. Pore bitches! . . . 'Ere!'

'What?'

'If you want a job, there's a noo place opened orf Leicester Square; place called the Silver Fox. They might give you some-fink to do there. It's a chance.'

'Thanks, I'll look in . . . By God, here comes the daylight!' exclaimed Adam, with relief.

'*Miaouw!*' cried the cat.

''Ere y'are, greedy!' said the watchman, dropping the debris of the last bloater. 'Bloody cats; they can always git a meal . . .'

The sky was getting pale. Day was coming. In the streets, ordinary life was beginning to stir. The iron clangour of milk-carts sounded in the side-streets. Trains muttered underground; a cock crowed; sparrows chirped at the sun. Faintly, very faintly, there arose the incoherent murmur of the awakening City. Even in the first feeble rays of the morning, the City took on a new aspect. The electric lamps burned yellow. Even the savage neon signs faded and became inconspicuous. Mighty is the daylight, mighty and merciless; the hammer of the night, the breaker of the spells of darkness!

'Starve a cat, and you gits pinched; starve a man, and nobody says nothink,' said the watchman . . .

People crept up from the night-clubs, and passed out into the cold, fresh morning. Glamour vanished, like smoke in a draught, and in its place there came the sodden nausea of the drunkard's dawn; heavy blue boozers' gloom; the sickness of stale air; the disgusting aftertaste of lost money and wasted time.

'Cats are only cats,' said Adam. 'Men are men.'

Dawn broke.

Book Two

IN HOW MANY WAYS CAN
A MAN LOSE HIMSELF?

EIGHT

But although the Silver Fox closed at half-past four, it was nearly nine o'clock before Vi, the dance-hostess, got home. The watchman was gone; the workmen were shivering at the handles of their pneumatic drills. Vi paused to watch. A tiny Cockney, covered with dirt, yelled: 'Blimey! Look 'oo's 'ere! Me ole pal the Duchess!' Vi walked on, with dignity, and went indoors. Before going into her own room she knocked at her neighbour's door, and called: 'Oh, Helen!'

'Who is it?'

'Me.'

'Oh, come in.'

Dressed only in an old blue dressing-gown, Helen was standing in front of her mirror, brushing her thick brown hair with a hard brush. Her strong white legs were set apart; she was balancing herself on the balls of her feet. The rustling of the brush mingled with the electric crackling of vigorous hair. With every down-stroke she sank back on her heels and uttered a short exclamation – 'Ou!' – then rose again on tiptoe for the next stroke.

'Knock-knock!' said Vi.

'Ou! . . . *Ou!* . . .' The skirt of her gown stretched taut between her thighs. The force of the brush-strokes made the room tremble.

'Lousy, or something?' asked Vi.

Helen relaxed, and combed her hair back.

'No,' she said, 'I do this every morning. It's good for the hair.' She tightened the cord of the gown about her waist, and sat down. Her large, dark-brown eyes, deeply set under thick black eyebrows, gazed curiously at Vi, who had fallen into a chair.

'You got too much energy,' said Vi. 'What you want is a man.'

Helen shrugged. 'Well, Vi?'

'Ooo, all right!' exclaimed Vi. 'Fine! How about you? Any luck?'

86

Helen pointed to a crumpled copy of the *Daily Telegraph*. 'Not a thing. No jobs going at all in my line. If this goes on much longer I'll have to look for a job as a cook or something.'

'Don't be a mug,' said Vi. 'Oh, my Gord, am I tired! Christ, did I have a night last night!'

'Have a good time?'

'Ooo, wonderful! I got so tight I tried to dance a Rumba with a copper in Oxford Street. Laugh? You would of died. I met ever such a nice feller. I pinched a quid off of him, and a fountain-pen. I gave the pen to a Greek boy that sells peanuts outside the club. More use to him than me. If I'd thought of it, I could of brought it back for you, though, couldn't I? Got any aspirins? Oh, listen; heard a marvellous Little Audrey. Listen, before I forget: Little Audrey said to her mother . . . Now what was it, what *was* it? Oh, never mind. This feller I was telling you about, so he wanted to marry me. Do you know what he said? He said: "Come away with me at once to Dublin, and we'll get married there." *Me,* mind you! Could you imagine me being such a mug as to marry anybody? Me! Doing the *house*work! Do you like Irish whiskey? I hate it. It made me queer: I had to go into the cloakroom and sit down; and the boss came up to me, and what d'you think he said? I must tell you before I . . . Oh, did I have a night last night or did I have a night? As I was coming in I nearly started to do a waltz with the umbrella-stand. I did! Laugh? You would of *died!* . . .

'Ow, did I have a night . . .

'Ooo, before I forget: I met ever such a nice feller. What I liked about him was, he was *straight.* I can't bear it when fellers say: "Oh, you're this . . . Oh, you're that . . ." I hate flattery. Well, this feller said to me, he said: "It's not that you're beautiful, but you've got character and personality." I like a feller to be straight with me. The boss said: "Young Vi's the best little grafter in the place." I don't flatter myself, but – oh, listen, I must tell you about this: we went into the Milk Bar, and I kept on taking taxis just across the road to the Ladies', and giving the driver a bob a time . . . Oh, Lord . . .'

Vi yawned, and from between her pale, painted lips there proceeded a breath such as might come from a pathological specimen in a jar when the alcohol is evaporating. Then she snatched up her bag, with an exclamation of dismay: 'Hey, wait a minute!' She shook out the contents of her bag on to the bedspread – cosmetics; a handkerchief stained with lip-rouge; a nailfile, white with spilled powder; and some loose silver . . . 'Five, ten, eleven-and-six. Christ, is that all I've got? I had a pound note and half a crown last night. That feller – the nice one – he wouldn't give me anything. He said: "I don't care how much I spend, but I ain't giving away money for nothing!" So I said: "How about my time? I spent five hours with you this evening." So he said: "I spent six quid on drinks and smokes with you tonight." So I said: "What about my rent?" So he said: "Listen," he said, "I ain't like other fellers who only go with a girl for what they can get out of her. I don't like a girl only for sex," he said, "I like a girl with personality and character," he said, "so you come back to my hotel with me, and I'll give you two quid." Well, then he finished off the third bottle, and fell off to sleep. Well, I saw he'd put his change in his waistcoat pocket, so I fished it out. One pound two-and-six. Then the doorman took him out. He only had ninepence left in his pockets. So they shoved him into a taxi and said: "Take him to 14 Rose Gardens, Edgware," and off he went.'

'Why, was that where he lived?' asked Helen.

'No, that's just the joke! He stays at the Paddington Palace Hotel. Laugh? You would of died. Can you imagine him waking up at Edgware, without a sausage to pay the taxi with? . . . But why've I only got eleven-and-six left? Ooo – listen – you know what I did? I threw away a shilling's worth of coppers – bang, crash! – they didn't half make a row! Tinkle, tinkle, tinkle, all down the street. Then I was sick. Ooo, did I have a night last night . . .'

'D'you want a cup of tea?'

'No . . . I think I'd like to go to the pictures.'

'Don't be crazy,' said Helen, 'you're going to bed.'

'Ooo, yes, that's right. So I am. I wanted to ask you to call me. Would you? Call me about five.'

'All right. Go to sleep now.'

'Good-night.' Vi went out. Then she came back again, and said: 'What I meant to say was, good morning!'

'Good morning.'

Vi went to her room and threw herself under blankets, fully clothed. Helen went for a walk.

* * *

At five o'clock in the afternoon she knocked at Vi's door.

'*Ehr* my Gord, *come* in . . .'

Vi's room was one of the smallest in the house, a mere closet, scarcely large enough to contain the bed, the dressing-table and the chair. It was lined with brownish paper – mottled, sickening brown paper with stripes like the tracks of balloon-tyres in rose-pink, and wide bands dotted with circles, crosses and things like broken fans in pale green. You can get such wallpaper for six-pence a roll in the region of Somers Town; but who can sit down at a drawing-board and actually *design* it? Nobody knows. The dressing-table was littered with empty chocolate-boxes, broken celluloid dolls, unidentifiable latchkeys, broken wrist-watches, odd ear-rings, empty aspirin bottle, lidless pots of dried-up face-cream, old tooth-brushes, clogged with black hair-dye, and, like shell-cases in the chaos of an amorous battlefield, the red-smeared brass tubes of several spent lipsticks. On the floor stood a three-day-old cup of tea, scummed with white, into which an old stocking hanging out of a drawer dipped, like a wick into oil. A pink evening dress lay in the fender. On the mantelpiece, between a photograph of Robert Taylor and a litho of the Virgin Mary, stood an uncorked lysol bottle, a bunch of decomposing violets in a milk bottle, a china cat for good luck and six long bars of ash where cigarettes had burned themselves out. The window was closed, and in the few cubic feet of space in the room there struggled the mingled odours of a dozen cheap perfumes, three months of stale cigarette smoke, unwashed underclothes, a hastily wrapped newspaper parcel under the bed and, above all, the penetrating smell of a tired and unhealthy woman – that curious, sneaking, characteristic odour of weariness and vice, which must have inspired a good deal of the mediæval theologians' disgust when they roared against hidden feminine corruption.

Helen looked down at Vi. '*What blind idiots men must be,*' she thought, '*to want to make love to . . . that!*'

Vi was still fully dressed, wrapped tightly in her teddy-bear coat. From under the bedclothes there protruded a foot, still gripped in a small satin shoe. Her head against the pillow was a study in all the indefinable pale colours of debauch. The pillow-case was grey, but Vi's face was greyer, tinged with the chlorotic greeny-yellow of anæmia. Rubbed smears of yesterday's rouge gave emphasis to this pallor. Under the laid-on red, her lips were pale pink and her teeth appeared yellow in the daylight. The pencilled lines of her eyebrows had been rubbed off on to the blanket; the metallic green paint with which she coloured her eyelids had become mixed with the blue mascara of her lashes, in an unearthly and poisonous bruise-colour picked out with flecks of silver. This was trickling down into the hollows under her eyes. One of her false eyelashes had come loose, and swung precariously against her cheek as she blinked. She seemed to be liquefying, falling to pieces.

'Oh, my Gord!' she groaned, 'have I got a hangover, or have I got a hangover? . . . Did I have a night last night, or did I have a night?'

'You'd better have a cup of tea. Come into my room, I'm just making one.'

'That'd be lovely . . . Oh, o-oh, oh, my Gord . . .'

Vi threw back the bedclothes and got up. I was too tight to take my clothes off when I got in this morning, and look what I done . . .' She had pushed one of her feet through the front of the flimsy black dress.

'I'll sew it for you, if you like,' said Helen.

'You *are* a dear.' Vi struggled out of her clothes. 'What do I look like? Am I getting nice and slim?'

From Vi's body, overheated with dancing overnight in the stuffy club-room, and wrapped for hours in a stale camel-hair coat under unwashed blankets, there proceeded an odour of decay mingled with Oppopponax – a perfume which is supposed to stimulate male desire. Vi was very slim. Her ribs and hip bones were visible. Under prominent collar-bones, little dead white breasts hung down, devitalised, on to her flat chest. Her waist was slender, but her abdomen bulged abruptly, like a bladder at bursting-point, incongruously supported by long, well-formed, dancer's legs. Pringling with goose-flesh in the sudden cold of the room she struck an attitude in front of Helen.

'Look, Lady Godiva!'

Vi peeled off her stockings, and wriggled her toes with a sigh of relief.

'Coming?' asked Helen.

'Just a minute . . . Look, how dancing busts up your feet.' Vi displayed five glutinous red toes, dotted with corns and blisters.

'Well, why don't you wear shoes that fit you?'

'I do!'

'You don't; you take a five, but you always wear a four and a half.'

'I feel terrible,' said Vi.

'Eat something.'

'Oh, don't talk about *food!*'

'A hot bath, then?'

'Can't be bothered.' Vi scrubbed at her teeth with pink denti-frice, spat out lingering strings of froth, then threw down the brush and polished her teeth on her camiknickers. 'Ah, that's better. Now, tea, eh?'

'I've got the kettle boiling.'

'Oh, Gord . . .' said Vi. She put on a dressing-gown and pushed her feet into slippers. 'I got to do some shopping. I ought to have a bath. I haven't had a bath for nearly a week. Still, I wash with cold cream; that's better for the skin than soap . . . Oh, I feel awful. Oh, I feel lousy. Oh, I didn't half have a lovely time last night. Was I drunk or was I drunk? And was I sick! I spoiled Yetta's new silver lamé . . . Something terrible's going to happen.'

'What?'

'I dunno.'

'Why?'

'Somebody sang "Danny Boy" last night; it's unlucky . . . Here, listen. You want a job, don't you?'

'Yes, why?'

'We want a girl, up at the club.'

'I don't think I'd be any good at that sort of thing.'

'What d'you mean? *I* keep respectable, don't I? A man asked me to go to a hotel with him last night: he offered me two quid. But I told him straight: "We're all decent girls down here; you won't get anything of *that* sort. We don't go with any Tom, Dick or Harry!" . . . Besides, it would of cost him at least three. All you've got to do is dance with 'em. They pay you for your time. A quid, ten bob – it's a living, isn't it?'

'Yes, but –'

'Then come along, you mug! There's room for one more. Gertie got the sack last night for taking liberties with the boss.'

'No, thanks all the same.'

They went into Helen's room. Vi took three sips of tea, and then pushed away her cup, saying: 'That was lovely . . . But I got to go and do some shopping. I got to get a brassiere and some stockings. Come with?'

'No, I don't think I will.'

'Oh, come on, come with me.'

'No, I'm not coming. I want to wash my undies.'

'You're always washing something. You got too much energy. What you need is a man.'

'Oh, shut up, Vi!'

'Well, you do.'

'If I do, it's my business.'

'Well, I'm going in a few minutes. You won't come and help me buy my stockings?'

'No, not now, Vi. I've been out.'

'Fed up?' asked Vi.

Helen shrugged her broad shoulders. 'A bit.'

'What you need is a –'

'Oh, shut *up*.'

Vi giggled as she went out.

* * *

She walked along, looking at the shops and rubbing shoulders with the plain, hard-working women of the neighbourhood who were out buying bread and soap.

'*If I had a lot of money*,' she thought, '*I'd buy a lot of furniture for cash, and have a flat . . . and get fifty evening dresses, and five day dresses, and a hundred pairs of shoes, and send my father ten shillings a week regular, and have champagne, and chicken, and whisky, and tongue sandwiches for breakfast every afternoon . . .'*

She stopped to look at a pair of orange-and-silver dance-slippers, priced at six-and-elevenpence. With the impulse, she went straight into the shop.

'I want those orange-and-silver shoes in the window.'

'What size, madam?'

'Um . . . er, fours.'

'Oh, I'm awfully sorry, madam, but those slippers are the last of a range; we only have them in threes and fives.'

'Oh . . . Well, can I try on a three?'

'Yes, certainly; but they're a very small-fitting three.'

Vi felt like a woman on the verge of a terrible bereavement; without those orange-and-silver slippers there would be nothing left for her to live for; nothing.

'I'll try 'em on.'

She squeezed her feet into them, and hobbled three paces in agony.

'Perhaps the five, madam?'

'No, I don't *take* size five . . . Could you stretch these?'

'Just a little, madam; but I'd try the five if I were you – it's a very small-fitting five.'

'Stretch these.' She followed the assistant with her eyes; she was afraid to let the orange-and-silver slippers out of her sight. They were as dear to her as life itself. She needed them more than anything else on earth.

'Now you might find them a little easier, madam.'

'Ooooo!' Vi put them on. This time she could walk five paces in them. 'Yes, that's better. They'll stretch a bit when I've worn them once or twice, won't they?'

'Oh, yes, madam.'

'All right, I'll take them.' The girl put the slippers in a box. Vi blinked: it seemed to her that they were far too beautiful to cover up. She left the shop, hugging the box to her bosom.

Two doors farther on she paused at the window of a stationer's shop in which there was displayed a range of coloured inks – red ink, yellow ink, blue ink, orange ink –

'*Orange ink! Then I could write letters to match my shoes!*' She almost ran into the shop.

'How much is orange ink?'

'Sixpence and ninepence, miss.'

'I'll have a sixpenny bottle.'

Vi put the ink in her bag. Then she remembered that she had come out to buy stockings and a brassiere. Well, the brassiere would have to wait; but stockings were a necessity. Grossman's had good stockings for one-and-eleven . . . But next door to the stationer's there was a Woolworth's store. She went in – not to buy anything, but only to look around. Nobody goes into Woolworth's shops to buy anything: one visits Woolworth's as a kind of museum, merely to look. And one comes out with a pot of paint, a hacksaw, a kettle, a pound of sweets, three egg-cups, a writing-pad, a lampshade, an electric-light bulb, a typewriter-rubber, an ice-cream cone, a rubber belt, two apostle spoons, a Swiss roll, a toilet roll and a packet of seeds.

The cosmetics counter drew Vi as a magnet.

DARK ALLURE PERFUMES said a show-card. Vi clutched at a bottle, as a starving man might clutch at a loaf. 'Oh, Miss!' . . . *Ting*! went the cash-register. Vi placed the perfume bottle in her pocket. Then her conscience muttered: '*Wasting money on scent when you've got a dozen bottles already! Get the stockings before all your money's gone!*' She set her jaw resolutely. But Woolworth is a tempter, a devil with women; a genius of shelf appeal, he displays feminine trimmings near the door; he catches them as they go in, and, as they go out, cashes in on their afterthoughts. Vi saw a display of artificial flowers.

These were things she could not resist – canvas camellias, cotton roses, velveteen violets – they were somehow close to her soul. She bought something resembling a sprig of yellow pansies. '*Stockings! Stockings!*' cried her conscience. She grasped the paper bag with the artificial flowers. Now she would go to Grossman's, she really and truly would . . .

Glass emeralds set in gilt metal on the jewellery counter winked at her like satanic eyes. She handled a pair of ear-rings: forty medium-sized diamonds set in solid lumps of platinum, complete with clasps, on a card – sixpence the lot. Woolworth must be mad to sell such lovely things so cheap. 'These, miss!' 'Thank you, madam.' *Ting!*

'*After all,*' thought Vi, '*I've still got about half a crown left . . .*' She went out and crossed the road, determined to buy her stockings. But she had to go out of her way to avoid a bus, and found herself outside the Black Horse.

Outside a public-house!

The swing-doors opened and shut like snapping jaws, and swallowed her.

'Johnnie Walker,' she said to the barmaid. She drank it, and felt better. 'Same again.'

'*Oh Jesus, my stockings!*' she thought, abruptly. But there was only a shilling left in her purse. Still, there was always Woolworth's. A pair of stockings, sixpence each stocking; just for this one evening . . . She finished her second drink, and went back to Woolworth's.

As she walked to the stocking-counter she looked neither to the right nor to the left. Stockings, stockings, stockings, stockin –

A spotted silk handkerchief caught her eye. She hesitated and advanced a hand towards it. '*No, no!*' cried the muffled voice of reason. Well, she would just feel it. She touched it, lingered over it, paused –

'Can I help you, madam?' asked a sales-girl.

'I'll have this one,' said Vi. She wanted to kick herself. Then an idea struck her, an inspiration. '*Coo! I can wear my sandals and paint my toenails –*'

She returned to the cosmetics counter. Varnish for toe-nails . . . dark red . . .

Ting! . . . 'Thank you, madam.'

Having no more money, she went home, and laid out her parcels on Helen's bed.

'Well, did you get your stuff?' asked Helen.

'Oh, yes.'

'What's in that box? Shoes?'

'Uh?' Vi opened the box, took out the shoes, held them up, made a grimace, threw them down, and said: 'Oh Christ, aren't they lousy!'

* * *

At nine o'clock, Vi started to dress. She danced up and down Helen's room, lashing herself into her nightly frenzy.

'Listen, Helen,' she said, 'why not come with me?'

'Don't be silly.'

'Why stay in and get fed up with yourself?'

'I'm not fed up with myself.'

'Yes you are, I can see you are . . . You know, Helen, you ought to find yourself a fellow.'

'There you go again!'

'Well, you ought.'

'Don't be ridiculous. What for?'

'You need a good –'

'– Oh, don't keep on!' Helen's face burned red; she fixed Vi with a sultry glare: 'I *know* I do! But it's my business! What do you expect me to do? Rush out into the street, and grab hold of any man who passes and drag him home? Go about screaming "A man! A man!"? Of course I want a man, but not just any man. I've got high standards.'

'Ah,' said Vi, with an air of infinite experience, 'I used to talk like that, too. I used to be crazy about Clive Brook –'

'I can't just go and fall into a man's arms. I'd have to be attracted to him, at least, ever such a lot, before I . . .'

'But what chance do you get of meeting any, the way you live?'

Helen shrugged. 'Not much.'

'Then why not come along with me tonight?'

'My dear Vi, do you imagine that I'm going to go around the night-clubs looking for men? Don't be –'

'What I mean to say is, you'll see a bit of *life*.'

'You call that life?'

'Call it what you like. I get a living out of it. You know, Helen, you are a mug.'

'All right,' said Helen, 'but you're a bigger one.'

'Me? Why am I?'

'Well, look at the way you live.'

Vi was offended; her mouth drooped. 'What d'you mean?'

'No sleep, no proper food; you ruin your health, and what for?'

96

'Who ruins whose health?'

'You ruin your health, and what have you got to show for it? A pair of six-and-elevenpenny shoes and a few artificial flowers . . . Ha!'

'I do not ruin my health!' cried Vi. 'I'm as strong as a lion! And I get a good living: I knock up my few quid a week –'

'And look how you waste it!' Superfluous nervous energy made Helen tap her foot against the floor.

'What the hell if I do waste it? It's my money. *I* earn it! At least, I get the money to waste. But what about you? You sit here, moping and worrying, and ruining your looks – that's good for your health, I don't think! You get a fat lot of grub, don't you? You can't *afford* to eat. And sleep – lying awake all night, wondering if you'll get a job for thirty-five bob a week tomorrow, and jumping out of bed first thing in the morning to grab the paper. *And* you're a fortnight behind with your rent. And when I say: "Come along and make yourself a few quid," you start going all bloody high-hat! If I'm a mug, what are you?'

Helen was silent. Vi continued: 'I'm saying it for your own good. Anybody would think I was asking you to go on the bash, or something. You can keep respectable in a night-club. Look at me!'

'After all, if one keeps one's wits about one, I daresay . . .' murmured Helen.

'I chuck my money away. All right. But it's only because I can always get some more.'

'Um; but for how long?'

'How long for? You should worry how long for! You've got to eat today and tomorrow, haven't you? How long do you think you can go on being a shorthand-typist for? A hundred years? A thousand years?'

'*Only too true*,' thought Helen; and a pensive expression came over her face.

'I'm only telling you for your own good,' said Vi, 'I'm your friend. You've got a lovely face and a smashing figure. You could *kid* fellows a bit, couldn't you? You don't have to sleep with a fellow just because you dance with him, do you?'

'*You do; I needn't*,' thought Helen; and she said: 'No, I suppose not . . .'

97

'You're a good dancer.'

'Fairly good.'

'Then what's stopping you from coming? Come just for one night, and see how you like it. Just one night! You can always walk out.'

'But . . . I've got nothing to wear.'

'You've got a dance-frock.'

'Only that bright-red one.'

'You look smashing in it; and red matches the colour of the place.'

'No, I don't think I'll come . . .'

'All right; sit here and mope. Today's Thursday. Can you get a job over the week-end?'

There was a knock at the door. The landlady looked in: a Scotch woman, with a voice like the skirl of wild bagpipes in a high wind. She asked Helen: 'Weel?'

Helen was embarrassed; she blushed.

'Have ye got anything for me, miss?'

'I-er . . .'

'Ye cannut go on like this.'

'No, I know; I'm awfully sorry . . . I expect to have some money tomorrow.'

'Is that defeenite?'

'Oh . . . yes, yes.'

'Hwit am I to do if me tenants don't pay me me rent?'

'I'll let you have some tomorrow, Mrs Anguish.'

'I dinnut want to be hard, but if ye cannut, you'll have to go on Saturday.'

She went out. Vi, who had been making herself inconspicuous, tossed her head and said, in a very low voice: 'The stingy bitch.'

Helen drew a deep breath – the deep breath of a diver about to plunge into dark water. 'I'll come!' she said.

Vi was elated. The greatest consolation of the degraded human being is the fact that there are others in the same mire. The lower you descend, the intenser grows your yearning for standardisation. The drunkard loves to see others get drunk; the prostitute would like to see all the women in the world on the streets. There is no satisfaction quite so deep and evil as that of the man who can say: 'Aha, now we're all in the same stew!' With what joyous melancholy, with how delicious a thrill of self-pity the out-of-work man sees the unemployment figures rise! 'Be exactly my size; no bigger, and no smaller,' says the dwarf; 'Damn your eyes!' whispers the blind man; 'Comrades!' yells the communist –

'Oh, Goody-goody!' cried Vi, dancing with joy. 'You stick with *me*. I'll show you the ropes. *I'll* learn you all you want to know . . .'

Whatever else goes to rot, the will to power persists, urgent but ineffectual, like an old man's lust, even in the last flat tundras of life.

'I'll show you what to do!' said Vi. She was excited: now she was a teacher, a mentor, an imparter of instruction. 'Now, let's see your dress.'

Helen took her red evening dress out of the wardrobe, and put it on. The bright silk clung to the strong salient curves of her body. She turned, displaying her back; the deep triangle of cream-coloured flesh seemed to glow in the dim little room.

A qualm of jealousy dulled the edge of Vi's triumph. 'Mm . . . And how you going to do your hair?'

'Oh, I shall just put a lot of brilliantine on it and leave it as it is.'

'Hm.' Vi was no longer pleased.

'I'll look better when I've made up.'

'Listen, try parting your hair on the side.'

'No, I don't like it that way.'

'Try; let's see.'

Helen parted her hair on the left-hand side. 'See? It's not so good that way.'

'Oh, I like it!' exclaimed Vi. 'Oh; you *must* do it that way. Oh, yes, Helen, keep it like that. It's marvellous – smashing!' At the back of her head a voice said: '*Now that's she gone into your racket, to which she thought herself so superior, take care she doesn't look too good, or do as well as you . . .*'

But Helen combed out the parting.

'Well, please yourself,' said Vi. 'I was only telling you for your own good, you know . . . Coo, Christ! I'll lend you my razor. Under your arms! My Gord, I've never seen anything like it!'

'Yes, it is a bit thick.'

'And your arms too.'

'Oh, no, I'm not going to shave the rest of my arms; it'll grow all bristly. Underneath, yes; but not the rest.'

'Oh, all right; I was just advising you for your own good. I haven't got a hair on my body, you know – well, except just one or two, of course. You going to have a bath?'

'No, just a wash. I had a bath this morning. I bath every morning.'

'Hm,' said Vi, with some irritation, 'you have time to.'

'You're not bathing, are you?'

'Of course I am! What d'you take me for?'

'Sorry; I thought you said you weren't going to.'

'Coo, I never! I bath every day, too, when I get the time.'

'But you've already made up.'

'Oh, Christ, so I have. Oh, well, I'll bath when I come home.'

Helen put a flat-iron on the gas-ring and took off the red dress. Vi watched her.

'I'll iron my dress,' said Helen. 'After all, you're right, you know. There's no need to let yourself go. As long as one keeps sober, and takes care what one does, there's no reason why one shouldn't get a living out of it. I'm not going to stand for any nonsense.'

'Mm, yes . . . but you don't want to be too strait-laced, you know.'

'No, I know. Are you annoyed about something?'

'Me? Ha-ha!'

'You know what? I think I'll even enjoy the change, for a little while, until I get something better.'

'*The mug! She thinks that once she starts she'll be able to leave off!*' sniggered the voice in Vi's brain. She was not pleased at Helen's attitude. More timidity, more uncertainty; come, but like a lamb to the slaughter! She replied: 'Oh, it's not *all* honey. You've got to *work*, damn it all, and there's a lot of brainwork in it.'

Bup! went the gas, and flame pricked at the flat-iron.

'Now, who will I see?' Helen asked.

Vi recovered her high spirits. 'Ah, *I'll* tell you. You'll have to be careful of a cow called Mary – she's Phil's wife; but if you ask me, they aren't really married at all –'

'Who's Phil?'

'The boss. Phil Nosseross . . .'

Helen laid out her dress on the table.

'That's a funny name. What's he like?'

NINE

Like Bagrag's, the Silver Fox was in a cellar; and like Bagrag, Phil Nosseross was something of a mystery. Most men are, who live by night. The past life of the night-club man is locked away; yet through the keyhole creeps a questionable smell, as of something hurriedly buried. How did he get into the business? When did he start? Why? What did he do before? If ordinary, honest commerce, then how did he come to associate with the people of the night so intimately as to acquire some of their slime – to learn the dodges and get connections? Where did he get the capital to start? These are questions which are seldom answered.

Nosseross was talkative, but not communicative. Red-hot irons could not have got reminiscences out of him. He was not exactly a liar, or even a prevaricator; he did not hide behind fictions, like Fabian, or wriggle round questions like Figler: he simply kept the facts of his life away from the light and covered their tracks with jokes. For example: people often asked him if he had been in the club business all his life. To this inquiry, he had at least fifty replies, all equally ridiculous. Sometimes he said: 'What, haven't you heard? I used to be a lieutenant in the Salvation Army'; sometimes: 'No, I used to have a moth farm; I sold moth-balls'; or: 'Don't breathe a word, but I used to be an international spy'; and so on. Nosseross might have been anything. He looked, most of all, like an old jockey: you could, somehow, imagine him in a jockey's cap, clinging like a monkey to the neck of a galloping horse. But then, it was equally easy to imagine him in a naval cap, sailing a ship; or in a clerical collar, reading a sermon; or in a conical hat with pompoms, throwing cart-wheels in a circus. He had a boiled-down figure and a dried-up face with a harsh, sand-blasted surface; and his bald scalp was of the colour of the light, durable leather with which the backs of ledgers are bound. His hands were small, hairy and sinewy – hard, with a rat-trap grip; spatulate, restless, quick to close and slow to open – clutching hands; and his hard little eyes glinted under fat black eyebrows that constantly arched themselves like furry caterpillars dying of thirst in the arid desert of his forehead. They enabled him to pull funny faces and make people laugh. Nosseross was good at making people laugh; genial, jocular, easy in his manner, but never off his guard. Catch a weasel asleep, then put one over on Phil Nosseross! He was humorous by habit, in the manner of a commercial traveller whose good fellowship is a professional attitude – a teller of limericks, a glad-hander who jovially prodded you in the ribs and slapped you on the backside to feel where you kept your wallet – dexterous at juggling and balancing tricks; adroit at making dogs and ballet-dancers out of paper serviettes; quick at figures as a bookmaker's clerk, and clairvoyant in the matter of good and bad cheques – hard as nails, slippery as a wagon-load of eels; an extraordinarily tough and wily little man who looked as if he had got away with things for which other men would have gone to prison for life.

No doubt he had.

He had discussed the Silver Fox with his wife Mary; a little, doll-faced blonde, twenty years old, with stupid blue eyes as large as walnuts.

She said: 'Oh, let's have the decorations in blue, darling; lovely electric-blue, with gold –'

'My little pet,' said Nosseross, 'haven't you got no psychology? Blue means misery: "I'm feeling blue"; but red means having a good time, making whoopee: "Let's paint the town red." So it'll be red, see, my lambkins?'

'In panels with gold edges, then?'

'No, my beautiful little baby doll. I'm going to paint this place quite different. I'm going to have a spiral design – you know what a spiral is; a thing like a, like a spiral – starting on the ceiling, not quite dead centre, and running round and round, right round the ceiling and the walls down to the floor, in great big thick bands of light red and dark red. Get the idea, duckie-duckie? Their natural instinct will be to follow that spiral round and round with their eyes. After they've had a few drinks, what with the band, they'll feel they're inside a damned great spinning-top; and it'll help 'em to get tighter and tighter. And the tighter they are, the more they spend.'

'Um. Lovely bright lights –'

'Now, lovey-dovey, where do you get ideas like that from? No bright lights! Dull lights. All the girls won't be as beautiful as you. *Revolving* lights; a revolving chandelier thing at the centre of the spiral. Hypnotise 'em, the fools! I'll skin 'em alive!'

'Mirrors?'

'Now, my precious; people love to see other people behaving like idiots, but not seeing themselves doing the same thing. No mirrors except in the lavatories, and there we're going to have pink mirrors, see?'

'Why pink?'

'They mustn't see themselves in their true colours, my love. When they go out to be sick, let 'em look as if they're having a good time. See, petsy-wetsy?'

'Clever little monkey-wunkey-face!'

'I use common sense.'

'But, darling; don't you think thirty-five bob is a bit steep for a bottle of Scotch?'

'They'll pay, my love.'

'*I* wouldn't.'

'No more would I, my angel. We're wise; we sell it. Only mugs buy it, and one is born every minute.'

'I can't understand why people *want* to get drunk.'

'Can't you, lovekins? I can. You know how a man can get so that he can't bear the sight of his wife?'

'Um?'

'Well, angel-face, people get so they can't bear the sight of themselves. So they get drunk and think they're somebody else. A man who's a coward to the backbone gets drunk and picks a fight. A man who goes red at the sound of his own voice, drinks a couple of whiskies, and insists on singing "Mother Machree". Get it?'

'Uum.'

'Boofie woofie!' crooned Nosseross: it was as if a granite kerb-stone were oozing honey. 'Diddlums! . . . Well, my pet: people are just a lot of sloppy, weak-kneed, pop-eyed, pasty-faced, herring-gutted, sodden, stupid, dribbling louts. Like rollmops – no spine and no guts. See, lambie?'

'Um-um.'

'They're no good for anything unless they're doped. If they're not doped one way, it's another. No virtue of their own. Some get tanked up on politics; others on booze. They know they're no damned good *themselves*, so they've got to go and get stuffed with something. Don't you have any respect for 'em. People!' He spat out the word.

Nosseross knew his fellow-men.

Man spends the first half of his life trying to find himself, and the other half trying to lose himself.

He runs in little circles, like a pup trying to nuzzle its own behind; he catches up with himself, sniffs, is disgusted, and runs away from his own smell.

He fears life; he flies from it. But in how many ways can a man escape from reality?

He can blindfold himself with religion or philosophy; but not until his body is almost dead. He can drug himself with dreams; but only before his body is awake. He is his own worst enemy: how can he hide from himself? He can always kill him-self, of course, but he never does. He lacks the courage to put his head in the gas-oven, so he says: 'That is the coward's way out' – and even thinks himself a hero for living on. This kind of self-aggrandisement is one of his hide-outs from encircling fact. He imagines a trouble, expects to be admired if he doesn't die of it, and hopes to be canonised as a martyr if he does. Apart from that, he takes to wine, women, laughter and song.

Woman – an ordinary necessity which he has fixed on a greasy pole – stings his vanity and makes him climb. Laughter elevates him, since it makes him feel superior to other men's woes; for he laughs at nothing but misfortune. Song enables him to enjoy his sorrows, and make toil a kind of dance. Alcohol simply stuns him, knocks him out; and he likes that best of all.

And so he runs in panic up and down these brief blind-alleys of ignominious escape, scuttling away from the hard and glorious possibilities of this superb earth – yapping to drown the hollow clatter of the tinpot conscience tied to his tail. And so it comes to pass that his soul is still in the cradle, and knows nothing but inarticulate grunts expressive of his emotions and blind needs: '*Ernh!*' – 'Pity me'; '*Gool*' – 'I am pleased'; '*Myer!*' – 'I hate you'; '*Ha-ha!*' – 'I despise you'; '*Ah-ah*' – 'I want to relieve myself'.

So, dandle the baby! Suck-dummies and rattles for his little brain, and Fuller's earth and vaseline for the sore backside of his soft pink soul! Distract him, pamper him; say 'ah-goo, ah-goo' and tickle his lip to make him smile; tell him about gooseberry bushes – God forbid that he should soil himself with the Facts of Life or get to learn What Every Boy Should Know. And above all – above all, give him a drink. Stuff his howling mouth with the nipples of oblivion! He wants to get away from the miserable little handful of silly falsehoods and tawdry half-truths which make up his life. Unconsciousness! Anæsthetise him: that is his greatest comfort – poor simulacrum; soft white maggot still unformed!

'People!' said Nosseross.

'And will you ever get so you can't bear the sight of *me*?' asked Mary.

'*My* little sweetie-pet.'

'My little bald-headed monkey-face.'

Nosseross was delighted. He could think of nothing to express his delight but the following: 'Izzy-wizzy-wizzy!'

Mary replied: 'Uzoo uvoo ickles? And will you fall in love with all the pretty hostesses?'

'Don't be ridiculous, lambie!'

Nosseross put his tough, bald head on Mary's scented shoulder, and sighed.

Unseen, Mary winked at the ceiling.

'Who says dynamite is powerful?'

Dynamite can only remove mountains. But one superfluous teaspoonful of seminal fluid can overturn the piled-up wisdom, pride and integrity of a hundred thousand years, as a child smacks down a sand-pie – rip open Troy like a hat-box, scatter Antioch like a handful of rice, shake the British Empire like a tablecloth and flap out kings!

Nosseross was wise: so was Solomon, who fell flat on his nose before the Baalim and went to the devil for the sake of a couple of Philistinian whores. Nosseross was subtle and tricky: so was Mark Antony, who exchanged an empire for the embraces of a stout Græco-Egyptian widow with a hook nose. Nosseross was strong; but not half as strong as Samson, who could tear up a lion as easily as a No Account cheque, but collapsed in Delilah's scissors-hold. Hercules could carry the weight of the heavens, but two grammes of spermatozoa would have been too heavy for him. What does strength or wisdom avail a man – or even experience of women? Nosseross had known hundreds of them during the sixty years of his life: he knew their habits, their souls and all the sensations that may proceed out of contact with their bodies, and could look at them with a diabolically knowing eye and laugh at them. He was not merely old enough to know better – he did know better. But the final wild flicker of a man's dying virility is more blinding than lightning. In his desire to alleviate that last intolerable prostatic irritation, an old man scratches out wisdom, knowledge, judgment, intuition, strength of will, shame, common sense – everything. And so he makes a fool of himself – a man in a dream – until there comes an hour when he looks in his mirror and sees that he is really old, shivering in impotence, while the woman scornfully dresses herself behind him; and then reason, limping painfully and wry with bitterness, comes creeping back in the cold grey daylight.

'And where is love when reason returns? Where is the itch of last summer's heat-bumps?'

'And are you going to give me that double silver fox?'

'I will if you give Phil a nice big kiss.'

Mary kissed him. His face, she thought, felt exactly like the seat of a leather chair after one has warmed it by sitting in it. Then she stroked the top of his head, and at the same time thought: '*There are plenty fellows with nice heads of hair; I can soon find one . . .*'

'Loppipops!' said Nosseross, fervently.

* * *

But to Helen and Vi Nosseross presented his real front: hard, calm and cunning.

'Ah, so you're the young lady Vi's been telling us so much about. What's your name?'

'Helen –'

'You don't have to tell me your surname unless you want to.'

'It's Arnold.'

'Helen Arnold. Well, so you want to work here, do you?'

'Yes, I'd like to try.'

'Why not?' said Nosseross. 'All right, you can try.'

'Thanks.' It was too quick. Helen could think of nothing to say.

'Well, Vi,' said Nosseross, 'if you just get a table for yourself I'll have a word with Helen . . .'

Vi went out. Nosseross grinned, and said in a confidential undertone: 'You know, that girl's a fool.'

'Is she?'

'Absolutely. But you ought to do well, you know.'

'I hope so.'

Nosseross had the air of a kindly uncle. 'Ye-es, I'm sure of it, Helen. You see, you've got some sense. I can tell by your face. You'll be about twenty-five, eh? . . . Yes, I thought so. A lovely age; you've got all your life before you. You've had some education, haven't you?'

'Secondary school.'

'And very nice, too. What kind of work have you done before?'

'I've been a secretary, mostly.'

'Very nice. And there aren't many jobs going, so you think you'd like to try your hand at something else, eh? Fine. That's the spirit. You get a chance to meet a lot of nice people in this business . . . Your family in London?'

'No, I've only got one sister, and she lives in the country.'

'Well, start here and see how you like it. I daresay Vi's told you what sort of terms a hostess works on?'

'Yes, I –'

'No wages; only what you pick up. But I'm pretty generous

with commission. It'll be easy for you. Now look here, I'll talk to you in confidence. About nine hundred and ninety-nine hostesses out of a thousand are mugs. They're the worst kind of mugs, because after they get one or two men who are dead drunk to give them a pound or two for nothing, they get such swelled heads that you can't teach 'em anything any more . . . Now actually they're just fools; greedy, but without any system, without any proper technique. You're intelligent. You've got polish. You'll beat 'em all hollow at this game. This is all you've got to do as far as I'm concerned: get men to buy drink. See? Whisky or gin, thirty-five shillings a bottle. Champagne, two pounds and up. Then there's other little things, like cigarettes. We charge two-and-six for an ordinary shilling packet, and so on, in that scale: a two-and-ninepenny Abdullas fetches six bob. You ask for a cigarette; tell 'em you only smoke Turkish – or if they're smoking Turkish, then you only smoke Virginia – and get 'em to buy you a packet. Try and get 'em to buy you cocktails; you get commission on cocktails. You see, we make a cocktail out of just plain lemon-juice, in a cocktail-glass. It costs three shillings; you get sixpence on every one you get. Got that?'

'Yes.'

'Now chocolates. We sell only fancy boxes. They cost me about three or four shillings, and I sell 'em at between thirty shillings and two pounds a box. You sell me back the box for ten shillings afterwards. That goes for dolls, too. It's like this: I pay about five shillings for a nice stuffed doll, and sell it for between thirty shillings and three pounds – the price varies according to how much the fellow's got and how tight he happens to be. You sell dolls back to me for a third of what the fellow pays. So you get ten bob on a thirty-bob doll, and so on. It's good profit for all of us. See?'

'Yes, I see. And exactly what do I have to do, apart from that?'

'Get 'em to spend. Keep 'em company; dance; talk to 'em. Talk intelligently. Parade all you've got. Display your education, so that they'll feel they're in good company. Help 'em to clean up the bottles.'

'You mean help them drink?'

'No, you won't drink much if you've got any sense. Splash the stuff around; waste it; get the customer to offer drinks to the band. See? Be hard, but don't look it. Graft. Get yourself some money, too. If a man wants to dance, tell him that'll cost him half a crown a dance. If he wants you to sit with him, your time for the evening costs anything from a pound up. Make it quite clear you've got to be paid; but don't nag, don't harp on money. If a man offers you ten shillings, take it first and look insulted afterwards. The average girl is an idiot – she only recognises a pound note. If you offered her a choice between a pound note and thirty shillings in silver, she'd take the note. That's because she comes from the gutter, where a pound note is a kind of god. They've got no arithmetic. They can't count. They don't realise 4 × 5s. = £1; the same as 20s. = £1.

'You know, I can't find any girls with sense. They can't use their judgement, and work according to the person they're sitting with. They either whine for money like a lousy beggar, or demand it like a rent-collector. Some men have to be bullied, more or less: but the best thing is to let 'em think they're being generous. Lead 'em gently, by the nose, especially if they come from the provinces. In general, you can push a Londoner about a bit; but never try that game on a man from Lancashire, or Yorkshire, or the Midlands, or Scotland. You don't take men home, I suppose, do you?'

'No, I don't do that.'

'Well, do as you like. That's your affair. The club closes about five in the morning. After that time you do exactly as you please. But while the club is open you're not allowed to leave the place, not even to go to the door and kiss a man good-night. See? Now about things like soda-water. Soda-water is five shillings a syphon. A man ordering whisky always orders soda; but you tell him you only drink ginger-ale, and that costs him one-and-six for a baby bottle. If he orders gin, then you've got to have lime-juice and tonic-water with it. Tonic, a shilling a baby bottle; lime-juice, seven-and-six. Is that clear?'

'Yes, thanks; quite clear.'

'Now, breakfasts. We like 'em to get a skinful of booze before eating, so no food is served before four in the morning; then we serve breakfast – an egg, a rasher of bacon, and toast: five shillings. Coffee, a shilling a cup, or two-and-six a pot, which holds two cups. They nearly always order pots, because they think they get more for the money that way. If there's nobody in and you want something to eat yourself, the same breakfast costs you a shilling; coffee, threepence. Never refuse anything. If you're offered ten breakfasts, one after another, take 'em all, mess 'em about if you don't want to eat 'em, and leave 'em. If you leave a breakfast, don't break up the egg; we serve it again. Remember, there's more profit in cocktails than in whisky. A man might not fancy laying out two pounds for a bottle and a syphon; but he's nearly always mug enough to spend about the same amount on several rounds of near-beer and cocktails. Near-beer costs two shillings a glass: call it just beer – forget the "near". See?'

'I see.'

'Then again, there's flowers. We send the chocolate-girl round with little bunches of violets; or perhaps a carnation with a bit of maidenhair fern tied on: two-and-six, five shillings, seven-and-six – price varies. But it's a thing no man likes to refuse a girl; a little bunch of shy violets, kind of thing. You get sixpence or a shilling commission on a bunch. If a man has spent over ten pounds, we sometimes give him a twopenny carnation: you know the idea – give a mug twopence back out of a tenner, and he'll be so pleased that he'll probably spend another fiver . . . Keep his glass filled; talk and dance all the time; keep his mind off the prices. No stealing.'

'Stealing?'

'Dipping; lifting money out of a mug's pocket. I don't like it. It makes trouble. Not in the club, anyway; what you do outside's no business of mine. Port or sherry costs twenty-five shillings to thirty shillings a bottle. Light wines, like Chablis, Graves, Barsac, and so on, we sell pretty reasonable: seventeen-and-six. They only cost us one-and-nine, anyway. If a man's very tight, and wants champagne, ask for *Special* Champagne: two pounds. You see, it's a kind of sparkling white wine, four bob a bottle: you get five shillings commission.'

'I see.'

'So you see we're generous to the girls here. You get more commission than in any other club in London. Concentrate, and look after yourself. If you know how to work, you can always get something out of a fellow. You'll make more down here than you would in an office, anyway. And bear this in mind: any man who'll pay five shillings or seven-and-six entrance fee to go into a place, and then lay out two pounds for a bottle of Scotch and a syphon of soda, is a *fool*. Therefore, skin him alive – but peel it off gently. Ask him if you can give the doorman a drink – and fill a tumbler: How can he refuse? Get him to offer drinks to the band, the waiters, to me, to everybody. Keep him moving and talking, whirl him round; keep his attention on the lights and the decorations. What d'you think of the decorations, by the way?'

'They make me giddy.'

'That's exactly what they're for. Everything's laid out, cut-and-dried for you. You won't have any difficulty. The men'll fall for you. Talk 'em into feeling big. Once a man starts an appearance, he'll sell the shirt off his mother's back to keep it up. Never hustle 'em, especially provincials, as I told you before. They're a bit shrewder than Londoners; but only about enough to give 'em a swelled head and make 'em bigger mugs in the long run. But you can't bully 'em. Give them their heads, and they'll skin themselves. Is that clear?'

'Absolutely.'

'That's good. Now I'll tell you frankly, between ourselves – I can see you've got brains and so I can talk to you – almost every girl in this racket is a common bloodsucker with about as much brain as a louse. Less even! A louse is at least clever at sucking blood: it knows how to pick out a soft spot on your belly. That's more than these girls know; They've got just one line: "Gimme, gimme, gimme!" I tell you all this quite openly, because I can see you're different.'

Helen was gratified. 'I think I see what you mean,' she said.

'Of course you do. You'll fall into the way of it like a duck into water. Remember – the average night-club hostess is a fool. If she wasn't a fool, she wouldn't stay a night-club hostess: she'd graft herself enough to start something of her own. Somebody once bought her a box of chocolates, and she never got over it.

For every ounce of sense she's got a ton of foolishness. Even if she happens to *have* some smartness, she always over-reaches herself. And if *she* can dig a fair living out of the game, what can you dig?'

'Well, Mr Nosseross –'

'Call me Phil.'

'Well . . . Phil; I'm out to make what I can, naturally, but I don't propose to make a career out of it.'

Couaaaaaaaaaaaaa! went a saxophone: the bandsmen were getting ready.

'Good. Well, now run along and get used to the atmosphere.' Nosseross shook Helen's hand for a second, in his dry, tight grip. When she had gone out he grinned at Mary. Her milky blue eyes, normally as expressionless as painted eyes in a bad water-colour portrait, were narrow with anger.

'What d'you think of her?' asked Nosseross.

'Awful! Phou! She's over-developed; and that accent – "Hwaw, hwaw, hwaw!" Hou!'

'Oh, she's not so bad. She's not bad looking, and she seems sensible and well-spoken –'

'Oh, be quiet! I don't know how you can make yourself look so cheap, flattering girls like that . . . "You've got sense!" and "You've got brains!" and – Ha! Blasted little swanker: "*Naturalluh*, Ai don't propose to make a *careeah* of it!"' sneered Mary, with bitter mockery. 'And you saying all hostesses are fools!'

'Well, darling, so they are, mostly.'

'Didn't I used to be one?'

'You're different, my precious. But you shouldn't worry what she says. Don't they all say they're only in the racket for the time being? And don't they always stay in? It's all talk. The fact remains: once they're in, they're in.'

'Why? They're not compelled to. They can come or go as they like, can't they?'

'No, lambie, they can't. It gets you. It gets you. If you work in a night-club long enough to wear out one pair of dancing-shoes, you're in for life. It's the hours, and everything. You're finished as far as daywork is concerned. Go to bed at seven and eight in the morning, and get up at nine and ten at night every day for a month, and you can say good-bye to the sun. How would you like to go into a routine job; get up at seven in the morning and go to bed at twelve – no noise, no drinks, no dancing; how would you like it?'

'Me?' said Mary, with dignity, 'I couldn't stick it. It's all right for the little office-girls –'

'There you are, then. Once you're in night-life, you're *in*.'

The doorman came into the office.

'Hey, Phil.'

'What?'

'Feller wants to see you.'

'Name?'

'Adam.'

'What's he want?'

'Talk to you.'

'Well dressed?'

'Ordinary . . . Big feller.'

'Send him in, then.'

Nosseross almost closed his eyes: they became like archers' windows in an impregnable old wall – stony slits, through which one could see a veiled glint of iron – while his lips curved into a humorous, chimpanzee-like smile.

Adam walked with a kind of loose-joined saunter, haphazard in his old blue flannel suit.

'Mr Nosseross?'

'Yes. Mr Adam?'

'Yes.'

'What can I do for you?'

'I heard you'd just opened.'

'That's right.'

'I thought you might have a job for me.'

Nosseross shook his head. 'What kind of a job?'

'Doorman.'

'Got one,' said Nosseross.

'Chucker-out?'

'Don't want one. A chucker-in would be more in my line.'

'Pianist. Accordion?'

113

Mary giggled. Nosseross also laughed, and said: 'Is this a joke of some kind?'

'No, quite serious.'

'You're a musician, then?'

'I'm pretty good on a piano: hot stuff.'

'What bands have you played in?'

'Nick's Nine Nitwits was the last.'

'Never heard of it. In any case, I'm fixed up.' As if in confirmation of this the pianist outside began to play 'The Cuban Cabby' while the saxophonist blew tentative notes. 'Leave your name and address, and perhaps –'

'Cloakroom attendant, then?' said Adam.

'Fixed up. Sorry.'

'Cook?'

'Don't be silly.'

'Waiter, then?'

'Jack-of-all-trades, eh?' said Nosseross.

'Why?' asked Adam. 'You could do any job about the place yourself, couldn't you?'

'But have you ever been a waiter before?'

'Yes, once. Olivier's Restaurant.'

'Why d'you leave?'

'Well, I don't mind taking an order from a customer: the customer is always right. He pays, so therefore he must be right. But the head waiter thought he was Mussolini. He made a threatening gesture when I was standing in a corner: I was legally entitled to hit him first.'

'And so you did, eh?'

'Not very hard.'

'Ever been in prison?'

'Not yet.'

Mary whispered: 'Give him a trial, Phil.'

Nosseross shrugged. 'I don't know . . . I can do with another waiter, but . . .'

'Oh, yes, Phil!' said Mary.

Nosseross hesitated. 'Well, look here,' he said, 'I'll tell you what. If I've got a coat to fit you, you can have a try tonight. If not, you're unlucky.'

'All right,' said Adam.

'What size chest do you take?'

'What size have you got?'

Nosseross took from a cupboard a bundle of white coats, embroidered on the breast pockets with the words SILVER FOX.

'Forty is the largest,' he said.

'Exactly my size!' said Adam.

'Let's see.'

Adam put on a white coat. The cloth at the corners of the button holes broke into wrinkles, like an old man's eyes, and from each cuff protruded two inches of heavy wrist.

'See?' said Adam.

'You damned liar, you go a good forty-four. No, I'm sorry; it looks bad –'

'Oh, Phil!' protested Mary.

'Oh, well, all right,' said Nosseross, 'I'll give you a trial tonight; but you'll have to get yourself a couple of white jackets tomorrow, size forty-four.'

'Very good,' said Adam.

'Go and get yourself brushed up. The doorman'll tell you where to hang your things. Then come back and I'll tell what to do.'

'Good. What wages?'

'No wages. Only tips. But the tips are good.'

'Hours?'

'Every night, all night.'

'As long as it's no more than seven nights a week,' said Adam, going out.

Nosseross turned to Mary, and, lighting a cigar, threw away the match with considerable violence.

'Why so eager to give him a job?' he asked. 'What's he to you?'

'Nothing; only I think he's rather nice.'

'Oh, you think he's rather nice! Just because he's about seven feet tall. Well, I don't like that. I'll kick him out –'

'Phil!' Her eyes filled with tears – the crocodile-tears of the voracious woman. 'How *can* you say things like that to me?'

'Oh, I'm sorry lambie; I didn't mean to upset you –'

'Go on, kick him out; kick him out, go on! Just because *I* say give him a job, kick him out!'

'But dear, I only took him on to please you!'

'Oh, don't do anything to please *me!* I'm nobody. I'm only a fool. You're jealous of me all the time.'

'I'm only jealous of you because I'm crazy about you, darling!'

'Aha, so you *are* jealous. So that means you don't trust me. Oh. Oh! I see. I'm as good as a prostitute, am I? Oh. Thank you.'

'But –'

'If he'd been a great big fat girl putting on an accent and making eyes at you, you'd have been all over him. "Oh, you've got sense, dear"; and "Oh, you've got brains, Helen". I'm fed up with you!'

'But I've given him the job, haven't I?'

'Well, you –'

'Ssh!'

'Ready,' said Adam, coming back.

'Then sit down and listen,' said Nosseross.

* * *

Like Fabian, Nosseross classified you according to your face. It would have been difficult to deceive him by means of an assumed expression, a false air. As he talked he kept his eyes on Adam's face. '*Now*,' he said to himself, '*let us place this fellow.*' But the switches and levers of experience and memory, and the connective wires of intuitive reasoning, led to no recognisable conclusion in his mind. The type of Adam was not classified in his filing-system: he was not in the dictionary.

Nosseross frowned.

Our faces are masks behind which we often try to hide our-selves. Sometimes a man endeavours, by conscious muscular effort, to give a different significance to his expression; but, as in a clumsily forged cheque, the alteration always emphasises the original value. We live only by false pretences – we go through life in the strait-jacket of Vanity, whose sleeves are Hunger and Fear – and the conditions of our souls may be diagnosed by the development of our cramped, false faces.

Hence, we would find it easier to live without food than without mirrors.

But Adam's appearance was ambiguous. It seemed to contain the unmixed parts of a dangerous compound: inert and soft things, like nitrogen and glycerine, ready to combine and form an explosive. His forehead was powerful but unlined, as clear as a child's. He had a broad, massive face, built upon big bones, and a thick, short nose. The expression of his mouth was not dissimilar to that of a good-tempered bulldog: he had the same kind of formidable jaws, made for crushing, and attached by tough tendons to an unbreakable neck – but relaxed, foolishly relaxed, in a perpetual half-smile of a lazy good nature.

Nosseross was puzzled. He looked straight at Adam, and their glances met. Adam's eyes were bright, light grey, like the mildest kind of steel, and set wide apart. '*Kid's eyes*,' thought Nosseross. He said: 'So you hit the head waiter at Olivier's?'

'Not really: it was more of a push than a blow.'

'Hurt him?'

'Oh, no; he came round in a few seconds.'

'Hm . . . You know you'll have to pretty lively if you want to work here. I doubt if you'll be any good. You don't look any too quick.'

'I can move fast. It's not necessary to rush up and down like a cat on hot bricks *all* the time, is it?'

'Maybe you're right.'

'All this hurrying – what for? If you've got to go somewhere, or do something, yes. But hustle for the sake of hustle? Not necessary.'

Nosseross nodded; he was beginning to understand. It occurred to him that this was the kind of man who moves slowly for years, gathering force; and then, when a predestined moment arrives, breaks out in inexhaustible energy. Such men are like cables for carrying electric power. Leave them in peace and lie still. But strong resistance makes them stir, glow, and give out a white light. Until that happens, however, they are inert. They can swallow strength. Like Antaeus, they can snore on the ground while pygmies pull their hair; but one day their pride says: 'Up!' – and then something is made, or broken. They await the stimulus that turns dead earth into a landslide, or a slumbering mountain into a volcano . . . '*No mug; slow but could move fast; hard to get started, but a bastard to stop,*' thought Nosseross. He said: 'Well, I've told you all I can tell you. The rest is practice. So get on the job.'

Adam rose.

'One minute,' said Nosseross. 'What kind of exercise do you take?'

'None at all.'

'But you've done some pretty rough work, I daresay?'

'Oh, yes, all kinds of rough work.'

'And yet you've had some education, haven't you?'

'A little. Ordinary sort of education and what I've read myself. Art school, and so on.'

'Painting?'

'Sculpture.'

'Do any good at it?'

'No money in it. Well, I'll get going.'

'Yes. Want a drink?'

'No. I don't drink much.'

'In that case, when you're offered a drink, don't say "no", but bring it into the office. See?'

'All right.'

Adam went out. Nosseross kissed Mary and said: 'You were right. I like that boy.'

'He's got nice eyes,' said Mary.

'Oh, to hell with his nice eyes!' Nosseross followed Adam out. Everything was ready. The girls waited, limp.

Then, faintly, an electric buzzer sounded, and the doorman appeared and said: 'Three good men!'

The girls sat up.

'Three good men!'

The pianist raised his hands. 'Give!' said Nosseross, and the band began to play 'I've Got You Under My Skin'.

'Three good men!' whispered the cigarette-girl. Mary came out, undulating her hips.

Vi threw away the cocktail-stick with which she had been picking her teeth, nudged Helen, and said: 'Three good men!'

Down into the Silver Fox came Harry Fabian, between Figler and the Black Strangler: three good men.

TEN

'What!' cried Nosseross. 'Do my eyes deceive me? Not Harry Fabian?'

'In person! Well, Nosseross, you dirty old crook, how are you? Meet my partner, Joe Figler.'

'We've met before, I think, Mr Nosseross.'

'I should just about say we have met before, Joe. And so you're in business with young Harry, eh?'

'Fabian Promotions!' shouted Fabian. 'All-in-wrestling. And Phil – this is Charlie Bamboo, the Black Strangler, coming heavy-weight champion of the world.'

Vi whispered: 'Oooo, Helen; see that little man, the fair one, all in blue? That's Harry Fabian, the song-writer. He's lovely.'

'What, Vi!' said Fabian, and, followed by Figler and the Strangler, he went over to her table and slapped her on the shoulder. Then he saw Helen, and his face expressed surprise and delight. 'Say, who's your friend? Boy, oh boy, that's what I call a pretty girl!'

'She's new to the business,' said Vi.

'Well, we all have to learn some time . . . Come on boys, park your bodies. We sit here.' Fabian sat close to Helen. The Strangler dropped his immense body into the chair next to Vi; while Figler, gingerly balancing himself on the edge of a little gilt arm-chair, blew his nose – *Plch-plch-plch* – on a large clean hand-kerchief, and took one cigarette from his pocket.

'And how about a girl friend for my old pal Joe?'

'No thanks; I'm all right as I am.'

'Drinks, then; drinks!' cried Fabian. 'Come on, boys, let's make whoopee. What's it going to be? . . . You know, Strangler, you mustn't drink too much. We're going to have you in Madison Square Garden, soon, slinging all the champs over the ropes; so we better make it champagne. What say, Joe?'

Figler replied, with a shrug: 'For all I care, order a glass of milk.'

'Ah, don't start getting miserable! Champagne, girls? Okey-doke, champagne.'

'Veuve Clicquot?' suggested Adam.

'You recommend it?'

'Oh, yes.'

'Okay.'

Adam went away.

'What a country!' said Fabian. 'Order a drink at a minute to eleven, and you're okay. Order it a minute after, and you've got to pay through the nose for it in bottles. What a racket! Now in the States –'

'Are you an American?' asked Helen.

'Nope. I lived most of my life there, though. I used to write songs. Hell!' cried Fabian, staring at Helen and slapping the table, 'I wish I'd known you then!'

'Do you? Why?'

'Hell, what wouldn't they have given for a girl with your personality and looks!'

'Who?'

'Who? Who? Jesus, Sam Goldwyn, that's who. He said to me: "Harry," he said, "find me a girl with real looks and personality, and I'll build her up," he said, "I'll make her a star, and you can be her agent on a ten per cent basis." But no. The only dame they could find was a girl called Anderson, Joan Anderson. Heard of her?'

'Of course.'

'Well, she had to have nearly a hundred operations to make her the right shape. Have you ever noticed her eyes?'

'Beautiful eyes –'

'Hah! Eyes! They're not real eyes, you know; they're made of celluloid.'

'No! You're joking.'

'I'm *telling* you – sort of celluloid things that fit over her real eyes. I thought you wouldn't believe it. Hah, people don't know what they're seeing. You've heard of a kid called Freddie Maxwell?'

'Um?'

'Well, how old do you think he is?'

'Is it ten or eleven?'

Fabian roared with delight, and then said: 'Just about thirty years old next March.'

'Surely not!'

Fabian laughed. 'I knew that'd surprise you. Isn't it marvellous? I can tell you that for a fact: in 1932 he was celebrating his twenty-fifth birthday. I was there. There were twenty-five candles on the cake. Mind you, he looks young, yes. But you see him without the make-up and the lines on his forehead are something wicked. He smokes over twenty cigars a day.'

'No!'

Fabian, who had already been drinking, became almost indignant. 'I give you my word of honour! I hope I may never see mother again if it isn't true. I've got papers to prove it. I admit nobody will believe it; but it's true. Did you know Rudolph Valentino was blind?'

'Blind?'

'Yes, it's the lights. Hah, I could tell stories about the studios that'd make your hair come out of curl . . . Boy, oh boy, oh boy, what a marvellous head of hair you got. Smashing! What wouldn't Myrna Loy give for a head of hair like yours!'

'But she's got nicer hair than mine –'

Fabian put his lips to her ear as he whispered: 'Bald as an egg. It's a wig.'

Adam returned with the champagne, and set out the glasses.

'Two pounds ten shillings, please, sir.'

Figler's eyes grew round, but Fabian, taking a thick packet of notes from his pocket, threw down three pounds.

'Keep the change.'

'Thank you, sir.'

Vi rolled her eyes. She was leaning towards Fabian with yearning in every line of her body. Adam poured out the wine.

'Now I'll tell you what I want you to do,' said Fabian, 'and you too, George' – he caught Adam by the coat – 'I want you to drink to Fabian Promotions; to my old friend and partner Joe Figler, and to the Black Strangler, the greatest wrestler in the world! Come on, drink!'

They drank. The cigarette-girl, who had been hovering over them like a kite, chose this moment to swoop.

'What, cigarettes?' said Fabian. 'Want some cigarettes, Helen?'

'Well, I only smoke Turkish.'

'Well, that's okay with me, baby . . . Hey, Flossie, Turkish for the lady.'

The girl picked out a presentation casket. 'One of these, sir?'

'I'd love one of those,' said Helen, 'if you don't think it would be too expensive, Mr Fabian.'

The cigarette-girl scowled. Nosseross knew his Fabian, and he smiled.

'Too expensive, hell!' cried Fabian. 'What am I, a piker? Don't make me laugh! . . . And call me Harry.'

'Twelve-and-six, please, sir.'

Fabian threw down fifteen shillings.

Vi crooned into the ear of Figler: 'Ooo, d'you think I could have some too?'

'D'you want a smoke?'

'I'm gasping for a smoke!'

'Then why didn't you say so before?' said Figler taking one cigarette out of his pocket.

'Oh, you *are* kind,' said Vi; but Figler, who was quite impervious to satire, replied: 'Kind? Listen. I buy a packet of twenty cigarettes in the morning, and I bet you I give away more than half of them before the day's out.'

Vi turned to the Strangler, who, holding a glass of champagne in an enormous ebony fist, was staring, fascinated, at the little bubbles which sprang over the rim.

'Ooo, I think it must be marvellous to be a wrestler. Can I call you Charlie?'

The Strangler simply grunted: 'Gnyuh.'

'The coming world champion!' cried Fabian, flushed with wine and swollen with a feeling of grandeur. 'He can break a leg like I can break a matchstick! He can tear two telephone directories in two as easy as I can tear a cigarette-card! He can straighten a horseshoe just like that – bing! They're scared of him; he gives 'em nightmares! He's a madman, I tell you, a savage! Mad Maguire thought he was a villain till he came up against the Strangler here; but you should of seen what we did to him! Blood? Three women fainted. God-damn it, when I take a man in hand . . . Hey, what the hell! This bottle's empty! Jesus, one bottle goes nowhere. Hah, it's a racket. It looks a big bottle, but the glass is an inch thick – and look at that great big dent in the bottom. Come on –'

'Well, who's going to dance?' asked Vi.

'Me and Helen,' said Fabian. He leapt up, seized Helen in a close, wiry grip and whirled her on to the dance-floor, calling over his shoulder at Adam: 'Another bottle of the same, Unconscious!'

They were the only couple dancing. Fabian felt the eyes of the club upon him. He shouted to the band: 'Put some life into it, and I'll buy you all a drink!' The hands of the pianist bounced on the keyboard. 'Faster! Faster!' cried Fabian, pressing against Helen. 'Come, on, baby, let's show 'em some life!' They spun round in wild circles to the tune of 'South American Joe', played at breakneck speed. The pink lights revolved above him; his eyes followed the spirals on the walls . . .

'Jesus, you dance well!' said Fabian, as the music stopped, and they went back to their table. 'Boy, oh boy, if Eleanor Powell danced half as well . . . Ouf, these God damned moving lights get you groggy. Hell, you're a nice girl . . . Hey, George! Come on, Unconscious, where's that bottle?'

'Here,' said Adam.

Ponk! The bottle opened. The golden wine seemed to dance with joy in the glasses.

'Two pounds ten shillings, please.'

'Who cares?' said Fabian, and dashed three pound notes on to the tray. 'Who cares about money?'

Vi gulped down her wine and, seizing one of Figler's flat white hands, said: 'This little piggy went to market, this little piggy stayed at home –'

'Don't be silly,' said Figler.

'Strangler!' cried Fabian, in a bullying voice. 'Don't forget this is your last drink tonight.'

'Right, Harry,' said the Strangler.

'I gotta keep an eye on him, see Helen? That guy's worth a million dollars to me. Hell, it's time I got back again into the big money. You'd hardly believe me, but in this lousy country I have to work – *work*, mind you – for a lousy fifty, sixty quid a week. What d'you know about that?'

'I wish I could make a quarter of that,' said Helen, 'all I have to live on is what people give me down here, you know.'

'I'll see you right,' said Fabian, pressing her hand. 'I know a girl's got to live. My God, I've been poor myself once. Hah, when I come to think of it! You might not believe it to look at me, but there used to be a time when I had to slave my guts out for ten or twelve pounds a week. Hell, I know what it is to go hungry! Oh, well, I'll be in the heavy sugar from now on.' He pulled out his bulky roll of pound notes, tossed it in the air, caught it, and put it back in his pocket.

'Harry!' said Figler, 'let me hold that for you.'

'Hell, Joe, I can take care of myself . . . Now listen, Helen, tell me all about yourself. You're new to this game, aren't you?'

'Yes, quite new.'

'Lived in London all your life?'

'No, I used to live in Sussex.'

'With your mother and father, I suppose?'

'No, I have only a sister.'

'Is that so? Well, well, well! Come on, come on, drink, drink. No more for you, Strangler – but I'll tell you what I'm going to do. I'm going to buy you a lovely fat cigar . . . Unconscious!'

'Yes, sir?' said Adam.

'Cigars.'

'A box?'

'No, just one for the coming heavyweight champion of the world. Would you like one too, Joe?'

'No. Listen, Harry, why be crazy? For Heaven's sake save some –'

'Lay off, lay off, Joe, and don't make any scenes. I can get as much money as I want,' said Fabian, in a low voice. 'Hiya, Toots, we want a cigar.'

The cigarette-girl came near to kissing the hem of Fabian's jacket. 'Oh, yes, sir! Cigars, sir. Corona-Corona or Bolivar? Romeo y Julieta?'

'By God, that's a grand idea for a song! "Romeo y Julieta . . . -a-a-a"' – he sang this to the tune of 'Oh Señora Señorita' – 'Or listen: "Corona, Corona, I need you, I need you, Corona oh come back to me!"'

'Marvellous,' said Helen.

'Well, Toots, give the biggest cigar in the place to the Heavyweight Champion.'

'Yes, sir.'

'And listen, Unconscious! Get us something to *drink*. This stuff's terrible. Get me a bottle of Scotch.'

'Yes, sir.'

'Now listen, Harry –'

'Ah, lay off me, you old tightwad. Am I asking you to lay out anything? We got to have a little cele*bration*, haven't we, before we start?'

'And by the time we've done celebrating? Where will the capital to start with be?'

'I'm telling you, Joe, I can get dough, I can get a thousand if I like . . . Come on, Helen, dance.'

He rose, reeling a little, holding Helen's arm, then began to dance with her. Figler watched him, moodily, until he returned.

'By God, can you dance!' said Fabian. 'Have you got rhythm! Have you got what it takes, or have you got what it takes? I'll tell you – you've got what it takes. Say –'

'Harry,' said Figler, 'let me hold your money.'

'That'll be thirty-five shillings, please,' said Adam putting the bottle of whisky on the table. 'Soda?'

'Sure, soda.'

'That'll be five shillings extra.'

'Do you mind if I have ginger-ale?' asked Helen.

'Do I mind! Everything I have is yours!'

'Two pounds three shillings altogether, please,' said Adam, opening the bottle.

Fabian gave him three pounds and a handful of silver.

'Harry! Once and for all – are you going to let me hold your money for you?'

'Ah, don't be crazy!'

'All right, Harry!' said Figler, with menace.

'Hold my money, he says! Huh! Gimme another drink. Give all the boys a drink. Come on, George, give all the boys a nice big drink!'

The whisky sank low in the bottle.

'By God, nobody could ever say I was mean. Hell, not me. "Spender Fabian" they used to call me, in the States. I think one day I'll maybe go back . . . Listen: a great idea for a song: "Oh, one day I'll . . . day I'll maybe come back some time . . ."'

Vi was stroking the Strangler's arm.

'Listen, Charlie: Knock, knock!'

'Unh?'

'Knock, knock.'

'Well?'

'Listen. I say "Knock, knock", and you say "Who's there?" and then I say – well, say "Smith" – and you say "Smith who?" See? . . . Now, knock, knock!'

'Who's there?'

'Phyllis.'

'Who's Phyllis?'

'Phyllis glass up, he wants a drink.'

'Wants a drink who?'

'Ehr, Christ! That's the joke, see? Phyllis – fill his. See?'

'Well, go on.'

'Oh, Gord. Listen, dear. You know you've got to pay us girls for our time.'

'What time?'

'The time we spend sitting with you.'

'Why?'

'Well . . . I got to pay my rent, dear, haven't I?'

'Well?'

'Well, that's why you've got to pay me. It's my living, see?'

'I ain't paying.'

'But I got to *live*, haven't I?'

'What for?'

Vi did not know what for. She emptied her glass and looked into it miserably. The place was nearly full, but men had brought their own women, and most of the girls were still disengaged, lounging disconsolately at their tables. The band pounded. Nosseross jumped on to the platform and shouted: 'Chord! Ladies and gentlemen – Siri Andersen!'

Under the revolving lights a slim blonde walked to the centre of the dance-floor. The band played 'Doing The Up-Town Low-

Down'. Tightly encased in a silver dress she flung herself round the room in the opening movements of a fantastic dance. Lights went out. From the spinning chandelier there fell only five feeble beams of dull red light, in which Siri Andersen twirled and swam like a wild silver fish, while her aluminium-shod feet rapped and crackled on the floor like electric sparks . . . The music went faster, struck a crescendo, stumbled, hesitated and changed to the 'Memphis Blues'. The dancer began to undulate . . . slower, slower; the fish was dying . . . her hips rolled from left to right . . .

The lights snapped up. The music ceased, and the dancer stopped dead, in front of Fabian, holding her left foot high above her shoulder. Then she ran out, while couples, still applauding, went back to the floor.

'That was clever,' said Fabian, 'dead clever. That girl's got brains.'

Adam whispered in Helen's ear: 'Who said "Love is blind"? It must have X-ray eyes. A fellow looks up a girl's skirts and sees brains.' Helen laughed.

'Drink!' said Fabian. 'Here you are, Unconscious – take this last drink and finish the bottle, and get us another one.'

Vi said to him: 'Oh, Harry; you going to buy me a nice doll?' The chocolate-girl held up a little woollen giraffe with protruding eyes.

'Did you say dolls, sir?'

'No, I did not, Toots. Who says I said "dolls"? It's a lie. I'll fill him full of lead. Listen, I got four choppers outside, with Tommy-guns; real gorillas, waiting for the guy that tries to take any liberties with me . . . Four men in a car, with pineapples, and Tommy-guns, and tear-gas, and sawn-off shotguns, and gats, and rods, and heaters, and razors, just waiting for a . . . a doll. Hey, Unconscious! Bottle!'

'Harry,' said Figler, 'the Strangler wants to get to bed.'

'Take him to bed, then.'

Figler rose. 'I'm going. I'll call you in the morning.'

'I'll bump you off if you're not damn careful. I'm small, but I'm wiry! I'll cut your legs off and tie 'em round your neck . . . Ever hear of Al Capone? Well –'

'Listen, Harry. I've had enough of this nonsense! Our deal is off.'

'Chocolates?' asked the girl.

'Joe,' said Fabian, 'I'm gonna buy you a lovely box of chocolates.'

'Rubbish! . . . Listen, Harry, for the last time. Will you let me hold the rest of your money till tomorrow? If not, go to the devil.'

'You're my buddy!' said Fabian, with a hiccough. 'Listen, I got a great idea for a song: "Buddy can you spare a dime?" Nice, hah? All right, Joe; hold on to this for me.' He took a packet of notes from his breast pocket. Figler counted them.

'Fifty. Where's the rest, Harry?'

'Ah, lay off!'

'All right, but I warn you! I'll see you tomorrow. Come on, Strangler.'

'Honest Joe Figler,' said Fabian, 'he never did a dirty stroke in his life . . . Would you like a teddy bear, Joe?'

'Don't be a mug. Let's go, Strangler.'

Three glasses of champagne had stunned the Strangler more effectively than a sledge-hammer could have done. He rose, like a somnambulist, and followed Figler to the door.

'Oh, Harry,' said Vi.

'Lea' me alone,' said Fabian. His American accent was falling from him like a cloak; his A's broadened, and his nasal inflexions took on something of the Cockney whine.

'Nice dolls?' said the cigarette-girl, holding up a goggle-eyed Cupid with a green bow.

'Wanna doll, Helen?'

'I'd love one.'

'Two pounds,' said the cigarette-girl, brazenly.

'Okay,' said Fabian.

'Oh Har-ry!' said Vi, 'aren't you going to buy me some cigarettes?'

'No . . . I'm going to buy my lil Helen some cigarettes, but not you . . . See?'

'Turkish?' The cigarette-girl took, from the back of the tray, an immense gilt-tin casket, stamped in a florid pattern, and decorated with black knobs, a lion's head, two scrolls and an artificial silk tassel. 'Very special ones, sir – real ladies' cigarettes, rosebud tips; three pounds –'

At the bottom of Fabian's mind a voice said: '*You fool! Sink your soul and risk your liberty for a hundred pounds, and then throw it away like this!*' 'Go to hell!' he shouted. 'Three pounds for cigarettes! What, am I a mug? Go and drown yourself!'

Nosseross said, audibly: 'Now, don't pester the gentleman if he can't afford to pay that much! Show him something for a couple of shillings or so.'

'What?' shrieked Fabian. '*I* can't afford it? Me? *Me*? Look!' He pulled out all his money and held it up in a clenched fist. 'I got a million dollars! I got a thousand pounds on me! Give her them cigarettes!'

'And what about me?' asked Vi.

'Oh, scram, you! . . . *Huc* . . . Oh . . .'

'Ain't I got to live?' asked Vi, almost in tears.

'Poor kid,' said Fabian, touched. 'Here, catch hold of this.' He took from a waistcoat pocket two cigarette-pictures and a little metal swastika. 'There's lucky numbers on those cards, and I wouldn't part with this lucky charm for five hundred thousand pounds, but you catch hold, go on –'

'Two pounds, three shillings, please,' said Adam, opening a bottle of whisky.

'Here, Unconscious, three quid and keep the change . . . Pour me a big 'un. Listen, Bozo, d'you want to make a thousand pounds a week? If you do, come and wrestle for me . . . I made the Strangler what he is today . . . Never goes out with less than a hundred quid in his kick . . . O-oh, my guts! Heartburn . . . Hell, did I pay you?' He counted out another two pounds, and added three shillings in silver.

'But –'

'Okay' said Nosseross, hovering behind Adam, 'it's easy to forget. Right, Adam.'

'Now what was I saying?' asked Fabian.

'Something about a doll,' said Nosseross. 'I think you were asking somebody if they'd like a doll.'

'Lovely black girl?' suggested the chocolate-girl, holding forward a stuffed negress with a pink loincloth. 'Two guineas?'

Fabian's mind was numb. He could see nothing except a whisky glass, and it seemed to him that this glass was multiplying like soap-bubbles. He tried to brush these bubbles away. His hand hit the whisky-bottle, which fell off the table and broke. He closed his eyes for a moment, boring down to the last layer of energy, the last feverish stronghold of consciousness.

'Drinks!' he yelled. 'Dri-i-i-i-inks! Drinks for the band! Gimme a drink! Drinks!'

'Adam,' said Nosseross, 'Mr Fabian would particularly like a couple of bottles of the Special Champagne.'

Adam made his way through the dancers like a man in a trance. This was too ridiculous to be real; yet his pockets were heavy with tips. Helen, also, had the same feeling of fantasy as she sat, with her cigarette-casket and her dolls, and looked about her at the noisy, smoke-filled club which seemed to spin like a wheel. She saw Adam returning with the tray. His luminous, and almost childish grey eyes held hers for a moment. Then the bottles were on the table, and his languid voice was saying: 'Four pounds, please, Mr Fabian.'

Fabian pulled out his money. It was reduced to a small, crumpled wad of stale-looking notes and some silver. His face lengthened. Then he shrugged, and stammered: 'Spender . . . spender . . .' and threw down four pounds and all his silver.

Corks popped. Fabian swallowed three glasses of the Special Champagne: a pale, acrid wine, pringling with gas. Nosseross, Helen, Vi, Adam and all the bandsmen raised their glasses to him. Fabian felt, for a moment, like a god at a creation. He shouted: 'Play "For He's A Jolly Good Fellow"'! . . . I wrote it.' The band played. Four struck. The chocolate-girl brought in sprays of flowers on a tray. Nosseross handed to Fabian a red carnation, saying: 'I'd like to make you a small gift.' Fabian stuck the flower, with an idiotic grin, between two buttons in his waistcoat.

'Would the-ladies like one?'

'Gi-give 'em . . .'

'Ten shillings, please.'

'Breakfast?'

'Breakfs . . .'

He looked down. From an egg and a rasher of bacon on the plate before him there seemed to rise the smoke of a thousand burning pigs, and the odours of all the eggs in the world.

'And I have to be paid for my time,' said Helen.

Fabian gave her two pounds.

'And what about me?'

Fabian felt in his pockets and said: 'No more money in the bank.' He put a little piece of bacon in his mouth, and held it there, fighting back nausea. Then he stood up, gulping.

Nosseross winked at Adam, who put an arm about Fabian's thin body, and led him to the door. The cloakroom attendant put his hat on his head, back to front . . . Cold air struck Fabian in the face, and then his entire body seemed to contract and thrust upwards, like the plunger of a syringe; and all the drinks of the night – the whisky, the champagne, and the bad white wine – gushed out in a sudden flood through his mouth and nostrils.

The carnation fell out of his waistcoat into the pool.

'Have you enough to pay a taxi?' asked Adam.

Fabian moaned: 'No.'

Adam gave him five shillings, and the doorman called a taxi. In the gutter, a little sharp-faced man, carrying a tray of flowers, stood and watched Fabian as he reeled in his own vomit, pale as death, shivering, held up by Adam and the doorman. This man was Bert, the Cockney. He came close to Fabian, and said: 'You ought to be ashamed of yourself.' He pointed to the carnation and to that in which it had fallen, and added, in a concentrated voice: 'You ponce! Is *that* what your Zoë walks the bloody streets for?' And then, with his open hand, calloused from the handles of his barrow and grimy with the dirt of the streets, he struck Fabian in the face.

Fabian burst into tears.

'Rupert Street,' said the doorman to the taxi-driver. The cab door slammed. Fabian disappeared. Bert paused, looked up at the lightening sky and down at the gaudy entrance to the club.

The doorman said to him: 'You shove off, or I'll sock yer.'

'I dare yer to!' said Bert.

Nobody touched him. He spat on the pavement, turned and walked away eastward.

ELEVEN

The Silver Fox closed at five. As Adam went upstairs, Vi called after him: 'Oh, Adam! Good-ni-ight!'

'Good-night.'

'Where you going?'

'Eat.'

'Wait for us,' said Vi, and ran upstairs after him, followed by Helen. They paused in the doorway, bracing themselves against the cold of the morning.

Vi screwed up her face, and said: 'Somebody hasn't half been sick.'

'That was Fabian,' said Adam; and pointing to the pavement, added: 'There's about thirty or forty pounds down there. God knows what the fool did to get that much money, but that's where it's gone to. Let's go.'

They walked towards Piccadilly.

'You're new tonight, aren't you?' asked Vi.

Adam nodded.

'So am I,' said Helen.

'Like it?' said Adam.

'Oh, yes, very much indeed. It's not half as bad as I thought it was going to be.'

'Bah!'

'Don't you like it?'

'It's a dirty game.'

'Oh, I don't know,' said Helen, 'you just dance, and get paid for your time. There's nothing so dirty about that.'

'When you come to think of five or six people, all hanging round one miserable little fellow too tight to know what he's doing – all cadging, and bowing and scraping, and hinting, and winking, and making parasites out of themselves, just so as to get a few shillings out of him . . . Bah! And then: "No more money – out you go!"'

'Oh, he's got tons,' said Vi, 'he's a song-writer.'

'Song-writer my eye.'

'But he is! He's American.'

'American my foot,' said Adam. 'Can't you recognise real American when you hear it spoken? Didn't you see how he talked more and more like a Cockney as he got more drunk? American! He just pretends to be American. All fools do when they want to look smart. That's because, for the last fifteen years or so, anything that looks big talks with an American accent. It's a tradition. You get people like that little Fabian remembering all the fake Yankee literature they ever read – slick finance, and gangsters, and all that kind of thing – and trying to talk like Pat O'Brien . . . Song-writer! He never wrote a note in his life.'

'But he must have money,' said Helen.

'Why? That suit he was wearing never cost a penny more than five pounds. The shirt he had on was a ten-and-sixpenny copy of the Barrymore Roll. Rich Americans dress better than that, especially if they want to make an impression. Don't let him fool you. He's not American, he's not a song-writer, and he's not rich. He's probably a pickpocket.'

'What right have you to say that?' asked Helen.

'Well, perhaps not a pickpocket. Perhaps he just lives on somebody. Yes, that's more likely.'

'All the same, I didn't notice you refusing to take any of his money,' said Helen.

'All right. Blame me for taking it if you like. But don't defend him just because he had it in his pocket.'

'If you feel that way, why did you come into the club at all?'

'Because I want to get some money, quick, by hook or by crook.'

'I suppose that's just the way Fabian feels about it,' said Helen.

'In my case there's a certain difference. That little louse; what does he want money for? A hundred suits? A thousand silk shirts? Now me . . . never mind. Let's go in here and eat.'

They went into an all-night restaurant in Coventry Street.

'Mixed grills,' said Adam, 'big mixed grills. I'm starving.'

Vi asked him: 'Where do you live?'

'Nowhere. I'm looking for a place. I'll stay around until nine o'clock or so and look for a room.'

'There's some empty rooms where we live,' said Vi.

'Decent rooms?'

'Quite good,' said Helen.

'Then if you let me have the address I'll go and see – good God, look who's coming in!'

It was Fabian, pale with a yellowish pallor, blinking unhappily with puffed-up eyes, and clinging to the arm of Zoë. He looked like some bedraggled little bird of prey which has rolled in a muddy puddle. His hat was still back to front as Adam had stuck it on his head. Zoë's weak, sensual face looked, somehow, weaker in anger. She led Fabian to a table, and began to rub at the lapels of his coat with a crumpled handkerchief.

'Shut up,' said Fabian, 'lay off, can't you? Making a whole s-scene . . .'

'Look at you! Look at you! Just *look* at yourself.'

'For crying out loud, Zoë, can't you wait till we get back?'

'Five and a half guineas that suit cost, and now look at it!'

'Oh, lay *off*, for Christ's sake! Can't you see I'm a sick man? O-oh, my guts!'

'Proper little drunkard,' said Zoë. 'Hey, waiter, give him a strong black coffee . . . I've been looking everywhere for you. Night after night! Who d'you think you are? And take your hat off when you're sitting down with a lady. You –'

'You shut up. I'll do what I like,' muttered Fabian.

'Oh. Oh. I see. You'll do what you like. And who keeps you –'

'Shut *up*!' said Fabian, in a terrible whisper. Caution drove away some of the whisky-fumes. His heel, under the table, came down with hard, steady pressure on Zoë's instep. He sucked in his upper lip and menaced her with the *chevaux-de-frise* of his profile.

'Be careful, Zoë!'

'Well, anyway, Harry, it's not fair. As soon as you get a few bob in your pocket, you leave me all alone and go pub-crawling.'

'Pub-crawling! Me! Me, pub-crawling! Listen. I've been doing business, big business. I run my legs off, and neglect my food so that I take one tiny little drink and it upsets my stomach – slaving myself sick, mind you, so that we can be in the big money soon – and all I get is insults. Pub-crawling. Sure, I've been pub-crawling. Sure, that's right. I haven't been starting Fabian Promotions. Oh, no. I've been pub-crawling. You make me tired.'

'Fabian Promotions! You and your nonsense. Ha! What about when you made a book at the dogs? That was another big idea. But what happened? You lost over thirty pounds. And now it's Fabian Promotions. Ha!'

'Who lost over thirty pounds?'

'You did. Oh, it was Rolls-Royces, and sable coats, and diamonds all over me – what wasn't I going to have when you made a book? How many Rolls-Royces was it? Five? Six? And what happens? The first week you win sixty pounds, and you come crying to me: "Oh, Zoë, Yosh ran away with the winnings." You! Gah!'

'I did not come crying!'

'You did. And what you wasn't going to do to Yosh! Ooo, you were going to cut his legs off, and tear his heart out, and poke his eyes out, and get him done, and boil him in oil, and break his arms off and tie them round his neck, and smack his teeth down his throat, and make him like it! And what happened when you met him in the street? You say: "Oh, hallo Yosh. Come to the milk-bar and have an apricot milk." Big shot! You're –'

'I did *not* say: "Come and have an apricot milk"!'

'All right, Coca-Cola. Just because you saw Wallace Beery drinking it in a picture. You! Ha.'

'And all the same, I tell you I'm on a hot proposition. I got financial backing.'

'I know. Me. I'm about all the financial backing you're ever likely to get.'

'Oh, yeah?'

'Yeah.'

'All right. You'll see.'

'Hm! . . . Well, tell me, what financial backing?'

'A famous chemist's putting up the dough for my all-in wrestling business, Fabian Promotions.'

'Drink your coffee. You're delirious.'

'Will you listen a minute?'

'I've heard it all before.'

Fabian ground his teeth and said: 'And I tell you, I could walk out of his place and come back with fifty pounds in my pocket.'

'Fifty pounds of what?'

'All right. I'll prove it.'

'I've heard that tale before,' said Zoë. Then, struck by an after-thought, she added: 'But listen, Harry. Don't start getting yourself into any trouble.'

'Listen, kid,' said Fabian, 'you can run me down and call me names just because you occasionally help me out with a few quid –'

'Few quid! I work for you. I keep you. I give you fifteen quid a week. I go without shoes –'

'I don't give a flying cattle if you give me fifteen thousand bloody pounds a week! When I get this racket going you'll be sorry for what you said. *I* know my onions, *I* know what I'm doing.'

'Yes?'

'Yes!' Fabian snarled and gripped Zoë's wrist. 'I could tell you a few things. I could make you jump out of your skin. I work slow, see? I play high, see? I don't play for pennies. Get me? And when I get going you'll see –'

'What, more Rolls-Royces?'

'Yeah! Rolls-Royces! I'll say it again – Rolls-Royces! If I said Fords, you'd believe it, wouldn't you? Well, you don't know me. I wait my time. I got ambition. I ain't small-time. I –'

'All right, Harry,' said Zoë.

'If I can't have a Rolls-Royce then I'll walk. See? If I can't buy a real diamond I'll buy nothing. See? If I can't buy a real sable coat you can stuff your lousy, cheap rabbits. See? And you go and say –'

'Ah, I was only joking, Harry.'

'And after I go out of my way to buy you something nobody else has got.'

'What's that?'

'Oh, nothing. Nothing. Never mind.'

'No, tell me, Harry, come on.'

'I think to myself: "I like Zoë. She don't understand me, but I like her. I want to get her something," I say to myself, "but it must be something nobody else has got." So I go to a lot of trouble to get you something . . . oh, never mind.'

'Oh, come on, Harry, tell me.'

Fabian had read, in *Hollywood*, that Lupe Velez owned several chihuahuas. He said: 'A little dog.'

'No, really? What sort?'

'A tiny little dog. So small it can stand up on the palm of your hand; and their ears are so thin, you can see right through them.'

'You're kidding.'

'I am not. It's called a chihuahua. You know I told you about a chemist, who's going to finance me? Well, he has a wife, and she's ill; see? Well, her brother brought one of these chihuahuas back with him from Mexico, and it had pups. See?'

'You mean he brought two of them, eh?'

'No, one. One chihuahua, and it was a bitch. See? A white bitch. Well, there's a certain dog-breeder, and he had a chihuahua dog. See? Well, this chemist friend of mine gave him twenty-five pounds to let his dog go with this bitch, see? And so she had black-and-white pups. See? It's the smallest dog in the world. The pups – honest to God, you could put all four of them in a sugar-basin.'

'Really and truly?'

'Would I lie?'

'When can I have it?'

'Well, I saw the fellow about two hours ago, and he said we'd have to wait a week or so until the pups get strong enough to give away.'

'Oh, *Harry!*'

'*I can always say they caught pneumonia and died,*' thought Fabian. He said, in an injured tone: 'Oh, go away from me. I'm a liar.'

'No you're not, Harry.'

'Yes I am.'

'No you're not.'

'Oh, don't talk to me. I'm imagining it all. Go on say it!'

'But, Harry! I was worried –'

'When I told you I was on a hot proposition –'

'I was in a temper, Harry.'

'You shouldn't have tempers. Did you ever see me in a temper?'

'But I had a hard day, Harry. Me and Dora met six fellers from Shanghai, and –'

'How d'you do?'

'Six quid, altogether, but I need a spring coat.'

'Gimme four.'

'But I can't, Harry darling. I –'

'Okay, *o-kay*. I run my legs off trying to get her a chihuahua . . .'
He saw Zoë opening her bag, and whispered: 'Outside, not here.'

He picked up the bill. They rose.

'What do you call that dog, Harry?' asked Zoë.

'Chi-hua-hua,' said Fabian. As they passed Adam's table, he said, with a suddenness that made Zoë start: 'Hell! Chihuahua! Jesus, what an idea for a Rumba!' And he began to sing, to the tune of 'La Cucuracha': 'Little chihuahua, little chihuahua – try it on your old guitar . . .'

* * *

Vi whispered: 'See that girl he was with? Isn't she fat?'

'I like fat girls,' said Adam.

'You're joking,' said Helen.

'I mean, I don't like thin girls. I like people to be well constructed; good bone, good muscle, plenty of healthy flesh.'

'Like Venus,' said Vi.

'The Venus de Medici,' said Adam, yawning.

'Do you like art?' asked Helen.

'Oh sure . . . sure . . .'

'So do I.'

'You do, do you?' said Adam, half asleep.

'Me, too,' said Vi.

'Are you interested in psychology?' asked Helen.

'Oh yes . . .'

'What's your favourite book?'

'God knows . . .'

'Do you like Beverley Nichols?' asked Vi.

'I'm just crazy about him. Boy, am I tired!'

'I know an artist,' said Vi.

'Good. What's the time?'

'Half-past six.'

'Give me your address. If your landlady has any rooms, I'll

take one. I'll go round there at about eight o'clock. Now you girls had better get some sleep.'

'If you're tired,' said Vi, looking down at Adam through eye-lashes like the ribs of umbrellas, 'you could come and sleep in my chair.'

'Go to bed, like good girls.'

When they were gone, he ordered more coffee, but he was too tired to drink it. He sat still, looking straight in front of him. The café was still sodden with the gloom of night, which seemed to cling like a film to the walls. Haggard waiters, petrified with sleep, lounged between the tables. Adam looked at the clock. He concentrated his eyes on the large hand.

Tick-tick, tick-tick, tick-tick . . .

'*I am caught in the wheels of that clock,*' thought Adam. '*Every time they move, they drag me a little farther back into the past . . . Then what am I doing, sitting here; just sitting, while life runs away?*'

His eyes slipped away from the face of the clock, down over the marble surface of the wall.

'*So much blank stone, only waiting to be carved . . .*'

He saw himself gripping a steel chisel and a mallet. He struck at the wall, and knocked out a great piece of it . . . Chips of marble flew like snowflakes. Huddled in the corners, the waiters covered their eyes against the downpour of splintered stone. The wall took shape. A head appeared; an arm; a shoulder. Sparks flew from the chisel. A colossal statue was taking form – a giant, with crude, corded muscles and a hang-dog head, struggling to free himself from something shapeless which clung to his waist. Crack! Crack! went the mallet on the chisel. Life seemed to flow through it into the stone. 'Out! Out!' yelled Adam, striking with all his might . . . Sweat fell from his fore-head on to the face of the stone giant. 'Out! Out!'

And then, in a murky, green, timeless gloom the statue stood finished – two things in one; part man, part ape, yearning out of a sea of slime, and tearing itself asunder . . . Then rain fell, a bright golden rain which tinkled as it struck the ground, turned to money and sank. And at this, the higher half of the creature tore itself away in one mighty spasm, leapt high into the air, and plunged headlong into the mud, grasping coins.

'Away!' said a voice; and like a reversed cinema-film, the chips of marble flew back into the places from which they had come. The colossus was wiping itself out. The marble became a wall. 'We want to clear away,' said the voice of the waiter.

'I must have dozed off,' Adam muttered. The clock said seven-thirty. He rose stiffly, and went to wash.

TWELVE

Fabian, meanwhile, had not gone to bed. He could not rest. He said to Zoë: 'You don't understand me. You don't get me right. You're like everybody else. But when I go out for a thing, I go all out. All out, I tell you. Is there any of that whisky left?' He looked in the kitchen, and found a quarter-bottle, half full; tore off the stopper with shaking hands, and gulped down a drink. 'I play for the top. See? And if I say I can get money, I mean it. Everybody ain't blind! Some people can tell a smart guy when they see one. You'll see.'

'Come to bed, Harry,' said Zoë.

'I don't want to come to bed. What do you take me for? Lazy? No. I'm going out.'

'No, come to *bed*, Harry! I've been waiting –'

'Oh, you've been waiting. I got *work* to do; work! D'you think I want to stay like this all my life? Say . . . say people found out you been . . . helping me out a bit while I built up my business, and sort of lending me maybe a quid or two once in a while while I worked out the schemes I got in mind . . .'

'What's the matter, dear? Come to bed.'

The memory of Bert writhed in his brain like a maggot in a wound. Fabian bit his knuckles. 'Say somebody came up to me and said: "Harry, what do you let your Zoë walk the streets for?" Say they said that to *me*? I . . . I . . they . . they'd be entitled to slap me right in the bloody face, and I wouldn't be able . . . No! You listen! You listen to me! I'm going right out of the door, and I'm coming back, and I'll put my hand in my pocket, and I'll pull out a hundred nicker in notes – new notes. I'll do that right now!'

'Ah, come to bed, Harry, and get some sleep.' Zoë had taken

off her clothes, and stood naked in the light of the gas-fire. 'Come *on*.'

But Fabian, having finished the whisky, had become crazy with the pain of his injured vanity – the savage, impotent shame of the kept man. He adjusted his tie with one vicious jerk, and put on his overcoat – the huge American overcoat which made him look twice as big.

'Har-*ry*!' said Zoë, clinging to him with her whole body.

'Go to bed.'

'No, not unless you come, too.'

'Leave *go* of me!'

'Not unless you come to bed with me.'

'I'm going out to get a hundred pounds.'

'I don't want a hundred pounds, Harry; I want you to come to *bed*.'

'No, I'm going.'

'You know as well as I do you'll never get a hundred pounds –'

'Oh yeah? Yeah? You sure? Yeah, you're sure? All right. Okay. I'll show you. Let me go!'

He pushed Zoë away, and rushed out.

'Taxi! Taxi! Taxi!' he shouted. He seized the driver by the lapels, and shouted into his face: '"The Nest", The Crescent, Turner's Green. Matter of life and death! Drive like hell! Do it quick and I'll give you half a quid!' He threw himself into the taxi, slamming the door; and as he felt himself moving away, flung himself from side to side on the cushions, biting his lips, and beating his knees with his fists.

* * *

He leapt out of the taxi before it had stopped moving, and threw the driver a ten-shilling note. 'The Nest' seemed to sleep in the morning sunlight. He grasped the door-knocker in a trembling fist, and beat it down with all his might – three times, four times. The noise of his knocking reverberated through the house. He knocked again and again. At last, he heard small, quiet footsteps; waited maliciously, until he felt that Mr Simpson had his hand on the lock, and then knocked once more, harder than before. The door opened.

The startled face of a middle-aged woman appeared.

'What do you want? What do you mean by knocking like that?' The venomous little face and the blue, bloodshot eyes of Harry Fabian menaced her in the shadow of the doorway. He replied: 'I want Arnold Simpson, quick.'

'But –'

'I *want* him! Get him!'

'But –'

'God-damn it!' Fabian pushed the woman aside, and went into the drawing-room. He paced the rug, kicking at the legs of chairs. The little man came in. He was wearing the same grey suit, the same round collar, from which there protruded his neat black tie. But he seemed to have slept a little since Fabian had seen him. His face was no less haggard, but it wore an expression of repose. The last bitter extremes of suffering bring with them their own bitter anodyne – the impregnable resignation of despair.

'Siddown,' said Fabian.

The little man sat. Fabian strutted before him, with his hat on one side.

'Well?' said the little man.

'What d'you mean, "Well"? Is that the way to talk? You better be careful, pal. I'm warning you.'

'You gave me your word of honour that you would never come here any more.'

'Who did?'

'You did. Word of honour of a blackmailer. Do you ever see yourself as I see you? Even a –'

'Shut up!' said Fabian. 'I want another word with you.'

'Well, say it and get out.'

'Listen, you dirty little louse,' said Fabian, grinning with hate, 'listen, you hypocrite, you stinking little –'

'I'm listening, man of honour. What do you want?'

'Don't you talk to me about honour. I'm not interested. Stick your honour! Who're you to talk, louse? Tart-chaser! Don't you talk that way to me! I'll smash you! I'll tear you up, you cowson bastard! I'll go and raise hell in the streets, I will! I'll flay you alive and rub you down with salt! Now listen –'

'I'm listening.'

'You better. I was going to let you off light. See? I was going to treat you soft. Get me? Now listen: because you talked to me the way you did just now, I'm going to nail your bloody hands and feet to the cross and tear your guts out. See?'

'I see. Well?'

'I was going to let you get away with a mere fifty. Now, I'm going to take you for a hundred. Gimme a hundred pounds.'

'Give you a hundred pounds?'

'Don't play for time, louse. That'll get you nowhere. I'll say it once more. I want one hundred pounds, now, this very minute; in one-pound notes, the same as before.'

'And then?'

'Then I'll go away.'

'And if I don't give it to you?'

'I'll go straight to the clinic.'

'But tell me; what good do you think that would do you?'

'Good? Me? No good. But I can make an example of you. Besides, nobody ever crosses me and gets away with it, see? Nobody, ever! See? By Christ, if anybody crosses *me*, by God, I'd *give* a hundred quid so as not to let him get away with it! So come across, and do it quick.'

The little man shook his head.

'Cut out that stuff, and get going. Come on. I'll go over to the bank with you. Get your coat. Write the cheque. Get going!'

'No. Now get out.'

'What?'

'I said no! Get out!'

'You know what that means?'

'You told me once before. Get out.'

Fabian's heart seemed to shrink and grow cold. He said, in a milder voice: 'Listen. You're delirious. You wouldn't have me go and tell your wife the whole story? Come on, now. Snap out of it. I wanna *help* you. Come on, give me fifty, and we'll call it a deal. Otherwise, I'll tell your wife.'

'You will?'

'You bet I will! On principle.'

'On principle,' said the little man. He took Fabian by the

arm, and led him into the next room. It was very dark. All the blinds were drawn. 'Look,' said the little man.

Fabian looked to the right, but could see nothing. Then he looked to the left, and uttered a startled grunt.

On two black trestles lay a coffin.

'Tell her,' said the little man.

Fabian was silent.

'Tell her!'

'She . . .'

'She died the same morning you came. Nothing you can say can hurt her or me any more. Now go away.'

He followed Fabian along the passage, and slammed the door in his face.

'And some people say there's a God!' said Fabian.

* * *

He went to Tavistock Place and called on Figler.

'Joe, I want that money of mine.'

'All right, Harry. There it is, exactly fifty pound. And our deal's off.'

'Off? Off? Why off?'

'Why? Because you're crazy. Throwing money away the way you did! No; I don't want to work with you any more.'

'Hell, Figler! I can get more!'

'I'm not interested. Call it off. Or if you like, deposit this fifty pounds with me, and come in with me on a seventy-thirty basis.'

'Seventy-thirty hell! I can get another fifty. But . . . Listen, Joe; would it still be called Fabian Promotions?'

'The name doesn't worry me. If you want the honour and the glory, have it. But I must have complete control of expenditure.'

'Well . . .'

'Yes or no?'

'Okay. Gimme a receipt for the fifty. It's a deal.'

'I'm taking the premises in Bristol Square. We'll start right away. Your business is to find programmes.'

'I can find a better programme than –'

'– Than any man in the world. Yes. I know. Then get on with it.'

'And listen, Figler. Do me a favour. Have some swell cards done. Something with class about 'em. Yes?'

'Very well.'

'I trust you, Joe.'

'You don't have to, Harry. I'm having an agreement drawn up.'

'Oh,' said Fabian. He felt quite crushed.

Fabian dreaded the moment when he should face Zoë: '*Well, big shot? Where's the hundred pounds? Where's the Rolls? You! Big shot!*'

He walked slowly back to Rupert Street; entered quietly, and undressed in silence. He was relieved to see that Zoë slept soundly.

He undressed and crept into bed beside her.

She sighed, and whispered: 'Chihuahua . . .'

'Oh, my God!' whispered Fabian, under his breath.

Exhausted by emotion, he slept like a child.

INTERLUDE: THE STRONG OLD MAN

One afternoon, a month later, Adam was sitting in a café, casually conversing with a fat old man who sat near him.

The old man said: 'You have a good body.'

'You look as if you might have been a pretty strong man yourself, in your time,' said Adam.

'Me? You know who I am?'

'No, who?'

'Ali.'

'Oh.'

'That name means nothing to you. I used to be called Ali the Terrible Turk.'

'What, the wrestler? Why, I remember having heard your name a dozen times. Of course; you were a heavyweight champion, weren't you?'

The old man's face brightened. 'Anybody who saw me,' he said, 'didn't forget me so quick. Eh? No, they didn't forget Ali.'

Ali the Terrible Turk was an immense old man; an ancient strangler and bone-breaker of the days before Hackenschmidt; but thrown by time, pinned by age, beaten down by the backhand blows of the years. Looking at him, one thought of a battered derelict, ignored and slowly sinking in a desolate sea. Too tough to die, he was already partly buried – he had left pieces of himself on a thousand mats, in a hundred strange cities. Sydney had his left eye; Paris and Montreal his front teeth; while in New York he had given back to the earth two fingers of his left hand, decomposed by blood-poisoning. He could tell a gruesome story of the night when he had fought the Denver Mauler for two hours, covered with mat-boils, and with a rib torn loose and protruding through the skin. 'What, plaster? And let him see I'm hurt? *Tfoo!*' He had never had a permanent home. His bread had always been well salted with sweat and blood. And what had he gained by all this? Fame? He was forgotten; he had outlived his generation. Money? He was hungry. What, then? Nothing but endurance – iron endurance – which is only one of the necessities of life. He still had a terrible fist, and a back strong enough to support the weight of a house. But his body had run to fat. He weighed twenty-five stone, and when he walked, floors trembled. His head was as round and hard as a cannon-ball, and almost as hairless; covered with shining skin of the colour of *café au lait*. His ruined ears looked like pieces of brain, squeezed out in a headlock and petrified. His nose tended to the left. Springing out of it, in a cascade of grey hair, a large moustache, soaped to fine points, swept out like the horns of a bull; and his purple, ponderous lower lip hung in a menacing droop towards his chin, which seemed as old and impregnable as Gibraltar.

He went on: 'No! Still, sometimes, somebody remembers. Anybody who ever saw me. You know what? Two years ago, a man wrote to me, an American man, and he says: "Ali, I saw you grapple the Denver Mauler in Chicago, and your temperature was a hundred and four degree, and you grapple the Mauler two hour: and pin him. If you want money, say just one word." See?'

'So you said that one word?'

'Me, young man? No. It would be not-nice. I never took nothing, from nobody. Giving, yes. I gave away plenty. Wrestling, my hand closes but never opens; money, my hand opens but never close. *I* should hold *my* hand out? *Hooff!*'

'So you manage to live all right?'

'I work. I am a trainer, for Fabian Promotions.'

'What, not Harry Fabian?'

'Yeh. You know Fabian?'

'Slightly. Do you like him?'

'I do not haf to like him. I work for him: he pays my wages; *voilà!*'

'Is he generous?'

'No, mean. Why should he be generous? I train his men; he pays me two pounds a week. So I am under no obligation to him.'

'And are the men any good?'

'*Tfoo!* Good wrestlers, with a girl in bed. On a mattress, oh yes. On a mat – *ptah!*'

'And how are the programmes going?'

'Oh, we will make a show. There is Legs Mahogany against the Black Strangler; Kration of Cyprus against Tiger Vitellio – oh, a lot of rubbish. Put them all in a line, and you could blow them down like postcards. Some of them are strong fellahs, like Kration. But wrestlers? *Oi!*'

'So Kration is pretty strong, eh?'

'You yourself could beat him. Come and try. What work you do?'

'I . . . I'm a waiter in a night-club.'

'Stinking night work! It will make you stale and soft, like last year's butter; like boiled rice. Come to the gym, yes? I like you. I will teach you. Yes? Come. I will show you my old holds. Yes, come. What do you weigh? Fourteen stones?'

'About that.'

'I can make you sixteen, seventeen stones, all fine muscle. Then people will turn round and look at you in the street, and say: "What a man; what shoulders; what a neck!" And you will say: "Ali did this." And one day you will have a son, and you will show him, also, to wrestle, and say: "Ali the Terrible Turk showed me this, fifteen, twenty, thirty years ago." I shall be dead then, but somebody will still mention my name. Eh?'

'Yes, I'd like to. I'll come.'

'To whom can I teach what I know? *Those* monkeys? *Tfoo!* After three weeks they think they know more than me. It is only that they are younger, now, and maybe quicker. But me, I stood on the mats one year, learning holds, before I was allowed to try to wrestle. Hah! . . . You like girls?'

'Well . . .'

'I like girls. I like nice plump girls. Women? Aha! Aha! But drink? *Ptoo!* Women, yes; a good rough fight with a man stronger than you, yes; a little wine but not much, yes; hot sunlight, yes; a good laugh a good hot bath, yes. But smoking, boozing, abusing yourself – *Pffft!*'

'You're right.'

'And you are wrong. Sleep all day and work all night? No. Who lives at night? Bugs, thieves, fools. Now your body is good; but already you have a white face, and under the eyes dark marks. What for?'

'I've got to make some money, I'm afraid.'

'What for? To make show, with nice clothes?'

'No. I want to do some real work, of my own.'

'What work?'

'Sculpture.'

'Making statues. What for? I seen statues. Over there there is the British Museum, full with statues. There is a nice Herakles. He was a Greek, yes; but a very nice back, and a good neck. But still, it's only stone. Could it grapple the Mauler? No. A navvy could smash it with a hammer. It's only a *copy* of a man. Be the real thing.'

'And after ten years, or twenty years, what then? The thing is gone. All the muscles are full of fat. But if I make a Farnese Hercules . . . well, I make it to stand for ever.'

'What for?'

'Do I know what for? It's a thing I feel I've got to do. What did you become a wrestler for?'

'I liked it. It was in my blood. It makes you big, and strong, and afraid of no man and no beast. It is what I could do best.'

'Well, and this business is in *my* blood, and it's what I can do best.'

'Then what are you doing in a night-club?'

'I've got to get some money before I can get down to work. See?'

'Young man, you mark my words. You listen to me: if you're looking for money first, then by the time you get it you won't be good for nothing else no more. Live! Work! Money? Money is lousy! Money is rotten! Money is an illness, like consumption, like pox! Wash your hands from it. I hate money! If I get it, I chuck it away – I throw it down the drain – I spit on it! *Fekh!* Take it! Dirty money! Ugh!'

'I don't care for money *as* money, but –'

'Be proud. Why chase money? Live. Do your best. Then money will chase you. What is the use of money? Can you sleep in two beds? Can you eat dinner ten times a day? Then what is the use of money? Who has money? Rockefeller? And he is dead, stinking with dirty money. Ten thousand million dollars could not make that man digest a pilaff. So who wants money? This is what you want: good blood, good bones, good nerves, good guts, good teeth, good brains. These, yes. But money? *Hou!* I have had money. I have spent it. *Bon!* Too much money is like too many friends. They make you good for nothing. Money and friends make you easy. They make you soft, good for nothing. Money and friends. If you wrestle with me, do not say: "This is my friend." Say: "This is my enemy." Then watch me, trick me, learn all I have to show you; and then, when you can pin me down, then shake my hand and say: "Ali, shake hands; we are friends." Your only friend is your equal, or your master. Friends and money, I poured them both away like water. Good. I am glad.'

'But if you'd kept some of it, then at least you'd be comfortable in your old age.'

'How much comfort does a man require? A meal, a rest, a talk. What more? Rolls-Royces? Diamond rings?'

'But when you're too old to work?'

'I die. I had a good life: plenty fights, plenty wins, plenty women. I am old now. I do not grumble. And I die on my feet.'

'But wouldn't you rather be your own master?'

'You talk like a tobacconist. I *am* my own master.'

'Yet you work for Fabian.'

'I work for myself. I give him work. He gives me money.'

'And if he gives you the sack?'

'What do I care? But why should he give me the sack? I give him more than he gives me; much more.'

'You realise that, then? You realise he exploits you?'

'Certainly. Better Fabian exploit Ali than Ali exploit Fabian. This way, I don't have to say: "Thank you, sir, much obliged, sir."'

'Hmmm . . .' Adam looked up, suddenly, at the threatening hands of the clock. 'Hell! I must start getting dressed.'

'The night-club, ha? A lovely boy, like you! Good body, good brain, wasting yourself in a filthy cellar! Learning to be a beggar, a cadger; holding out your hand for tips – shillings people throw at you – being polite so as to find your twopence under the plate. Bah!'

Adam's face was red as he replied: ' I know all about that. But I've got to get some money to do some work with, and I'll put up with anything to do that.'

'You'll ruin yourself.'

'No, I won't.'

'Yes. You are ashamed of what you do.'

'I . . .'

'You are ashamed. You are foolish. Well, at least, come sometimes down to the gym, and I will remind you that you are a man, not a waiter.'

'Thanks; I'll come.'

'I will give you an eighteen-inch neck and a chest of fifty inches. Yes?'

'Yes. Good-bye.'

Ali stayed in the café. Adam went to the club.

Book Three

. . . BUT A MAN CAN ALSO FIND HIMSELF!

THIRTEEN

The sun rose earlier now. By the time the Silver Fox closed it was already broad daylight; a bright blue morning.

'Shall we walk?' asked Adam.

'No,' said Helen, 'let's get a taxi.'

'Tired?'

'No, not tired, not a bit tired, Adam. Only I don't like walking through the streets in evening dress, and made up like this. Let's get a taxi.'

They rode back. Adam sighed, and said: 'At this time of the morning – a morning like this – we ought to be just waking up. Then we ought to jump out of bed, and run down to the sea, and dive in, and swim, and then come back and eat a good breakfast; and then start work.'

'Did you have a good night tonight?' asked Helen.

'Yes. But I'm sick of this life.'

'Oh, but Adam, you do quite well.'

'Yes, I know. I made fifteen pounds last week. But it's not worth it. I'm fed up with it. Just think of lying asleep all through these spring days! I'm going to give it up.'

'What, leave the club?'

'Yes. I would have left long ago, if . . .'

'If what?'

Adam looked at her. 'The money's all right,' he said, 'but it would take more than that to keep me there, much as I need it.'

'What?'

'Oh, I had my reasons. But now I think it's time I left. I . . .'

'Adam,' said Helen, 'don't leave. I should feel lost without you.'

'You've got kind of used to seeing me about the place, eh?'

'No. I . . . But don't go, anyway, Adam!'

Adam said suddenly: 'Listen, Helen, let's both go. This night-life's no good for anybody.'

'Oh, I don't know. I make more at this than I could get out of any other job. And I've got quite used to the hours.'

'I know; that's the trouble. It's easy money, but dirty all the same. I get mine by waiting on drunks, and you get yours by false pretences. Let's give it up.'

'Why false pretences?'

'You kid them. You make up to them. You promise them more than you intend to give. You lower yourself by asking for money. You talk them into feeling they've got to give you something.'

'That's the wrong way to look at it, Adam. They pay me for my time. It's a job like any other job. If a typist expects her wages, why not a hostess? I don't pretend to be in the club for just pleasure, do I?'

'It's the *right* way to look at it. You're getting the wrong attitude, Helen. You're getting too accustomed to this racket. You're an intelligent girl, but you know, in some ways you're a terrible fool. Don't you realise that you never keep on one level in a business like this? You sink and sink, without knowing it. Look at Vi. Twelve months ago she was a waitress, and if anybody had made a suggestion to her then, she would have slapped his face . . . well, said "no", anyway. But now look at her: she'd sleep with any Tom, Dick or Harry for two or three pounds. And that's the way this life gets everybody. Let's –'

'You don't imagine that I'd do things like that, do you?'

'Like what?'

'Sleeping with a man.'

'Why not? Haven't you ever?'

Helen looked at Adam without indignation, and replied: 'No. What do you take me for?'

'Helen, I take you for a woman like any other woman – only better looking and rather more intelligent. You've got to sleep with a man some time. You must, sooner or later. You've got physical needs like anybody else – probably more than most.'

'Why more?'

'Because you're bigger, stronger and healthier. You're young, you're beautiful, you're full of life and blood. And one can see it when you dance, and in the way you walk, and the way you look –'

'I don't look like that!'

'You do. Apart from the fact that you're young and beautiful, do you know what attracts men to you so strongly? It's a sort of expression in your face that says: "I need the love of a man more than food and drink." And you do. You know perfectly well you do!'

'Perhaps,' said Helen softly. 'But not just any man –'

The taxi stopped. 'Let's have some coffee,' said Adam.

'All right. But I'll go and change, and wipe this make-up off first.'

Five minutes later, she came into Adam's room. Rouge, powder, and blue eye-shadow had gone with the white satin evening-dress. Above her blue dressing-gown, her face glowed with cold water.

'You look good,' said Adam.

'Do you think so?' Helen looked about the room. 'Good heavens, aren't you untidy?'

She sat on the divan. Adam pushed it into a corner to make room for a large mound of red clay, which, balanced on a sugar-box and covered with damp cloths, occupied the centre of the floor. Beside it stood a pail of water, amidst a litter of wire loops and little boxwood spatulæ.

'Look at it!' said Adam, slapping the clay with a heavy hand. 'Two hundredweight of it. And not touched. Not a mark on it! Yet, you know, I have such ideas; I want to do such things! I feel I only have to start pushing that clay about, to make it walk and talk. And then, as soon as I begin, that damned clock says "Get out!" and out I go, back to that stinking club; and all that lovely clay lies there . . .'

'Perhaps later on, when you find time?' Helen suggested.

'Perhaps and perhaps and perhaps! No! I'm going to give this up. It's ridiculous to fool about for the sake of a few pounds, when times goes so fast. No. I'm going.'

'Don't go, Adam.'

'You really *want* me to stay in the club?'

'Yes, I want you to stay.'

Adam sat next to her, a little behind her, his hands on her shoulders. He could feel, under his palms, the stirring and the surging of her body. He said unsteadily: 'I've only stayed there so long on account of you, Helen.'

'Adam, I should hate you to go. I should miss you horribly.'

She leaned back against him. His arms rose and closed about her. Then he paused for a second, like an athlete gathering and organising his strength; picked her up, and laid her on the divan beside him. In Helen's mind, one tiny dry inhibitory impulse rustled like a dead leaf. 'No,' she said. 'Yes,' said Adam. Something inside her seemed to blaze like oil. All thought and all sentience melted, boiled and poured in one thick and intolerable flood down to the base of her spine – stopped there; gathered; swelled to bursting-point –

She uttered one exclamation: 'Oh, God . . .'

They appeared like enraged enemies, locked in a last desperate struggle.

On the surface of the water in the pail by the clay, ripples began to spread and break, rhythmically.

* * *

Later, they talked.

'I can't think why I waited so long,' said Adam.

'Did you want to . . . make love to me before?'

'Yes, I did. The first time I saw you.'

'Did you really? You know, I think I must have felt the same way about you, Adam. I kept on looking at you. I kept thinking about you ever such a lot. I used to watch you going from table to table, and whenever you came to my table, I was ever so pleased. I don't know why – at least, I didn't know why. I know now. I must have been in love with you.'

'Helen, my dear, I've been in love with you for weeks. I've actually stayed awake thinking about you. I used to hear you getting into bed: it disturbed me. I'm the kind of fellow who sleeps and sleeps. Nothing ever kept me awake before, let alone a woman.'

'Darling!' Helen rubbed her cheek against his shoulder. 'Why are you so marvellous?'

Adam went on, in a low, bewildered voice: 'I never loved anybody before. Now, I appear to be crazy about you. It's funny.'

154

'I never let anybody make love to me before, Adam. I dare say you've made love to dozens and dozens of women.'

'Yes; but that's nothing.'

'Oh, Adam, I used to think and think about you . . . and Vi used to keep talking to me, until I wanted to say: "Oh, go away! Shut up! Let me just think about Adam." I used to want to be alone, so that I could think about you. You know, sometimes, I used to burst into tears. That was because I wanted you so much.'

'And are you happy now?'

'Perfectly happy.' After a little while, she said: 'I'm only afraid of one thing.'

Adam asked drowsily: 'What?'

'Now that I . . . Now that we . . . Say you left me. It would be so hard to live without you . . .'

'I shan't leave you.'

'Ever?'

'Never.'

'I want to be with you always.'

'You shall.'

'I shall be jealous of you. I shouldn't want to let you out of my sight. If you left the club, I should be horribly miserable . . .'

'My dear little Helen, don't worry.'

'You're not going to leave, are you?'

'We'll see, later.'

'Promise me you won't leave.'

'All right, dear.'

'Promise!'

'I . . . All right, I promise,' said Adam; and a small voice in his brain said: '*Weakling!*'

'Now tell me: do you – oh, Adam, you're so big, and strong, and marvellous! – tell me, do you really love me? Or did you only want to . . .'

'Both.'

'Oh . . . *darling!*'

Soon, Helen fell asleep, but Adam could not sleep. He lay quietly, in order not to disturb her; contentedly aware of the pressure of her warm, strong body. He caressed her very gently as she slept. His left hand crept over her, carefully exploring the smooth white neck, the rubbery deltoids; palpating the heavy and resilient breasts; tracing the course of the ribs; prowling over the firm softness of the abdomen; through the humid maquis of dense virgin hair, down to the powerful thighs that relaxed in sleep.

'*What, a shape!*' thought Adam. '*What structure! This is what sculpture is for; to make this form everlasting; to catch it, at this moment, before time drags down these breasts and folds this belly in creases . . .*

'*. . . Yet every moment old age and death come nearer. Life runs away, like a road behind a fast runner . . . And I lie here!*'

He opened his eyes, and looked towards the clay. His mind was clearer now. Idea jostled idea. There recurred the conception of the resurgent man, the man forcing his way out of the ape. Then, from that, there came the vision of a group, a group of huge figures, a hundred feet high: four lives, all intertwined. At the base, the beast; the thing that was neither ape nor man. Struggling out of this a kind of human being – a man without a forehead; squat, hideous, whose hangdog shoulders bulged with bestial strength. His enormous arms and gnarled fingers clutched the legs of two perfect human beings, a man and a woman, interlaced. They strained upwards, still in the grip of the ape-man. The man's right hand was highest: his arm was tired, but he still held it high above his head, while the right hand of the woman supported his wrist. His left pressed down on the head of the ape-man. On his face was a radiance. Upon his uplifted palm, at the very peak of everything, he held something alive – a child, newly born, laughing . . .

'*I would call it "Evolution"*,' thought Adam.

He wanted to leap out of bed and begin at once. He clenched a fist. With this for a mallet, he would hammer the clay into its first shape. His whole body grew tense. Instinctively, Helen's arms closed about him. She turned in her sleep, moved closer to him. He relaxed and, through a triangular aperture between the curtains, watched the vivid daylight. Realising, then, that he was tired, he, also, slept.

* * *

It was three o'clock when they awoke. Helen smiled at Adam, and said: 'And you didn't give me that coffee, after all . . . But I'd better get back to my room before Vi comes in, hadn't I?'

'Who cares about Vi?'

'I know, but . . . Oh, darling, I don't want to leave you!'

'Then stay, my child.'

'No, I'd better go. I've got some sewing to do. And I must have a bath. Did you want to use the bath first? Yes, you bath first. I'll bath later, before we go. Will you come up in a little while?'

'Of course I will.'

'Kiss me then . . . 'Bye!' The door closed behind her. Adam put on a dressing-gown, caught up soap, towel and loofah, and went to the bathroom. He scrubbed himself savagely with ice-cold water. Drying, he saw his reflection in the long mirror: tensed a massive arm, and shook his fist at himself: 'Idiot! Wasting daylight!' He hurried back to dress, and went out.

He walked fast, through Euston Road and past King's Cross; faster and faster, and deeper and deeper into the sombre, rumbling gut of north-west London – nightmare land of blank, black walls eroded by the acrid breath of the railways – past Battle Bridge, through Farringdon Road, across Ludgate Circus, and down Fleet Street. He found himself in Kingsway, and remembered Ali the Terrible Turk.

'Bristol Square?' he asked, of a passer-by.

'Orf Sarfampton Row, second or fird on yer left.'

Adam walked more slowly. The offices of Fabian Promotions were not difficult to find: Fabian was not the man to shun the conspicuous. He had marked his headquarters with a big blue board, on which gold letters said: FABIAN PROMOTIONS: HEAD OFFICE AND GYMNASIUM: MESSRS H FABIAN & J FIGLER. He had even caused the area-railings to be painted to match the sign-board. Adam paused at the top of the stairs, and listened. He could hear the sound of Ali's deep, hoarse voice, punctuated by an intermittent thumping. He went down. Fabian opened the door.

FOURTEEN

'What can I do for you, buddy?' asked Fabian genially. Then his eye narrowed. 'Say, where have I seen you before?'

'At the Silver Fox.'

'O-oh! That's right . . . Yeah. Was I tight that night?'

'Somewhat. Anybody would have been, the amount you got through.'

'Hell, that? You call that drinking? Jesus, I could drink that much before breakfast, if only I've had a night's rest. Only I hadn't been to bed for more than four days, that evening; and I didn't get the chance to eat for twenty-four hours. Otherwise . . . How's Phil? And that nice girl?'

'Phil's fit. Which nice girl?'

'The one I was with that night.'

'Oh, Helen? She's fine.'

'You're telling me she's fine. Phil Nosseross knows how to pick 'em. Come in. Take a look at my place. It's only temp'ry headquarters, till our new place is fixed. We're getting a place in Regent Street – chromium plate, a cocktail-bar, special mats, everything. Take a look at those two guys sitting by the wall over there. See the big nigger? Get an eyeful of those biceps. That's Charlie Bamboo, the Black Strangler. I discovered him. Hell, six months ago he was a punk. I took him off a Jamaica banana-boat, and made a world-beater out of him. See? Londos? O'Mahoney? Ha! Listen: the Strangler could beat 'em both, with one hand tied. It's a bet! I'd bet a thousand quid on it. The other guy's Legs Mahogany. He's good, too. He's got a scissors-hold – may I be paralysed, he could cut a bullock in two between his legs. And take a look at the fat old mug on the mat, now, with that youngster. He's Ali the Terrible Turk. Boyoboyoboy, did that man used to be a big shot in his day! He came to me on his bended knees, and he said: "Mr Fabian, sir, I'm starving to death; please give me work." We-ell, you know how it is, I wouldn't see a dog starve. I'm funny like that. I couldn't see a dog starve. So I gave him a job, sort of training the boys, kind of style, and sort of massaging 'em a bit. See? He worships me like a god. He's a good old-timer –' Words poured out of Fabian's mouth, like rice out of a burst sack – 'Live and let live is my motto, live and let live, if you get what I mean. Jesus, are we getting a programme, or are we getting a programme? I'll tell you: we're getting a programme. I'll show 'em. Bielinsky thinks he can run a show. I'll show you a show . . . Look at poor old Ali. That guy with him is a coming champ: Siegfried the Murderer, I think I'm going to call him.'

Ali, who, stripped to trousers and a singlet, seemed to fill most of the gymnasium, was shouting: 'Again! Try again!'

His huge arms flapped out like bolsters. Siegfried the Murderer, a big, long-legged Lancashire man, grinned sheepishly. He was trying to catch Ali by the neck. But the neck of Ali, thick and ponderous as a tree-trunk, moved under its fat on muscles like steel springs.

'Eh, I can't,' said Siegfried.

'Try!'

Siegfried's fingers closed on air as Ali ducked. The Lancashire-man giggled. Ali uttered a roar of rage, and slapped him on the side of the head, knocking him down. He got up, and said indignantly: 'Eh, go easy!'

'Easy? Easy?' Ali menaced him with a closed fist. 'Be serious!'

'But I'm only a beginner.'

'Put your heart and your soul into this! I will teach you to wrestle by force, through pain! Coward!'

'Tha better be careful!'

'Coward! Your father before you was a coward! You were born in a whore-house, and your mother was a negress!'

Siegfried leapt at Ali's throat with a growl. Ali bellowed with delight. The two men struggled for a few seconds. The Lancashireman's fists sank into the fat on Ali's stomach. Ali grunted; heaved. Siegfried cried out sharply: 'You're breaking my arm!'

'Lay off all that crap, Ali,' said Fabian, 'and just show him some of the holds. He'll pick things up as he goes along.'

Ali saw Adam, and released Siegfried the Murderer. He lumbered over the mats, and came forward, holding out his hand. 'You, ha?'

'You know each other?' said Fabian.

'We've met. Well, Ali, how are you?'

'Good. Have you come to join us?'

'I don't know. I just came to . . . well, say hallo to you, Ali, and have a look at your place.'

Fabian asked: 'You wrestle, eh?'

'Hardly at all; just a little catch-as-catch-can.'

'Okey-doke!' said Fabian. 'Then, listen. I can make a world-beater out of you!'

'Don't make me laugh.'

'Listen. Come, in here a minute.' Fabian led Adam into a little blue office. 'Seat.' He indicated an easy chair, and threw himself into a big directorial swivel-seat at a new oak desk. On the wall above him, wrestling and boxing champions sparred and clutched at space. Hackenschmidt insolently thrust out a Herculean chest at Jimmy Wilde; Jim Londos shrugged a shoulder as formidable as an armoured car at a little Herrera the Skull-Crusher; moustachioed George la Blanche poked a tentative left towards the implacable bulk of Hans Steinke, who scowled above the homely head and shoulders of Strangler Lewis. The entire wall was plastered with photographs – plain Jack Sherrys, common Jack Dempseys, ordinary Jack Johnsons and unadorned Yussufs, together with the inevitable gathering of awe-inspiring Tigers, Leopards, Assassins, Butchers, Slaughterers, Rippers, Panthers, Masked Miracles, Thunderbolts, Bulls, Lions and Man Mountains.

'What's your name?' asked Fabian.

'Adam.'

'Well, listen, Adam. You want to be a wrestler. Is that it?'

'I wasn't exactly thinking of making a career out of it. I only proposed to do it for exercise.'

'Good enough. Now listen. I can make a big shot out of you. See? I can train you. I can give you fights. I can bill you. I can get you publicity. I got all the newspapers in my vest pocket. I can see you're as strong as a horse. The minute I set eyes on you, I said to myself: "Jesus! That guy's got a figure like Adonis." Adonis, the Greek Wrestler; you know. Get it? Sign on with me. I can make a career for you. I'm building guys up now. I got the best trainer in the world – Ali the Terrible Turk. He could make muscles come up on a rice-pudding. He could train Little Tich to pull down St Paul's Cathedral. I pay him plenty. I bought him off Bielinsky at a fat wage. He does me a favour by being here. I got money to put into this racket. See? Listen. I'm putting wrestling on an American basis in this country. There'll be heavy sugar for all. Inside two months, you'll be making fifty pounds a week, and then some.'

'But what's your proposition?'

'My proposition, buddy? Listen. You sign a contract to wrestle for me, and nobody else, for the next four years. See? Well, you start at a sort of nominal wage – *nominal*, mind you, purely *nominal* – of round about a couple of quid a week. But that's only nominal, while we're training you for the big money. See? After all, I spend scratch on you, I fix you up, I build you, I start you off, I *make* you. It costs me a packet, so I can't run the risk of you walking out on me. Ask yourself, can I?'

'No. Well? And what do I do for the two pounds a week?'

'Just keep fit, and learn wrestling. And maybe wrestle sometimes, when I tell you. See? And after two years, then you go on the basis of so-much a fight.'

'Ah-hah! After two years. And then, how much a fight?'

'Well, I'll tell you frankly; I don't quite know. But it couldn't possibly be less than a fiver. I'd see to that. We'd come to some sort of friendly agreement about it – a gentlemen's agreement, if you get what I mean. See?'

'I see.'

'I make you a star, a top-liner. Thirty, forty, fifty, sixty, seventy, eighty, ninety pounds a week, there's no limit. And later, when we go to America, on tour . . . hell, Jesus, figure it out for yourself: some Yank wrestlers make tens of thousands! They live like princes. Women run miles to see 'em. All you need do is sign. The contract's only nominal. See? Nominal. It just means to say, I pay you two quid a week as a retainer, and you just wrestle when I tell you, while I'm making a champ out of you. See?'

'Well, thanks for telling me all this.'

'I'll get you a blank contract.'

'Don't bother.'

'You think it over. You're a mug if you don't.'

'All right, I'll think it over.'

Fabian sprang out of his chair. 'Listen. You got brains. I'll tell you. Wrestling is a fine sport, yes. But Hell, who wants to see it now? It's a thing of the past. See? The public wants a show. They want acting, and rough stuff. All right, they're mugs. Okey-doke, we're clever. Give 'em what they'll pay for. You know wrestling is a lot of hooey. I know wrestling's a lot of hooey. They know it themselves, and still they get a kick out of it. So what am I going to do? I say to myself: "These mugs go to wrestling the same as they go to the pictures. They know it ain't genuine. They know the Black Strangler doesn't really draw with Legs Mahogany, just the same as they know Clark Gable doesn't really marry Jean Harlow in the films. Well, they like to be fooled. See, Adam? The public are mugs, bloody mugs. Kid 'em! They like to have illusion. See? Well, that's life . . . Hey! Hell! Hell, what a smacker of an idea for a song!' Fabian sang, to the tune of 'It's My Mother's Birthday Today': '"It's just an illusion; that's life . . ." Well, listen, Adam. If you stick around a minute, you'll see what I mean. See? Look, come out here a minute. The Strangler and Mahogany are working over the fight a bit.'

Adam followed him back to the gymnasium.

* * *

The Strangler had a superb back, black and glossy as carbon-paper, loaded with muscles that jumped and squirmed like snakes in a bag. It would have taken a battering-ram to shake the ebony balustrade of his legs, or knock the wind out of his corrugated-iron stomach, or damage the japanned-steel cuirass of his pectorals. As he turned his head, the tendons of his neck snapped up under the skin, like a handful of twanging steel cables, and Adam saw his face. Supported by a neck as thick as a thigh that grew, with the curve of an oak-trunk, out of shoulders as broad as a door, the Strangler's head was mean and small. His brow belonged to the beginnings; the Pithecanthropus lingered in his jaw. Above all, his eyes were as lifeless as two bits of mica mounted on mother-o'-pearl and glued to his face.

'*Carved meat*,' thought Adam.

Legs Mahogany, also, was a big man, but his torso was cylin-drical – nothing to look at, but padded with the fast-moving, rubbery wrestlers' muscles, such as one may see in the pictures of men like Madrali, Roeber or Pojello. At forty, his nose was still unbroken, though he had the ears of the hardened matman, rubbed and squeezed and smudged until they resembled fungi on the bark of a tree. The tow-coloured hair on his head was clipped down like the pile of an Afghan rug. His chest and arms were furred with a similar growth, sprinkled with grey. (It is something of a tragedy for a wrestler, when the hair on his chest turns grey.) He spoke out of the corners of his mouth: 'Now listen, Strangler. You want to keep calm. Just keep your temper. If you lose your temper, you'll hurt me, and if you hurt me, I'll murder you. Get this right. I get the first fall, see? You rush me, I sidestep, and you fall out of the ring. Right?'

'An' I come back, an' I kick you in the belly, an' you falls down. Then the referee warns me, an' I chase him round the ring.'

'That's it. Now: I catches you, and I shoves a scissors on you, and you groans.'

'I groans.'

'And groan as if you meant it, see? Then you gets my toes.'

'And that breaks your hold.'

'Yes. Then you do some of your rough stuff. You gets my foot and you bite my toe, see? And you shout out – well, what?'

'Quit or I bite your toe off!'

'Correct. But I gets your head, and gives you a head-lock. But you break, and we go down, and you gives me a Boston Crab. Then I get away, and we better rest a bit after that. You know, I holds you, and you holds me.'

'Legs. This is too tame.'

'Listen to me. I've wrestled for fifteen years, and you're trying to tell me! It'll be all right, as long as you put a bit of life into it. But you won't listen, Strangler. You either play about or go mad. Be a showman. Make an act.'

'I'm a wrestler, not an actor.'

'You are, like hell.'

'I pull some hair off your chest, eh?'

'It'll be cut short, cock, so don't kid yourself. We can mix it a bit after that, and I'll tell you what you can do; you can gouge me – only no fingers, mind. Knuckles. Bend your fingers over, and screw them round and round; only don't press too hard. Try it.'

The Strangler pushed a knuckle into Mahogany's eye, and twisted it like a screwdriver. Mahogany shrieked aloud: 'Oh! Oh! My eyes! I can't see! . . . Get that, Strangler? That's the way to groan. Put some pain into it. Learn to be a showman, Strangler. I'm telling you for your own good. I used to be a Græco-Roman champion, but I starved until I learned how to put up a show; and I'm telling you.'

'I want the second fall.'

'Yes. You get the second fall. But don't forget; I win on a knock-out. I'd let you have the first fall, only I can't trust you not to double-cross me. Anyway, I win on a knock-out, and don't forget.'

'No. Better make it a straight fall.'

'Strangler, don't argue.'

'I say a fall.'

'Now look here –'

'Aw, I'm a villain. I can't be knocked out. I'm a villain, see?'

'Strangler, don't you be a bloody fool. Ain't I going to give you opportunities?'

'I don't care. You can't knock me out. And don't get me mad. If you get me mad, I fight straight. You be careful. Look what happened to the Greek.'

'Listen, Strangler. If you want to shoot straight, shoot straight. I don't give two hoots for your Greeks. I can pin you in five minutes, straight wrestling. But be reasonable. All I want is a knock-out. It's no disgrace to you. I knock everybody out. Anyway, I can wrestle you off your feet.'

'And am I a mug? I can maul you so your own mother wouldn't recognise you. My line's rough stuff.'

'Well, ask Harry Fabian.'

'All right, ask Fabian.'

Fabian stepped forward. 'Hey, what *is* all this? Why can't you guys make up your minds? What's the quarrel? What I want is a show. See? I don't give a flying cattle if you kill each other, but I got to have a show. See? Legs, what are you worrying about a knock-out for? Don't let me have any more of this bickering.

And listen, Strangler: here's another line for you – crown Legs with the basin. That raises a laugh. And afterwards, grab your towel and wind it round his neck and throttle him with it. See? Good, eh? Or else, I tell you what, blindfold him with the towel, and kick him out of the ring.'

The Strangler grinned.

'And what am I supposed to do while he's doing that?' asked Mahogany.

'You got more experience: use your own common sense. But I tell you what: this is a good gag. Hide a match under the belt of your shorts, and then afterwards, put a scissors on him and set light to the top of his shoe –'

'Heh –'

'– Now don't get excited, Strangler! Listen: the referee throws water over you. Nice, eh?'

'Not my line,' said Legs.

'Well, it suits me,' said the Strangler.

'Okay,' said Fabian, 'let it go at that . . . You see, Legs, you *got* to let the Strangler do some funny stuff. You got to. You're the more experienced man. You got to make a *show*. People have got to *talk*. It's going to be a big chance for you boys. Now's your chance. Get yourselves in the limelight. Now you be good boys and give me a show, eh? Work it over a bit more, then eat. Eh? Listen: I look after you like a father. Don't I? Well, don't you worry. I'll stand by you. I –'

'Oh, Harry,' said the Strangler, 'what about the red silk dressing-gown?"

'What dressing-gown?'

'The one you promised me, with my name in gold letters on the back.'

'Oh, that one! Hell, give a guy a chance to *breathe!* I'll see to it, don't worry. Now, be a good feller, and let me get on with what I've got to do, eh?'

'I want my red silk dressing-gown!'

Fabian drew himself up, thrusting out his jaw. The top of his head barely reached to the point of the Strangler's chin. He said: 'On the job, or I'll smash you!'

The Strangler could have cracked Fabian between his two

thumb-nails. But he only said: 'Right, Harry,' and went back to the mat.

'Dog!' said Ali.

Fabian raised his eyebrows. 'Why dog?'

'Because you talk to him like a dog, and he obeys like a dog.'

Fabian grinned. 'You see what it is, pal? He's got brawn: I got brains. Get the angle?'

'*Ptcha!*' said Ali.

Fabian went back to his office. Ali followed him.

* * *

'Well listen, Ali,' said Fabian, 'what d'you think of Kration?'

'He is a very strong boy. But a wrestler? Never.'

'Yeah, yeah, yeah, I know, I know. I know all about that. But what sort of show does he put up?'

'As for show; yes, he makes a good show. But what is show?'

'Ah, you got the wrong angle. You don't like Kration, do you?'

'Why should I like Kration? Is he a girl, that I should like him?'

'But admit, you don't like him.'

'All right. I don't. What is he? A kitchen-boy, whom you have put on top of a bill. His head is swollen. One day I teach him what.'

'Well, now!' Fabian laughed. 'He said just that very thing about you.'

'What?'

'Ssh! . . .'

'Tell me what he said!'

'No, Ali, honest to God, I don't want to start any ill-feeling.'

'I have no ill-feeling.'

'Well, if you promise not to repeat a word; he said you were an old has-been. "If I wanted to," he said, "I could pin Ali in two seconds."'

'*Hou!*'

'But don't say anything.'

'Say anything? *Say* anything! Oh, no. I will not say anything. But I will just take him to bits, and see what he is made of, only that!'

Fabian protested, in the tone of an adult talking to a difficult child: 'Now Ali; don't go and strain yourself. You know you've got to be very careful.'

'Me? Why?'

'Your heart –'

'*My* heart –'

'Besides, the Greek's a much younger man, and well, Jesus, Ali; we all know you *used* to be a champion, and all that; but, hell . . .'

Ali trembled with rage. 'But what? Tell me?'

'Well, Ali, we all like you, and we wouldn't like to see you starting anything you couldn't finish. You take my advice, and let well alone.'

'I swear by God, I could beat Kration with one hand tied!'

'Sure you could. Sure, sure. Forget it.'

'I am telling you, I can beat him with one hand tied to my left foot!' cried Ali, at the top of his voice.

'Oh, yeah, yeah, sure, sure: oh, sure you could!'

'Why are you laughing at me?'

'Who, me? Laughing at you?, Oh-ho-ho-ho; ahem; not me, Ali! Me? Don't *I* know you're not afraid of Kration? I know it, so I don't care what anybody says –'

'Anybody? Who said I was afraid? Who? What is his name?

'Oh, forget it. Everybody *says* so, but nobody believes it. Forget it.'

'Do you think I could not beat Kration?'

'Now listen, Ali; you're old enough not to worry what anybody thinks.'

'I am not old. I am still quite young.'

'Sure you are. Oh, sure. You don't look old. You still look good for three ten-minute rounds –'

'Three? Six!'

'Sure. *I* didn't believe it when they said you were nearly eighty.'

'Who said that? Who?'

'Listen,' said Fabian, 'I don't want any quarrels down here. If you want to fight Kration, then fight him in a ring.'

'So it was Kration who said that?'

'I didn't say so.'

'I would like to meet him in a ring.'

'Ssh! Don't upset yourself. You want to be careful about getting too excited.'

'Why do you say that? Tell me!'

'Nothing. Only you can't be too careful.'

'Will you stop tormenting me? I tell you, I am strong; my heart is strong. Make me a match with Kration, and I will show you. Yes?'

'No, Ali, no. I wouldn't have it on my conscience.'

'Then I shall wait until he comes down, and I shall tear him to pieces in the gymnasium!'

'No, joking aside, Ali. Would you really take the Greek on?'

'Willingly!'

'And is your heart really all right?'

'I swear; my heart is like rock.'

'Then I might fix a match for you. Keep quiet, and I'll see what I can do.'

'I should be very grateful.'

Ali went out. Fabian looked at him, and wrote on a sheet of paper: '*Sensational Come-Back. Ali the Terrible Turk, 60-year-old undefeated Champion, versus Kration . . .*' He thought of Ali's vast bulk, of his burden of fat and years, his purple lips and his strenuous breathing. He said to himself: '*Oh boy, oh boy; say he dropped dead in the ring? It'd be in every paper in the country! . . .*'

The Strangler pushed his rudimentary head into the office.

'Harry. You going to give me that red silk dressing-gown soon?'

'Yes.'

'With my name in gold letters?'

'Yes, yes.'

'Big letters?'

'Yes, *yes*, YES!' The door closed. Fabian wrote: '*The needle fight of the century! Ali the Terrible Turk makes a sensational come-back!!!*' Then he could see black headlines: 'DEATH OF TERRIBLE TURK . . . TERRIBLE TURK FALLS DEAD IN RING . . . FAMOUS WRESTLER DEAD.' . . . And somewhere down the column: '*Mr Harry Fabian said, this morning: "I didn't know Ali's heart was bad. He was a great guy and a swell wrestler. He hated Kration like poison. I don't know why. Kration is a fine, clean lad. I taught him all he knew . . ."'*

'Jesus!' said Fabian. He opened the door, and shouted: 'Oh, Ali!'

'Yeh?'

'Come in here. Listen, Ali. You want to fight this guy Kration?'

'Yes.'

'Okay, then. I'll fix it up for you.'

'Good!'

'I'll make it worth your while. You can make a come-back. I'll put you on top of the bill. I'll pay you three quid for the fight. Well?'

'What do I care for money?' said Ali.

FIFTEEN

'I'd do murder for money,' said Vi, 'if I could get away with it. I saw a picture about a feller, and so he bashed a money-lender with a poker. Ooo, I want some money, I want some money bad!'

'Haven't you got any at all? You ought to have some, surely,' said Helen.

'Me? Why? Why ought I? Christ; it's not as if I *waste* what I get. I only spend money on what's necessary. But look what happened to me last night.'

'Did you go home with that Australian?'

'Dirty swine,' said Vi. 'You ought to know what happened. He took me to a hotel in Paddington: he had about fifty or sixty quid on him, in notes mark you. Well, I said to myself: "*Blimey, I'll have some of that.*" So I starts playing about; you know, putting my hand in his coat, and tickling him, and all that Fanny Adams, but I couldn't find out where he kept the money. Well, so I go to a hotel with him, see? And I thinks: "*Blimey, he's tight as an owl. All I got to do is wait till he falls off to sleep.*" See? It wasn't,' said Vi, indignantly, 'it wasn't as if I was going to take *all* his money and leave him penniless, like some girls would. I would have left him* with at least a tenner: you know, just take *some*. But a fat lot of appreciation I get. And did I have a job making him go to sleep! Cor! I thought to myself: "*As soon as he drops off, I'll creep out of bed and sort of roust round.*" My Gord, I got to *live*, haven't I? Well – oh, before I forget: I heard a lovely new "Knock-knock". Listen: Knock-knock.'

'Who's there?'

'Buddha.'

'Buddha who?'

'Buddha can you spare a dime. What was I saying? Oh, yes, this Australian. I kidded him along all right. I kept on saying: "Over the top and the best of luck, Digger," and all that kind of thing. Funny thing, if you say that to an Australian you can take his trousers off of him. I mean, you can get quids. Well, whenever I gets him off to sleep and starts to move, he wakes up again and starts all over again. Talk about doing his knitting! Sex. Gah! Well, in the end, I creeps out of bed as quiet as a bloody mouse, and I goes all over his pockets. Not a light! He must of hid it somewhere.'

'You should have tried his shoe,' said Helen.

'Well, it's funny thing you saying that, because I did. I felt in one of his shoes, and there it was – a roll of fivers and pound notes as fat as a toilet roll. And just then he wakes up and says: "You come back here." And he makes me go back to bed, and he starts all over again; you would of thought he hadn't seen a woman for twenty years. So in the end I falls off to sleep, and when I wakes up he's gone. Of all the lousy tricks to play! He must of had at least a hundred quid on him. All right. Say he'd given me twenty. That's a fifth of a hundred. It's just like giving a person a penny if you've got five pence. If I was a man . . .'

'You should have asked for some money first.'

'No, it's not nice. It's making yourself look like a tart.'

'Well, anyway, you ought to have asked.'

'As a matter of fact, I did, but he said: "Afterwards." Ooo, what wouldn't I do for some money! If I had a gun, you know what I'd do? I'd go into a bank, and I'd put down half a dollar, and say: "Could you give me change?" and just as the man put his hand out, I'd say: "Stick 'em up!" Joe's girl friend's had an abortion, and Yetta says it was a black one. I always thought she was a pinkie. Got any money?'

Helen said, reluctantly: 'I could lend you half a crown if you like.'

'Thanks,' said Vi, gloomily. 'How much did you make this week?'

'About six pounds.'

'But you can save. I can't. I'm not like that. If I see a thing I fancy, I've got to have it. But you . . . I bet you've got money saved up.'

'Not much.'

'How much?'

'About twenty pounds.'

'You're lucky. If I had twenty quid, d'you know what I'd do? I'd buy eight dresses from the Guinea Dress Shop, and six pairs of shoes, and send a quid to my father; and then d'you know what I'd do? I'd change a pound note into bloody halfpennies, and I'd go down to the club when it was full, and chuck the whole lot – bang, crash! – all over the floor. Eh?'

'You're crazy.'

'Why am I?'

'You ought to save.'

'What's the use of saving?'

'Well, one day I want to have a proper home of my own,' said Helen, 'a roof over my head; my own furniture.'

'So do I, but I'm going to find a rich man. Aren't you? Oh, no, I forgot – you're still crazy about Adam, aren't you?'

'Yes,' said Helen.

'Well, you might do worse. He's a nice boy. What's he like?'

'You've seen him almost as often as I have.'

'I mean, what's he *like*? You know.'

'Well, I think he's marvellous.'

'Are you going to live with him?'

'I don't know.'

Vi lit a cigarette. 'Isn't it funny?' she said, 'about two months ago you used to go right up in the air whenever I mentioned anything like that. Now, why, I bet you're worse than me.'

'What d'you mean, worse than you?'

'Well . . . I've got sort of fed up with sleeping with fellers. But you like it.'

'What if I do? It's only natural, isn't it?'

'That's what I always told you, only you never listened. He's a funny kind of feller, Adam, isn't he? Kind of moody, funny sort of bloke.'

'He's an artist, a sculptor.'

'Where does he think that'll get him?'

'Oh, anyway,' said Helen. 'It's only a kind of hobby. He doesn't waste any time on it. He's marvellous, really. Ever so hardworking. He saves quite a bit.'

'Oh, well, I don't know. The best thing is a feller with money. Look at Harry Fabian.'

'Yes, Fabian's quite nice; but not my type.'

'Oh, you'd be surprised; some of these small men . . . anyway he's clever, dead clever. He doesn't half make some money. He's always got hundreds on him. All business, but lively with it. You know, Helen, he likes you.'

'I know he does. But I don't take much notice of him.'

'You should. You know what? If you went home with him, I bet you he'd give you ten quid.'

'I wouldn't think of such a thing.'

'Why not? You go with Adam, for nothing.'

'That's entirely different.'

'Why is it? Tell me why?'

'I happen to be in love with Adam, if you want to know.'

'So does that mean to say you can't make yourself a tenner? You can still be in love with him, if you like. Ah, I used to be just like that. Christ, when I used to be a waitress at Spanglers, people used to offer me a quid, two quid, a fiver even. And me working my guts out for a lousy seventeen-and-six a week and tips! But I wouldn't. I only did it for love. And where did it get me? In the family way, that's where it got me; and then I *had* to batter a bit for a few quid. You're a mug, Helen, that's what you are. You can sit down in the club and soak a mug for all he's got, and then come back home and talk about "not dreaming of taking money for sleeping with a man". I think you're crazy.'

'Oh, don't be a fool.'

'I'm a fool. Yes, sure, I'm a fool! But you more or less promise to go home with the fellers, don't you? Well, that's taking money under false pretences,' said Vi, with an air of virtue. 'So pick the bones out of that. Are you going to marry Adam?'

'I don't know. If I do, I want a proper home, and everything; and we couldn't have anything like that just now. Perhaps if we saved up a lot more, we might.'

'Has he asked you to?'

'As good as.'

'Ah,' said Vi, bitterly, 'men are a selfish lot of bastards. What dress are you wearing tonight?'

'The white, I think.'

'I shouldn't. Mary's got a new white dress.'

'What do I care about Mary's new white dress?'

'She'll be annoyed. Besides, she doesn't like you.'

'No, I don't suppose she does.'

'She's jealous. She thinks you're making eyes at Mr Nosseross.'

'Me? Making eyes at him? She's mad!'

'You know Phil likes you.'

'You're crazy. If he does, it's just platonic. Everybody can see he's just wild about Mary; though God knows why.'

'She's a bitch,' said Vi. 'She talks about you behind your back.'

'What does she say?' asked Helen.

'Oh, nothing much.'

'Tell me.'

'Well, promise you won't repeat it; but she said to Yetta that you were a Lesbian.'

'What?'

'Don't take any notice of it, though –'

'She can't say things like that about me! Wait till I see her. I'll tell her off.'

'That's right,' said Vi, eagerly. 'You do.'

'I'll tell her what I think of her.'

'But be careful,' said Vi. 'Remember she's more the boss there than Nosseross. She could get you slung out.'

'I don't care!'

'*She'll get the sack!*' thought Vi, with exultation; and she said: 'After all, you're the best worker in the place. Phil said so. They'd never sack you.'

'Why should they? I make pounds and pounds for them . . . I wish I owned that place. I bet Nosseross makes a hundred pounds a week out of it.'

'More!' said Vi. Then an inspiration struck her. She cried: 'Helen! You could start a place like the Silver Fox. It needn't cost much. Adam could be the manager. You could be chief hostess, and have the pick of all the best men, and you could give me a job, and you and me would work together!'

Helen looked at Vi. 'That wouldn't be a bad idea.'

'Then why not do it?'

'I'd need more money.'

'You can get it . . . one way or another; and you and Adam could start.'

'But Adam probably wouldn't want to.'

'Why not?'

'He doesn't like the life. He wants to do his own kind of work, sculpture.'

'Then you run the show while he does sculpture. Or you and him could run it together for, say, a year. Well, say you only make fifty or sixty quid a week clear profit. How much would that make in a year?'

'Two thousand five hundred or three thousand pounds.'

'Christ! Then there's the Coronation coming. You can clear hundreds over that alone. London'll be *lousy* with money. Then, when you've made a few thousand quid, go and do sculpture.'

'You know, Vi, once in a while you get a good idea!'

'What would you call it? Helen's Club?'

'No. What about the Adam and Eve? Or the Forbidden Fruit!'

'Smashing!' said Vi. 'And it wouldn't cost very much to start. Only you'd have to be quick, to be in time for the Coronation. You've got about twenty quid. I bet Adam's got fifty. That makes seventy . . .'

'Not enough,' said Helen.

'Well, God Almighty, *get* some more. It's not as if you're a virgin any more. Graft a bit on the side. Who's to know?'

'Oh, I couldn't. Adam would never have anything more to do with me.'

'Well, you can use your loaf a bit. Why, a girl I know, a French girl, she makes as much as a fiver an afternoon while her husband's at work. She's been doing it over a year, and he doesn't know yet.'

'No. I couldn't do that.'

'I mean to say, it wouldn't be as if you were doing it just for the sake of doing it. It'd be for *business* – God Almighty, people do worse things than that every day. You say, for instance, some old man makes his daughter marry a feller in business, so he can get something out of it. Well? Isn't that just the same sort of thing?'

'Perhaps. But it's not my line.'

'And, my God, there was a woman used to have a club, a woman called Battleship Maggie. Some people used to call her Caso Maggie. She got her money out of girls, if anybody did; and she married some lord. He only married her for her money, and she got it going caso. And if lords can do it, then blimey! Why not get a flat for afternoons, and work up a quiet connection. Do some indoor bashing –'

'No, I couldn't. Still, perhaps I might have some luck. I'm sorry we started talking about it. I'll keep thinking of it, now; and once I set my mind on a thing, I have to do it in the end . . .'

'Now listen. For instance, say next time a feller like Fabian came in you went back with him for an hour. You might get a fiver. And what would you lose?'

'Self-respect.'

'Oh, don't make me laugh! Is it any worse to *say* you're going back with him, and then shake him after you've touched him for a quid?'

'Perhaps not, but –'

Heavy footsteps sounded in the passage.

'Adam!' said Helen. 'Not a word to him about clubs!'

She went to Adam's room. He was standing at his mirror examining a bruise on his neck.

'Darling!' said Helen. 'Have you hurt yourself?'

'No. Old Ali's a bit rough when he plays, that's all. I wish you could see him. "Fight, damn you, fight! *Ptoo!* Beat me if you can! Make yourself the better man!" And smack, smack, smack! He's a grand old man.'

'He sounds horrible. But what's that?' She pointed to a big square parcel on the divan.

'Just clay.'

'But, Adam dear, you haven't even started to use all that clay you've got!'

'I will, I will, when I get time.'

'You know, dear, you ought not to spend more money on this kind of thing just now. We ought to save.'

'Save? Of course. But isn't this the kind of thing we're saving for?'

Helen did not say 'No'. She simply said: 'Sit down here and kiss me.'

* * *

'It's good to see you again,' said Adam.

Helen asked: 'Adam, I want to ask you something. How much have you saved?'

'I don't know exactly, but somewhere around forty-five pounds, or so.'

'Well, you know, Adam, I was thinking . . . we do need money so badly . . .'

'Well? Aren't I trying to get it? Aren't I at the club all night? Do you think I ought to rob a bank, or something, in the afternoon?'

Helen's fingers stroked the back of his head. 'No, Adam darling, don't be annoyed –'

'I'm not annoyed.'

'I was only thinking . . .'

'What?'

'Well; we're only in this business for just a very little while . . .'

'I hope so.'

'Just a *very* little while. But for the time we're in it – it was only a kind of idea that occurred to me, mind you – it did seem so silly to let Nosseross get most of the benefit out of all our hard work.'

'You call it hard work? It strikes me as being the easiest money in the world.'

'Yes, darling. But you must admit that Nosseross gets most of the profit, and well . . . for the little while we're in the business, it seemed to me that the quickest way of getting some *real* money together would be –' She paused, took a deep breath, and said, very quickly: '– to pool what we have, and start a place of our own.'

'What place?'

'A bottle-party; a club. What do you think?'

'I think it's a rotten idea. I'm trying to get out of the business not further and further into it.'

'But, darling, it would only be for a little while.'

Adam replied: 'No it wouldn't. It would be for ever.'

'But it wouldn't! In a year or so, we could make as much as three or four thousand pounds.'

'It's possible,' said Adam, 'but that's just the point. Does anybody in the world ever walk out on three or four thousand pounds?'

'But we need the money, darling; we do need the money, don't we?'

'It's no use, my dear; I'm not going to discuss it.'

A little experience of men had taught Helen subtlety. She said: 'All right, darling. Don't be annoyed with me.'

'Annoyed with *you*?' said Adam. 'My dear Helen!'

She kissed him, pressing her whole body against him; and in spite of the fact that this kiss, and Adam's immediate response to it, stirred up in her a veritable maelstrom of desire, she retained, deep in her consciousness, a little cold corner from which her critical faculties watched him. Adam's big hand twitched the curtains together. He went back to the divan and kissed her again.

'No, not yet,' said Helen.

'Why, what's the matter? Aren't you –'

'Oh, I'm all right. I want to talk to you a little first. I'm . . . oh, I don't know, I'm worried.'

'What about?'

'Oh, Adam, isn't money a curse?'

'It is,' Adam began to caress her, with the slow, steady movements of a masseur.

Helen quivered from head to foot. She put her lips against his ear, and murmured: 'Dearest, don't you think . . . don't you think we might consider what I said just now? It wouldn't be for long, and then you could work in comfort, in peace and quiet –'

'No!'

Helen turned away from him, and burst into tears. 'I think you're selfish, and perfectly horrible!'

'No, but Helen! Helen, darling, do listen! Once we really get right into the club business we're finished as far as anything else is concerned. Don't you understand that? Did you ever hear of a gambler who could get up from a roulette-table with his winnings? No, Helen, we mustn't get too deeply into this business, or else we'll never get out at all.'

'Oh . . . you've got no will-power, that's what it is! Anybody with real will-power wouldn't talk like that. I'm only suggesting something for your good, and mine . . .'

'Don't cry. For heaven's sake don't cry!' said Adam, who could not bear the sight of women's tears. 'Listen, Helen . . . Helen . . .'

'Oh . . . don't talk to me! You've done all sorts of stupid jobs for years, and never made a penny out of them. And now you've got some idiotic idea into your head about not wanting to make too much money! I –'

'But I haven't! I –'

'Oh, yes you have! Afraid of life being too easy! I never heard anything more ridiculous in my life. And so I suppose we've got to spend the rest of our lives in one dirty little furnished room, being noble, and talking about sculpture, which you never do, anyway. What sculpture? I've never seen anything you've done. Oh, don't talk to me. Go away! I think you're stupid! I think you're weak! I think you're foolish!'

'But Helen! You don't understand what I mean! I want money just as much as you do. I like money, to spend. But I just don't *like* this night-club business of working all night and sleeping all day. It's all rotten. I hate it!'

'Oh! And I suppose if you were a coal miner, that would be all right? You'd think it was very noble, I suppose? But just because you don't get corns all over you, and have to wear a stiff shirt, so this business is rotten!'

'It's parasitic –'

'Parasitic! You get hold of a word, just like a baby. What do you mean by parasitic, anyway? I suppose you'd rather starve in one room, and not even do any sculpture, anyway, rather than spend two or three months doing something you don't like so as to be able to work hard at sculpture for a year afterwards? Oh . . .'

It seemed to Adam that the most important thing in the world was to put an end to this argument, and take Helen in his arms again.

Helen sensed this, and pushed away his soothing hand. 'You're foolish! Just think what lovely work you could do if you had a quiet house, and plenty of money, and a studio, and models, and tons and tons of clay and stone and things! If you had time to work all day long! If –'

'But, darling, there's only one drawback. It we began to open clubs, we might have houses, and money, and studios, and everything you can think of; but there's one thing we wouldn't have any more – we wouldn't have what it takes to make a good thing out of clay. Helen, I tell you, you can't shelve a creative impulse indefinitely. Not at my age. The longer I delay now, the less likely I am ever to do anything. And if I had all the money in the world, and all the houses in the world, and everything in the world, what good would it do me if I couldn't do what I had come into the world to do?'

'Why should a few months make all that much difference?' asked Helen, scornfully.

'It wouldn't be only a few months. It would be years and years – as long as it made money; and then, if it failed, we'd start looking for more money-making propositions. Did *you* start this racket meaning to make it your career?'

Helen was silent. Adam pulled her towards him. Her body remained tense. She said: 'Anyway, dear, don't say no, yet. Think about it, eh?'

'There's nothing to think about.'

She encircled him with all her limbs. 'You'll just think it over, eh? Darling!'

'Well . . . I'll think about it, then.'

Helen kissed him.

SIXTEEN

That evening Fabian walked the streets aimlessly, in an evil temper, an unaccountable anger; deep in thought, yet thinking of nothing definable. He looked up, caught a glimpse of flapping bunting, and said 'Suckers!' Shopkeepers were already hanging out flags and coloured plaques for the coronation of George the Sixth. The vanguard of the Coronation visitors was already in the streets: gaunt Colonials with wrinkled necks; bulky, dry-cleaned Americans in expensive overcoats; bearded men; men in berets. 'Mugs!' said Fabian. At Oxford Circus, a fat man, wearing a beautiful mauve scarf, took off his hat to Fabian, and asked: 'Eexcuse mee pleese, ees thees, Peecadeelee, pleese?'

'Couldn't say, pal, I'm a stranger here myself,' said Fabian. He walked on. He envied that man's scarf. '*Peecadeelee!* The steamer! Can't these here lousy foreigners learn English?' And what right had they to be so wealthy? Who were they to wear overcoats for fifteen guineas, and three-guinea hats, and scarves of vivid mauve *crêpe de Chine*? Fabian wished he had misdirected the man; sent him to Marble Arch.

In Regent Street, another man accosted him; a tall, pale young man, with a beige hat pulled down over his left eye.

'Hallo, Charlie,' said Fabian, 'you look worried.'

'About look worried! I am worried.'

'Smatter?'

'Bloody Coronation.'

'The Coronation's jam, you mug,' said Fabian. 'London'll be stinking with money.'

'Is that so? Well, the bloody bogies are cleaning the streets up. There won't be a girl about.'

'Shut up, you fool. It's a gag. They only want something to put in the papers.'

'You know what they do?' said Charlie, biting his nails. 'They pinch a girl, see? Then they find out where she lives, see? Then they go there and wait till her boy friend comes in, and they lumber him, and give him half a stretch.'

'You should worry. Your Joan's a smart kid.'

'Yeh, yeh, I know. But they've lumbered her.'

'They've what?'

'Lumbered her, I tell you,' said Charlie, almost weeping. 'They pinched her two hours ago, down Oxford Street, and I tell you straight, I'm scared to go home. It's a frame-up. The bastards, the dirty bastards, they won't let you live!'

'They'll fine her forty bob. So what you worrying about?'

'If they come and pinch me, I'm entitled to six months.'

'Ain't you got an alibi?'

'What alibi?'

Fabian swelled with a sense of power. 'Listen, Charlie, if they lumber you, say you're working for me, Fabian Promotions. See? Here's my card. You're my contact man. Get it? Hand 'em this. I'm your employer. If they come to me, I'll talk to 'em. You're all over the country contacting new talent for me, see? And you don't know what your lady-friend does in your absence.'

'Jesus Christ, Harry, you've got brains!'

'Sure I got brains. Well, I got to be moving. 'Bye.'

Fabian walked, thrusting out his chest. Visions formed in his mind. He was Harry Fabian, a kind of Robin Hood; an outlaw; a lord of the underworld; subtle, elegant, adroit, debonair. He lit a cigarette with a gesture, and flicked the match away. Harry Fabian, the Brain; Fabian the Terrible. He went, automatically, towards a pin-table saloon: he remembered that they had a new thing in the rifle range, a machine-gun. He would have two shillings-worth of shots, and fill a target with holes . . . Nurtured on the gangster pictures of the era before the G-Men; suckled on the legends of Capone, Torrio and Dillinger; weaned on *American Detective* and *Black Mask*; the queer little brain of Fabian floated in pleasant conjecture . . .

He was riding in his bullet-proof car, with four hard-faced men armed with machine-guns. All his enemies lined the road. 'Okey-doke, boys; give 'em the business!' *Tatatatatat – Tatatatatatatatat!*

went the Tommy-guns, roaring like pneumatic drills. Ejected shells fell in shining showers; people dropped like skittles, one after another, in a line. Whoosh! – the great car took a hairpin bend at eighty miles an hour, with a thundering of exhaust –

A sharp little voice, filed jagged by years of shouting in open air, slit this pleasant screen of dreams from top to bottom: ''Lo, 'Arry!'

It was Bert, the costermonger, passing with a barrowload of bananas. The machine-gun in Fabian's imagination gave a last, vicious stutter. Bert completed the pile of dead.

'What the hell d'you want?' asked Fabian.

'Wanna tell you somethink.'

'Yeah? Yeah? And now I'll tell you something: I don't speak your language, see? So you can shove off. Get me, pal?'

Bert laughed. 'You bloody fool. D'you think you're kidding me, with that madam? Don't speak my language! What other language *do* you speak, you bloody steamer! Think you can fool me with your Wallace Beery stuff? I –'

Fabian gnawed his upper lip. 'Well, what? Say it, and scram.'

'I wanna give you a tip. The bogies are everywhere, see? They're pinching all the tarts, and they're lumbering all the Johnny Ronces. See? I'm warning yer: if you gets lumbered it means a shopping. So nark it now, while there's time. That's all.'

'You silly bloody fool, d'you think I don't know my onions?'

'All right. You think you're smart. Only just remember I warned yer. You deserve to get it in the bleedn' neck, 'Arry. You're a dirty, rotten dog –'

'Lay off, you –'

'– but after all, you're my –'

'Bert! Cut that out! I don't know you, and I don't want to. You louse, d'you think I was too tight to remember what you did to me the other night?'

'No,' said Bert, 'I should 'ope you ain't. I smacked yer round the bloody face. An' I'd do it again. I'd do it to me own farver, if 'e be'aved like what you do. I'd do it to Jesus Christ! You're a bloody kept boy. Zoë keeps you, and what do you do? You takes the bloody money she walks the streets for, and drinks yerself sick! You sicks 'er life out on to the bloody pavement! Why, you ponce! If you was a stranger to me, I wouldn't say nothink. But you're my relative. You ain't fit to live. I'd screw yer 'ead orf, if I thought I could git away with it. I smacked you in the face, and I'll do it agin; but I'm warnin' yer, for the last time – turn it in and go and do some work! Or go and be a straightforward tea-leaf – thieve, rob, do bloody murder – do anythink except ponce on a woman!'

Fabian snarled like a wolf. 'You better shut up!'

'*You* shut up, and let me finish! Turn it in! You're goin' bloody rotten! You stink!' Bert sniffed. 'Yers, you stink like a ponce. You stink of bloody rotten scent. Gertcher! Lettin' a woman bash on the bloody streets to buy you brilliantine for yer 'air! And you used to be a good kid. You used to be as good as gold, till you got lazy. And now look at yerself!'

'Well? And look at you!' said Fabian. 'Look at your trousers! Look at your boots! Push your lousy barrow round the streets: "Buy! Buy! Buy!" And where does it get you? Your old woman's in stinking dirty rags, and you run like a bloody dog with the cops pushing you around from corner to corner, and your kids' arses sticking out of their pants –'

'– My Gord-forbids might be runnin' around in the gutter, stark naked, but their old pot-an'-pan won't ever 'ave to 'ide 'is face away from 'em, or crawl round the back-doubles in case somebody comes up to 'im and shouts: "Ponce!"'

'Say that word again, and I'll smash you! Strike me paralysed, I'll smash you!'

'You? You can't smash me. You know I'm right. See? It's made you crawl on yer belly like a bloody worm. And a few years back you 'ad a 'eart like a lion! But now you're ashamed. I smacked yer face in the street the other night, in front of a crahd of people, and you couldn't raise a 'and back to me. No, you burst aht cryin'. That's what it's turned you into. An' I tell you, 'Arry, I'd do it again; I would! If it was in the middle o' Piccadilly, in front o' the King and Queen, I would!'

The two men looked at each other. Fabian shrugged. Bert laid his hands on the shafts of his barrow, and heaved it up on to the wheels. Fabian forced a scornful smile – but the corners of his mouth were even heavier to lift.

Without another word, they went their ways.

Fabian felt sick. He went to Bagrag's for a drink. But the club was almost empty. Mike was standing by the door with his unholy, wound-like mouth clamped on a dead cigarette. Bagrag was looking at an evening paper.

'Hiya, Bagrag,' said Fabian.

'Uh-uh.'

'You're quiet down here.'

'Um.'

'Seen Louis?'

Mike lifted a corner of his mouth, and let out one word: 'Pinched.'

Fabian experienced a curious qualm. 'What for?'

'Loitering with intent,' said Mike.

The pianist, who was sweeping the floor, added: 'They're cleaning up all the boys; everybody they know. It's the Coronation.'

'What the hell do I care?' said Fabian. 'They don't know me.'

He gulped his drink. Bagrag stared at his paper, reading nothing; deep in secret thought.

''Night,' said Fabian. He went out, depressed. Outside the Oxford Corner House a middle-aged man whose head looked like that of Caracalla, soaked in brandy, said to him: 'Aha, Harry. Heard about Charlie?'

'I saw him only a little while ago. What?'

'Lumbered?'

'What? When?'

'Ten minutes ago, up at his place. Well, that's how it is; here today, gone tomorrow . . .'

Something in Fabian's stomach began to flutter.

'Well, what the hell do I care?' he said. 'Charlie's a mug. He let 'em get something on him. I –'

A touch on his shoulder sent his heart bouncing. He turned, grey in the face, and saw Mr Arthur Mayo Clark standing behind him. Fabian laughed with relief: 'Hah! You made me jump!'

'Guilty conscience?' said Mr Clark, baring one tooth in a prim little smile.

At that moment an idea occurred to Harry Fabian. He said:
'I was wondering if I'd see you. I want to have a word – business.'

'Walk along with me, then.'

Fabian accompanied Mr Clark towards Oxford Circus.

'Mr Clark . . . you know my Zoë?'

'Yes.'

'She's getting fed up with London.'

'Oh?'

'She's been thinking of going abroad.'

'Really? Where?'

'Well . . . where would you say?'

'Oh. You want me to say where?'

'Yes.'

'Oh. So it's like that, is it?' said Mr Clark. 'Zoë. Mmm . . .'

'Well?'

'Well. There are drawbacks. First of all, she's dark. They prefer ladies fair, abroad. Then again, the whole thing gets more and more difficult . . .'

'But she's a smashing good-looker.'

'But dark.'

'And young!'

'Twenty-four. I'm not terribly keen, Fabian; not desperately keen. Anyway, what's her attitude?'

'Leave her attitude to me. All being well, what would it be worth?'

Mr Clark shrugged, and said: 'Between a hundred and a hundred and fifty pounds, perhaps.'

'Christ! Have a heart!'

'My side of the matter gets increasingly hard. It's not as if she were a child straight from home.'

'But you know as well as I do, a good girl like Zoë is no trouble.'

'Well, there the matter rests. I can probably manage a hundred and fifty pounds, all being well. If you don't like that, well . . .' A gesture of Mr Clark's right hand said: '*You can go to the devil.*'

'How soon?'

'Valdes leaves Cardiff in three weeks' time.'

'No sooner?'

'No. I'll be seeing you in the meantime, but if you want to do this deal, have Zoë with you in Cardiff next Friday a fortnight.'

'All right,' said Fabian, 'I'll give you a ring.'

'I turn off here. You needn't come any farther. Good-night, Fabian.'

There was something about Mr Clark that made Fabian feel cold and uneasy. The man was of ice, hard ice. Fabian went to a café, and ordered hot soup. He began to think again . . .

A hundred and fifty pounds was a lot of money to have in a lump. But sell Zoë? Send Zoë away? *'She's worked hard for you,'* said his conscience. *'She's crazy about you. She would even die for you.'* Again, reason protested: *'She's your living!'* Then he thought of a hundred and fifty pounds. With that much money he could take a holiday at Monte Carlo, and play at the Casino. He had seen movies about the place . . . glittering crowds, princes, beautiful women, long tables, piles of chips, spinning wheel, and a little ball that went *pitapit*. Then he saw himself, in a beautiful dress-suit, sitting at a table, toying with a heap of money and counters as high as an ant-hill. At his back bejewelled women murmured: 'Lord Fabian has broken the bank. He has won ten million francs, *mon dieu!' Pitapitapita-pitapitapit;* and the croupier's rake pushed another hundred thousand over to him. 'The bank is broken.'

And then, like a man who suddenly sees a simple solution to an overwhelming problem, Fabian was struck by the conviction that, with a hundred and fifty pounds, he could break the bank at Monte Carlo. He felt this as an absolute certainty.

'Check!' he cried. The serial number of his bill was 1253897. This added up to 35. Five and three made eight. Eight, Fabian had always believed, was his lucky number. He could not have been more pleased if he had picked up a ten-pound note. 'Here's where I hit my lucky streak,' he said. The occasion seemed to demand some celebration. He counted his money: he had five pounds in cash.

Fabian called a taxi. 'Silver Fox,' he said to the driver.

He would have a bottle of champagne, and a dance with the

big brunette. This would cost him all he had in his pockets; but it was of no consequence. Soon, he would break the bank.

SEVENTEEN

He was the first customer of the evening. Nosseross greeted him with enthusiasm: 'Harry! It's good to see you again! You're looking well. And prosperous! Tell me, who have you been knocking down?'

'Hiya, Phil! Hell, you're looking good!'

'Come and sit down, Harry. Come and sit down and tell me all about it.'

'I wanna give you a couple of tickets for my first show.'

'That's nice of you, Harry. I appreciate that, I really do.' Nosseross looked over his shoulder, and called: 'Oh, Helen, my dear! Here's an old friend of yours.'

'Why, Mis-ter *Fa*bian! I've been thinking about you,' said Helen.

'And I been thinking about you, too, baby,' said Fabian. 'I thought to myself: "Hell, I'll come down to Phil's place, and see the best-looking brunette in the West End." . . . Phil, what about some champagne?'

'Need you ask twice, Harry? . . . Adam!' Nosseross left the table. Fabian moved a little nearer to Helen.

'You look very pleased with yourself, Mr Fabian.'

'Harry, to you. Yes, I am pleased with myself. I've got things going nicely. Soon, I shall be in the real money. I've got to go over to Monte Carlo in a week or so.'

'Oh, that must be lovely.'

'You get used to it.'

'Do you often go?'

'Aw, about two or three times in a year. I have to go on business. I don't get no pleasure out of it. I just do what I've got to do, play the Casino a bit, and come back.'

'It must be awfully exciting. Do you win much?'

'A bit. They call me "Lucky".'

'You are lucky.'

'No, I'm not, Helen, honest to God I'm not. I'm lonely.'

'You? Lonely? But you must have thousands of friends, surely?'

'Helen, I haven't got a friend in the world! I know millions of people, yes. And I'm a soft-hearted kind of sucker – I'm always helping people out. "Lend us a fiver, Harry," and "I got my rates to pay, lend me twenty-five quid, Harry," and all that. And I never say no. But I ask myself: "If you didn't have a sausage to your name, where would they be then, all these pals of yours?" I'm fed up. I've got to the stage where I know how to make dough, yes. But you know what my ambition is now?'

'What?'

'To find one good woman, and have a home, full of nice furniture – settle down, have a little peace and quiet. It may sound crazy to you, but there it is.'

Fabian had never known this method of attack to fail.

Helen said, warmly: 'What's crazy about it?' She imagined herself in a flowered afternoon-frock, presiding at tea in a drawing-room which was an exact replica of one of Heal's shop-windows. On the third finger of her left hand, above a chaste band of platinum, a large diamond flashed. Fabian was smiling at her over the rim of a cone-shaped teacup. Behind him, through folding doors, Helen could see a piano littered with manuscript-paper speckled with creative dots and dashes . . . 'Well, Harry dear, have you been working hard?' 'Oh you bet, honey. I've just composed the hit of the century. You're going to have a sable coat and a Bentley.' 'Oh, Harry! . . .'

'What are you thinking about?' asked Fabian.

'Nothing much.'

'Wanna dance?'

'In a minute. Let's talk a bit.' She looked from Fabian to Adam. Fabian was wearing a new grey spring suit, a light-grey shirt, a light-grey tie and light-grey socks. He looked like something out of a hosier's window; too unruffled to be real. Adolescent boys stare at such figures, sighing, while they vow that when they become very rich, they, too, will dress like that. Adam's wide back strained against the white jacket. A lock of hair fell across his forehead, and he made his way to the table, balancing a tray.

She thought: '*I like Adam, yes. But after all, he's a man with no ambition. Even if he did make good at his sculpture – and how can he? – he'd still be only a kind of working-man . . . Now l bet I could get a man like Fabian just by putting out my hand . . .'*

She looked at Fabian's hands. They were soft, white, manicured. She thought: *'Artistic hands. At the worst, they'd only get a little inky. Adam would slop about the house in a sweater, and he has navvy's hands even now.'*

'You have nice hands,' she said.

Fabian had the gift of pathos – part of the stock-in-trade essential to the man who lives on women. He could open his eyes, and look like a little wounded bird until women felt a desire to take him in their arms and stroke him.

He did so now. 'Yes,' he said, 'I got nice hands. I got all sorts of things. But I still got nobody who really loves me. You know, Helen, I could fall for you.'

'Oh, come on now, don't be ridiculous.'

'I'm not. I think you're wonderful.'

'What's wonderful about me?'

'Everything. You got beauty, and you got brains. Gee, I'd like to be with you always! Wouldn't it be swell? Just you 'n me. We could go places together; cruises, dancing, Paris, New York . . . Hell, can't you see us, coming out of a great big cream-coloured Rolls-Royce – you in furs, me in tails, walking into some swell place with a big band playing . . . maybe playing one of my own numbers! How'd you like that?'

'Mmmm!' Helen glanced at Adam. His face was sombre. The lassitude had departed from it, giving place to a brooding gloom. *'He would never think of things like that; and if I wanted to dance with him, he'd talk about evolution, or something.'* 'But how's the wrestling going?'

'Getting going, baby. Soon, I'll be taking the money to the bank in wheelbarrows.'

'You're a funny man.'

'Why?'

'Writing songs, and running wrestling, and all that kind of thing.'

'Hell, I can't lie idle. Action, gimme action! I'll only stop when I've made a million.'

'Pounds or dollars?'

'Pounds, kid, pounds. Hell, a million dollars is only two hundred thousand quid. Jesus, what's two hundred thousand?'

'It's a lot of money to me!'

'Y-es, maybe. I admit I haven't got that much right now – less than half that much, to be quite frank. But I'll get a million, you mark my words. A million is *money*. I stop at that; not before.'

'Yet some men have no ambition.'

'A man without ambition's no damn good,' said Fabian.

'Look at Adam, for instance; the waiter. He doesn't care about money. He's crazy about sculpture.'

Fabian laughed. 'What can you make out of that?'

'Well, I don't suppose the most successful sculptor makes much more than three or four thousand a year.'

'I spend nearly that much on clothes and entertaining,' said Fabian. 'Besides . . . hell, I bet it takes 'em weeks to finish a sculpture. Now me, I write a song in two or three hours. *Ping!* A thousand.'

'But he's quite nice,' said Helen.

'Who, the waiter? Sure. He works out down in my gym. But listen, Helen. I like you.'

'Well, I like you.'

'Have tea with me tomorrow?'

'I'd love to.'

'That's great! Where?'

'Shall we say Raoul's, in Bond Street?'

'Sure! Four o'clock?'

'Five.'

'Okay, five. I wanna have a chance to talk to you quietly . . . You know, Helen, I'm keen on you. I ain't a sentimental guy, but . . . Jesus, I don't know how it is. I –'

'Two pounds, please,' said Adam.

Fabian threw down two-pounds-ten; and *Puk!* went the cork of the champagne-bottle.

* * *

Mary had been staring at Helen with the fascinated gaze of a woman in the grip of a good hate. At length she said to Nosseross: 'Phil, I wish you'd get rid of that girl.'

'Who, Helen? Why?'

'I've got my reasons.'

Nosseross laughed. 'You're crazy, darling.'

'Oh. I see. I'm crazy. *I* see. Oh, all right.'

'What's the matter with you, baby love? Helen's a good worker, one of the best in the place. What have you got against her?'

'She talks about us behind our backs.'

'Well, they all do. Let her talk. What can she say?'

'Phil, you've got to get rid of her!'

'Now, angel! The way you go on, anybody would think you were jealous of her!'

'What? *Me*? Jealous of *that*? That horrible, fat, common, over-developed, sexy-looking –'

'Now, Mary, my pet –'

'Me, jealous of a hostess! I see. You're insulting me, now. Oh, all right! *Very* well.'

'But –'

'Don't talk to me, Phil Nosseross! I hate you!' Mary turned her back on him, and walked away. She went into the office; then came out again, passed unobtrusively between the tables in the dim, moving light, and sat at a table behind Fabian.

He was saying: 'I tell you, kid, the more women you've known, the better you appreciate the real thing when you come across it. You're right – I've known plenty dames. When I lived in Hollywood – this is between you and me – I used to go around with Jean Harlow.'

'But you're not going to tell me that you like me better than Jean Harlow.'

'I am! You got more glamour in your little finger. But it's more than that. I don't know what it is. You ain't so sort of *beautiful*, but you *got* more. Besides, I could never fall for a blonde.'

'Most men like blondes.'

'The hell with blondes.'

Mary bit her lip.

'Oh, I don't know,' said Helen, 'some of them are quite pretty. Look at Mrs Nosseross, for instance. She's quite popular with the men – with the lower types of men, it's true; but still, she seems to have a certain amount of attraction for them.'

'Pooey!' said Fabian, and made, with his right hand, the gesture of pulling down a chain. 'Attraction! Who for? Old suckers like Phil Nosseross. Jesus, kid, I knew Mary when she was doing a kind of strip-tease in Saxophone Joe's, over in Golden Square. There's hardly a musician –'

'But don't you think she has nice eyes,' said Helen, 'in a cowish sort of way?'

'Baby, you've got more glamour in your toenails.'

'It's true she's got no brains,' said Helen, 'and she's horribly jealous.'

'She's entitled to be,' said Fabian, squeezing Helen's wrist. 'Anyway, to hell with Mary. Who cares about Mary? It's you I like, not Mary. Come on, now; finish that drink and let's dance. You do a good Rumba, don't you? . . . Hiya, Unconscious! Tell that band to play "La Cucuracha". Say, do you like dogs?'

'I love them. Why?'

'Well, I'm going to give you a chihuahua.'

The band began to play. The drummer yelled into a megaphone:

'La cucuracha, la cucuracha
Marijuana que fumar . . .'

'Boyoboy, can this dame dance!' cried Fabian in an ecstasy.

Mary rose, shaking with anger, and went back to Nosseross. 'You coward! You beast!' she said.

'Why, darling –'

'Don't darling me! Go back to your Helen!'

'But what is it now?' asked Nosseross.

'I'm not going to argue! I tell you one thing – either that girl leaves this place, this very minute, or I do. I mean it! I swear! Unless you kick that filthy bitch out of this club, I'm going to leave you! I *won't* be insulted, do you hear? I won't! I won't!' Mary began to weep.

'Who's been upsetting you?'

'You ought to have heard the things Helen was saying . . . oh . . . oh . . .'

'What things?'

'She called me a prostitute, and said you were an old sucker . . .'

Nosseross patted her shoulder, and said, with magnificent loftiness: 'My darling, if you go to Hyde Park, you'll hear all sorts of layabouts shouting things like that about the King and the Government. But who takes any notice?'

'You're standing up for her!' cried Mary. 'All right! I'm going.'

'Darling, don't be silly –'

'I'm going, I tell you!'

'All right, all right, my lamb. I'll sack her tonight.'

'Now!'

'But –'

'This very minute!'

Nosseross shrugged. The music stopped. Fabian's shrill voice exclaimed: 'Can you Rumba, or can you Rumba!'

Nosseross went to his table, and said to Helen: 'You're wanted on the 'phone.'

'Me? I wonder who that can be.' She followed Nosseross to his office; looked towards the telephone, and saw the microphone lay on the hooks. 'You said –'

'It's all right. There's no 'phone-call. I just wanted a word with you, Helen.'

'What is it?'

'You're a nice girl. I like you. But you'll have to go.'

Helen's face became pale. 'Go? Why?' Then colour came back into her cheeks and forehead like the red glow breaking through the coils of an electric heater. She said: 'But . . . but Mr Nosseross! If . . . if it's on account of that ginger-ale the other evening –'

'No, it's nothing like that. You're the best grafter in the place. But the fact is, you make trouble among the other girls.'

'How?'

'Why,' said Nosseross, soothingly, 'they're jealous of you. You know how it is, you're a superior type, and they resent it. It makes 'em discontented.'

Helen showed her teeth in an angry smile. 'Oh, I see. I think I understand. Mary put her foot down, eh?'

'Ah, come, come, come . . .'

'Oh, yes. I know she doesn't like me,' said Helen, 'and I know just what she's been saying behind my back. Very well. She's the boss –'

'I'm the boss.'

'You're not. You know you're not. I despise a man who has to do whatever his wife tells him.'

Nosseross grinned.

'But before I go, Mr Nosseross, I'd like to tell you one thing. You're a perfect old fool.'

It was impossible to make Phil Nosseross lose his temper. He said: 'Am I?'

'Don't you know what everybody else knows – or are you just pretending not to know?'

'Not to know what?'

'About Mary and –'

'Keep that beautiful little mouth clean, Helen, my dear, or I might scrub it out with a dishcloth,' said Nosseross, amiably.

'Oh, you can't frighten me. Listen. Do you know Sir William Cheshunt?'

'Well?' said Nosseross, calmly.

'Well, the next time he sits at a table with Mary, get somebody to listen to what they say.'

The smile of Nosseross became narrower. 'Why?'

'You'll see.'

His hand closed suddenly, like a break-back rat-trap, on Helen's wrist. 'Spit it out,' he said

'Don't try and terrorise me! I'll tell you because I want to tell you. Mary's carrying on an affair with Sir William Cheshunt, behind your back.'

'You lie,' said Nosseross.

'Very well, you know best. Now let go of my wrist.'

Nosseross's grip tightened for a second, then relaxed. Helen rubbed her hand. 'What else?' asked Nosseross.

'Mary is making a fool of you. I know for a fact that she went to his flat last Friday afternoon, between two and three. And she intends to go away with him.'

There was no change of expression in Nosseross's face.

'Last Friday afternoon?' he said.

'Yes. I heard them talking. She said she'd tell you she was going to a dressmaker.'

'Dressmaker,' said Nosseross.

'He asked her to go with him in his launch for a Mediterranean tour. She said "Yes". If you use your ears, you'll hear more. That's all.'

'Get your things and go,' said Nosseross.

'You wanted to know, and now you know,' said Helen.

'You misunderstood what they were talking about. You're simply trying to make trouble. Get out!' shouted Nosseross, in a strangled voice.

'You owe me fifteen shillings commission for cocktails.'

Nosseross pushed a hand into his waistcoat, and pulled out two pounds; crumpled the notes into a ball, and threw them at Helen. They struck her shoulder, and fell to the floor. She stooped to pick them up. Nosseross jerked a thumb towards the door.

Helen got her overcoat, and left the club.

* * *

Ten minutes later Adam came into the office.

'Oh, Phil,' he said, 'Cheshunt wants to know if you'll cash him a cheque.'

'Tell him,' said Nosseross, 'that I'll cash him a cheque for as much as he likes. And Adam . . . take his order, and then say: "Please accept this, with Phil's compliments; Mr Nosseross will be honoured if Sir William will be his guest for this evening."'

Adam looked at him. 'What's the matter? You don't look too good.'

'I'm a bit sick.'

'Stomach?'

'That's right, stomach. Listen, Adam . . . shut that door a minute. Will you do me a favour? I know I can trust you.'

'Anything in reason.'

'Is Mary sitting with Cheshunt?'

'Yes. Why?'

'Will you stick around and use your ears? I want to know what's said.'

'No. I don't like that sort of thing.'

'Not as a personal favour to me?'

'No. I'm sorry. Not even as a personal favour to you.'

'All right,' said Nosseross, 'forget it. You're a good boy. Shake hands; I like you.' There was warmth in his grip as he grasped Adam's hand.

Nosseross straightened his tie, with particular care, and went into the clubroom. Mary was sitting at one of the obscurest tables with a blond giant in a dinner suit. Nosseross watched her face. She was smiling. Nosseross approached the table.

She saw him. Her lips moved, and her eyes became blank; flat and empty, like holes punched in a magazine-cover, with specks of sky visible through them.

'Thanks for the hospitality,' said Sir William.

'Great pleasure, Sir William.'

'You'll take a drink, Phil?'

'Of course I will. Cheers! . . . Well, don't lead Mary astray.'

'Oh, you be careful, Phil,' said Sir William, with a laugh. 'Mary and I are getting ready to elope.'

They all laughed heartily. Nosseross moved away; then returned, in a roundabout route, and stood near their table.

> 'I got you under my skin
> I feel you deep in the heart of me . . .'

sang the drummer . . .

Nosseross heard Sir William Cheshunt's voice saying: 'What is there to be scared of?'

Mary replied: 'He can scare other people, but he can't scare me.'

> 'So deep in my heart, you're really a part of me
> I've got you under my skin . . .'

Nosseross felt that his body was being crushed between two forces: a cold weight pressing downwards, and a flaming rage pressing upwards. The music stopped. There was a crackle of applause.

'How are you doing, Sir William?' asked Nosseross, with a smile. He felt, at this moment, that if he had an axe, he could split Sir William Cheshunt in two equal halves, from head to groin, in one fearful stroke.

'Magnificent! We're just deciding when to run away. I say now, but Mary says no, next week. When do you suggest?'

Nosseross roared with laughter. 'Well, I don't know, make it next week. Mary's just ordered a fur coat: wait till I've paid the bill, and then run away with her, eh?'

'Ho-ho-ho-ho-ho! Well, just as you say, Phil, just as you say.' Cheshunt's knee touched Mary's under the table. Nosseross, watching with gimlet eyes, saw the movement.

'Excuse me, won't you?' he said, still smiling.

Adam, passing with a tray, asked: 'Where's Helen?'

'Gone,' said Nosseross.

'Where to?'

'Hell, I hope. I sacked her.' Rats were gnawing his heart. 'Adam, get a bottle of brandy, Courvoisier, and put it in the office.'

'Phil . . . don't start making a fool of yourself.'

'Do as I tell you. I got a bad heart.'

Fabian shouted: 'Helen! Where's my Helen?' The champagne was going to his head. 'Gimme Helen!'

The band drowned his voice.

Vi, who had already consumed half a bottle of whisky, threw her arms round his neck, and said: 'Harr-y! Har-ry! Help me out! My landlady's going to kick me out into the street and keep my furs for back rent!'

Fabian gave her a handful of silver and pennies, and pushed her away. Vi went back to her table, clutching the money in a hot hand. She remembered having seen, in a shop in Holborn, a kind of pop-gun. It looked like a revolver, but when you pressed the trigger, a long green snake jumped out. Next day, she decided, as soon as the shops opened, she would go and buy one of these pop-guns, and frighten everybody in the club.

'Bing-bing!' she said, and shrieked with laughter.

EIGHTEEN

On a previous drunken morning, Vi had bought a cuckoo-clock – one of those complicated masses of woodwork surmounted by a phoenix, which the Swiss peasantry carve with pen-knives. Why had she bought a cuckoo-clock? She liked to see the cuckoo pop out. It made her start, and then laugh. For two or three days she spent most of her spare time sitting under the clock, anxiously looking at her wrist-watch and waiting for the hours to strike. Sometimes, her impatience overcoming her, she would urge on the hands of the clock with surreptitious pushes. Then something went wrong with the machinery. Sometimes, the cuckoo only half emerged, with one feeble pipe. Sometimes – especially at ten minutes past three – it rushed out with maniacal vigour, and shrieked *Cuckoo!* fifteen times. On such occasions, Vi would jump up, whirl round, stare, open-mouthed, and finally sigh, and say: 'Isn't it lovely?' But after a week or so she had grown tired of it, and given it to Helen in exchange for a powder-bowl shaped like a lady in a crinoline, and a cylindrical box which, when picked up, mooed like a cow.

The cuckoo-clock now hung in Helen's room. Helen, who was adroit with her fingers, had adjusted it to keep accurate time.

This afternoon, the cuckoo – evil, clamorous bird; vulture screeching over the corpses of dying hours! – jumped out of its hole and cried four times.

'I don't know,' said Vi. 'You're lucky. *I* couldn't do anything with him. Lousy cuckoo! He always went off when I was just getting to sleep. Once, he let out twenty-five pips . . .' She laughed. It occurred to her that it would be an excellent joke to buy an egg, and break it on the floor under the clock, and then say that the cuckoo had laid it.

'Why, d'you want it back again?' asked Helen.

'N-o, no, that's all right.'

'Say so if you do.'

'*I* don't want it. I tell you what; I'll give you my orange shoes for it, and a pop-gun. When you pull the trigger, a snake jumps out. Laugh! You'd die.'

'What happened last night?' asked Helen.

'I made about thirty bob.'

'I mean, after I left; what was said?'

'Fabian kept asking for you. Phil got tight. He got through two bottles of brandy.'

Helen smiled. 'Why?

'Gord knows. He got tight. Adam had to stay behind with him. Mary didn't half create. She said it was disgusting. Old Bill Cheshunt saw her home in a taxi . . . Christ, was old Phil tight! He gave Adam a black eye.'

'*Did* he? And what did Adam do?'

'Oh, he was ever so nice about it. He just said: "Take it easy, Phil," and he picked him up like a chair, and laid him down. Why did you leave so sudden? Did you get the sack?'

'Mary made mischief. Nosseross started to argue, so I left. But I told him something first . . . Mary and Sir William Cheshunt! I can't understand men falling for such types. He must have an awful lot of money. I once saw his photo in the *Bystander*.'

Vi replied: 'He owns the whole of Yorkshire.'

'Don't be silly.'

'My oath! He once took a girl out of the Red Rose, and he gave her a banking account, and a car, and Christ knows what all. She used to come in, sometimes, and show the girls a cheque-book with about two hundred pages in it. Little blue cheques. Luck, eh? That's what Mary's after. Well, so what you going to do now?'

'I'm certainly not going to starve! I'm going to make some big money, some real money, instead of all these silly little pounds.'

'Fabian gave me fifteen bob,' said Vi.

'I'm finished with shillings. He's quite nice, isn't he?' said Helen.

'These little fellers often have more go in them than some of these great big 'uns. Most little men are clever,' said Vi, 'look at Nosseross. Look at whatsiname.'

'Fabian's got money, I believe?' asked Helen.

'Never goes out with less than a hundred quid in his pocket. He's got property.'

'What property?'

'Oh, just property.'

'Oh.'

Vi lit a cigarette, and said: 'You know, a girl with your looks could do a lot better for herself than Adam.'

'What d'you mean?'

'Oh, I'm not saying anything against Adam, but he . . . well, you know, sort of . . .'

'Ssh! He's coming in now.'

Vi rose, with a wink. 'I'll leave you two!'

Adam knocked at the door.

* * *

'What happened, Helen?' he asked.

'Mary had it her way after all. I got the sack.'

Adam laughed.

'I suppose, on the whole, you're rather pleased!' said Helen.

'Not altogether sorry.'

'And now say: "It's a rotten business." Well, suggest something better, then, instead of giggling and trying to look superior! But, whatever you say, you can't deny that we've got to *eat*; at least, I have –'

'Don't let's quarrel, Helen. I'm tired.'

'I hear Nosseross was drunk.'

'Drunk as a coot. Poor old Nosseross! When a man like that goes off the wagon, he bites dust.'

'What happened?'

'I took him home and put him to bed. He offered me a fiver, but I couldn't very well take it.'

'Adam, you're crazy! How far do you think you're going to get if you behave like that?'

'Oh . . . Nosseross is a good fellow. I like him. So do you expect me to take five pounds off him for putting him to bed? I'd do that much for my worst enemy.'

'You know we need every farthing –'

'That doesn't mean to say I eat dirt, Helen! But what do you propose to do now?'

Helen said firmly: 'I propose to raise money and start a club in time for the Coronation. You're going to help me, eh?'

'Helen, I don't *want* to!'

'You promised!'

'I didn't promise. I –'

'All right, if you want to wriggle out. But I despise people who wriggle out. Why didn't you say in the first place –'

'I did! And I'm not trying to wriggle out. Only I never promised.'

'You did; well, practically, anyway . . . But you're tired. Lie down, and rest . . . Adam, my poor darling, what have you done to your eye?'

'Nosseross did it, accidentally. My God, I'm tired . . .'

'Just relax. Oh, Adam, I do want to see you famous and successful. But how can we ever get anywhere if we have to keep struggling and struggling?'

'I don't know.'

'We could be quite well off, in a little while –'

'Oh, Helen, forget about your club for a little while!'

Adam's eyes closed. Helen watched the clock. At ten past four she began to dress, with great care, in her new blue-and-white two-piece. Adam awoke, and asked, sleepily: 'Where are you going?'

'Shopping.'

She reached Raoul's, in Bond Street, at five past five.

Fabian was waiting for her.

* * *

'You're marvellous,' said Fabian, staring at her. 'Now who'd imagine you worked in the Silver Fox all night long? What a figure! What a skin! You look like real class, and you know how to carry your clothes. Boy, what a woman!'

'Well, I'm glad you approve,' said Helen, pouring tea. 'One lump?'

'Huh? Oh, sure . . .'

Helen said, suddenly: 'I got the sack last night.'

'You got the sack? Jesus, Nosseross must be crazy. So what are you going to do for a job now?'

'D'you know what I'm going to do, Harry? I'm going to make some big money myself. I'm going to open a club of my own.'

'That takes jack.'

'I know; that's the trouble.'

Fabian asked: 'Got any saved up?'

'Not one single penny..'

'You know, it's not a bad idea,' said Fabian, very thoughtfully. 'There's money in that racket . . .'

'I calculate it wouldn't take very much to start. I'd start with a smallish one, big enough to seat sixty or seventy people. I want to open it in time for the Coronation. I've watched, and I know exactly how they're run. There'll be about ten million people pouring into the West End during Coronation week, and millions of pounds spent. I'd like to get hold of some of it.'

Fabian gaped. 'By God, you're smart! You're a smart girl! You're going to go a long way.'

Helen replied, frankly: 'I propose to. I came into this night-club business for what I could get out of it. I don't propose to stay in it all my life. I'm going to make some large money, quickly. I'm *going* to go a long way. Finance me.'

'Uh?'

'Finance me,' said Helen, coolly. 'Invest a hundred pounds or so with me and you'll see.'

Fabian was disconcerted. He coughed, and said: 'Listen, kid. Sometimes I may be a bit of a mug. I do all sorts of crazy things, and I've slung thousands and thousands down the drain.' He said this slowly and earnestly, to give himself time to think. Then he went on, rapidly: 'But when it comes to judging people, I never go wrong. I like you. You got brains and ambition. You want a hundred?'

'At the very least.'

'Then I'll give it to you.'

Helen looked at him. Fabian, by day, was not the same as Fabian by night. There was something uneasy about him. The machine-gun speed of his speech suggested hurry. His glance flickered about the tea-room, as if he half feared to see some long-expected enemy.

Fabian added: 'All being well, I'll let you have it in the next few days.'

Helen had almost hoped that he might dig a hand into a fat

wallet, throw down a bundle of white banknotes, and say: 'There!' But she reasoned: '*He's a business-man. He wouldn't be where he is today if he weren't cautious.*' She decided to meet caution with caution, and said: 'Very well. It would, of course, be a purely business arrangement –' She looked deep into his eyes for a moment – 'quite apart from our private affairs, of course, Harry . . . How soon can you let me know, definitely?'

'I can let you know definitely in two or three days' time,' said Fabian. 'Most of my English money's tied up at the moment, and I'm waiting for a royalty cheque from New York. You see, kid, this wrestling racket has cost me a packet in ready cash, and I don't want to sell any of my shares . . .'

'No, of course not,' said Helen. 'I only want to know if I can rely on you.'

'Oh, you can rely on me all right.'

'There's another friend of mine, with capital, who wants to come in.'

'A man-friend?'

'Only a friend,' said Helen.

'Count me in!' said Fabian, slapping the table. 'I'm your partner . . . But, Helen; you and me are going to get along together, ain't we?'

Helen pressed his hand, and said, in a voice like warm cream: 'We certainly are, Harry!'

Fabian's voice was unsteady, as he said: 'I'm a guy that goes the whole hog. Are you?'

'All or nothing,' said Helen, nodding. 'I like a man who knows what he wants and goes all out to get it. That's what attracted me to you from the start.'

Fabian loved a compliment. He smiled.

'You've got vitality and force,' said Helen.

'Jesus, kid, I'm *crazy* about you!' he said.

'To get back to business –'

'To hell with business,' said Fabian, red in the face. 'I'm with you. You can have the hundred quid. We'll be partners in business . . . and pleasure.'

'Then I can rely absolutely on you,' said Helen.

'Absolutely,' said Fabian. 'Absolutely!'

'I can be sure of it?'

'On my honour.' As he said this, Fabian experienced a curious sensation of misery. What was it? Was it that for the first time in his life he had become aware of the appalling burden of accumulating lies with which he loaded his soul from hour to hour – the closing coils of deceit which he spun about himself day after day? There passed through his mind a vision of life free from vanity, fiction and subterfuge – one flicker of retrospect, in which he saw, with the heart-breaking nostalgia of a plainsman lost in a forest, a bygone period in his life when black was black and white was white; when one sinned, and confessed, and breathed again. *'Why do I always have to start these tales? They aren't necessary!'* he said to himself.

But all this passed in the blink of an eye. Even as he said: 'On my honour,' he was conceiving one of his tortuous plans of campaign: *'Okay . . . I can probably raise fifty, and flash it . . . Keep her waiting a bit: "The rest is coming." In the meantime, date her. What dame stands a chance against me? She falls, lock, stock and barrel. Zoë takes a trip. I have some money in hand. Okay, then; I start a bottle-party with this bride. Why not? Nosseross makes plenty, and she's got brains . . .'*

Helen, watching him from behind a friendly smile; thought: *'If I can rely oh him, well and good. If he's got the money I'll even let him have me – once. Once only makes them want all the more. Who's to know? I shan't lose my head. There's always Adam; between us we ought to be able to raise enough, if Fabian fails . . . If not . . .'*

'Bill!' said Fabian to the waitress. 'Hell, I got to get back to the gym . . .'

NINETEEN

The Strangler was waiting for him. He put two fingers against Fabian's chest and stopped him. 'Listen, Harry, did you forget?'

'Did I forget what?'

Fabian sucked in his upper lip. 'For crying out loud, Strangler, don't hand me no riddles. I'm worried. Can't you guys see when a guy's *worried*? I got the whole world on my shoulders. So say what you want to say, and shut up.'

'Don't you remember what you promised to bring me?'

'What?'

'Red silk dressing-gown –'

'Oh, hell, yes; with your name in gold letters across the back . . . Sure, sure, sure. Sure, Strangler, I been along to the shop. And listen; you're such a big feller, such a tremendous big feller, they got to make it specially for you. So listen; you got to wait a day or two more, see? So be a good boy, eh?'

'You not kiddin'?'

'Listen,' said Fabian, 'do you want me to beat you up? Did you ever know me to tell a lie? By God, I'll tie your legs round your neck if you call me a liar.'

'Well, when do I get it?'

'God's truth, give 'em a chance to *make* it! Two days; maybe three.'

'You won't let me down?'

'I wouldn't let my worst enemy down, Strangler, let alone you, and you're my best friend.'

'Then don't forget, Harry. I need that red silk dressing-gown with my name in gold letters 'cross the back. I got a woman to meet.'

Fabian went downstairs. In the entrance to the gymnasium Bert was waiting. Fabian turned pale. They stood face to face in the passage.

'You, eh? What you want?'

'Word wiv you.'

'Another word, eh? Well, before you start – I warn you once and for all; if you start any stuff like you started last time, I'll –'

'Listen,' said Bert. He put both hands behind him, and stuck out his chin. 'I got a proposition. Don't go up in the air before I finished: listen. You wanna be a big noise. All right. I got a proposition.'

'What proposition? And make it snappy.'

'I wanna take three pitches in Diamond Road Market; green-grocery: fruit, vegetables, salads. It's more than one can 'andle, and 'ard graft for two or three. There's a good livin' in it. A few quid would start it. What d'you say?'

Fabian was unable to repress a laugh.

'Will yer listen. You want money; I want money; and there's money in it, and nothink to be ashamed of. Well?'

'Are you seriously suggesting I should go in a market? Me? Shouting by a stall? I'm Fabian Promotions. What do you take me for?'

Bert said, persuasively: 'You wouldn't have to look like a coster. We'd wear white coats.'

'Can you imagine *me* in a white coat?'

'Why not? There's quids in it. In the end we could 'ave shops. Other big firms have started small. Look at Beecham's Pills – old man Beecham used to stand in a market, in a 'igh 'at, shahtin' 'is guts aht . . .'

'Shut up,' said Fabian. 'Me a shopkeeper! You're crazy.'

'Look at the fives. Look at Lyons –'

'How much would it take.'

'We could start in style on a pony.'

'Chicken-feed!' said Fabian. 'Twenty-five quid!'

'Well? What d'you say, 'Arry?'

'I'll finance you,' said Fabian. 'I'll give you twenty-five quid, and you give me a third of the profits.'

Bert uttered an impatient exclamation: 'Kah! You don't see what I mean. I wanna be friends wiv yer. Come in wiv me and go straight. You 'and a few bob over to Zoë for a change – you'll feel different, 'Arry –'

'Pipe down. I got a business here that's going to mean thousands.'

'It might and it mightn't. I wouldn't give yer a tosser for it.'

'Listen, Bert; you've shoved that bloody barrow till you've shoved your bloody brains out. You're ignorant, ignorant as dirt. I've stood for a lot from you, just because you're ignorant, ignorant! But I'll tell you one thing; when you come to *me* with your boloney about *me* standing in market with a barrow of lousy fruit – that's an insult.'

'It's you wot's bloody ignorant! I'm tryin' to *save* yer. All this fanny about wrestlin', all this madam –'

'You go to the Salvation bloody Army, but don't come here saving me!'

'*Aw*-right, *aw*-right, go to 'ell! I'm finished wiv yer.'

Bert went out. Fabian called after him: 'Bert! Just a minute!'
'Wot?'
'Listen, Bert, you're a . . . well, listen. Wanna couple o' quid?'
'No.'
'Independent, eh? Listen, you want to start that fruit racket?'
'Wiv you, yes.'
'I'm otherwise engaged. But if you want to start it, I can find you a pony. I don't want no share of the profits, see? I'll get you a pony, and you can pay me back when you can. If you want a pony, say so, and I can go right inside this very minute and raise it for you. Well?'
'I can't understand yer, 'Arry. Even when you was a nipper, you was like that. You used to 'arf-inch suckers orf the barrers, and give 'em away afterwards. Yet you go and . . . Nah listen, 'Arry; come in wiv me. You won't 'ave to shaht in the market if you don't want to. You won't 'ave to wear a white coat, even. You can do the books, an' I'll teach you 'ow to buy. I'll –'
'No. But if you *want* a pony –'
'So long, 'Arry,' said Bert, sadly. He held out his hand. Fabian hesitated, then shook it. Bert added, looking at his boots: 'I'm sorry if I showed yer up the other night, only . . .'
'Forget it,' said Fabian, and went indoors.

* * *

He found Figler in the office, making calculations on the back of an old envelope.
'Joe,' he said, 'I want to borrow fifty quid.'
'Yeh? I wish you luck.'
'Would you lend me it?'
'Who, me? Fifty pounds? All the cash I've got is tied up here . . . And don't ask me to let you take any money out of the business. I'm getting fed up with it as it is.'
'You're getting fed up with it?'
Figler made a weary gesture. From the gymnasium came the noise of muffled shouts and the slapping of hands on bare flesh. 'I'm not used to this kind of business. I try anything once; but this is too tame.'
'What's tame about it?'

'There isn't any life in it. Besides . . . overheads; staff; bills, bills, bills; all this paying cash all the time – I don't like it.'

'You're crazy! We're right on the point of big money, only just starting. And you get fed up! Hell, I thought you was a man with guts! We'll make a clear eighty or a hundred quid on the next show alone.'

'It isn't my line. I'm used to a business where I handle property without paying out a penny in cash. And here? What do I do? Sit and wait. Everything's in the air. It's all guess-work. It's like playing cards. Perhaps people will come; perhaps they won't come. Perhaps and perhaps and perhaps! And we've got money tied up. And if there's an earthquake? And if there's a war? I don't like having capital tied up in anything. I don't like it.'

'But this next show's going to be a sensation.'

'What guarantee have you?'

'What guarantee, you say? Every guarantee! We got popular names. We got a good hall. We got posters everywhere in every café. I've made special arrangements for a surprise item – I'm getting it into the papers. Old Ali's making a come-back – it'll be a scream. People will come a thousand miles to see it. Old Ali'll drag in all the Coronation Yanks – he used to be a top-liner in the States. They still put his picture in *The Ring*. And you say what guarantee!'

'Uh . . .'

'Well what do you want to do, then?'

'Pack it up,' said Figler.

'What? You're crazy! We're going right ahead.'

'You forget that I have two-thirds of the say in this business.'

'So what?'

'You furthermore forget that I am the actual proprietor of Fabian Promotions, and that you are employed by me, accord-ing to the agreement.'

'That's a lie! I didn't sign any such agreement.'

Figler addressed the ceiling: 'That's how these people are! They sign an agreement, without looking at what they sign . . . I've got the paper with your signature; so what more do you want? I have the right to close up the business if I think fit.'

Fabian shrieked: 'What? If you're trying any funny stuff with me, I'll tear your legs off and smash you over the head with 'em!'

Figler replied: 'I'm shivering with fright.'

Fabian stabbed the desk with a paper-knife. There was something invincible about Figler – all the power of black and white, seals, signatures, stamps and the soft, octopus-strength of the law. Fabian's little hollow soul swelled with hatred like a balloon. But he swallowed his anger, and said: 'What d'you want?'

'What are you so annoyed about? I'm not trying to take anything away from you. I'm going to wind up Fabian Promotions.'

'I see. You ain't taking nothing away from me, but you're going to wind up the racket, eh? And I lose my fifty quid, eh?'

'On the contrary, you get your fifty pounds back.'

'And how much have we got in the bank?'

'Less than a hundred pounds.'

'And you're going to give me back all of my fifty?'

'Yes.'

Fabian exploded again: 'You double-crossing old bastard! You got something up your sleeve!'

'Keep calm. I only want to cut losses.'

'We haven't started yet! Hell –'

'I'm hoping we'll get our money back on the show. After the next show, I quit.'

'Yeah? Well, if you want to quit, I don't. We stand to make money. You can draw out your hundred quid, and I'll carry on.'

'You can do what you like. I'm getting out. As a matter of fact, there's another proposition I'm interested in, and I shan't have time for this.'

'What other proposition?'

'It doesn't concern you, Harry. I'll take my hundred, you take your fifty, and anything left over, we'll divide fifty-fifty; and finished. Yes?'

'Okay,' said Fabian, 'but I'd like to know what you've got up your sleeve.'

'Ah, you know *me*,' said Figler, with a curious smile. 'I got to have life, I got to be on the go, I got to change about from one thing to another. I don't like a business where you have to sit about. What are you worrying for? We'll each get out with our money back, and a profit, a few pounds profit. We've made a living out of it while we've been in it, haven't we? Ah, you're a silly boy, Harry . . .'

'I still think you've got something up your sleeve.'

'I haven't, Harry. I never stay in one business long. If I did, I might make a fortune, but I can't. I got to move about – make a few pounds, and then try something else . . .'

'I bet you're trying some funny business.'

'Honest to God! Besides, a boy with brains like yours can carry on without me . . . If you don't want to draw your fifty pounds out, *in cash* . . .'

'I need fifty pounds in cash.'

'Then you can take it out, almost at once, if you like; and I'll rely on the proceeds of the show.'

'We're splitting that, fifty-fifty.'

'Certainly; *after* I cover my original hundred pounds, we divide the rest fifty-fifty.'

Fabian hesitated; but how could he resist the idea of fifty pounds in cash? He said, sullenly: 'I need that fifty; I need it bad. Okay, I'll draw it out . . . I got another proposition, too. And after the next show we split fifty-fifty, and quit . . . But I still think you got something up your sleeve.'

From the gymnasium came the noise of two men shouting together.

'That's Ali and the boy from Cyprus,' said Figler. 'I wish you'd talk to them . . . squabbling day and night.'

'I'll tear their legs off,' said Fabian, going out.

As the door closed, Figler smiled to himself.

* * *

Kration was roaring with laughter, while Ali grunted with rage. Adam stood between them.

'What's the trouble?' said Fabian.

Ali replied: 'There is only two kinds of Cypriot. There is the Cypriot who always giggles, and the Cypriot who never smiles.'

'Hoh-hoh-hoh!' laughed Kration.

'The first kind laughs all the time because he is too stupid to see that he is really something to weep at; the other frowns all the time because he is too foolish to see how ridiculous he is.'

Kration still laughed. Ali went on, at the top of his voice: 'They all wave their hair. They have only three trades. There is no Cypriot who is not a barber, a tailor or a kitchen-boy. In the end they all call themselves wrestlers. But damn it, their national sport is dominoes. They bang down the dominoes, and shout – that is the game. They make love to servant-girls who take them to the pictures. Then they are national heroes. And they all fight like slaves. *Ptoo*, and *ptoo* on the Cypriot!'

'Big belly!' laughed Kration, showing twenty brilliant teeth. When Kration laughed he looked like a man who was completely satisfied with himself. The expression of his smiling face said: 'If I were not Kration, I should be God Almighty.' But as soon as his mouth closed his face changed. Savagery came into it. He looked strong and ferocious enough to tear himself apart. His hair crouched low on his forehead, trying to obliterate his eyebrows; his eyebrows, colliding over his nose in a spray of black hair, endeavoured to smother his eyes; and only the flat, heavy prow of his nose kept his eyes apart – otherwise, they would have snapped at each other. Meanwhile they waited, smouldering, while his upper lip snarled in triumph over the lower, which, from time to time, jumped up and clamped down on it. Turkey, Greece and Africa waged war in his veins. Even his hair carried on ancient warfare. There was antagonism in his very follicles, and the hair writhed out, enormously thick, twisted, rebellious, kinked, frizzled and dried up.

He said to Adam: 'He too old to hit. I hit him once, he die. One finger enough. Tiss finger: look!' He wagged a forefinger.

'Lay off!' said Fabian.

'He said I was old! He said I was fat.'

Fabian grinned. 'Old? Fat? Hell, can't we all see you're a two-year-old? Ain't you wasting away to a shadow?'

'You may joke, yes. But let me fight him. I will show him how old I am . . . *Tfoo*, I say! Didn't your grandmother learn that a Turk was a better man than a Cypriot while your grandfather hid under the bed? Mongrel!'

'You –'

'Hold um!' yelled Fabian, and attached himself, like a mosquito, to Ali's wrist, while Adam threw his arms round Kration and held him. The Cypriot shook himself. Adam's feet left the floor.

'Listen! Listen!' shouted Fabian. 'What's the excitement? You two are having a chance to fight it out in the ring. I'm billing you as a surprise item for next show. Why waste your energy down here, mugs? Ali is making a come-back, see? Ali the Terrible Turk, and Kration. See?'

'Good,' said Ali.

'No,' said Kration, 'my friends will laugh at me for fighting an old man.'

'Two guineas apiece!' said Fabian.

'No,' said Kration.

Ali suggested: 'Give him four, my two and his two. I will fight him for nothing.'

'Well?' said Fabian.

'Right,' said Kration.

Ali sneered. 'They can be bought, these champions. *Ptoo!* He would sell his brother and sister for a small cup of coffee. His friends would laugh at him! *Hou!* They will laugh all the more when I tie him up like a brown-paper parcel.'

Kration replied, over his shoulder: 'Fat guts, say your prayers.'

Adam took Fabian aside, and said: 'Seriously, are you going to let those two fight?'

'Why not?'

'It's a crime! Ali's nearly seventy; Kration's not yet thirty. Ali's old, but he won't admit it. And he's sick.'

'Boloney! He's a tiger.'

'But –'

'What are you worrying about? Afraid he'll drop dead, or something?'

'I'm afraid he'll take a beating, and I don't want to see it.'

'Then stay away.'

'I'll give you a fiver if you'll call the fight off.'

'Are you trying to offer me money to interfere with sport? Besides, there's more than that in it for me.'

'Oh, go and drown yourself.' Adam went to the dressing-room, and found Ali. 'Ali, do me a favour. Call this crazy fight off.'

'Why?'

'Why? You get nothing for it, and besides, Kration's not a wrestler; he's rough-house specialist; a killer.'

'Yah? And I am a hangman.'

'But Ali!'

Ali turned with bulging eyes. 'Go to the devil! Go to the night-club! Leave me alone!'

Adam went home. Helen had not returned. He dressed, and went to the club.

TWENTY

He arrived at half-past nine. The doorman said to him: 'I'm glad you've come. Phil's gone off his nut. He's got a bottle of brandy in the office, there. He's been asking for you. He's got a black eye. You better go in.'

Adam opened the office door. Nosseross was sitting at his desk – or rather, writhing. His shoulders twisted; he slid from side to side in his chair, clenching his fists, and his face was sucked together in an expression horribly compounded of pain and shame. A black bruise kept his left eye closed. In front of him stood a brandy bottle.

'Phil! What's the matter?'

'Matter?' said Nosseross, in a level voice. 'Matter? Nothing. Why?'

'Who gave you that eye?'

Nosseross said: 'I got his front teeth anyway. He won't be able to kiss her, much, not tonight, he won't.'

'Whose front teeth?'

'Cheshunt's.'

'Why, has he –'

'Yes, he has. He's gone off with Mary. Paris. And that's that. See?'

'How did it happen?'

'They came in here about six this evening. The two of 'em together. She had a case packed. She said: "Phil, I'm sorry. I found somebody I like better than you. We're going away." Just like that.'

'What did you say?'

'I just said: "Once a hostess, always a hostess. You always were a bit of a whore. Get out and stay out." That's what I said. I wasn't going to go down on my knees and say: "Don't go." Then he said: "You can't say things like that to the woman I love," and he gave me this eye.'

'And then?'

'I gave him a left-right, right in the teeth. That knocked the fight out of him. Then I said: "You louse. You came in looking for tarts, and you found one," I said, "I picked her up out of the gutter, and I'm slinging her back." And I said to her: "You're a fool, a fool to yourself, like all cheap whores. You were okay for ever with me," I said, "I've got more money than you ever thought I had, and you could have done what you liked with me as long as you played straight," I said. "But now, finish as you started. How long d'you think he'll keep you hanging around. Three months? Six months? And then you can go back on the clubs, and try and dance, and go to bed with the agents to get a two-quid engagement; and you'll end up like all the rest," I said. I said: "You played me for a mug. I'd cut your throat from ear to ear," I said, "but when you're dead, you're finished, you're out of everything, you're free, free as the air. Nobody ever double-crossed me and got away with it, nobody, ever. So get out and live. Live and suffer. And if you ever try and come back to me, I'll spit in your face and kick you out."'

Nosseross drank a tumblerful of brandy, and then went on: 'D'you know what she said then? She said . . . She said . . . She . . . Adam, get me another bottle.'

'No, no more,' said Adam, 'don't drink any more.'

'For Christ's sake, Adam, do as I say!'

Adam went out. When he returned, with the bottle, Nosseross had opened a drawer. He saw the blue glint of steel, leapt across the office, and gripped Nosseross's wrist. For a second or two, the wiry strength of Nosseross contended with the heavy force of Adam. Then the pistol lay in Adam's hand – a sinister old blue Parabellum, with a thin snout. He took out the clip of cartridges, and gave the pistol back to Nosseross.

'Is any woman worth that?' he asked.

Nosseross replied, in a cracked voice: 'I've had a million women. This one got me. What do I want to go on for? What for? I'm used up, I'm finished.'

'Take it easy,' said Adam, 'there are other things to do besides making love to women. God Almighty, there's about ten stone of you. That odd few ounces isn't all you've got.'

'D'you know what she said?' asked Nosseross. 'She said: "You're old enough to be my grandfather, you horrible old Egyptian mummy; and if you had all the money in the world I couldn't stay with you another night. Every time you touch me, you make me sick" – she said this in front of him, mind you! – "And anyway, I might as well be with a mummy, for all the good you are. I get as much thrill out of sleeping on my own – more," she said; and she said: "You old monkey, you think you're clever, but what's the use of that? You're not even a man any more." And then she went out with Cheshunt. Oh, I wish to Christ I'd remembered that gun then! I'd given them a bullet each.'

'And hung?'

'Why not? You mark my words, Adam, when you get to my age . . . open that bottle . . . there's nothing much more to live for. It's not so much . . . losing a woman; not so much that alone; but it's the *shame*. You want to kick yourself, tear yourself to bits! I'm clever, Adam, and I've had enough women to . . . to . . . But when a thing like this happens, there's nothing you can do! Stay here. Don't go . . . fill that glass . . .'

Adam thought: '*What are women, that a man should make them his life? What are women that a man should sacrifice his work to them? Blind-alleys. A man's a fool to pour everything he has into a woman's lap.*'

He said: 'What can I do to help you?'

Nosseross replied: 'Damn all. I can't help myself. You can't help me . . . But the disgrace of it is, Adam; the bloody, crying disgrace of it is, Adam, that I know she'll come back when Cheshunt's done with her, *and I'll take her back*! I shan't be able to help myself. I shan't even be able to look like a man any more.'

'I can't understand that,' said Adam. '*Are* you a man? Use your will. If I thought a thing like that might happen, God, I'd go away; thousands of miles! I'd like to see the woman who could do that to me . . .' He paused as he thought of the naked body of Helen, and how it could draw him away from the red clay as a vortex draws down a straw. He became angry, and added: 'You can fight against it. You can beat it! It stings, like salt in a cut; but it passes! If you get grit in your eye, cry it out and forget it! By God, even now I wouldn't let a woman do that to me – and you're twice as old as me!'

'Yes. I know. You're young. You're twice as young as me. A hundred women are ready for you, for every one that finishes with you. But me, I'm old, and this is my last.'

'What if it is? Isn't there anything else to interest you, except twenty minutes on top of a girl?'

'I ask you . . . give me another drink . . . I ask you, once you cut out eating, drinking and women, what is there left? I used to be able to get a kick out of a hard fight, a rough house, competition, tricky business, danger. I'm beyond that now. Besides, I got money, plenty money. I don't eat much, I don't enjoy drinking, I never sleep more than four hours – and there's twenty-four in a day! And I tell you, that woman was the last thing in my life!'

'Then you've built your life up wrong. You're old. I'm young. You know a lot. I know very little. But I can tell you one thing. If you've got to rely on tickling your guts for the pleasure you get out of life, then you're little more than a beast on two legs, and this kind of thing is bound to happen.'

Nosseross shook with drunken laughter. 'Then what? Reading poetry? Looking at the stars?'

'Well, why not?'

'Why not? I'll tell you why not. Because I'm alive. I'm a live man. I've always worked hard and played hard. I've got no regrets –'

'No regrets? I always hear that. People who make a mess of their lives always say: "I've got no regrets." But they whine all the same.'

'Who's whining?'

'You are!' cried Adam, moved to an inexplicable anger. 'You're whining. "I worked hard and I played hard." What does that mean, tell me! I'll tell you! It means that you fiddled and chiselled and chased money till you got a headache, and then swallowed a bottle of booze and went to bed with a bird! A great life! You call that living hard? Fool!' shouted Adam. 'You don't live at all! You live only for your belly! Make something before you die! Make something, if only a family! You can't live only for yourself. You've got to make *something* beyond yourself – otherwise you end up as you're ending up now, crying into a bloody bottle.'

'You think you're smart,' muttered Nosseross, 'but wait, wait!'

'When I think of a man like you, I could spit! I could spit blood. You've got everything, yet you're only manure for a grave-yard. You're clever. A brain like yours, with a proper will behind it . . . what couldn't you do? But no, you have to go chasing after rubbish.'

'Wait. Wait. You're smart. But wait. Old age'll get you, too. Ten years, twenty years, thirty years . . . wait, wait, you wait . . .'

And, his body deadened with alcohol, cut adrift from his senses by an encompassing fog of brandy-fumes, his mind turned in upon itself. He seemed to be looking into his own skull, but it had become as vast as the dome of the sky, and spangled with stars, and filled with a heaving sea. He felt, for a moment, the surge of a mighty eloquence; but words lost themselves in mist before they reached his lips. He only said: 'And then . . .'

After that he was silent.

* * *

This is a fact: arranged in order, the mind of Nosseross the night-club man, would be as rich as the mind of Da Vinci.

There is a memory behind the consciousness, and here, as in a deep sea, are hidden incalculable jewels of wisdom – every thought, word, sound, fear, hope, passion – all experience – everything in life. The few things we know and remember are like a pinch of dried salt on the shore of this ocean of knowledge that flows in chaos within us. Behind the things of which we are aware lies a dim and profound wilderness of moving shadows, encrusted with the eggs of forgotten inspirations, piled with sunken treasures, and the cracked shells of rejected things.

But because we are still animals, our minds must remain hungry in the midst of this abundance. We are the apes that have not yet learned to fish – the cavemen who have not yet discovered fire – still only mammals! We still blink, without comprehension and without desire, at the wild horizons of the universe.

Between ourselves and our undiscovered souls we build impenetrable walls. And so it seems that man suffers and dies in vain; that he is an insect, caught in the ticking cogs of time. But beyond the dictates of his little loves and hungers, mightier laws ordain the life of man.

All life is a cycle of ripening and decay. The seed which you plant in the soil goes back to the dirt in dung; the seed which you plant in the womb goes back to the earth in abominable putrefaction – yet life stirs in the rottenness; life struggles upwards, from change to change; and death and decay beget higher life. Out of the rottenness of dead leaves creep higher and more fruitful trees. Tree fights tree, until out of the frenzy of the wrestling jungle climbs the tree that seems to touch the sky. Even the grass strives, blade against blade, towards the sun – rising, falling, and growing again. Life moves eternally upwards.

And if a man dies with his promise unfulfilled, his seed shall keep alive that promise until it shall be fulfilled. A tongueless man may pass through his loins his unsung music, to gladden the hearts of another generation. The harlot may carry in her womb the builder, the cleanser, the healer or the lawgiver of tomorrow, just as the seeds of beautiful shrubs are carried out to replenish the wastelands in the dung of bedraggled wild birds. Nothing can be lost!

And there are some seeds which time and the wandering wind drive from place to place, until they are dried up. But, in wandering, these seeds sometimes gather virtue, because they are destined to blossom and fructify later on.

There descended over the brain of Nosseross a blanket of resignation; a sense of predestination; a hollow feeling of doom.

He said: 'Next time . . .'

Adam asked: 'Black coffee?'

'No . . . no. I'm going to finish this bottle, and sleep for an hour. You take charge of the club. I can't go out there with this eye . . . and anyway . . . Get that white coat off; get into your dinner-jacket . . . Take over. Authority; you're manager. I'm asleep. Phil Nosseross is . . . indisposed.'

Adam picked him up and laid him on the couch; then turned out the light and went out into the club.

* * *

At dawn, he shook Nosseross, who awoke with a groan.

'Wake up, Phil. We're closing.'

'What's . . . what's . . . Oh-oh, my head . . .'

Nosseross blinked and dragged himself back to consciousness. 'How did we do?'

'It was a good night,' said Adam. 'We cleared about forty to forty-five pounds.' He handed Nosseross a bundle of notes and some silver.

'Good boy. Take a tenner.'

'No, that's all right.'

'Do as I tell you. You were the manager. Take a tenner. Here, take it.'

Adam put ten pound notes in his pocket. 'Come and eat something,' he said.

'Listen, Adam, I like you. You're honest. You're sensible, too. I feel all shaken up. I want to be, sort of, away from things for a bit. I want you to take charge of the club for a couple of weeks or so. I'll give you a third of the profits.'

Adam offered Nosseross tomato-juice in a teacup. 'No,' he said, 'I'm not keen.'

'What d'you mean? This place clears on an average a hundred and fifty pounds a week. I'm offering you about fifty!'

'I'm quitting this business, anyway.'

'You're what? Listen, Adam, you wouldn't do that! Why, my God, you're the only person in the world I feel I can trust! Listen, Adam, I like you. What d'you want to leave for?'

'I've got a fancy to do some sculpture.'

'Adam, I like you, and I regard you as a friend; and now you want to walk out on me. Why? Have I treated you wrong? Stick by me a bit, now, for Christ's sake! You've got time for sculpture – tons of time, tons of time, all your life before you! I'm only asking you to stand by me for a few weeks. You'd make yourself some money, too. You'd get about fifty a week. Do you want more?'

'It's not that, but –'

'Didn't I give you a job when you came in here with no soles to your shoes?'

'Yes, I know, but –'

Nosseross suddenly shouted, in astonishment: 'What the bloody hell am I sitting here begging you to stand by me for? Damn your eyes! Get out and go to hell! I just ask you to stay with me for a week or two when I'm down, and you choose that moment to walk out on me. Get to hell out of here, then, if you want to quit when I'm sick. You dirty rat!'

'Well, look, Phil, if you like I'll stay a little longer, till you kind of pull together a bit.'

'Don't pity me!'

'I don't pity you. I'll stay because I like you.'

'Then shake,' said Nosseross. 'My Christ, my nerves are all upset . . . You're my manager, on a thirty-three and one-third of the profits basis . . . And remember, you'll have Coronation week. That'll put a hundred quid in your pocket.'

'*After all,*' thought Adam, '*a few weeks more won't make much difference, and then I could have enough money in hand to work for a year in comfort.*'

'That's agreed,' he said. 'And now you've got to walk out and eat something.'

They walked through the sharp air of the morning, to the Corner House.

'Oh, my Christ,' said Nosseross, 'look who's here!'

It was Fabian, somewhat flushed with excitement, drinking coffee at an adjacent table. Even as Nosseross spoke, Fabian cried: 'Oh boy oh boy, do my eyes deceive me?' and came to their table. 'What, Phil Nosseross, you old crook, you! Listen, Phil, if you wanna see a show, come and see the one I'm running. Listen, Phil, you've heard of Ali the Terrible Turk? He's making a comeback. And is that man in form or is he in form? I'll tell you – he's in form. Is this gonna be a needle-fight, or is this gonna be a needle-fight? Boy, will they tear lumps out of each other!'

Adam said: 'I have half a mind to smack you on the nose.'

'Go on, then, smack me on the nose!' said Fabian. 'Am I supposed to be scared?'

'What is all this, anyway?' asked Nosseross.

'The fight of the century. Ali the Terrible Turk against Kration. Coming?'

'What, old Ali? He must be getting on for seventy. I saw him thirty years ago, and he wasn't anybody's chicken then. But what a fighter!' said Nosseross. 'Not much skill, mind you, and no psychology; but what a terror! Heart of a lion, and about as strong as a bear. Is he still alive?'

'You'll see,' said Fabian.

'Listen,' said Adam, 'let me referee that fight.'

'I'm refereeing it myself,' said Fabian. He grinned at Nosseross: 'He's scared in case Ali . . .'

'It's not that. Poor old Ali's finished, and you know it. He can't win. About the only thing he's got left is his pride. He's only got one eye. The only thing that keeps him going is the fact that he's never been defeated. And now you match him against a man forty years younger. You ought to be ashamed of yourself!'

'Any betting on this fight?' asked Fabian, grinning.

'With you refereeing it?' said Adam. 'Thanks.'

'Betting?' said Nosseross. 'You're crazy. Dog-racing is dirty; boxing isn't clean; racing stinks a bit; but wrestling! There hasn't been a straight match in forty years.'

Fabian grinned in Adam's face. 'I thought you'd be scared to bet on Ali,' he said.

'What odds are you laying?'

'Twenties on Kration.'

'I'll take you,' said Adam. 'Give me forty pounds to two.'

'You're on.'

'Idiot,' said Nosseross, when Fabian had gone. 'Why d'you let him rib you into giving him two pounds?'

'I'm not so sure. Old Ali'll never lie down while there's any breath in him. But I'd give a tenner to have this fight called off,' said Adam.

Helen was hardly awake; flushed, replenished by sleep, charged with energy like a powerful battery. She grasped Adam's hand with fingers as hot as the bars of a fire, and said: 'Kiss me good morning . . . Again! . . . Now tell me, did you have a good night?'

'Nosseross wants me to be manager.'

Helen sat up in bed, and cried aloud with joy. 'No! Manager? Not really? Why, that would be worth at least ten or twelve pounds a week!'

There was something infectious about her excitement. Adam laughed, and said: 'On a commission basis. I'm to get a third of all the profits.'

'A third! No, you're joking. Tell me honestly, how much?'

'Word of honour.'

'But . . . he must make nearly a hundred pounds a week!'

'He averages a hundred and fifty.'

'Then you'll get fifty?'

'Or thereabout.'

'A-dam!' cried Helen, and dragged his head down to her bosom. 'Adam! Oh *boy*!'

'You're suffocating me . . .'

He undressed, and got into bed.

'*Fif*-ty pounds a *week*! Oh, Ad-*am*!' She pounded his chest with her fists; leapt out of bed, and danced round the room, flinging her nightdress into a corner, throwing out her hands in bacchanalian gestures. Then she returned, with a stifled squeal of happiness, and pinched Adam's cheek until he grunted with pain.

'Hey! That hurts!'

'It's cold . . .' She went back to bed, and covered herself, clinging to Adam, and shivering. 'Isn't that absolutely marvellous? But you don't seem very excited, darling.'

'Oh, I am. We can save some money. It's good.'

'Good? Adam, you're marvellous! You're wonderful!'

'Ssh! D'you want Mrs Anguish to hear?'

Helen crept back to bed. 'Soon, we'll be away from this place and Mrs Anguish. Oh, Adam, you're wonderful. Why are you so marvellous?'

He thought. '*What money can do! If I produced the Elgin Marbles with one flick of my wrist, she couldn't be half as pleased . . .*'

Joking heavily, he replied: 'It runs in the family.'

TWENTY-ONE

In the office of Fabian Promotions, Fabian tapped the floor with an impatient foot, while Figler droned laboriously into the telephone: 'Yes . . . I shall want some more "God Save the King" flags, about twelve gross of them. Got it? Twelve gross of "God Save the King". And about two gross of "God Bless Their Majesties"'. Then six gross of the threepenny Union Jacks, and five hundred of those little oval heads of the King and Queen . . . Okay, all right, yes. Yes, that's the lot.' He said to Fabian, as he hung up the receiver: 'These Coronation decorations are going like hot cakes. I've got twenty-five girls on piece-work, making little King Georges and Queen Elizabeths to wear in the buttonhole, and they can't turn them out quick enough. But cardboard periscopes, you can't sell for love or money. It's funny, Harry. There's lots of money in this town, if you know how to get it.'

'Coming to the fight tonight?'

'It's old Ali, ain't it? Poor old man. Oh, listen, Harry. You promised that black fellow a red silk dressing-gown. Why don't you give it to him? It's dangerous to mess about with people like that, black men, savages. He carries a razor, and he's got a terrible temper. For fifteen shillings you can be safe and look like a gentleman at the same time. Why break promises when it only costs you a few shillings to keep them?'

'Maybe you're right. Anyway, in a few days time, we won't be in the racket any more. But it seems a pity, somehow, just as we get going . . .'

The Strangler came in, carrying a Gladstone bag. 'Harry, you got it?'

'The gown? Sure, you'll have it tomorrow.'

The Black Strangler's eyes suddenly became bloodshot. Figler saw this and said: 'Yes. They spelt your name wrong. They had to embroider it, in special gold thread, but they spelt "Strangler" wrong. You ought to have it by tomorrow, though.'

'I got to have it tomorrow.'

'You will, you will,' said Fabian.

'You promise?'

'I swear.'

'Say: "Cut my throat if I lie."'

'Cut my throat if I lie. Now scram.'

'Okay,' said the Strangler, going out.

'I didn't like the way he said that,' said Fabian. 'Oh well, hell, I got to go to the hall . . . Hey, Strangler, hold on! I'll give you a lift in my taxi . . . Coming, Joe?'

'Later.'

Figler sat quietly, smoking a cigarette. Ten minutes later, another man came down; a small, fat, dark man, with little bright eyes that glittered like black pinheads under the rim of a bowler hat.

'Hallo, Lew,' said Figler.

'Aha, Joe.' The man called Lew sat down. 'Well?'

'Oh, it'll be all right. Fabian will be out tomorrow. I'm paying him his fifty pounds, and everything will be clear. Then we can start right away.'

'Did you put the proposition to any of the wrestlers yet?'

'Not yet. But that's easy.'

'Yes, I suppose so. Poor devils; the things they do for a square meal and a flop! Give 'em a reasonable wage and their expenses paid, and they'd do murder . . . I've thought of a better name than "Embrocation".'

'What?'

'Muscle-rub. "Zok Brand Muscle-Rub". Isn't that better?'

'Not bad, not bad.'

'In times like these you've got to give things clever-sounding names, Joe. If you call Aspirin acetyl-salicylic acid, you can sell it at three times the price, although the fact remains that it's still only acetyl-salicylic acid. "Muscle-rub" carries ten times more weight than "Embrocation". When I was in the States, I was talking to a comedian. It's surprising, the effect of one word on the public. He used to try out gags. There was one gag, when he threw his watch into a wash-basin, and said: "Better rusty than lost." Not a laugh. Then, when he said, next time: "Better rusty than *missing*," it brought the house down. It's funny, but there it is.'

'Yes. You talk about America. Have you ever heard Harry Fabian trying to talk like an American?'

'No. I heard he's a smart fellow. Is he?'

'Smart? Yes and no. He could be clever, if he wasn't such a lazy little creature, and if he didn't like showing off so much. He must always look bigger than he is. Yet he's got nerve, he's got cheek, and he's even got some brains. But he reads American magazines, and pretends, just like a little boy.'

'I don't know why people have to pretend to be Americans. I suppose it's the films.'

'And again, he can't keep his thoughts on one thing for five seconds. One minute he wants to write a song; next minute he wants to buy a race-horse. A little while ago, he was crazy about wrestling. Now he's got a craze to open a club. Ah, let him go to the devil. I've lost nothing. Come and see the show?'

'We may as well.'

'You know old Ali the Terrible Turk? Fabian persuaded him to make a return to the ring. He's fighting a Greek.'

'Not old Ali! Lord, I saw him thirty years ago. He tore a muscle out of some fellow's arm – *phip!* – like that. Now this is a good idea. Ali's about sixty-eight or seventy. Well, how does he keep his strength and suppleness at his age? Why, he takes Zok Brand Rejuvenating Wafers, and massages himself with Zok Brand Muscle-Rub. See? The more you think about it, the better it looks, eh?'

'Ah, it's a pleasure . . . Have you arranged about the bottles?'

'Yes. We're having the square bottle with the moulded cap.'

'But that costs us an extra penny a bottle.'

'Joe, people *buy* bottles. Bottles are publicity. Goods don't sell on their merits. A man doesn't buy medicine because it's already cured him; he buys it because he thinks it might.'

'After all the rubbish I've been hearing, it's a pleasure to hear sensible talk for a change.'

'How does that fellow Fabian live, then?'

'On show. He'd go without food to buy you a cigar for three shillings. Actually, he lives on a woman. He thinks nobody knows.

Everybody knows. And he's always running, and hurrying . . . He works harder doing nothing than I do getting my living.'

'Well, let's go and see your fight. It'll be good to see poor old Ali again. Thirty years! Isn't it wicked, the way time flies?'

'What do you expect it to do? Stop still?'

Lew muttered: 'Last time I went to see Ali fight, I rode in a horse-bus. Those were the days!'

'Uh . . . You were younger then. It's better now, really.'

Lew trod on the accelerator of his brand-new Buick. 'I don't know. You could live on a couple of quid a week, and there were plenty of opportunities for everybody.'

'There are now, too.'

'I know, but you've got to cut everybody's throat to get any-where.'

'You always did, believe me. It's harder, now, because you're older. Competition is hotter, yes. But what do you want? Pound notes to *fall* into your pocket?'

'I want to make enough to retire on, and it's now or never.'

'How much would you retire with?'

'Twenty thousand.'

'I'd retire on half of that. What would you do if you retired?'

'God knows. Nothing. And you?'

'Nothing.'

Lew laughed. 'Silly, eh?'

'What?'

'Graft hard all your life, so as to end up doing nothing. Like a lunatic banging his head against the wall – so pleasant when you leave off.'

'So what do you want? The stars?'

'No. But it seems crazy to end where you started. I should have married and had a family.'

'What for?'

'I don't know.'

The car stopped outside the Olympia, Marylebone.

* * *

Here, in one of the dressing-rooms, Ali was preparing for the fight. Ali was fat, fantastically fat. When he was naked, one could see

226

how malevolently time had dealt with him; blowing him up like a balloon, and dragging him down like a bursting sack. His pectorals hung flabbily, like the breasts of an old woman. His belly sagged!

He brushed his moustache, pinched out a length of Hungarian Pomade, and moulded the ends to needle-points with a dexterous twirl.

'Kration'll try and grab that,' said Adam, 'just to give the lads a laugh.'

'Let him try!'

'Ali, why not trim it down?'

Ali swore that he would as soon trim down another essentially masculine attribute. He put on a curious belt, nearly a foot wide, made of canvas and rubber. 'Pull this tight, please; as tight as you can,' he said, and muttered, with an apologetic look: 'I do not want the people to be under an impression that I have been getting a leetle bit fat . . .'

Adam pulled at the straps, and, like toothpaste in a tube, soft fat oozed up above Ali's waistline.

'Ali, is this wise? This belt squeezes your guts together. If Kration hits you, or kicks you there –'

'Let him try.' Ali writhed into a set of long black tights, and pulled over them a pair of red silk shorts. 'Now, help me with this sash.' He held up a long band of frayed red satin, embroidered with Arabic characters. 'This was a present from Abdul Hamid . . .'

'Ali, you're crazy to press your belly in like that!'

'*Ptah!*' Ali drew himself up, and stood with folded arms. 'Tell me, do I look good?'

Adam felt an impulse to shed tears. 'Fine!'

'One day, I let you sculpture me.'

'Thanks, Ali. Listen, Ali; be cautious, for heaven's sake.'

'My little friend, you forget that I have won hundreds of fights – that I have never been beaten!'

'I know. But I should hate like hell to see you hurt.'

Ali laughed. 'Professor Froehner tore one of my ribs right out of the skin, but I beat him; and I fought again next day. In all my life, nobody ever heard me cry out! Nobody ever saw me tap the mat. Leblond had me by the foot in a ju-jitsu hold. "Give in, or I break your ankle," he said. I said: "Break on, Leblond: Ali never gives in." And he broke my ankle, and I got up on one foot, and pinned him. I said: "You cannot hurt Ali. But he whom Ali grips, God forgets!" That is me!'

'Oh, I'm sure you'll win. I've betted on you.'

'Good boy! What odds did they lay against me?'

'Very small.'

'You're lying. They think I'm an old man. They laugh. Good, let them. And in the end, when they laugh on the other side of the face, I shall laugh, too – I shall laugh right into their eyes, and say: "The old wolf still has teeth." Do I look good?'

'You look like a champion, Ali, you really do.'

Ali laughed, until the fat on his stomach bounced like a cat in a sack. 'Ha-ha-ha! I surprised you, eh? . . . They think I'm going to fool about with this Greek, this Cypriot. No. I shall walk in – one, two, three; up with the legs, back with the head – dash him down, pick him up like a child, shake him like a kitten; then over my head, bim-bam, and pin him. Back again – forward with his head, under my arm with it, and *khaaa!* my old stranglehold, until his eyes pop out. Then I shall pick him up like a dumb-bell, and hold him above my head, and say to the crowd: "This is the man who thought he could beat Ali the Turk!" Then –'

An open door let in the shouting of a crowd. Legs Mahogany came through, bleeding from the nose, followed by the Black Strangler, who staggered as he walked. An attendant came in, and said: 'Ali!'

Ali put on a dressing-gown of quilted red silk, thirty years old and eroded by moths. 'Smart, eh? A woman gave me this in Vienna, in . . . I forget the date . . .'

Adam whispered: 'Give me your glass eye: it's madness to wrestle in one of those things.'

'Rubbish! And let him see I have a blind side?'

'Give it to me, I tell you!'

'If you insist, then, take it.' Ali slid out his left eye, and gave it to Adam, who put it in his waistcoat pocket. Then he strode, with slow dignity, out to the ringside, while through his head ran the cheerful rhythm of the 'March Of The Gladiators', the tune to which the old wrestlers at the International Tournaments had strutted in glory round the arenas.

There was a roar of applause. Ali raised his hands to acknowledge it, when he saw Kration, already in the ring, bowing and smiling. Ali grasped the ropes and swung himself up. There was a pause. A little trickle of clapping broke out; then laughter, which rose and swelled, pierced by high cat-calls and shrill whistles . . .

'Hoooi! Laurel and 'Ardy!'

'Where d'you get them trousis?'

'Take yer whiskers orf. We can't see yer!'

Somebody began to sing, in a good tenor voice: 'It happened on the beach at Belly-Belly!'

Figler's friend, Lew, rose and shouted, in a voice trained in the market-places of the earth: 'Good old Ali! We remember you!'

Ali tore off his dressing-gown, and threw it to Adam.

'Go on, laugh!' he cried.

They laughed.

Fabian shrieked into a megaphone: 'Ladies and gentlemen! On my right, two hundred and forty pounds of bone, muscle, brain and nerve, Kration of Cyprus, contender for championship honours! . . . On my left –'

'Father Christmas!' said a voice; and there was another shout of laughter –

'Ali the Terrible Turk, ex-heavyweight champion of the world, now making a sensational come-back –'

'Champion of wot world?' yelled a thin, Cockney voice.

'Lad-eez and gentlemen! The name of Ali the Terrible Turk was a household word at the beginning of the century –'

'Wot century?'

('That's what you get, if you get old without any money,' said Lew to Figler.)

Fabian stepped back. Kration and Ali went to their corners. Kration still smiled. It was best, he decided, to let it seem that this affair was an elaborate joke. Ali was as grim as death.

'Now don't forget – take it easy!' whispered Adam.

Ali replied: 'I shall have pinned him within twenty seconds. Count twenty, slowly –'

The gong clanged.

The wrestlers went out into the ring.

TWENTY-TWO

Kration advanced with the grace of a dancer. Ali moved slowly, jaws clamped, chin down. They circled about each other, feinting. Then there was a sound like the crack of a whip. Before Ali's fat-clogged, time-laden muscles could co-ordinate in a counter-attack, Kration had slapped him on the buttocks.

'Get 'im by the 'orns!' somebody shouted.

'Right,' said Kration, and grabbed at Ali's moustache. But next moment, a grip like pincers closed on his wrist, a force like an earthquake twirled him round, and his hand went back over his head towards his shoulder-blades.

Kration broke out into a sweat. It occurred to him that Ali was in savage earnest. He had not sufficient skill to break the hold. Resisting Ali's pressure with all his strength, he butted backwards with his head. The hard, round skull, padded with kinky black hair, jolted against Ali's jaw. The Turk snarled, and tried to knock Kration's feet from under him; but, between himself and his opponent, his vast abdomen stood like a wall. Kration's head jerked back again. In Ali's nose, something like a lever in a pump, and bright-red blood began to run on to his moustache.

Kration broke away, whirled round, and, in turning, struck Ali on the jaw with his forearm. It seemed to Ali that the Cypriot was swimming in a sea of red water reticulated with a network of dazzling light, and that the voice of this sea was laughter. But even as his brain wavered, his ancient instincts were sending him lumbering after Kration, while his consciousness automatically juggled with the logic of a hundred different forms of attack . . .

'He's too fast! Waste no strength chasing! Get close and crush!' His huge right hand hooked Kration's neck. Kration's fingers, forked like a snake's tongue, flickered towards his eyes. Ali ducked. Kration's nails scratched his forehead. Then Ali had his right hand in an irresistible grip. Adam saw his back quiver.

'Flying mare!' screamed a woman's voice.

Ali heaved Kration off his feet by his right arm; stooped to throw him over his shoulder; then stopped. The edge of his belt had cut him short. They stayed, for a moment, in this ignominious posture. Then Kration, wriggling like a python, caught Ali's throat between his biceps and forearm, twisted a leg between Ali's thighs, grunted, tugged; then writhed away as they fell. The Turk's body struck the mat with the dead thud of a falling tree. Something snapped: his belt had burst. Kration uttered a triumphant yell and pulled it away; leapt back and held it over his head.

Laughter roared through the spectators like a wind through trees. Ali was up, growling. Fabian took the belt from Kration's hands, muttering, as he did so: 'Liven it up a bit, can't you, you two? Don't play about like kids in a bloody nursery! Come on, now!'

Kration evaded Ali's slashing right hand, threw himself back against the ropes, and fired himself across the ring like a stone from a catapult. His right shoulder struck Ali in the abdomen. Ali fell backwards, with a tremendous gasp, but even as he fell, rolled over with a grunt and caught Kration below the ribs in a scissors-hold.

Kration felt like a man in a train-smash, pinned by a fallen ceiling. He writhed, but Ali held fast. The crowd screamed. Kration breathed in short coughs – '*Assss . . . Assss . . . Asssss.*' He tensed all the iron muscles of his stomach. Ali still struggled for breath; every exhalation, blowing through the blood which still ran from his nose, spattered the mat with red drops: '*Prup-aghhh . . . prup-aghhh . . .*' He realised that he could not hold Kration for more than another ten seconds. Cramp crawled in the muscles of his thighs.

Kration ground the heel of his hand into Ali's mouth, and broke loose; leapt high in the air, and came down backside first. Ali saw him coming, but could not move quickly enough. Kration's fifteen stone dropped, like a flour-sack falling from a loft, on to Ali's chest. Wind rushed out – '*Ahffffffffffff!*' – with a fine spray of blood. Darkness descended on the Turk; for perhaps one second, he became unconscious. His mind floundered up out of a darkness as deep and cold as Siberian midnight. He found himself struggling to his feet.

Adam's voice reached his ears as from an immense distance: 'Careful, Ali, careful!' Kration was upon him again, on his blind side, and had caught him in a wrist-lock.

Ali's brain flickered and wavered like a candle-flame in a draught. There was a counter-move; something . . . something . . . he could not remember. He put out all his might, and caught one of the Cypriot's wrists; grunted 'Hup!' like a coal-heaver, and used his tremendous weight to spin Kration round and swing him off his feet. As Kration staggered, Ali caught one of his ankles, twirled him round, six inches off the mat, in the manner of an acrobatic dancer, then let go. The Cypriot fell on his face, kicking and heaving like a wounded leopard. 'Ahai!' yelled Ali, springing forward as Kration rose to his hands and knees. 'Waho!'

'Nice work!' screamed Adam.

Ali had Kration in a headlock. Kration crouched, gathering his strength; then began to strain left and right in spasmodic jerks. Blood from Ali's nose fell like rain on Kration's back. Both men were red to the waist, slippery with blood. Ali's grip was slipping: Kration was as hard to hold as a flapping sail in a raging wind . . . Kration's head was free. Ali caught a glimpse of his face, purple, swollen, split by a grin of anger that displayed all his teeth, white as peeled almonds. Then Kration swung his left arm. His hard, flat palm struck Ali in the face: one of his nails scraped the surface of Ali's eye.

A blank, bleak horror came into the heart of the Turk. '*My eye! My last eye! If lose this eye, too!*' Then he roared like a maddened lion, buried his ringers in the softer flesh above Kration's hips, lifted him above his head by sheer force, threw him across the ring, and followed him, growling unintelligible insults and spitting blood –

Clang! went the gong.

Ali groped his way back to his corner, and sat limply. Adam sponged him with cold water, adjusted his sash, and wiped the blood from his face: 'My eye,' said Ali, 'my eye!'

'It's badly scratched,' said Adam.

Ali's eye was closing. The lids, dark and swollen, were creeping together to cover the blood-coloured eyeball.

The crowd shouted. One voice screamed: 'Carm on, Nelson! Carm on, whiskers!'

Ali sucked up a mouthful of water and, like a spouting whale, sprayed it towards the crowd. 'Cowards!' he shouted. 'Cowards!'

Figler muttered: 'This is disgusting. Let's go.'

Lew, shaken by emotion, did not answer, but raised his piercing voice and called to Ali: 'Good work, Ali! I've not seen anything better since you beat Red Shreckhorn in Manchester!'

Ali called back: 'Thank you for that!'

'Go easy; for God's sake go easy,' said Adam.

The gong sounded. Kration advanced, smiling. To Ali, he looked like a man half-formed out of red dust. He thought: '*If I do not get him within five minutes, this eye will close, and then I shall be a man fighting in the dark.*' This thought was indescribably terrifying. The curtain of mist was darkening. Now, by straining the muscles of his forehead and cheeks, and holding his mouth wide open, he could barely manage to see.

A voice cried: 'Look out, Kration! He's going to swallow you!' Another shouted: 'Oo-er! Look at 'is whiskers! They're coming unstuck!'

Ali's moustache had, indeed, fallen into a ludicrous Nietzschean droop, matted to a spiky fringe with congealing blood. Kration snarled, leapt in, struck Ali across the neck with a flailing arm, and seized his moustache. He tugged. If the hair had not been slippery with the blood from Ali's nose, Kration might have pulled it out. But it slid through his fingers. Ali, weeping huge tears of pain, grasped blindly, and caught the Cypriot by the biceps of his right arm. The darkness had come. He knew that if he relaxed that grip, he was lost. As Kration jerked back, Ali followed. The Cypriot began to gasp with pain: '*Ess-ha; ess-ha . . .*' Everything in Ali's body and soul focused in the five small points of his finger-tips. He was blind, now, utterly blind, lost in a roaring, spinning ring, dumb with agony, choked with blood, deafened with howls of derision and encouragement which seemed to have no end – and, in this world of sickening pain, there was only one real thing, and that was the arm of his enemy, in which he was burying his fingers . . .

They clung together, spinning round and round like two twigs in a whirlpool; the Cypriot groaning, now; Ali silent. He felt cold. A ring-post ground into his back. He groped with his other hand, and found nothing. The noise of the crowd was becoming fainter; his face seemed to be swelling and swelling, while in his breast his heart thundered like horses galloping over a wooden bridge. Something knocked his feet from the mat. He fell, still clutching Kration's arm. The Cypriot said: 'For Christ's sake!' Ali replied: 'You feel my grip, eh?'

Voices were shouting: 'Stop the fight! Stop it!'

Out of his midnight, Ali roared: 'Stop nothing! Ali never stops!'

Suddenly, he released Kration's biceps, slid his hand down until it reached the wrist, where it shut like a bear-trap; swung his other hand to the elbow. The Cypriot's arm broke. Ali heard his scream of pain, but still held on. Kration became limp. Ali held his eye open, with the first and second fingers of his free hand. He could see nothing except an interminable, fiery redness. Somebody tried to prise open his fingers, which still gripped Kration's wrist. Ali struck out blindly. A voice said: 'Stop! You've won! It's me, Adam!'

'By God,' said Ali, 'that Greek went down like bricks.'

The crowd was delirious. Fabian said: 'You certainly gave those sons of bitches their money's worth.'

Adam led him back to the dressing-room.

Ali found his voice: 'Did you see how I beat him? Did you see how I broke him up? Did you see how I pulled him down? Did you see how his arm went? Did you see my grip? I could have beaten him in the first ten seconds, only I wanted the public to see a *fight*. Did you see my grip? What Ali grips, God forgets!'

'You were great, Ali.'

'Now am I fat?'

'No, Ali.'

'Now am I old?'

'No, Ali.'

'Now have I no teeth?'

'Teeth like a tiger.'

'Now can I wrestle?'

'Better than ever, Ali.'

'Now am I undefeated?'

'Still undefeated, Ali.'

Ali raised his head, brushed back his moustache, twirled it

again to fine points, and said: 'Nobody on God's earth ever beat me. Nobody ever will. Look at me. If he hadn't scratched my eye, I should be as right as rain.'

'Have a rest, Ali.'

'Close the windows,' said Ali, 'there's a devil of a cold wind.'

The windows were already closed.

Ali muttered: 'I wonder if my eye is badly damaged? Get me some boracic acid crystals and a little warm water –' He stopped abruptly, and said: 'Put your hand on my chest!'

Adam did so. In Ali's chest he felt something rattling, like a loose plate in a racing engine.

Ali exclaimed, with an astounded expression: 'The clock is stopping!'

'Nonsense, Ali! Rest.'

Ali struck his vast belly with a colossal fist, and murmured: 'What a meal for the worms!'

Those were the last words he ever uttered.

That night he died.

* * *

Later on, Adam met Fabian and said to him: 'Well? What have you got to say for yourself?'

'I didn't know he had a weak heart.'

'Didn't I warn you?'

'Well, you're not a doctor.'

Adam gulped. 'Do you know what's going to happen to you one day, Fabian?'

'Well, what?'

'Somebody's going to jump on your face till your teeth stick out at the back of your head.'

'You mind your own business.'

'And by the way, you owe me forty pounds.'

'I owe you what?'

'You laid me forty pounds to two pounds Kration would win.'

Fabian looked up into Adam's face, and said: 'Well, Ali didn't win. Kration retired with injuries, so there's no bet.'

'You dirty rat, you refereed the fight.'

'Certainly.'

Adam was quite astounded. Fabian continued: 'I mean, break holds – hell! You got to draw the line somewhere, you know.'

'I want forty pounds off you,' said Adam, seizing Fabian by the lapels and shaking him. 'And if I don't get it –'

'Well,' said Fabian, 'what?'

'I'll come along and smash you.'

'Try it,' said Fabian. 'Do you think I'm scared of you?'

'You'll see.'

Adam hurried back to the club. Fabian went to the office. The Strangler was there, with a swollen nose.

'Harry, I want my dressing-gown.'

Fabian yelled curses: 'You bloody nuisance! May you die! May you be run over by a bus, you big black nuisance! May you go blind and dumb, you ignorant coon! You mug! You duff wrestler! You great big polooka! How many times are you going to nag me about that lousy red silk dressing-gown? Haven't I promised, not once but a thousand times? By God! I've a good mind to smash you.'

The Strangler put one hand in the waistband of Fabian's trousers, and, without effort, lifted him clear of the floor, as he said: 'Harry, I told you, I want that dressing-gown, because I got a girl to meet, and if I don't get it, Harry, I'm coming round with a razor.'

The Strangler produced from his pocket an old, bone-handled, hollow-ground cut-throat, flicked it open with his thumb, and held the edge a quarter of an inch away from Fabian's nose. He could actually feel the coldness of the steel.

Fabian said: 'Listen, Strangler, haven't I promised?'

The Strangler replied: 'You keep your promise, or I'll keep mine.'

A woman's footsteps sounded on the stairs.

'Let me down,' said Fabian. The Strangler released him and went out. Helen came down . . .

'What's the matter?' she asked. 'You look flustered.'

'I was just showing that nigger a few holds. They all come to me, I have to teach 'em everything. Darling, I'm so glad you've come. Let's go and have some coffee.'

TWENTY-THREE

Next morning, at ten o'clock, Fabian sat down to an early breakfast of tea and boiled eggs with Zoë. His first care, when he got up, was to brush his hair very carefully, until he thought he could see golden tints in it. As he ate his breakfast, he radiated assurance. Zoë's heart went out to him. There is nothing a woman loves more in a man than self-confidence. A man who appears to know precisely what he wants, and how to get it, can win more hearts than Robert Taylor. Fabian had this air.

He said: 'You know the little dog I promised you?'

'Mm.'

'It'll be big enough to be taken away from its mother in a few days' time.'

'Will it really?'

'Yeah. What a lovely little dog it is, too! A pure-bred chihuahua.'

Zoë asked, for the twentieth time: 'What do they look like?'

'You'll like it,' said Fabian. 'They're hairless Mexican dogs. Not a hair on their bodies; and when they're full grown they're only six inches long, with legs as thin as pencils and funny big ears. You could tie a bit of blue ribbon round its neck, and lead it about, see? Only you'll be careful not to let it catch cold because they're very delicate, see, delicate.' And he thought: '*I better kill this chihuahua; I'm getting fed up with it . . .*'

'Oh! Harry!' screamed Zoë, throwing down her egg spoon, and running round the table to kiss him.

'Well listen, kid,' said Fabian. 'We're going to be on the up and up. We're going to touch heavy sugar. I've got a great deal on. An absolute cert. And I've got to run down to Cardiff in about a week's time, to see a couple of fellows, and I thought it'd be a nice little break for you, if you came with me. I could borrow a car, and we'd pack up some food and a bottle of wine, and go down by road. Make a sort of picnic of it, and you could take the little dog with you. What do you think?'

'Oh, Harry! I think it'd be lovely! You *are* a dear. Really you are. You know I do love you, Harry, you *are* marvellous, honest to God you are.'

'Sure I'm marvellous. But that's nothing. You wait. You're

going to have diamonds, Zoë, silver foxes, sables, a car of your own. You wait and see. I give you my word, you don't know what's coming to you. You don't know me, yet.'

It gave Fabian an intense pleasure, a sense of indescribable power, to speak in riddles. He became drunk with ambiguity, as a poet might become drunk with beautiful words.

'And I've got a surprise up my sleeve for you too. You wait. You'll hardly be able to believe it. Boy, boy, boy, I can imagine your face!'

'Oh, what is it?' asked Zoë. 'Tell me what it is?'

'Well, I wanted it to be a surprise, but I'll tell you. I'm on a proposition that might take me – guess where?'

'Tell me,' said Zoë. 'I can't guess.'

'Havana,' said Fabian, 'Cuba. What do you think of that? The place where the Rumbas come from. Good old Havana. How'd you like to go?'

'You're joking.'

'No, I'm telling God's truth. I shall have to go to Cuba, and I'm going to take you with me; and I'll let you in on another thing; you know I told you we were going to Cardiff? We're going to take a week-end trip to Ostend. What do you think of that?'

Zoë begged: 'Harry, don't kid me.'

'I'm telling you the honest truth, or may I be struck dead where I sit. Next week, you and me are going first of all to Cardiff, on business, and we'll come away from Cardiff with big dough in our pockets; and from there, you and I are going to have a little holiday, for two or three days, no more, in Brussels.'

'Brussels?'

'Certainly. First Ostend, then Brussels.'

'But,' said Zoë, 'could we take the dog over with us?'

'You leave that to me,' said Fabian.

'I bet you're only kidding me.'

'Look here,' said Fabian, 'I'm giving you my word of honour. I might kid people, sometimes, but I never break my word of honour, never.'

'Well, I tell you a funny thing,' said Zoë. 'I had my fortune told the other day, and they told me I was going on a sea voyage. Isn't that funny?'

'Well, there you are, you see. Now do you think I'm kidding you? You ought to have a little more faith in what I say, Zoë. I don't like all this stuff about kidding people. When I tell the truth, I expect to be believed.'

'I believe you, Harry. Honest to God I do.'

'Well, listen,' said Fabian, 'it's not a thing I want talked about, so keep your lip buttoned.'

'You're not going to get yourself in any trouble?'

'Don't you worry,' said Fabian. 'Don't you worry. Just don't talk about it, that's all. It's between ourselves, see?'

'All right, Harry. I won't say a word.'

'Well, mind you don't. You know what people are. You can't trust 'em with anything.'

They finished their meal. Fabian washed and dressed.

'Where are you going?' asked Zoë. 'To the office?'

'Yeh. Well, so long. Be good.'

* * *

Fabian went out. He went into the subway at Piccadilly, and telephoned Arthur Mayo Clark: 'Hallo, Clark? Fabian here. Listen, Clark, will that thing be all right for when you said?'

'Yes.'

'Definitely?'

'Definitely.'

'I can rely on it?'

'Absolutely.'

'Valdes'll be there?'

'Yes.'

'And you too, I suppose, with the money?'

'Yes.'

'Will I be able to borrow a car?'

'I think so.'

'And listen; the tale is, a trip to Ostend.'

'Zoë thinks that?'

'Yes.'

'I see, all right. Don't say any more now.'

'But it is all right, isn't it?'

'Quite.'

'And you'll have the money in cash?'

'In pound notes.'

'Good-bye.'

Then he rang Figler.

'Listen, Joe, can I have my fifty?'

'All right.'

'Today?'

'If you like.'

'When?'

'Today if you like. The sooner the better. You made a mistake over that Ali fight, Harry. I think you done wrong, very wrong indeed. The poor old man!'

'Jesus Christ, what am I to do? Go around feeling everybody's pulse or something? Have a little sense, Joe.'

'Well, see you later.'

'Oh, Joe, can you find me a very cheap red dressing-gown, and get the Black Strangler's name written on it in gold?'

'How much do you want to pay?'

'Not more than a quid.'

'Did you say red?'

'Yeh.'

'What size?'

'Fifty-inch chest.'

'All right. But it'll have to be specially made. You're crazy, Harry! That fellow's dangerous to play with, I warn you. Well, goo'-bye.'

Fabian went back into Piccadilly and walked around. He paused for a long time outside a hosier's shop, where there was a display of hats and shirts labelled: GENUINE AMERICAN GENTS' STYLES. Finally, he went in and said, in his best American accent: 'I'd like to try on that Harvard model, light-grey Fedora.'

'Certainly sir, size?'

'Six and five-eights.'

Fabian tried on the hat. The assistant said: 'If you're interested in a rather wider brim, sir, we have a model, the Cicero, exactly as worn by Al Capone.'

Fabian's eyes sparkled.

'Show me.'

He tried on the Cicero hat, in dark blue.

'I'll take it,' he said. 'Hell, that's a great idea for a song ". . . Honey, oh, honey, I'll take it . . ."' he sang to the tune of 'Oh, Honey, Do Something'.

'Very good, sir. Do you write songs?'

Fabian replied: 'Ever see the *Love Parade*? I wrote it.'

'Really, sir? Would you be interested in the Humphrey Bogart shirt? Exactly the same as he wore in *The Petrified Forest*?'

'Show me.'

The assistant produced a dark brown shirt.

'And it doesn't show the dirt either, sir.'

'I change my shirt four times a day,' said Fabian, loftily. 'So this is the Humphrey Bogart. I know Bogart well . . . No, I don't like it.'

'And would you care to see the Stepin Fetchit bowtie?'

'No,' said Fabian, 'I guess not.'

'Or the Barrymore socks?'

'No, I'll just take the hat now. I got to meet a guy at the Waldorf.'

'Twenty-five shillings, sir. Will you wear the hat now?'

'Sure.'

'Where shall we send the other one?'

Fabian looked at the hat he had just taken off – a little pale green hat which he had bought only a week before: the Fred MacMurray, for which he had yearned with all his soul.

'Give it to the poor,' he said, and swaggered out.

Zoë, meanwhile, had dressed in a black two-piece, an imitation silver fox and a little black hat with a veil, and had gone to drink a cup of coffee in a nearby café. As she went in, another girl called to her: 'Hi, Zoë.'

'Hallo, Greta.'

The girl called Greta was a tall, rather angular blonde. Somebody had once told her that she looked like Greta Garbo, and she had never got over it. She wore her hair in a long bob, used a tragic lipstick, and even spoke in a guttural monotone.

'How's everything?' asked Zoë. Greta shrugged.

'You know how life is,' she said.

'How's Wilf?'

'As usual; how's Harry?'

'Marvellous.'

Greta said, philosophically: 'All men are marvellous till you find them out.'

'Oh, I don't know,' said Zoë. 'They're not all so bad. I've come across nice ones, though some of them are a bit lousy. Look at my Harry, he's the best boy in the world. Do you know what he's getting me? A Hotcha.'

'A what?'

'A Hotcha dog.'

'Don't be silly. There's no such thing.'

'All right, it's a dog without hair.'

'He told you and you believed it. All dogs have got hair. How can you have a dog without hair? It wouldn't be a dog if it didn't have hair.'

'Anyway,' said Zoë, with some irritation, 'he's getting me one, I don't care what you say.'

Greta shrugged loftily, and said: 'By the way, how's your rival?'

'What do you mean?' asked Zoë.

'Just what I say. Harry's other girl friend.'

'You're lying,' said Zoë. 'My Harry wouldn't look at another woman.'

'Oh, well, I'm sorry; I wouldn't have said anything, dear, but I thought you knew.'

'Tell me,' said Zoë. 'Tell me. What is it? What is it all about?'

'Oh, it's nothing,' said Greta. 'I don't suppose there's anything in it. It's just that I saw Harry with some girl, and I wondered who she was, that's all.'

Zoë endeavoured to appear indifferent.

'What sort of girl?' she asked.

'Well, it's like this,' said Greta. 'I happened to be in a very expensive restaurant the other day – Raoul's, in Bond Street – with a gentleman friend, and who should come in but Harry, with a girl, rather dark, very good looking, and marvellously dressed. My dear, and the way she spoke! Obviously, a well-educated girl, and he was sitting down with her, and they had quite an expensive sort of meal, and seemed, well, very friendly, and I just wondered if you knew about her.'

'Did you hear what they said?' asked Zoë.

'Well,' said Greta, 'I never listen to people's conversations, but I thought I heard him call her Ellen, or Helen, or something. Still, don't take it too seriously, Zoë, my dear, there's probably nothing in it. He wasn't doing anything much, I must admit, just holding her hand, and there's nothing in that.'

'When I think of all I've done for that bloody man. He came to me with his backside sticking out of his trousers, and starving like a bloody dog, and I took him in and I fed him, and I dressed him, and I've kept him ever since, and that's what I get for it. Starving! Starving, he was!'

'Sh, don't shout.'

Zoë went on in a quieter tone. 'He was starving when I took him in, and I give him most of what I make, and he goes about spending it on other women. My God! I'm gonna kill him. I'm gonna buy a knife, and I'm gonna kill him. I'm gonna cut him to pieces. I know a fella that's got a gun. I'm gonna borrow it, and shoot him, and blow him to pieces. What a fool I've been! Are you telling me the truth, Greta?'

'Of course I am.'

'All right, then,' said Zoë, 'I'm gonna murder him. I don't care if I get hung for it. I'm gonna kill him. I'll tear him to pieces, you see if I don't. After all I've done for him. I've gone short of things myself to give him money, and that's all the thanks I get. Sometimes, when he's been late back at nights, I've lain awake and worried about it, and then he goes and . . .' Zoë burst into tears.

'There, there,' said Greta. 'There, there.'

'Now, I'm finished with him,' said Zoë. 'Now I really am finished with him. Ponce! Dirty little ponce! Going about, show-ing off. Telling everybody he's this and that. Why, he'd starve it if wasn't for me. He'd be dead of starvation by now, if I hadn't kept him. And what for? What for? While he's been spending my hard-earned money . . . the money I work and graft for, on some other bloody woman.'

'Mind you,' said Greta, 'she seemed a very well-educated girl.'

'I'll kill her too,' said Zoë, 'honest to God I will. I'll kill them both. You see if I don't; And some people say there is a God. But perhaps you're lying?'

'I never lie,' said Greta.

'Well, I'll soon find out,' said Zoë.

* * *

Zoë left the café. In the doorway, one of her friends, coming in leading a baby Alsatian, said: 'Hallo, Zoë, you look as if you had lost a shilling and picked up a halfpenny. How do you like my little dog? Isn't he lovely? I'm going to call him Archie. Isn't he sweet?'

Zoë managed to say in a dead voice: 'That's nothing, I'm going to get a Hotcha dog.'

'A hot dog?'

'A Hotchacha dog.'

'Never heard of it. I say, Zoë, listen. Walk quick when you get outside, don't hang around. The bloody street's alive with busies.'

'Thanks,' said Zoë. 'I'm going home anyway.'

She walked quickly back to Rupert Street, and sat down in the little living-room; then she began to cry, very miserably, thinking: '*I take him out of the gutter, and that's all the thanks I get. Starving, he was, starving, and that's the way he pays me. I went all the winter without a proper coat. He's had hundreds and hundreds out of me, and now he's going around with other women.*' Then she began to bite her lips.

The prostitute is sentimental and unhappy. Why does she walk interminably, in utter degradation, and then give all her money to a man? Because he alone, in a faithless world, remains faithful to her: he is her home, her husband, her child, her anchor. He is, in her consciousness, the last human being in the world to whom, by virtue of her self-sacrifice, she can feel superior, and therefore she loves him with a curious desperate love.

'*And now,*' thought Zoë, '*he's got hold of somebody else with my money.*'

Rage, the hysterical rage of the prostitute, rose within her. She picked up a heavy glass flower-bowl and threw it into the fireplace. It broke with a heavy crash. The noise infuriated her, and she wanted to be infuriated. She took an orange from a dish on the table and began to squeeze it between her hands until the juice ran out, lacerating the skin with her nails until it came asunder in dripping pulp.

'*This is Harry, and I'm tearing him to pieces.*' She began to laugh wildly, and threw the orange away. The halves struck the opposite wall, in two grey stains of juice. She kicked over a chair.

'*I'll wait for him,*' she thought. '*When he comes in I'll kill him. I'll cut his throat with something.*' She went into the kitchen, searched methodically until she found a little black-handled vegetable knife with a needle point.

'*I'll stab him as he comes in at the door, stab him right in the chest, and keep on stabbing him, and then I'll be hung . . .*' The idea of death presented itself. She imagined that death must, somehow, be like black ring velvet . . . an immense box, pitch dark, very soft, full of velvet. She had dreamed of it and knew exactly what it must be like – simply black, and you floated about, like smoke. But first of all she must kill Harry, with this little black knife. Automatically she switched on the wireless, and through the room, in sombre and awful magnificence, there suddenly roared the undying agony of tortured giants, as an invisible orchestra played the third movement of Beethoven's Fifth Symphony. Normally she could not have listened to this, but now she liked it. Agony called to agony, she sat and listened, hacking at the edge of the table with a knife.

* * *

Fabian, meanwhile, was having a drink in Leicester Square with a racing tipster.

'Well, Freddie,' he was asking, 'what do you think of Old Boot for tomorrow?'

'No good.'

'What do you mean, no good?'

'What I say, no good.'

'Well, I fancy it.'

'What, did you pick it out with a pin?'

'No, I just fancy it.'

'Well, forget it, Harry, forget it. It don't stand a chance on

Gawd's earth . . . and, by the way, what you done with my book?'

'What book?'

'The book I lent you.'

'Oh, Christ, you mean *How To Beat The Book*. I've got it at home. You in a hurry for it?'

'I am a bit. You promised me it back a week ago. It ain't mine.'

'Well, blimey,' said Fabian, 'I just got it up at the flat there. I tell you what, wait for me here; I'll nip round and get it for you.'

'Will you? I wish you would.'

'All right, wait here.'

Fabian went out, and then, as automatically he looked at himself in the mirror behind the bar, he was horrified to observe that the bow in his hat was hanging loose. He left the public-house hurriedly, grinding his teeth, and went back to the hosier's as fast as he could walk, burst into the shop shouting: 'Look at this! Look at this, God-damn it, I buy a hat, it isn't ten minutes ago, and now it's falling to bits. What's the idea?'

A horrified assistant examined the band.

'I'm so sorry, sir; it's just one of the stitches come loose. We can put that right at once.'

'You'd better,' said Fabian darkly. He took from his pocket a two-shilling cigar, lit it with a flourish, and blew smoke towards every face in sight. The assistant returned with the hat.

'You'll find that quite all right, sir.'

Fabian examined it minutely.

'You can't do things like that and get away with it, not with me.'

'No, sir.'

'I know it's not your fault, but you ought to be more careful.'

'Yes, I'm very sorry, sir.'

* * *

'*Isn't that bastard ever coming?*' thought Zoë. '*My God, isn't he ever going to come?*'

She fidgeted in her chair, and her knees trembled. Fabian remembered the book again, and went towards the door, then paused as something caught his eye. It was a little showcase full of clips, with bars and chains, embellished with monograms in black and gold. He asked the assistant: 'Say, have you got an HF?'

'I'll just see, sir. We can do any initials you like while you wait.'

'Well do me an HF while I wait,' snapped Fabian.

'With pleasure, sir. What sort would you like?'

Fabian selected a tie-clip with a little American flag on it.

'How much is this one?'

'Seven-and-six, sir.'

'Okay, do me an HF on this one.'

'Thank you, sir, ready in two minutes, sir.'

'It'd better be. You guys in this country have got no idea of time, no idea at all.'

He waited. Ten minutes passed. Zoë was ripping up the stuffed arm of the chair with the knife, and tearing out handfuls of flock. The concert came to an end . . . 'The concert of gramophone records of old favourites,' said the voice of the announcer, and in a sentimental tenor voice, a man began to sing: 'Ah, sweet mystery of life at last I've found thee.' Zoë burst into tears. Her whole body shook with the force of her sobs. Tears ran out between her fingers. Fabian went back to the flat and found Zoë sitting like this, weeping in the chaos of the disordered room.

'Why, what the Hell!'

Zoë's rage was being washed out of her body by her tears.

'Oh, you, you, you . . .'

'Why, what's the matter?'

'Oh,' said Zoë, 'how could you do a thing like that to me, Harry . . . meee . . . after I've worked for you and grafted for you. After I took you out of the gutter, and made you what you are today.'

Through Fabian's brain, quicker than lightning, flashed the thought: '*Somebody saw me with Helen.*'

'Why, what the hell!' he said indignantly. 'What the hell are you talking about?'

'Going about . . . spending my money – the money I work for, on other women.'

Fabian exclaimed in a loud, clear voice: 'May I be struck dead where I stand, I don't know what you're talking about.'

'You know what I'm talking about. Greta saw you in Raoul's with a girl.'

'Raoul's? Who's Raoul's? I've never been there in my life.'

Zoë looked at him. His face expressed blank astonishment. He went on: 'Do you think, do you honestly think I'm interested in any other dame? Do you honestly think so? Because, if you do, you must be crazy . . . Here I run all over the bloody town, arranging holidays for you, getting you chihuahuas, thinking of you all the time, working for you, scheming for you, breaking my head to think in what way I can please you –' Fabian seized her by the shoulders, and shook her violently – 'Why, you!'

'Harry,' asked Zoë, 'is that the honest truth?'

'Greta's a liar. A dirty liar. A dirty, lousy liar. I'll cut her throat. Strike me dead, I'll cut her throat! I'll bump her off. I'll rub her out. I'll smack her down.'

'She said her name was Ellen.'

Fabian uttered a shout. 'As God's my judge, I've never met anybody named Helen in my life, and I've never been to Raoul's in my life.'

'Swear.'

'On the soul of my poor mother, God rest her soul,' said Fabian.

Zoë began to laugh, hysterical with relief: 'Oh . . . Harry . . .'

'But say, what's been going on here?'

'Oh, Harry, honestly, when Greta told me that . . . honest to God . . . I went crazy. I would have killed you if you'd come in ten minutes earlier. I would. I was waiting behind the door with a knife. I'd die rather than let anybody else have you. I would! I would!'

Sweat poured out on Fabian's upper lip, as he looked at the slashed armchair and the scarred table-top. *And some guys say there's no God*, he thought, fingering his tie-clip.

'Where'd you get that, Harry?' asked Zoë.

'Joe Figler gave it to me. It's a lucky mascot. I wouldn't part with it for a thousand pounds. An American millionaire, a guy called Henry Ford, gave it to Figler and Figler gave it to me, because the initials are the same . . . HF. See? . . . Well, angel, are you going for a walk?'

'Listen, Harry, the streets are full of plain-clothes men. They pinched French Simon just because she winked at a man.'

'Boloney.'

'But –'

'Remember,' said Fabian, with irony, 'we'll need some furniture . . . Helen, you're nuts! What's she supposed to be like anyway?'

'A good-looking dark girl.'

'Well Greta had better introduce me.'

'Really? Do you mean that?'

'Oh, sure, sure. I hate the sight of you. That's why I'm running my feet off for your sake.'

'Well, I hope that mascot brings us some luck.'

'Well it brought Henry Ford luck. I wouldn't part with it for one thousand pounds.'

Fabian saw a vision of himself, twenty years hence, sitting in a luxurious office. Touching the tie-clip with a finger on which shone a diamond worth £10,000, and saying, through the smoke of a 25s. cigar: 'Gentlemen of the Press, my mascot . . .'

'Now run along, sweety,' he said.

Zoë went to wash away the tear stains.

* * *

Fabian, who felt that so emotional a scene must have ruffled him, changed his tie and, polishing his shoes on the backs of his trousers, adjusted his hat with microscopic accuracy, and went out again. At the doorway it occurred to him that he had forgotten his book.

'Oh, well, what the Hell!' he thought. 'I'll tell him I locked it in a drawer, and Zoë has the key.'

He went into a telephone box and rang Helen. He felt more than ever like a man of destiny, a master of puppets, a puller of strings. As her warm contralto voice vibrated in his ear, he felt a quiver of pleasant anticipation run through his back. He said: 'Listen, honey baby, I been thinking over that club racket very carefully, and I've decided we're going to go in for it in a big way.'

Helen asked: 'Have you got the money to put into it then?'

Fabian replied: 'I'm selling some of my shares. By next week

I expect to have five thousand pounds in hand. Now listen, Helen, can you meet me tonight?'

'Why, of course.'

'Fairly late?'

'Any time you like.'

'Eleven o'clock, same place?'

'Very well.'

'Well, good-bye.'

Fabian rang off. Then like an inspiration, a thought occurred to him: '*Now what say the two of them made the grand tour? Say I had three, four, five hundred quid in hand? Francs are a hundred to the pound. Say I had fifty thousand francs and betted, say, five hundred times in succession on, say, number nine . . . or, say, I kept on betting on the red a thousand francs a time, and broke the bank at Monte Carlo. Oh boy, oh boy! Say I did that?*'

Every film he had ever seen, and every book he had ever read, rushed together in his brain to form one blazing and magnificent composite, in which he, Fabian, fantastically enlarged, fantastically dressed, leaned backwards in a wild photomontage of champagne bubbles, limousines, diamonds, galloping horses, baize tables and beautiful women; all whirling and weaving in a deluge of white and yellow chips and large bank-notes; an eternal reduplication of breasts and legs of every conceivable shape, size and colour.

'*That,*' he said to himself, '*is what I'm going to do . . . Plunger Fabian, the playboy who broke the bank at Monte Carlo. Afterwards, I can buy plenty dames.*'

TWENTY-FOUR

And the earth, roaring up in its orbit, came nearer and nearer the sun, and the hot spring blazed out in the City, with its expansive urge, its tendency to growth and opening. The trees put out leaves; in the parks tulips opened their mouths to gape at the sky; and the curious, intangible influence of spring sent new impulses pouring into the veins of the population. Men began to breathe deeply and throw out their chests again at the sight of the sunlight, like people, who, lost in a dark forest, suddenly break out of the trees into a wide free plain. Only at this season, this brief season of spring, does man forget his ancient craving for oblivion, in the light of the ancient pro-creative instincts.

But Nosseross, in whom life was already dying, still remained in his office, a pale convict condemned to spiritual death, and irretrievably shackled in a cellar to his waiter's chits. He was speaking to Adam: 'Listen, Adam, I'll tell you something: you're too soft.'

'Who, me?'

'Yes, you; do you know you threw away twenty-five quid last night?'

'How did I?'

'Well, I'll tell you. That little Japanese who was down here had about fifty pounds more in his pocket.'

'I know that, so what?'

'Well, you as good as told him to go.'

'Damn it all, the man had just spent twenty-five pound, and he asked if I thought he'd had enough to drink.'

'He was tight or he wouldn't have asked.'

'I know he was tight. He asked me and I said: "Yes, you've had enough." What should I have said?'

Nosseross made an impatient gesture.

'You're a mug. You should have said: "No, sir," you should have said: "An intelligent man never has enough to drink, sir, besides, sir," you should have said, "*we*'ll look after you even you *have* too much to drink." See? Then you should have said: "Try some of our special champagne."'

'Oh, the hell with that!' said Adam.

'Now don't start talking like a fool, Adam. What do you think we're in this business for: love?'

'No, money. But there's a limit. The trouble with you, Phil, is you're a mug, like all the rest of you smart Alecs. I used to think you were pretty smart, but it seems to me you're just as big a fool as any nit-wit hostess in the place. You can't see an inch farther than the end of your nose. I mean, quite apart from the principle of the thing, it pays you better to treat people decently. Why be such a fool? You chisel them and you never see them again.'

'A bird in the hand is worth two in the bush,' said Nosseross, 'and don't call me a mug.'

'A bird in the hand is not worth two in the bush. Not in business, anyway. The trouble with you people is all you know is ready cash.'

'You trying to go high hat on me or something? What do you mean, you people?'

'What I say, you people, you and the girls here.'

'Are you trying to put me in the same class?'

'You are in the same class. You're a mug like the rest of them.'

'Don't start getting insulting, and don't start handing me any philosophy, because I knew this business before you got the cradle marks off your backside.'

'I don't give a damn for that, I'm just telling you. You're exactly like Vi, only a little bit smarter, that's all, chisel, chisel, chisel, without a tuppenny damn's worth of thought to your credit, and in the end business falls off. And, of course, you never realised it's because customers have said to each other: "Nosseross skins you alive." No, you don't realise that at all. You start grumbling about bad luck, I suppose.'

'Never mind that,' said Nosseross. 'I'm just telling you. I don't want you to lecture me, because I've forgotten more about the club business than you'll ever know. Don't you start getting high-principled and generous on *my* money. I'm just telling you, you handled that Jap dead wrong.'

'You're crazy. Have you noticed any drop in the takings since I've been running this show?'

'Well, there has been a little.'

'That's on account of the Coronation.'

'Don't make excuses, Adam. I'm prepared to make allowances because you don't know the ropes, yet. But don't start getting a swelled head already.'

'Oh, go to hell,' said Adam. 'I'm fed up with you, anyway.'

'You're what?'

'I'm fed up with you, and I'm fed up with the business too.'

'Well, by God!' said Nosseross, 'I like that. You come here as a waiter, and I put you in the way of making more money in a month than you've ever made in a year, and now you're getting cheeky. So that's the sort of fellow you are. Are you trying to tell me you've been doing me a favour by working here, or something?'

'Well, what would you call it? You know perfectly well you practically begged me to take over when Mary ran off with Cheshunt. You were sitting in that very chair, simply sodden with drink, as you are now, and you practically begged me to stay with you and you know it, and now you can go to the devil, because I'm leaving. Run your lousy dive on your own, because I'm leaving.'

'Now wait a minute, Adam, wait a minute.'

'Go to hell,' said Adam, 'I'm finished. Pay me what you owe me and I'll clear off.'

Exhilaration took possession of him. He cried: 'To hell with your lousy club, and to hell with the club business, anyway. To hell with being polite. To hell with money. To hell with the whole stinking racket, I say. You vultures! You parasites and imbeciles. You crooks and you fools! You greedy little degraded idiots! I'm going to quit this and go to work.'

'Don't be a fool,' said Nosseross. 'Can't you take a joke?'

'Of course I can take a joke, but I just don't want to take a joke. I'm leaving, now.'

Nosseross got between Adam and the door, and said: 'Wait a minute, listen. If I upset you, I apologise. Isn't that fair enough? Sit down a minute, just a minute, sit down. I just want one word, that's all, one word. Don't be so hasty.'

'What is it, Phil?'

'Listen, Adam, do you know you're the only friend I've got? Honest to God you are. Don't be rotten. Don't let me down. Don't walk out on me, just on account of a hasty word. I've been on the booze. I'm all broken up. I'm shot to pieces.'

Adam interrupted him, with an angry, exclamation: 'Now, for God's sake, Phil, don't start making me pity you again, because I'm getting to hate the sight of people who want me to pity them.'

'I'm not asking you to pity me,' said Nosseross. 'But, boy, at my age a man feels lonely. A fellow needs somebody to stand by him. Christ Almighty, if it's only a dog . . . and I haven't even a dog. Hell, Adam, I'm sick, I'm lonely, don't walk out on me.'

Adam replied: 'Listen, Nosseross, I like you. Don't talk like that any more, or I'll start despising you. I stayed with you when you needed me most, didn't I?'

'Yes, you did.'

'And now,' said Adam, 'I've got work to do.'

Nosseross replied: 'Listen, Adam, I've lived a hell of a lot longer than you, and I know more than you think I know. You think you're going to do sculpture, don't you?'

'Well?'

'Well, I'll tell you something. Give it up, because you don't stand a dog's chance. You haven't got enough training, you haven't got enough money to be trained properly. You're just like an obstinate kid that gets an idea in its head. You want to be a sculptor. Bah! You're crazy, I tell you. How can you be? What have you ever done? Show us some of your sculpture, can you?'

'No,' said Adam, grinding his teeth, 'I can't, because I've smashed up all the things I've ever done, because they were rotten, no damn good for anything. But I know perfectly well, Phil, that I'm going to do it, see? If it kills me I am, and something seems to tell me that if I start, and I get going, I shall make something which won't have to be broken up and thrown away; something that the world will look at, and that's what I'm going to do, Phil, and I've made up my mind, and I can tell you one thing, much as I pity you, I'm not going to let pity stop me any more. What good is pity? Am I going to let pity chain me up in a cellar? When I might, at this very moment, be producing a *Thinker*, or a *Winged Victory*, or a *Venus of Syracuse*. No, Phil, I'm finished with this nonsense, I really am. This is the end of it. I'm quitting. It's not because of what you said just now, it's because I've got work to do.'

'You'll starve,' said Nosseross.

'I'll live.'

'You won't. In the end you'll turn it all in, and say to yourself: "By God, Phil was right!"'

'Not in my lifetime,' said Adam.

'Do you realise that you're chucking away fifty pound a week?'

'I do.'

'Just for the sake of making a few statues?'

'Yes.'

'And if you make 'em, what then?'

'Nothing. I make them, and when they're made, I make more.'

'And so what? You make 'em and you starve – all right. You say you don't mind starving. You haven't done any yet. All right, let us say you'll learn to be a famous sculptor, and make Venus and Apollo, and all the rest of them. Say you do that, you can't get any dough out of it. You'll be bloody lucky to get a living out of it, and in the end you'll be the same as me – just when you feel you know enough to really do something, you'll be too old, and too tired, too bloody worn out to do it, and then you'll peg out, and the most you can hope for is that they'll shove your stuff in a museum. Just dead stuff. But you won't be there to see it. No, you'll be dead and stinking, a mile underground, and that'll be the end of you.'

'I know all about that,' said Adam. 'I've heard it before, and I've thought it before, and it's a lot of crap, because you don't understand, as old as you are, you don't understand that a soft bed is not what a man was made for. A belly full of meat and a good kennel is a very nice ambition for a dog. The world is still no good, just because people have been too concerned with resting and comfort. All right, comfort's not for me. There's something I've got to do. There's something in me that seems to have been collecting for a hundred thousand years, and when I find out what it is, and let it ride, then I tell you, Phil, things'll be broken, and things'll be made, too. You whine because you're lonely. I'm lonely, but I'm proud of it. But we're different people, from different worlds. You're lonely, just because you put everything you had into your belly, because you locked yourself up in your cellar. But I'm lonely among ordinary people because I'm flying higher, see? I got things to make and break, and at this point, Phil, I quit. I like you, because you're clever and you're tough, and I'm sorry for you, because you've cracked up, but I'm not going to let pity hold me back any longer, so good-bye.'

Nosseross looked at him, and shrugged his shoulders, and said: 'Adam, you're a bloody lunatic, and you'll see that I'm right, but even if you begged me to let you stay now, I wouldn't. I'd kick you right out of the door. Pity me! Pity *me*! My God Almighty, my God Almighty! Nobody ever pitied me. I've gone through more than you'll ever know – fire, water, hell, mud – and I got through it without having to be pitied. You bloody fool, I've walked through the fire.'

'And for what?'

'To do what I wanted to do.'

Adam was silent and thought: '*Clever, strong and hard as nails, and the peak of his ambition was a night-club.*'

He smiled and held out his hand. Nosseross thrust a hand into his fob-pocket and pulled out a fat roll of pound notes.

'All the same, I like you, Adam. Hang on to this. There's a hundred quid there, and come and see me sometimes.'

'Put it away,' said Adam.

'Take it.'

'No.'

They clasped hands. Nosseross dropped the money on the desk, struck Adam a tremendous blow on the chest, cursed him, and said: 'You lousy bastard, I love you like my own son. If ever you're bust, slip me the word. If ever you need a pal, call on me, my door is always wide open. Look in sometimes, and even if you don't, don't forget your old pal, Phil Nosseross, now scram.'

As Adam left he caught a last glimpse of the office – the files, the white, dead gas fire, the blank back of the big black desk, and Nosseross pouring out brandy with the grim concentration of one who believed that truth, happiness and the consummation of human endeavour lie at the bottom of a bottle.

* * *

Helen looked at Adam in astonishment as he returned.

'You're back?' she cried.

'Yes.'

'But, it's half-past ten, you'll be late.'

'Late for what?'

'For the club.'

'I've left the club.'

'What?'

'I've left the club,' said Adam, smiling.

'But why?'

256

'Oh, I just decided I'd leave and I've left.'

'You must have had a quarrel with Nosseross.'

'No, we parted on the best of terms; in fact, he begged me to stay.'

'You mean you've left of your own accord?'

'Yes.'

'Don't keep on saying "Yes, yes". Tell me about it, what happened? What on earth made you do such a thing?'

'Well, first of all,' said Adam, in a good-humoured tone, 'Nosseross and I were having a little argument. There was a Japanese man in, and he asked me if I thought he'd had enough to drink, and since the man had spent twenty-five pound, I said: "Yes, save your money and go home, and Banzai Nippon."'

'That was a perfectly idiotic thing to go and do,' said Helen, beating her hands together. 'And Nosseross was quite right to tell you off about it. You should have apologised.'

'On the contrary, I told him to go to the devil.'

'You really are a perfect idiot, Adam.'

'Well,' said Adam, 'then Nosseross begged me to stay.'

'He actually asked you to stay, and you refused?'

'I did. I said "Mr Nosseross, I'm giving up night-life in order to find my place in the sun."'

'And your place in the sun means sculpture, I suppose?'

'I think so.'

'Oh my God! And what did Nosseross say then?

'He said: "Well, since you're going, here's a hundred pounds," and he took out a roll of money as big as a jam-jar and offered it to me.'

'Well, that's not so bad,' said Helen, somewhat mollified. 'We can open our place quite nicely with that and what we've got.'

'We can, my child, but we won't, because I indignantly refused his tainted gold, and he put it back in his pocket.'

'You utter lunatic, and what do you propose to do now, may I ask?'

Adam executed an uncouth tap-dance on the floor, seized Helen by the elbows and swung her off her feet, as he replied with an uproarious burst of laughter: 'Lock you up in a leaky attic, feed you on bread and water, and model you in the nude.'

'Put me down.'

There was such a concentration of anger in her voice that Adam stopped, quite astonished. 'Eh?'

'Put me down.'

She pushed him away, and said: 'Well, this finishes it. I thought you might have something in you. I thought I might be able to make something out of you. I thought you might get to be somebody, get somewhere. But you're hopeless. I often had my doubts of your sanity, now I'm convinced you've got a kink somewhere. You're crazy. You're worse than crazy, you're selfish, utterly selfish, horribly selfish. You've thrown up a job that was worth forty pound a week to you, just so you can play about with the perfectly idiotic idea of being a sculptor.'

'Correct,' said Adam. 'That's exactly what I've done.'

'And you expect me to have anything more to do with you, after that?'

'Certainly; why not?'

'Well, all I can say is you must be crazy. And I don't mind telling you once and for all, that I'm fed up with you and your wild ideas. You're just like a little boy who wants to be a pirate or something. It's just as mad, and just as impossible. I think you're utterly mean and selfish; if you consider nothing else, Adam, you might at least have considered me, because it's not as if you'll even be able to get a living on it.'

'I've got enough to live on for about a year.'

'Live on! What do you call living?'

'Just living; about three pounds a week.'

'Oh, just living at about three pound a week, for about a year, and then what?'

'By then I ought to have done something.'

'Oh, by then you ought to have done something. It's all very nice and vague, isn't it?'

'I don't see anything vague about it,' his temper rising. 'Why vague? I know exactly what I mean to do.'

'Yes, of course, play with clay.'

'No, not play with clay, work with clay; and stone too.'

'Quite romantic. Some girls would be quite impressed. I'm not.'

'No, I don't suppose you are. The limit of your ambition is a sable coat and a Rolls-Royce.'

'Well, at least a sable coat would look nice and keep me warm. I can't imagine your sculpture doing either of those things.'

'Now you're being insulting.'

'Of course, the truth is often insulting.'

'What the devil have you got to do with truth? Your whole life is a wild goose chase after nonsense. Nice furniture, nice holidays, nice clothes, nice people, a nice bank-balance, nice parties –'

'Of course, you're above all those things.'

'No, I'm not, but there's something I want to achieve, something more important.'

'Oh, I forgot, you're a great sculptor. And I'm supposed to sit down and watch you work and count the pennies?'

'You've counted pennies before, and you didn't die of it. Anyway, you're not supposed to do anything you don't want to do.'

'After all the promises you've made, you go and spoil everything,' said Helen, beginning to cry.

Her tears infuriated Adam. He replied: 'If, when I've been on the point of making love to you, you've said: "Will you do this or that," I suppose I have been foolish enough to say: "Yes, YES," but such promises have to be broken in the end. What the devil! Selling one's birthright for a . . .'

'Well I tell you once and for all, I'm not going to starve in an attic, for you or anybody. I've had enough of poverty. You say you love me?'

'I do. I'd find it very hard to live without you.'

'Adam, I'm going to start this club. I'm going to make some money. You've got to come and work with me.'

'I can't work with you, Helen; you've got to work with me.'

'No,' said Helen.

'Then that's the rock we split against,' said Adam, heavily.

'I shan't see you any more,' said Helen.

Adam sighed.

'It means good-bye,' said Helen.

'Yes.'

'Then, good-bye, Adam.'

'Good-bye.' He held out his huge right hand. Helen grasped it.

'Adam, won't you kiss me good-bye?'

He kissed her on the forehead.

'That's a very cold farewell kiss, Adam.'

'If I kissed you properly I should end up by making promises I couldn't possibly keep.'

She went out. The door closed firmly. Adam stood, automatically pulling at the points of his dress-coat. Oh, black heartache; oh, desolation. Upstairs, a door slammed. Silence came down upon the house. Outside, in a sky devoid of stars, the waning moon glimmered indeterminably, melting into encompassing blackness.

Adam put out his hand in a mechanical gesture. His fingers slipped on to something cold and wet. He found himself playing, listlessly, with a piece of red clay. He confronted it, thrusting out his jaw. Then steadily, without removing his coat, he began to work on it, in crude deliberate strokes.

Helen's footsteps came downstairs again, and the street door closed.

Sweat began to moisten the edge of Adam's collar.

TWENTY-FIVE

A sense of perfect calm had taken possession of Helen. She reasoned simply: '*There is nothing to hope for from Adam; he's finished. The only thing to do is to take Fabian for what he's worth. Start a club. Make some money. Get somewhere, be somebody, by hook or by crook.*'

She walked quickly and overtook Vi, who was trotting along in high-heeled slippers, her long evening dress brushing the pavement, eighteen inches below the hem of her camel-hair coat.

'Oh, hallo Helen.'

'Hallo.'

'I'm late. Bloody buses . . . they say there's going to be a bus strike for the Coronation. Won't it be a lark?'

'I don't care.'

'How's Adam?'

'Damn Adam,' said Helen.

'What, you had a row with him?'

'No, I just can't be bothered with him any more.'

'What, you found another boy friend or something?'

'Oh,' said Helen loftily, 'I can always find plenty of boy friends, if I want them. I'm going to make some money.'

'What,' cried Vi, 'are you going to open your club?'

'I don't know. Somebody offered to put the money up for me, but I don't know. Anyway, I'm determined to open it. I'll show you how to run a night-club.'

'And could I come and work for you?'

'We'll see.' Mentally, she added: '*You can go to the devil, I'm fed up with you and everybody else. I'll work alone.*'

'Wouldn't it be nice?' said Vi. 'I say, do you notice that there's no girls about here?'

'Yes,' said Helen, without bothering to look.

'I bet you would hardly find a prostitute the whole length of Charing Cross Road.'

'Why?'

'I tell you the police have been absolutely clearing 'em off the streets, for the Coronation visitors, lot of bastards, they won't let you live. They want to make out there aren't any tarts in London, see? And all the poor old soldiers, they've been lumbering them too, bloody lot of hypocrites, and nobody dares to stand about and wait for a friend, or anything. It's getting terrible, and they call this a free country. Did you know Marion? They pinched her, and then they went round to her place, and waited for her boy friend, Spots, and they pinched him when he came in, and gave him six months straight away. I mean it ain't right, especially when everybody was looking forward to the Coronation, to make themselves a few bob. I mean to say it's mean. They ought to let you live, didn't they? Don't they do the same thing to their wives? Well, then. A girl's got to live the same as anybody else, hasn't she? I tell you, it's got me scared. Bloody coppers! Well, anyway, I might make myself a few quid over the Coronation, down the club. I got myself a new red, white and blue dress, Coronation colours, see? And listen, Marjorie's getting a white dress, with GOD SAVE THE

KING embroidered on it, in red and blue letters. But what I wanted to ask you, do you think I ought to go blonde, so as to be a pure English type for the Coronation?'

'Good idea,' said Helen.

'Some people think I'm a mug, but I'm pretty wide all the same. I don't want to flatter myself, but I do get an idea sometimes. Blonde, eh? Would you say honey blonde, or platinum?'

'Platinum,' said Helen.

'More English, eh? What's the matter, Helen, you upset? Don't you be upset, men aren't worth it. They're all a lot of bastards. I picked up a fellow at the club last night, and I went home with him, and do you know what he gave me? He gave me a cheque for ten pounds.'

'Lucky,' said Helen.

'Oh, I say, Helen, could you lend me two bob? I've got to get a taxi.'

'Where's your cheque for ten pounds?'

'I sent it to my mother.'

'All of it?'

'Yes, I am like that. Could you lend me the two shillings?'

'No, I can't,' said Helen.

'You can't?'

'Didn't bring any money out with me.'

'Oh, all right. I say, Helen, listen, I been offered another job up at the Sugar Mill club. The girls make a tenner a night, only they're expected to go home with customers. Do you think I should?'

'Why not?' asked Helen.

'After all,' said Vi delicately, 'it is prostitution.'

Helen shrugged. 'You should worry,' she said.

'Isn't it funny?' said Vi, with gusto. 'A little while ago you couldn't have said "Boo" to a goose, and now look at you. Isn't it funny how the club business broadens your mind?'

'Oh, I suppose I used to be soft,' said Helen. 'But I'm not any more. What does it matter how you get your money, so long as you get it and get somewhere? Did people like Rockefeller get theirs any better? It's all very well talking about prostitution, but is sleeping with a man for money any worse than marrying him for money? Is opening a night-club any worse than opening a tea-shop? I'm sick of all this silly talk I hear of this and that . . . morals and all that nonsense. How is anybody going to get anywhere if they are going to be fussy about what they do?'

'You're quite right,' said Vi, affectionately holding Helen's arm. 'Coo, we both think the same way, isn't that marvellous? I say, Helen, look, what say you and me get a flat together, and do a bit of indoor bashing?'

'I don't know,' said Helen. 'I'm going to try and open my club, and give some orders for a change. Oh, I could show you how to run a club.'

Vi did not speak for a minute or two, then said enviously: 'You can save your money, can't you? And you've got brains, too. I admire people with brains. Blimey, I bet you end up with a club of your own, and furs and a rich man to keep you.'

'That's because I've got ambition,' said Helen. 'I'm determined to get somewhere before I die. You're a fool, Vi, you ought to have some ambition. You ought to try and become something.'

'Oh, I've got my ambitions. Do you know what I want to do? I want to take a little café, with a house upstairs, and get all the boys and girls in . . . are you listening? And let the girls use the rooms at ten shillings a time, and if they want drinks they can have it under the table. People think I've got no ambition, but you see, that's all.'

'Oh, well, we'll see,' said Helen.

'Which way are you going?' asked Vi.

'Bristol Square.'

'What for?'

'To meet somebody,' said Helen.

'Who?'

'Nobody you know.'

'Harry Fabian?'

'Well, what if it is?'

'You know, Helen, I don't want to tell you what to do, but you didn't ought to associate with that type of fellow.'

'Why not?'

'He's not much good.'

'Oh, don't be stupid, I can take care of myself.'

'Do you know what I heard?'

'Well, what?'

'Well I heard he was a white slaver.'

Helen laughed. 'You're mad,' she said. 'Such things don't happen any more.'

'Well, anyway, somebody told me he was a bit of a ponce.'

'Oh, don't be an idiot, why should he be?'

'Well, listen, would you come along to the Sugar Mill with me if I went?'

'I might, I don't know.'

They reached Great Russell Street.

'Well, good-bye,' said Helen, turning off to the left.

'Bye-bye, dear,' said Vi, and walked on biting her lips.

'*The mean cow,*' she thought, '*I bloody well educated her, I teach her all she knows, and now she starts going high hat on me. All right, all right, and wouldn't even lend me two shillings, and I made her what she is; she comes to me starving, and I help her to get somewhere, and that's all the thanks I get.*'

She hurried down Shaftesbury Avenue. Near Wardour Street, a dark full-bosomed woman stopped in the kerb, to smile at a passing man. He walked on. From out of the shadows of a shop-front, two tall men appeared and seized the dark woman's arms.

'Come on, Zoë.'

Zoë went pale.

'What do you mean?'

'Now, be sensible.'

'What do you mean, be sensible? Leave go of me.'

'Come on, you're under arrest, and don't argue and be a good girl.'

'You dirty lot of bastards,' screamed Zoë.

'Now, why not come quietly? I mean, Zoë, you've got to come. You know you've got to come, so why not come quietly, like a lady. You are a lady, aren't you, Zoë?'

'Course I'm a lady,' said Zoë. 'Let go of my arms, and I'll come quietly.'

The detective said to her: 'I always knew you were a sensible girl.' Courteously he offered his arm, and led her towards the station. As they walked, he said to her in a conversational way: 'How's Harry?'

'Don't know what you're talking about.'

'Now why be like that?'

The other detective said, with a wink: 'Ah, don't you know, she doesn't see Harry any more, he's got somebody else.'

'That's a lie,' said Zoë.

'Love is blind,' said the first detective. 'Oh well, Zoë, and I thought you were wide. Why, didn't you know Harry's been carrying on with some tart from Phil Nosseross's club?'

'It's a lie,' cried Zoë. 'What's her name?'

'Girl called Helen.'

At the mention of this name, Zoë almost fainted. Then, bitterness choked her: she could say nothing. The first detective said, soothingly: 'Poor old Zoë. After the way you've kept that man, too.'

'I've given him thousands,' said Zoë.

The detectives exchanged a wink.

'Never mind, Zoë, you'll get your own back, all you've got to do is make a little statement.'

Zoë nodded. They stopped under a blue lamp.

'Up you go, ducky.' Zoë went up the steps between the two detectives.

* * *

Fabian, meanwhile, was sitting in Anna Siberia's club playing poker dice with two men. He loved this game, which smacked somehow of the gangster films, about which he had constructed all those elaborate affectations, which went to build up his life. In his pocket lay the fifty pounds which he had just received from Figler. He called for drinks; Anna Siberia said to him: 'You like American drinks?'

'Sure I like American drinks.'

'Well, I got some rye.'

'By God!' cried Fabian. 'Let's have double ryes.'

The other two players drew up their chairs. One of them was a very fat, silent man, whose upper lip was merely a dry line, but whose lower lip protruded beyond the edge of his nose; the other was tall, thin, silent and dried up.

'Remember,' said Fabian, 'you guys promised me revenge.'

The fat man said soothingly: 'Sure.'

'You guys got dough?'

'I got a pony,' said the thin man.

'And I got a pony,' said the fat man.

'And I got a pair of ponies,' said Fabian, slapping his pocket. 'Well, what do we ante?'

'Ten shillings a throw?'

'Make this a quid game,' said Fabian, 'a pound a throw.'

'Right.'

Fabian fingered his tie-clip, for luck.

'When I got this thing on me I can't lose. Come on, boys, ante up, ante up, ante up.'

Three pound-notes fluttered down on the table. Fabian snatched up the dice, and whispered at them as he rattled them, just as he had seen negroes and gangsters on the pictures.

'I smell 'em, I smell 'em, I smell 'em, come on, come on, roll, roll!'

He threw. The dice rolled over quietly on the baize cloth.

'Two tens,' cried Fabian. 'Two tens, two tens, two tens.' He threw the other three dice. 'And three little kings. Full house, gentlemen. Full house with kings on the roof.'

He sat back and let the acrid, American whiskey trickle down his throat. The fat man threw three aces.

'Hm,' said the thin man, and, with a casual hand, threw four aces at a single throw.

'That's all right,' said Fabian, as the thin man took out the money. 'That's quite all right, brother. I hate to take out first go. It's dead unlucky to take out the first go, dead unlucky. Now, Slim, throw 'em and I'll show you something, and I'll show you something, this time. Ante up, boys, two nines . . . and a nine . . . ooh! and a jack and a king . . . three little nines for Slim, oh Jesus, me beads! Gimme, gimme, gimme, whoa!' screamed Fabian, shaking the dice high above his head. 'Life is just a bowl of cherries. Crash bang! I say, crash bang!'

He threw the dice.

'Four aces in one! Beat that.'

The fat man shovelled up the dice with a languid hand, and threw.

'For Holy Jesus,' said Fabian, somewhat disconcerted, 'five kings.'

The fat man dragged in the money with a weary hand, and grunted: 'Ante up.'

Fabian peeled off another note. At the back of his mind, a little fear said: '*Now, Jesus, say I lose all my money, all my hard-earned money?*' Then he touched his tie-clip, and thought: '*A way to win a game like this is to say you can't lose . . . I can't lose, I can't lose, I can't lose.*'

'What have I got to beat?' he asked. 'What? Only a straight? Gimme these dice . . . Oh, little kitty, little kitty, little kitty, come down the river to Grandma. Atcha! Three tensie-wensies . . . widjiwidjiwidjiwidji, and another ten, four tens, you little babes in the wood, four tensie-wensies.'

He scooped in the kitty.

'Now gentlemen, now, gentlemen, here's where you break down.'

He threw three aces.

'Three aces in one. Let her ride.'

The fat man exclaimed suddenly: 'Side bet of a quid I beat that throw.'

'Okay.'

The fat man threw.

'Full house in one, nines on the roof.'

The fat man collected the kitty again, together with Fabian's side stake. The telephone rang, and Anna Siberia began to shriek into the mouthpiece.

'Who is it? I can't hear you. Can't you speak properly? I can't hear what you're saying . . . Oh, Fabian, just a minute. Harry, telephone.'

'Oh, Jesus, who is it?'

'Figler.'

'What does he want?'

He snatched up the telephone. Figler's gurgling voice came through the receiver.

'There's a girl here called Helen.'

'Oh, Jesus Christ!' said Fabian. 'I forgot.'

He covered the mouthpiece with his hand, and turned to the other players.

'Listen, boys, I wonder if you'd be able to excuse me? There's a dame I promised to see.'

The fat man replied, talking to the ceiling: 'He makes arrangements for a quiet game and I come miles to play, and now he tries to wriggle out.'

The thin man muttered, in a sour voice: 'Well, he lost his nerve.'

'Listen, Figler,' snapped Fabian, 'send her along here, will you? That's a good boy. Okay. I say, did you get the Strangler's dressing-gown?'

'I haven't had time,' said Figler.

'Oh, Christ! Never mind. If he comes, tell him you don't know where I am, see? . . . No time now, good-bye.'

He dashed the receiver back on the hooks, and snapped: 'Who's lost whose nerve? Who's trying to wriggle out of what? By God! I'll show you. Make it a quick game. Raise the stakes to a fiver a throw.'

'Okay,' said the fat man.

'Okay.'

'Ante up then, and make it quick.' At the sight of fifteen pound on the table, his heart began to thump.

'Well,' he thought, 'now I can really win some money.'

'Three queens in one,' said the fat man. 'Let it ride.'

The thin man threw.

'Two lousy pair,' he muttered, pushing the dice over to Fabian. Fabian scooped the dice into his left hand; he remembered that it was luckier to throw with his left hand.

'I can't lose, I can't lose,' he said, and threw the dice hard. 'Straight to the ace!' he yelled, reaching out his hand for the money.

'Cock dice,' said the fat man.

Fabian stared. It was right; the king was tilted at an angle against the foot of his glass. Fabian's heart sank. He threw the dice again, and then groaned: 'Three rotten, stinking jacks!'

Collecting the money, the fat man permitted himself to joke: 'Harry, maybe you'd rather play ping-pong.'

Fabian ground his teeth.

'Don't talk so much, and throw,' he said.

'Side bet, Harry?' asked the fat man.

'Sure.'

'A fiver, Harry?'

Fabian hesitated. 'Well, say a quid,' he replied.

The fat man grinned meaningly and grunted: 'In like a lion, and out like a lamb. First of all, quids aren't big enough, but as soon as they lose one or two goes, phooey!'

'Oh, yeah?' said Fabian, in a grating voice, thrusting out his jaw, and dragging out all his money. 'Oh, yeah? Side bet for a fiver then, shoot!'

'Popeye,' said the fat man.

'He's a tough guy,' said the thin man.

The fat man grunted as he shook the dice: 'He chews nails and spits rust . . . Two nines . . . He's a rich man, he is . . . Three nines, four nines in three!'

Fabian's face burned red. He closed his lips tightly and said nothing.

'Lousy full house,' muttered the thin man, throwing away the dice. Fabian collected them, and shook them fervently, actually praying: *Christ Almighty, let me skin these bastards alive, and I'll give ten quid to the Salvation Army!*

He kept his mouth tightly closed so as not to let bad luck get in, and threw.

'Three aces in the first throw, and very nice, too,' said the fat man.

'*God,*' prayed Fabian, with all his might, '*send me a fourth ace.*'

'Still only three aces,' said the thin man.

Fabian shook the dice till his hands tingled and dashed them down in the third throw.

'Hard luck,' said the fat man, moistening a finger to pick up the money.

'*All right,*' said Fabian to God, '*I'm through with you!*'

'Throw on,' he said, caressing his tie-clip.

'Straight in three,' said the fat man.

'Full house, aces high,' said the thin man.

Fabian shook the dice again, and addressed God: '*This is your last chance, otherwise I do something desperate.*'

'Pair of jacks,' said the fat man, 'I lay you an even quid you don't get four.'

'I'll take you,' said Fabian, throwing again. 'Whooey! Three jacks.' He shook the dice again. 'Werch! Oh, gimme, gimme, gimme! Four jacks!'

He collected the stakes. 'Come on, now, let's really get going! Here's where I start! Ante, ante!'

'Side bet, Harry?' asked the thin man.

'Okay, fiver?'

'All right.'

Fabian snapped his fingers as the dice rolled.

'Three kings in one and let her ride.'

'Bah!' said the fat man, throwing three jacks.

The thin man threw. 'I tie you up, Harry, three kings. Come on, throw it out.'

'Okey-doke, like to add a bit to the kitty?'

'Well, I'll add another quid if you like.'

'Haha!' laughed Fabian, rolling the dice between his fingers. 'Haha! They soon come down to quids, these big shots. Haha! Haha! Come up the alley to poppa! Three tens!'

The thin man threw three queens.

'Three bitches,' he said, and dragged the money towards him.

Fabian lit a cigarette with an unsteady hand. The fat man said pityingly: 'Listen, Harry, don't lose more than you can afford.'

'Don't you worry about me,' said Fabian.

'Perhaps you'd like to go back to smaller stakes?'

Fabian hesitated, then said: 'No, I got plenty.'

'Rich man,' murmured the thin man, in a tone of such maddening irony that Fabian shouted: 'Yeah, plenty, you poor lice! And I'll say so with ten pounds a throw.'

The fat man chuckled: 'So now he wants to play for a tenner a throw.'

'I want to get this game over: I got a dame to meet. So come and be skinned,' said Fabian. 'A tenner a throw.'

'Ten a throw,' said the thin man, counting his money. The fat man said: 'Well, Harry, I respect a man who can gamble sugar or bust on a few throws.'

'I'm like that,' said Fabian; then he wished he had bitten his tongue out. The fat man was laughing at him. He bit his lip and became silent.

'Harry,' said Anna. 'There's a man wants to talk to you. Urgent.'

Fabian went to the telephone. It was Figler.

'Harry, for God's sake lie low for tonight.'

'Why?'

'The Strangler's been here. He's raving mad. He's gone to look for you. He's got a razor, he's going to kill you.'

'I'd like to see him try.'

'I tell you, you fool, that nigger set his heart on that dressing-gown. Why couldn't you have given him a dressing-gown for twenty-five shillings? He's not responsible for his actions. He's going to cut you to pieces.'

'You got nerves, Joe.'

'I tell you, I know the difference between a man that's dangerous and one that isn't, Harry. Have you forgotten that time when . . .'

'Skip it, I'm not interested. Has Helen left?'

'She's on her way, Harry. I'm warning you, he's been drinking double whiskies.'

'Go to Hell!'

Fabian returned to the table.

'What's the trouble, Harry?'

'Nothing, shoot.'

'One ace . . . two aces . . . three aces in three,' said the thin man.

Fabian threw. His throat was dry, and he breathed like a man who is suffocating.

'Ace, king, queen, jack nine. Bleeding Jesus!' he shouted, and threw all the dice again. 'Pair of queens . . .' He threw for the last time. 'And two more. Beat four queens!'

'One king,' said the fat man, throwing the dice, 'and two is three kings, and by God! I got it! Four kings.'

'Take the money!' said Fabian dully. 'Christ, if I got five aces somebody'd get six. There's a jinx riding me. Ante up and shoot.'

The doorman came in.

'Harry, Bert wants you,' he said.

'Tell him to go to Hell,' shouted Fabian.

'He says it's urgent.'

'Then send him in, and let him say what he wants to say here.'

'Two pair, aces and kings in one,' said the fat man. 'Let it go.'

'Pair of lousy tens,' grunted the thin man.

'Here's where you break down,' said Fabian. 'Come over the precipice, snake eyes!' He threw.

'Kings and queens, hard luck,' said the fat man, taking out the money.

'Well ante up and shoot,' said Fabian.

Bert came in.

'Harry, just a tick,' he said. 'If you don't want to get murdered. Take a ball o' chalk. That big nigger's after you, with a bloody cut-throat as long as me arm. Lie low till 'e's slept it orf. 'E's on 'is way 'ere from the Duchess, an' 'e's raving mad.'

'Scram,' said Fabian.

'I'm telling yer!'

'— off!'

'But –'

'Get out, I'm fed up with you. Scram out of here before I kick you out.'

'And there's another thing,' said Bert.

Fabian leapt up, and pushed him to the door.

'All right, you fool,' said Bert.

'Ante up, and shoot,' said Fabian, sitting down again. Helen came in and stood by Fabian's chair.

'My mascot,' said Fabian. 'By God! I bet you, here's where my luck changes. Come and sit by me, Helen . . .' He fumbled in his pockets, and his heart became heavy and cold, as he found only thirteen pounds. He said, in a small dispirited voice: 'We'll make this a three pound ante, boys.'

The fat man grinned, and threw.

'Full house, kings high, in one.'

'Bah,' said the thin man. The dice dropped from his hands. 'Pair of tens. Shoot Harry.'

'Watch,' said Fabian, pressing Helen's knee. 'Whooey! Four aces. What did I tell you?' He took out the kitty.

Helen whispered: 'Did you get that money, by the way?'

'Sure,' said Fabian. 'Come on, boys, back to the ten-pound ante. Come on, kids, make or break.'

'Side bet, Harry?'

'Sure.'

'Fiver?'

'Sure.'

Fabian threw. 'Two tens and three aces, in two. Come on, your dice, boys.'

The fat man threw.

'Four aces, in one,' he said.

'Ace, king, queen, jack, nine,' said the thin man, in disgust.

The fat man arranged a large pile of notes.

'That skins you, Harry.'

Fabian's mind went back to the fever of the hunt for the £100; the weariness, the danger and the shame; and returned, step by step, down and down to the intolerable depression of this present moment. He gulped, and said: 'Skins me my foot. Skins me my left tit. I can lay my mitt on two hundred pounds any time I want.' It was true, he reflected, that there was always Zoë, and within a week, a trip to Cardiff. He laughed. 'Skinned! Haha! Let's have a drink. Sherry, Helen? Anna, three double whiskies and a sherry.'

'What's all that noise outside?' asked the fat man, hastily pocketing the dice.

A voice said: 'There's no use arguing.'

Two tall men walked in.

'We're police officers,' one of them said. 'We're here on a warrant. This club is raided. Nobody move.'

The other approached Fabian, and said: 'Hallo, Harry, we want you.'

Fabian's face became blue. He swallowed, and said: 'What do you mean, you want me?'

'Got a warrant here for your arrest.'

'Warrant? What for? What warrant? Why a warrant? What have you got on me?'

'Living on the immoral earnings of a woman.'

'It's a lie.'

'Come on.'

The club seemed suddenly to be crowded with policemen. An inspector said to Helen: 'Keep calm. We only want your name and address, you can go soon.'

Fabian, who had been silent, suddenly shouted at the top of his voice: 'It's a frame-up!'

As a man who reasons with a child, the detective replied: 'Zoë made a statement.'

Fabian became limp, and then said in a voice which seemed to contain all the bitterness in the world: 'And some fools say there's a God!'

* * *

Helen found Bert still waiting outside. He spoke to her: 'They got 'Arry?'

'Yes.'

The little man's voice grew hoarse, until it blurred to a whisper. He said: 'It's for the best.'

'I suppose so.'

'Worse was coming to 'im tonight.'

'Was it?'

'To 'im, to Zoë, and maybe to you, too. Things always 'appen for the best.'

Fabian came out between two policemen. He turned his head, and said to Bert: 'Come on, you louse, now throw a few rotten oranges.'

A policeman said: 'Now come on.'

''E could of made somethink of 'mself, but 'e was too conceited. 'E 'ad brains, but 'e was lazy. 'E 'ad nerve, only 'e didn't like soiling 'is 'ands. It's a shame. 'E made 'eroes of the wrong kind of people. If 'e'd only kept steady, blimey, 'e might 'ave been somebody. Instead of being disgraced, blimey, 'e might 'ave been running a dozen shops by now . . .'

'Do you know him well?' asked Helen.

'I ought to,' said Bert. "E's me brother . . . Would you like a banana?'

'No, thanks.'

'Yer welcome yer know. Did you see a great big nigger go by just now?'

'Yes, why?'

"E was waiting for 'Arry, wiv a razor; and 'Arry says there's no God!'

'Why did God allow him to sink so low then?'

Bert laid hold of the shafts of his barrow, and replied: 'God knows. Good-night.'

'Good-night.'

Helen walked away. The night was dark: the city was sombre under its pitiful lamps, still struggling against the universality of darkness.

'*Perhaps,*' she thought, '*I could still open my club, and get some credit to begin with. Or is it worth it, just to spend my youth trying to make money? . . . Is Adam right? . . . Starve, go cold and miserable, age quickly and die young, just to make statues? . . . If one has money one can buy statues . . . I want Adam, yes . . . but any man, any strong man, could satisfy me just as well . . . and there must be men just as strong and masculine, who would devote their lives to me, and worship me . . . No, no more of Adam, there are other men . . .*'

Helen stopped walking, and sat in a café for a little while . . .

* * *

High, high, oh, infinitely high! white and mysterious stars burn with pure clear light. Each, in itself, lost in eternities of empty black space, seems to roll on a meaningless orbit in empty loneliness. But, even when seen from this planet, through the weak little eyes of us who cling to it, they form a pattern.

The darkness fades a little . . .

Under electric light, Adam still works steadily, with all his force; straining every muscle; filthy with mud, smelling of perspiration. His clothes are covered with red clay. From time to time he wipes his face, smearing his face with clay, and the clay with his sweat. The mass takes form. As Adam's outlines become blurred, the shape of the clay becomes clearer. Soon, perhaps, it will mean something. His hands strive against the deadness and the coldness of it. He looks himself like a clay man – he, too, is a mass of struggling earth. Form! Form! Shape! Shape! Order out of the amorphous! Life out of the dead mud! So orders his will.

Outside, the dull moon – little, fickle satellite – trails after the advancing earth, like a prostitute at the heels of a battered soldier, marching on in blind obedience to incomprehensible orders, across the desert of the skies.

The night bursts open. Blood and life soak into the sky. Torn at the edge by the black silhouettes of spiky spires and cold chimneys – polluted but bright, ragged but triumphant – dawn breaks over the city.

LONDON CLASSICS

THE GILT KID

JAMES CURTIS

The Gilt Kid is fresh out of prison, a burglar with communist sympathies who isn't thinking about rehabilitation. Society is unfair and he wants some cash in his pocket and a place to live, and he quickly lines up a couple of burglaries in the London suburbs. But complications arise, and he finds himself dodging the police, checking the newspapers and looking over his shoulder, fearing the ultimate punishment for a crime he hasn't committed. He remains defiant throughout, right up until the book's final, ironic conclusion.

James Curtis recreates the excitement of 1930s London as he delves into the sleazy glamour of the underworld mindset; a world of low-level criminals and prostitutes. His vibrant use of slang is as snappy as anything around today, his dialogue cosh-like as the Gilt Kid moves through the pubs and clubs and caffs of Soho. Curtis knew his subject matter, and this cult novel doubles as a powerful social observation.

This new edition comes with an introduction by Paul Willetts, author of *Fear And Loathing In Fitzrovia*, the best-selling biography of author Julian Maclaren-Ross, and an interview with Curtis's daughter, Nicolette Edwards.

London Books
£11.99 hardback
ISBN 978-0-9551851-2-0
www.london-books.co.uk

LONDON CLASSICS

A START IN LIFE

ALAN SILLITOE

Alan Sillitoe's first novel, *Saturday Night And Sunday Morning*, was published in 1958, *The Loneliness Of The Long-Distance Runner* arriving the following year. Both were hits and led to high-profile films, which is turn cemented his reputation. Tagged an 'Angry Young Man' by the media, Sillitoe's ability to record and interpret the lives of ordinary people was nothing short of revolutionary. He has been prolific ever since and remains one of England's greatest contemporary authors.

A Start In Life tells the story of Michael Cullen, who abandons his pregnant girlfriend and heads 'to the lollipop-metropolis of London in the 1960s'. Cullen is, in theory, leaving his problems behind, but he is 'the Devil on two sticks' and becomes involved in a smuggling ring with Moggerhanger, a man who believes 'that you must get anything you want no matter at what cost to others'. Cullen is an optimist, with an eye for the ladies, but his new swinging lifestyle is soon under threat.

Includes a new introduction by Alan Sillitoe

London Books
£11.99 hardback
ISBN 978-0-9551851-1-3
www.london-books.co.uk

NORTH SOHO 999
A True Story Of Gangs And Gun-Crime In 1940s London

PAUL WILLETTS

Just before 2:30pm on 29 April 1947, three masked gunmen entered a shop in Soho. Little did they realise that they were about to take part in the climax to the unprecedented crime wave afflicting post-war Britain. *North Soho 999* is a vivid, non-fiction police procedural, focusing on what would become one of the twentieth-century's biggest and most ingenious murder investigations – an investigation which later inspired *The Blue Lamp*, starring Dirk Bogarde.

'A brilliant snapshot of '40s London, peopled by crooks, coppers and creeps. Willetts slices through time with the skill of a razor-flashing wide boy. Essential reading' – John King

Dewi Lewis Publishing
£9.99 paperback
ISBN 978-1-904587-45-3
www.dewilewispublishing.com

LONDON BOOKS RECOMMENDS

THE GORSE TRILOGY
The West Pier / Mr Stimpson And Mr Gorse / Unknown Assailant

PATRICK HAMILTON

In Ernest Ralph Gorse, Patrick Hamilton creates one of
fiction's most captivating anti-heroes, whose heartlessness and
lack of scruples are matched only by the inventiveness and
panache with which he swindles his victims. With great deftness
and precision Hamilton exposes how his dupes' own naivety,
snobbery or greed make them perfect targets. These three
novels are shot through with the brooding menace and sense
of bleak inevitability so characteristic of the author. There is
also vivid satire and caustic humour. Gorse is thought to be
based on the real-life Neville Heath, hanged in 1946.

'The entertainment value of this brilliantly told story
could hardly be higher' – LP Hartley

Black Spring Press
£9.95 paperback original
ISBN 978-0-948238-34-5
www.blackspringpress.co.uk

LONDON BOOKS

FLYING THE FLAG FOR
FREE-THINKING LITERATURE

www.london-books.co.uk

PLEASE VISIT OUR WEBSITE FOR

- Current and forthcoming books
- Author and title profiles
- Regular column by contemporary writers
- A lively, interactive message board
- Events and news
- Secure on-line bookshop
- Recommendations and links
- An alternative view of London literature